The Luminary

Elle J Rossi

CRIMSON
ROMANCE
Avon, Massachusetts

This edition published by
Crimson Romance
an imprint of F+W Media, Inc.
10151 Carver Road, Suite 200
Blue Ash, Ohio 45242

www.crimsonromance.com

ISBN 10: 1-4405-5468-4
ISBN 13: 978-1-4405-5468-1
eISBN 10: 1-4405-5469-2
eISBN 13: 978-1-4405-5469-8

This is a work of fiction.

Names, characters, corporations, institutions, organizations, events, or locales in this novel are either the product of the author's imagination or, if real, used fictitiously. The resemblance of any character to actual persons (living or dead) is entirely coincidental.

Dedication

WITH SPECIAL THANKS TO JENNIFER LAWLER FOR BELIEVING IN ME AND MY WITCHES, TO KATRIENA KNIGHTS FOR TEACHING ME SO MUCH, AND TO ALYSON REUBEN WHO WALKED ALONG MEERA AND GHANEM'S PATH WITH ME FROM DAY ONE.

WICKED LOVE TO BERINN RAE. IF IT WEREN'T FOR YOU, MY VOCABULARY AND SANITY WOULD BE IN SERIOUS JEOPARDY.

BETH, THE POT THICKENS AND WE PERSEVERE. WHAT A RIDE! BRENDA, THERE REALLY ARE NO WORDS. WELL, MAYBE FOUR WORDS: "IS THAT THE GUY?" BEVERLY, YOU NEVER HESITATE TO ANSWER MY QUESTIONS AND HELP ME WITH MY RESEARCH. I LOVE YOU AND YOUR SPIRIT, SISTER OF MINE. BRANDY, FOR SATURDAY MORNING COUNTRY MUSIC, LAUGHTER, AND CLINKING GLASSES OF MIMOSA. MARY, SHALL WE UGLY DANCE? THIS TIME THE SONG IS "MOUNTAIN MUSIC" BY ALABAMA. PAM, SIMPLY THANK YOU. I COULDN'T ASK FOR A BETTER SEVENTH SISTER. MOM, I LOVE YOU.

TO THE ENTIRE TEAM AT CRIMSON ROMANCE. THIS HAS BEEN AN INCREDIBLE EXPERIENCE AND I THANK YOU ALL FOR THAT.

AND TO MY BROTHER. WHEN WE HEAR THE SOUND OF THUNDER, OUR HEARTS WILL SING. RIDE, BOBBY, RIDE.

FOR LARRY, BECAUSE DREAMS ARE NEVER A SOLITARY ENDEAVOR.

Prologue

Realm of the Oracles

Time was running out, and if what lurked in the shadows of the horizon didn't kill him, the stench in this room would. Who knew grotesque had a smell?

"You're not looking well, Ryken. Perhaps we should continue this another time." The faceless one pushed back from the oak table, the gnarled legs of its chair scraping across the stone floor.

Not accustomed to being so easily dismissed, King Ryken reached out and grabbed the oracle's bony wrist. He'd traveled through two portals to get here and the fuck if he would leave without answers. "I'm fine. Go on." He swallowed past the bile in his throat, practically gagged forcing out his next word. "Please."

In this realm it was harder to keep the glamour in place, but so very necessary. Ryken despised anything unattractive, and to say his true form was hideous would be an understatement. It made him nauseous to think about it. The gray-hued skin, the lidless eyes . . . Sweat beaded on his brow as the first signs of transition took hold. Any second now, his skin would start to separate and thin at the base of his skull. Ryken doubled his efforts. He could ill afford to show his true self. Not when the oracle scrutinized him as if it needed to confirm his worth.

The sight of the oracle, with its tattered hood covering what should have been a face, was quite simply repulsive. Why would a being with so much power choose to stay in its natural form—a revolting, grotesque state? Ryken wished the robe covered even more. Though its legs weren't exposed, he imagined them to be no different from the arms—abnormally long and covered with blisters. Those sores oozed a pungent substance that now covered Ryken's own hand—his once clean hand.

5

More bile collected in his stomach, mixing with the already uneasy feeling that had settled over the past several days. He released the oracle's wrist and eased back in his chair, feigning confidence. He refused to wipe off the sticky matter, knowing it would offend the foreshadower, though it almost killed him to leave it on his pristine body, a body that had taken hours to create. Granted those had been pleasurable hours, but valuable time nonetheless.

"Very well." The oracle's voice floated through the room in haunting waves that seemed to come from every direction. It stood and crossed to the far corner, its movements careful and slow.

Ryken watched the retreating form and wondered, not for the first time, why the oracle chose to live as it did. Its knowledge of the future was priceless. The oracle could ask for anything, and many would gladly pay the price for a glimpse of what the future held—even if it cost them their souls. His own soul had fled centuries ago, and he'd never had the desire to get it back. Souls: bothersome and needless. It wasn't just the oracle's appearance that intrigued Ryken. He found the solitude and the view outside the hovel equally disturbing.

Ryken had taken one look at the forsaken land and had almost returned to the other side of the portal. He'd instead forced his body to take the first step and then trekked miles through mud, sullying his treasured boots, bypassing other hovels, until he had finally spotted the building only someone as crazy as this oracle would call home. This one, the eldest of all oracles, the keeper of past, present, and future, held the knowledge Ryken so desperately needed. Dark and damp, with the smell of death bleeding from the walls, the one-roomed hut was the complete opposite of his expansive home. Yet another reason to hurry this along.

He repressed a shudder and focused once again on the ancient being across the room. The oracle lifted its arm. Moments passed before one spindly finger pointed into the air and then to a spot behind Ryken's head.

He turned in his chair, followed the oracle's all-seeing gaze. He'd been told it wasn't always easy to decipher the predictions and many times impossible. A dirt-smudged window flanked by crooked, sagging rags sat alone within the stone wall. He wanted to go to it but hesitated to have the oracle at his back. He'd made the tiring trip through the portals because he'd sensed something was amiss, something that could threaten his throne and his future.

Knowledge is power.

Ryken stood and waited for the dizziness to abate. Retaining his glamour in this place proved exhausting. Once he got back to his kingdom, all would be well again. His entire body hardened at the thought, making him even more eager to return to Lemra. But he couldn't go without knowing what was coming. Coming for him. The oracle was the only being who could give him the answers he needed.

As it made its way to the window, the oracle spoke, its voice resonating through the small stone structure. "Two. Two will come. One should be king, the other full of light."

King? He alone was king. King of Lemra and nothing—no one—would take that from him. He'd fought to take over the throne and he had won. Now he craved more. And he would have it. Already his orders were being carried out for the next phase in his plan. "Who? Who is coming and how do I stop them?"

The laugh that followed echoed off the walls. Ryken spun around. Trying to control his anger as well as maintain his glamour was nearly impossible. The tip of his tongue tingled as it prepared to split. He couldn't take much more. "Who, oracle? Who is coming?"

"Two. Two come for you. Light comes for you. A fallen one comes for you. They must."

"What can I do to stop them?"

"Naught. They will come. They must. But only one will win. Only one *can* win."

Ryken closed the distance and stood before the oracle. With barely restrained fury, he whispered, "And that will be me."

The oracle's foul breath hit him in a rush as a laugh of mockery filled the entire room. It surrounded him, cackled in his sensitive ears.

"Sssstop." Ryken's tongue, fully forked now, flicked and shuttered. His skin sloughed, peeling away from his body in layers. "Sssstop laughing."

The oracle's laughter grew louder. Ryken held his hands to his ears but couldn't block the sound. He looked down at the floor and saw his fine attire lying in a puddle at his feet. He stood before the laughing oracle in his true form, the form he despised, and let his anger consume him. He wrapped his hand around the fabric of the oracle's hood and pulled it back. Immediately the laughter ceased.

What Ryken saw was unlike anything he had ever seen before. The oracle had a face, a face too small for its body and covered with the same infection that leached from its arms. A face that held no eyes, just black holes that told too much.

Those gaping cavities would never reveal the future again.

The oracle's laughter turned to screams as Ryken let the slayer—his true form—take over. Piece by piece, he ripped the oracle to shreds until there was nothing left but its tattered robe and walls full of that sticky, putrid infection.

Odd that it hadn't predicted its own death.

Chest heaving, Ryken stood near the window and stared beyond the mud to the shimmering portal beyond. Time to go back. Time to refuel. Then and only then would he be ready. "Let them come."

Chapter One

"It's happened again, hasn't it?"

Meera Jones didn't have to say anything. The cards said it all. They always did. She twisted her long black braid around her fist and stared at the images laid out on the table in front of her.

The Chariot. The Tower. And worst of all, the Moon.

The picture of two brightly clothed, dancing marionettes held upright with thin strings controlled by a scouring moon sent chills down her spine. She'd always felt like two sides of a coin on any given day—bright and cheery one moment, hauntingly shadowy and tarnished the next. The Moon card, which represented dark influences, trickery, and illusion, had just confirmed her earlier suspicion: She could very well be losing her mind. Some scoffed, but Meera trusted the power of the tarot, and more importantly Carrine, the woman who had become her sole confidant over the past several months.

After a deep breath, she finally pulled her gaze away from the cards and met Carrine's. So much wisdom shone in those dark green eyes, but an underlying current of sorrow shadowed their depths. Her dark hair and bright red lip stain seemed even more pronounced than usual against her pale skin. She'd always reminded Meera of a porcelain doll—although she highly doubted Carrine would break quite as easily—today even more so as her painted lips pursed in concentration. One day Meera would discover the truth about her new friend, but for now she'd answer the question.

"Another episode, yes. The strongest yet."

Sighing, Carrine reached out with long, slim fingers, her rings gleaming in the beam of the overhead lights, and moved to put the tarot cards away. "You better tell me about it."

Meera stopped her with a gentle and slightly shaky hand. "Leave them. I don't think we're quite finished."

Nodding, Carrine smoothed her long black dress, scooted back on the couch and placed one pale hand over the other on her lap. "Very well. I'm all ears."

A fact. Carrine was the best listener she had ever met, and, considering the way she kept her attention focused solely on Meera, this time would be no different. "I'll get us some more wine first, and I need to stir the soup. Be right back." Meera hurried out of the room, more to gather her thoughts than anything. She was rattled and didn't work well that way. The only way to fix her current situation was to remain calm and talk it through. Thank goodness she'd met Carrine when she had, or these last several months would have really messed with her psyche.

Meera pulled the lid off the crockpot and stirred the contents, having whipped up a batch of chicken and noodles before she'd gone out for a run that morning. Her muscles were still tight. Probably because she didn't exercise nearly enough. Her love of homemade comfort food had prompted her to get her butt in gear. That and the need to combat her mounting stress.

She snagged the open bottle of merlot from the counter and made her way back to the living room. Perhaps she should have kept said butt inside today. Maybe then she wouldn't have been assaulted on the beach.

"How about some music?" she asked while topping off Carrine's glass, the deep red wine sloshing precariously before settling.

Carrine laughed. "I don't think you can really call what you listen to music."

"Sure I can. It gets the blood pumping." She poured wine into her own glass, lifted it to her mouth and sipped, her lips curling upon the glass at Carrine's next words.

"And causes migraines."

"Ha. If you turn it up loud enough you can't even feel your

head pounding. Shall we try it?" She placed her glass on the bright red coaster and lifted a brow in question.

"I'll pass, and you're stalling."

True. But Meera walked to the entertainment console anyway and flicked on her state-of-the-art system. Opting for a compromise, she let the media player pick the tunes in the adult contemporary genre.

"Ah," Carrine said. "This I can handle."

Meera smiled. Celine she would deal with. Pavarotti she could not. "I think you're showing your age." Though to be honest, she had no idea just how old Carrine was. Her astuteness spoke of years that belied her appearance and constant energy. She'd learned so much and still so little about her friend since the day she'd bumped into her at the mystic market. Literally bumped into her like she'd been pushed from behind even though the crowd had been sparse at best. If she'd been able to discover the source of the shove that had catapulted her into the Carrine's tent, she would have paid them her gratitude. That chance meeting had changed her life for the better, and thanks to Carrine the downward spiral of her life had been slowed.

Until recently.

Meera adjusted the volume to a comfortable setting before plopping down on the other end of the suede couch—the color, so soft and calming, reminded her of the creamiest butter. She pulled one leg under the other. Another lingering sip of wine, and she was finally ready to talk about the day's events.

"Well, I was running on the beach and—"

"You were exercising?" Carrine asked with wide eyes as though even the thought were an impossibility.

"Funny. I do exercise on occasion."

"Like when?"

"Like when I want to eat three bowls of fattening soup for dinner. Speaking of, I think it's ready. I'll go get us a couple of bowls."

Wide eyes changed to slits as Carrine's red lips turned down. "Later. First I want to hear about what happened."

Meera closed her eyes and blew out a long breath. "It started with that hum again." The hum that grated on her already fragile nerves like a swarm of killer bees she could never escape no matter how freakin' fast she ran. Now she knew how hamsters felt. Constantly spinning that damn wheel, but never getting anywhere.

"Go on."

"Okay." Meera blew out a breath and picked at the end of her braid. So I was running and probably cussing . . . definitely cussing."

Carrine smiled.

Her next words sucked the tentative, lighter tone out of the room. "Out of the corner of my eye I saw a shadow form. Then it was gone." She snapped her fingers. "Just like that. I tripped and nearly ate the sand." She tugged on the collar of her shirt, the room's temperature seeming to rise with each staccato thump of her heart. "I knew what was coming, Carrine. It happens almost every day now. So I stopped, faced the lake, and prepared myself. The dark water churned and the wind . . . " Meera's heart nearly pounded out of her chest as she remembered how scared she'd been. Still was. "God, I can't even explain how hard the wind blew."

"It's okay, child. What happened next?"

"My breath, it formed swirling patterns. Almost hypnotic, really. Like it was dancing in front of me. Seductive. Kind of like that air belonged to someone else, and I was just there to watch the show. I wasn't even cold. I should have been, but I wasn't. I didn't feel anything except scared and angry and maybe a little determined to beat it this time." A lot determined to kick some ass and take back control.

"Good for you." Carrine squeezed her hand, her black eyebrows drawn together against snowy skin.

"That's when the voices started, almost as if the wind was calling to me."

"What did the voices say?"

She shrugged. "Same thing they always say. 'Meera. It is time.'"

She'd whispered the last four words when she'd really wanted to scream them. Scream until her throat was raw and ripped. Scream until the whispers and the hum went away.

"How does it make you feel?"

Squashing the anger that desperately wanted to grab hold, Meera cocked her head and gave a half grin. "Psych 101, huh?"

Carrine's lips formed a thin line. "You can call it that. Or you could call it like it is. Two friends talking something out and maybe finding a solution."

"You're right. My sarcasm sneaks up on me sometimes."

"Certainly does, but that's part of what makes you *you*."

"And that is the question of the hour, isn't it? Who am I?" Meera watched as Carrine averted her gaze, something her friend did when she was troubled. "What's wrong?"

"I think those voices may be right. Perhaps it is time."

"Time for what?" Meera tamped down her frustration and lowered her voice. "I think something bad is about to happen, Carrine. Really bad." She waved her hand, gesturing to the table. "Look at these cards. The Chariot . . . Venturing into the unknown. And the Tower. I . . . "

"I know," Carrine interrupted. "The Tower means ruin and upheaval. On paper this doesn't look good."

Moving to the edge of the couch, Meera said, "Clearly."

"However, sometimes we can turn things around for ourselves."

Meera harrumphed. "Not if we don't understand what's happening."

"I think I can make some things a bit more clear."

Did Meera dare get her hopes up? "How?" she asked, and then cleared the clog from her throat with another sip of wine.

"Do you trust me?"

Now Meera's smile came easily. "You know I do."

Carrine rose. "I need to contact some people. I'll be back tomorrow, if that's okay?"

"You don't need an invitation. You're always welcome." She

left it at that rather than begging Carrine to stay. Being alone tonight didn't appeal to Meera in the least. She glanced at the large round clock hanging above the fireplace and then out the picture window. Only five o'clock and already pitch dark. She had a long night ahead of her. Hopefully she'd get through it without another *episode*, as she liked to call her moments of insanity.

After loading her up with some crockpot goodies, Meera walked Carrine to the door. Her friend, who looked so much like her with the long black hair, pale skin and troubled eyes, turned and hugged her. Meera squeezed her tight. The contact brought a semblance of calm to her tattered mind.

"I'll be back tomorrow and we'll get started." Carrine pulled the door closed behind her.

With loneliness already settling in, Meera went back to the couch and grabbed her journal.

*

"Hey, Gannon?"

Ghanem's fingers stopped typing as he looked up at his boss. On the verge of correcting the man, yet again, he bit his tongue. It wasn't worth it. The idiot would never pronounce his name right. Few did. But really? How hard could it be?

"Gan" rhymes with "can" and " um" as in "um, you're an idiot." Harold was both an idiot and an ass. The accurate stereotype of an insurance salesman never ceased to amaze Ghanem, and Harold was as cookie cutter as they came.

"Yes, Harold. What can I do for you?" What bothered Ghanem most was having to work for this brown-nosing, three-pack-a-day cigarette-smoking fucker. Out of all the jobs he'd had—and there had been many—this had been, by far, the worst. Stuck in a literal corner, day after day, typing up insurance forms. He couldn't even call himself a salesman—no, nothing as glorified as that. Nothing more than a paper pusher. The monotony was killing him, but he had to work, and more importantly Ghanem needed to blend. As if that were a problem.

He scrubbed his head, looked up at his boss, and tried to ignore the stench of stale cigarettes. Harold would bend over backward for a potential customer, then do whatever he could to screw them out of their money. Ghanem had his number. The problem was, he couldn't do anything about it. Not outwardly. But on the sly he'd slowly begun to give a handful of clients their due. His father took Ghanem's birthright, but he could never take his fundamental core.

"Someone's here to see you." Idiot adjusted his pants, pulling them up another inch past his navel. The motion had Ghanem's own nads aching at the potential assault. How did any man find that comfortable? "Now, you know how I feel about personal interruptions at work, but he claims it's an emergency." Harold lifted a bushy, salt and pepper eyebrow.

Ghanem glanced past Harold, all the while giving the perception of keeping eye contact. Unfortunately, he couldn't see who waited for him, but now that he focused his attention, he could tell *what* waited beyond the short row of cubicles. Usually, he would have detected the being sooner. He was slipping. No surprise there. He practically choked on his next words. "I apologize, sir. I'll make this brief."

"Be sure that you do. Oh, and punch out first." Harold nodded and stomped back to his office, a whole four feet from Ghanem's cubicle.

Ghanem clenched his fists and waited for Harold to shut his office door. Better that than to jump over the desk and break his scrawny-ass neck. A flick of the wrist was all it would take. Ghanem's six-five frame dwarfed Harold by about a foot. Weight was a whole other issue, but he didn't have the time to beat the shit out of Harold. The visitor waited. Ghanem had another matter to deal with. Again.

He always hoped for the best, but braced for the worst. Hope was a bitch that had his balls in a noose, because even after all these years he'd never been given another chance.

After logging out of his computer but skipping the clock-out instructions—Harold owed him more than the few minutes this would take, and it was already past five—Ghanem walked past the piles of insurance claims, manila folders, and other crap paper, trying not to let the heaps get to him. He hated the mess. Hated the confinement. You'd think with so many pissed-off people waiting for insurance money, Harold would hire someone to come in and organize. But that wasn't really the point, was it? You didn't own an insurance company because you wanted to pay claims. Ghanem had pegged the insurance business as a scam from day one, but he had to do something, and this job currently paid the bills, and, more importantly, sucked up several hours of the endless days. Just like all the other jobs he'd had for the last two hundred years.

As Ghanem neared the door, his senses became more acute, more intense. If they knew he'd retained this fragment of his power, he could only imagine what they would do to strip him even more bare. But retain it he did, and because of that, Ghanem now had no doubt of who waited on the other side. *Well, well, well.* This should be interesting. He opened the door and came face to face with his father's personal messenger.

"Dominic has summoned you."

"Nice to see you too, Derek."

The messenger narrowed his bright blue eyes. "My name is Drake."

"Ah, yes. It's been so long I must have forgotten." Of course he hadn't forgotten. He just enjoyed fucking with the lesser guardian. Ghanem eyed Drake's long mane of blond hair, but managed to hide his envy. He'd shaved his own head moments after being shunned, the length no longer necessary.

"Dominic has summoned you."

"What does my father want? Are Thane and Amella okay?" Forcing the panic out of his voice, he glared at Drake. What if something had happened to his brother or sister? His father hadn't sent for him in years. Which had to mean something had happened. Guardians protected the innocent. No matter the cost. That he couldn't protect his own any longer gnawed at his gut and sliced at his soul.

"Dominic has summoned you."

"I fucking heard you the first time. I asked you a question." Ghanem shoved Drake against the wall and yanked him off his feet by his lapels. "Answer me."

Drake didn't quiver, but Ghanem sensed nervousness even as the messenger shifted his eyes to look down at him. They hadn't seen each other in years. Many years. Years in which Ghanem's appearance had drastically changed. Once, he had been on the verge of being one of the strongest and mightiest guardians ever to exist in the Adamo family. A family of warriors, a family with power whose sole task in life was to guard and protect the innocents of the world, human and non-human alike. But Ghanem was no longer part of the family, and with his banishment had come the loss of his prized horns, the tribal tattoos, and the ever-changing color of his eyes. Eyes that at one time had changed to brilliant shades of the most vibrant of gemstones depending on his mood. Emerald, blue topaz, diamond, and the deep crimson of a ruby. Now? Now they were as brown as the dirt beneath his feet. Human brown.

"I cannot give any other information. Dominic has summoned you."

Ghanem lowered him to his feet. He knew this as the truth. Dominic would punish Drake severely if he uttered any other words. The fault did not lie with Drake, just his unfortunate station in life.

"When?"

Drake cocked his head.

"When am I to go to him?"

"Dominic has summoned you," Drake repeated, his eyes widening slightly for emphasis.

"Apparently I'm to go now." The only way to get there was with

Drake's assistance. Just one of many things they'd done to make Ghanem appear weak and less of a guardian. If they'd wanted to embarrass him, they'd succeeded. With one last glance over his shoulder and a silent *good riddance* to Harold The Idiot, Ghanem placed his hand on Drake's shoulder, and, within a moment, they disappeared.

They materialized mere seconds later in his father's study, a place in which he had spent countless hours centuries ago. He took in the familiar leather furniture and antiques Dominic had collected. The room should have invoked good memories, but those memories were overshadowed by the event that had changed the course of his life.

After Drake disappeared through the outer door, Ghanem wandered around the room, careful not to touch anything. If he laid his hands on even one of his father's prized possessions, he'd probably smash it against the nearest wall. His emotions were perilously close to the surface, a dangerous mixture of anger, rage, despair, and that bitch, hope.

He closed his eyes and found it easier in this realm to conjure a memory of his siblings. He allowed it to sweep him away to a better time, a better place. In his mind he saw purple skies. He saw the alluring woods behind their home, trees towering over them in a canopy of wonder, orange sunlight filtering through the dense foliage as they ran and taunted one another. He saw two dark-haired boys and one fair girl. As she wove in and out of the trees, her hair, the color of the purest cotton, danced. Out of the three of them, he was the oldest. His brother, Thane, a mere two years younger, had practically been his twin. They were two halves of a whole. Together, they'd both been protective of their baby sister, Amella. And though she could hold her own, she never squawked at their need to come to her defense.

Ghanem remembered a time when they had no worries. Their days had been filled with laughter, intrigue, and unlimited amounts of energy. Thane had been the thinker, Ghanem the doer, and Amella the constant voice of reason. If only he'd listened to her words of wisdom instead of dismissing them as those of a child. He'd learned since—far too late to save himself—that one should never rule out someone's advice as nonsense, but should take the time to study it from all angles. *Take the time to see how your choices will affect the rest of your life.*

The sound of voices outside the door interrupted his disturbing thoughts. Ghanem should have been thankful for that, but he wasn't. Any memories of his siblings—even troubling ones—were always welcome. The voice outside the door was not.

His father, the mighty Dominic Adamo, was about to enter the room. The last time he'd seen him, Ghanem's heart had been filled with hope. Hope that he would get his chance to join his family once again. That hope had been squashed in seconds and with it, Ghanem's heart. This time he wouldn't make the same mistake. His father would use him before condemning him, again, to spend his life with humans—humans who had a life span of about eighty years. His would be endless.

Dominic entered the room, filling the width of the doorway with his massive form. To Ghanem, he had always seemed larger than life. Time had not diminished Ghanem's awe. Dominic wore a black Armani suit custom-made to fit his immense stature. His hair, as intense as ever with its varying shades of black and white, was shorter than the last time Ghanem had seen him, the style emphasizing the curl of his horns. Horns that twisted and curled back from his forehead. While all guardians had horns—unless they were stripped of them—the look of their horns was uniquely their own.

Dominic's were black in color, giving them an ominous appearance. Feared but revered within their community, he'd been branded throughout this realm, the realm known as Saharren, as one of the mightiest warriors of all time, a trait he would have passed on to his sons. A trait that did not just exist but one that had to be taught, melded and perfected over time. A trait his brother Thane no doubt not only possessed but oozed.

Ghanem stood erect, awaiting some form of acknowledgment from the mighty guardian. What he got was a flash of color within the depths of Dominic's eyes. The red, as if blood had seeped into his irises, could have been sorrow, anger, regret or disdain. Ghanem would never know. Without a word, Dominic handed him a scroll of parchment paper and disappeared.

He should have expected as much, but the hurt could not be denied. Only his father could make him feel so worthless. Ghanem's shoulders slumped as he sank to the floor, his back supported against the wall, his heart thudding against his chest, his breathing shallow. He carefully untied the corded rope and then just as carefully unrolled the fragile and aged scroll. The words swam before his eyes before he could focus his vision, but when he finally did his heart no longer thudded, but slammed against his ribcage, causing an ache, a longing so intense he could scarcely breathe.

Chapter Two

Propped against two overstuffed pillows, Meera pulled her sock-covered feet beneath her and chewed on the end of her purple pen. Earlier she'd written a gloomy entry in her journal, but, ever the optimist, she always forced herself to combat her dark thoughts with lighter ones. Plus, Carrine had promised to help, albeit cryptically, and she had to believe the two of them could figure this out.

Her alternate plan of hiding beneath the covers with a flashlight and pepper spray hadn't had the desired effect. Instead the action had pushed her closer to a state of despair she feared would end up consuming her very soul. *That* she could never let happen. Meera sighed and put pen to paper. She scribbled rapidly and then capped the pen. Five words. Five simple words full of hope.

I will find the truth.

The complete opposite tone to her words from that morning. She preferred this side of her personality. The determined side. If that side had to mix with the darker side in order to get the answers she needed, so be it, because one thing she knew for certain: The truth had to come out.

Her so-called family made the top of the ever-growing list of suspects to question. Meera popped a raspberry and chocolate truffle in her mouth, pushed a stray braid away from her face, and considered her lineage. Her hair had been only one reason she'd suspected she wasn't a biological descendant of the Jones family. *Hello?* They all had blond hair and blue eyes—mother, father, sister, brother—it didn't take a genetic scientist to figure this one out. Two blue-eyed people could not make a green-eyed baby. Okay, so that wasn't exactly true. She ought to know. She'd researched the theory to death. It wasn't impossible, but add the fact that no one, including her father, stood over five foot six while she towered over them at five foot ten, and they all had freckles while her skin was as pale and clear as a geisha, and it was no wonder her suspicions had grown by the day.

When she'd asked, they'd all changed the subject in each of their unique ways. Her father simply left the room. Her mother, on the other hand, threw accusations meant to place the blame on Meera. *Aren't we good enough? Haven't we given you everything?* And her siblings? They were too self-absorbed to even listen.

Meera glanced at the clock again. Only thirty minutes had passed since Carrine had left. She stood and stretched her tight muscles, intent on changing into her pajamas and settling into bed with a good book. As an afterthought, she reached down and turned over the next card in the tarot circle.

The Lovers.

This card, with a nearly nude couple embracing one another with so much emotion evident in the arch of their bodies, gave her chills for another reason entirely. She hadn't had a lover in quite some time. The loss of affection weighed on her mind frequently, but she couldn't have any sort of relationship until she got her life under control. Unfair to all parties involved.

No longer hungry, she stopped by the kitchen to unplug the crockpot and put the food away before heading to her bedroom. The menial tasks helped to quiet the questions in her mind, though nothing could completely silence them once she got going.

Opening the door to her expansive walk-in closet, she stepped in and sighed. Like a lot of women, she had a weakness for clothes. Meera's fingers stroked the different fabrics as she walked by, the textures calling to her sense of style. She adored fashion, not necessarily the latest trend, but fashion that suited her. Lately her style had leaned toward slightly gothic with a hint of eccentricity. Gothic chic.

Her current must-have? Cloaks.

Cloaks in every color and texture imaginable. She couldn't explain why suddenly in this past year she'd been consumed with the need to search out cloaks. They weren't easy to find. Not real ones anyway. Thanks to her *parents*, she had unlimited funds at her disposal, making it easy for consignment shops and online auction sites to become her new best friends. Actually, the Internet had become one of her only sources of interaction. Each weird episode had caused her to distance herself more and more from people until she had all but pushed her friends away. Right or wrong, she just couldn't handle the looks of judgment and pity cast her way when she tranced out, so to speak. Which made her time with Carrine that much more important.

These past few months had been full of unpleasant surprises. Nightmares, dreams, trances, and a family who refused to talk to her about any of her concerns. The list grew endless. It had all started on her birthday. Started with a hum. Then the voices—two voices calling to her, struggling against each other like a tug-of-war in her brain, competing for her attention. One a whisper washing over her in a soothing caress, the other a hiss that scraped against her skin like the sharpest of blades.

Meera squashed the feelings of helplessness and allowed the fires of fury to take over. *Enough!* Tomorrow would be the beginning of the end. She wasn't helpless, just uninformed. Something wasn't right, and she couldn't let fear keep her from finding out the truth. The complete truth. If they weren't her family, who was? Did her *real* family suffer from the same ailment? She didn't want their money. She wanted their answers, and, if she were being honest with herself, she wanted their love.

Snagging her favorite pair of flannel pajamas, Meera threw her clothes in the hamper and pulled the soft fabric over her skin. She brushed her teeth, slipped into bed, and turned off her lamp in favor of a small reading light she had attached to her book.

Opening the pages to her favorite modern day fairytale, she let the characters take her to another world and cast herself as the heroine who kept the chocolate-eyed hero on his toes.

*

Ghanem slowly lowered the parchment after reading it no less than ten times. His mother, the mother he missed so much his heart ached as if the splintered fragments had never healed properly, had written to him when he'd been nothing more than an infant. Written of things he knew nothing about. Things he didn't understand. This letter presented a challenge.

No.

Not just a challenge but also a chance.

Dare he believe it? So many times he had wished for a chance at redemption, only to have the very thought crushed. Now, his own mother had offered up the opportunity he had thought impossible.

He searched deep in his mind, weeding through memories of a time so long ago. He vaguely recalled hearing about the particular veiled she wrote about but couldn't remember what or who they were exactly. He'd run into many veiled species in the human realm over the past two centuries, but no longer considered himself to be part of that community, a community made up of anything and everything non-human.

He pushed to his feet, parchment in hand, and paced the length of the library. Stolen souls? Underground realm? Morphing into humans? The fate of all lay on his shoulders?

Blast it. What was he supposed to do with all this information? One thing was certain. He had to do something. If this were in fact his one chance to return to his rightful life, nothing and no one would stand in his way. With that in mind, Ghanem spun, fists up, when the door behind him swung open.

"Whoa." A striking guardian with hair the color of midnight, horns the color of hell, walked through the door and came to a stop, arms raised, smirk firmly in place. "First time you see me in over two hundred years and I get this as a greeting? Good to see you too, big brother." He studied Ghanem. "Or by the looks of you maybe I should start calling you little brother. And what's up with the button-down and khakis? Are you for real with that shit?"

"Thane?"

"Great. Now you pretend you don't even know me." Thane crossed his arms and leaned smugly against the wall. "One would think you'd be a little happier to see me. It's not as if I'm the one who banished your ass."

Just when Ghanem thought his heart couldn't take anymore, it swelled a million times over. His baby brother stood before him looking just as rebellious as ever with jet-black, wavy hair hanging halfway down his powerful back. His jeans, baggy. His T-shirt, graffiti covered. Just the type of look that would disgust their father and probably the precise reason he dressed that way.

Words failed as he closed the distance and embraced him so tightly Thane gasped for air. Ghanem held him a moment longer before shoving him away. "You're still a smartass."

"Yeah, maybe. But obviously you missed this smartass." Thane straightened his shirt.

Ghanem didn't need to confirm or deny. He and Thane had always been close, and two hundred years could never take that away. "I'm surprised he let you see me."

"What do you mean, let? Don't you know I run this place?"

"Riiiiiight." Gut clenching, he asked, "Where's Amella?" If Dominic allowed Thane to be in the same room with him, maybe, just maybe he'd get to see his sister, too.

"She's away. Some sort of excursion or something. She rarely stays here anymore." Thane angled his head toward the scroll still clenched in Ghanem's right hand. "What's that?"

Ghanem clutched it tighter, his thoughts twisted with regret.

He just hoped he wouldn't have to go another century before he could embrace Amella.

"Relax," Thane said. "I just asked what it was. No big deal. If you don't want to tell me . . . whatever, man."

Ghanem forced himself to loosen up. He knew Thane better than that, and he was one of only two people who would never take anything from him. "Sorry, *fratello*."

Thane smiled at the familiar Italian word for brother. "No worries."

Ghanem looked down at the scroll. "It's a letter."

"Clearly it's an important letter. Mind if I ask who wrote it?"

"Mother."

"Our *mitera*?" Thane lowered himself onto the leather couch.

"Yeah, *Mitera*." Ghanem's thoughts drifted to a better time. A time before he'd made a catastrophic mistake that forever changed so many lives. "Funny how she never liked to be called *Madre*. She always preferred *Mitera*." He shrugged. "I guess she held on to what little Greek she could in a home filled with strong Italian men."

"Nah. I think she did it just to rile Dominic."

"You're probably right. Anyway, this is from her. She wrote it a long time ago." Ghanem remained standing.

"How long ago?"

He shrugged. "I guess I was only a couple months old."

"Damn," Thane said. "That was a loooooong time ago."

"Smartass."

"I'm pretty sure we covered that already. So, what's the letter about?"

"It's probably easier if I let you read it." Ghanem offered the scroll.

Thane gently wrapped his hand around it. "Yeah, Ghan? I can't read it if you won't give it to me."

He reluctantly loosened his hold, but not before saying, "Be careful, and you have to give it back." He didn't care that he sounded all of nine years old. He would get the scroll back. He had no treasures in the human realm. Nothing he considered truly his. This letter would be a part of him until . . . Always.

"Man, the human world must be rough. Don't worry. I'll be very careful and when I'm done . . . it's all yours." Thane carefully smoothed the paper with his hands. He took several moments to read through. "Shit."

"Nicely put. Any suggestions?"

"Well, now I get it." Thane carefully returned the scroll, leaned back, and watched as Ghanem meticulously tied the rope to keep the scroll from unrolling.

Ghanem looked up. "Get what?"

"I *get* what Dominic's been rambling about. He's been going on and on for days about how I had to help someone. I questioned him numerous times as to who I was to help." Thane waved a dismissive hand. "But you know him. Need to know basis only."

"I don't understand. Whom does Dominic want you to help?"

"You, Ghanem. He wants me to help you."

Chapter Three

Panic set in with the first drawn-out note of the hum—the telltale sign of an episode.

A wave of dizziness washed over Meera and the room went pitch black, her tiny reading light snuffed, the beam from the moon shining in her window stolen.

An evil darkness surrounded her. Nothing tangible—more like an essence, a spirit. She had to fight, but how could she fight what she couldn't see?

The weight of the oppressed air seemed to crush her lungs. Meera closed her eyes and tried to take slow, even breaths, but it was too hot, too much, too painful. She squeezed her eyes shut even tighter and held her breath. When would it stop? What did it want?

Meera.

Oh, God. She could hear it calling to her. Not a voice really, but more like a hiss on the wind, digging and scratching against her nerves. She opened her eyes in an attempt to see something, anything.

Total darkness.

Absolute darkness.

The kind of darkness that crushed and paralyzed. *Damn it!* Where was the light? She desperately needed the warmth of light. A world without light would be cruel. Evil.

Meera. It is time.

Time for what? A sequence of tarot cards flashed before her eyes. Each one bleaker than the next. She didn't understand. Evil didn't flow through her veins. She was normal, good.

The voice came at her from all directions now. Behind her, then beside her, hissing in her ear. The hot air swirled, wrapping her body in its wicked current. *Come to us. It is time.*

With a string of rampant curses, Meera woke, her body shivering. She was drenched in sweat and her head pounded like the bass in a Bose system. She breathed through the pain. Nightmare. One that had seemed so real. They always did. The voices. Calling to her, screaming at her . . . begging her.

She whipped the twisted sheet off her body and stumbled out of bed toward the bathroom. She knew from almost a year of experience that the nightmare would fade in mere moments and with it most, if not all the details and memories it conjured. The voices would remain.

Meera braced herself, her hands clamped tightly to the sides of her pedestal sink. Slowly lifting her head, she studied herself in the mirror. The face of a stranger greeted her. She recoiled, but then realized she was staring at her own reflection. The dark shadows under her green eyes, making her look every bit as tired and drained as she felt, were more than just the remnants of yesterday's make-up. Meera removed a cotton ball and make-up remover from the cabinet and gently wiped away mascara and fatigue. She washed her face and then stole one more glance in the mirror.

After several calming breaths, she wandered toward the kitchen, the need for coffee so strong she could already smell it. She turned the corner and came to a complete, sudden stop, her hand flying to her throat.

"Holy cheeseballs, Carrine," Meera whispered. "You scared the crap out of me." She tried to laugh, but the sound came out jagged and brittle.

"I apologize for that. But you were asleep and I didn't want to wake you. I hope you don't mind me letting myself in."

"No, of course not. But how did you get in?" She didn't remember giving Carrine a key, but maybe she had in one of her unfocused moments.

"The door wasn't locked."

She couldn't tell if Carrine had just uttered a statement or a question. Something about her friend seemed different this morning. Very different. Maybe it was just the lingering effects of the terrible dream. That or perhaps she had yet to wake at all. Was it possible the nightmare could completely take over and become the total hell she feared?

"I should have said good morning. Good morning, Meera. I've brewed you some coffee. Please have a seat." Carrine pulled out the chair next to her own.

Still trying to figure out why Carrine was acting so oddly, Meera lowered herself into the chair, drew her legs up, and wrapped her arms around them. Resting her chin on her knees, she said, "I don't understand. Did I miss something? Why are you here so early?" *And why are you acting so bizarre?* That was the question she really wanted to ask. Though Carrine seemed calm, Meera detected much emotion in her friend's eyes.

Carrine slid a mug of steaming coffee toward her then sat regally in her chair, her back straight, her hands folded and placed on the edge of the table in front of her. "You have many questions. You must be patient and I will explain everything." She waved a dismissive hand when Meera tried to interrupt. "Learning patience will serve you well in the future. Drink your coffee, child. This is going to be a very long day and will require a great deal of energy."

"I—" Meera began to protest. Why was Carrine acting so superior all of a sudden? She'd called her child before, but never in a condescending tone, as if she weren't a confident and capable adult. Who was she kidding? Certainly not herself, and, by the look in Carrine's eyes, she wouldn't be fooled either. She needed help, and Carrine had been the first person, the only person, to offer any form of it. The least Meera could do was hear her out. If nothing else, she owed it to herself. So instead of protesting the harsh tone, she slumped back in her chair and sipped her black coffee, which, she might add, had been made to perfection.

"Ah, you are a fast learner. I expected as much. If you can master patience, that will go a long way in helping you on this journey."

They sat in silence, each one studying the other in an attempt to learn the mysteries that lay beneath the façade they both wore this morning. Meera knew the story behind her own attitude. Crap-ass nightmares would do that to a person.

Carrine, though, proved to be an enigma. Like always, Carrine was impeccably dressed. Her corset-style top accented her slim waist and the magenta color set off her green eyes in such a way she looked almost enchanting. Her hands remained folded. Her nails were pristine and buffed to a high polish, her make-up subtle yet striking. They'd had an ongoing, though never spoken of, fashion battle playing out between them for months. Meera glanced down at her blue-and-white flannel pajamas. She'd lost this round. No doubt about it.

As though she knew she were being scrutinized, and seemingly proud of it, the better-dressed woman nodded her head, a slight movement but unmistakable. The silence grew uncomfortably long. Carrine drew a breath as if she were preparing a long speech, but instead closed her eyes, her brows drawn, her lips pursed. Meera wondered if that was how she looked when she went into one of her trances. She cleared her throat and received no response. Moments went by before Carrine opened her eyes again and rose, her features oddly void of any emotion. "The council needs me. I must go."

"But—the who?" Meera interrupted.

"I must go."

"You can't go. You just got here and you ditched me last night, too. You didn't even . . . why did you—"

"I will be back as soon as I can. One thing I can tell you now is I am no longer your friend. I am your mentor. Now, I really have to go. Remember to preserve your energy. Remember . . . "

"What did you just say? Remember what?" More confused than ever, Meera questioned the retreating woman and wondered again what had gotten into her friend. "Remember what?" She never got her answer. Carrine shut the door with a concluding click.

*

Ghanem and Thane quickly perused the bronze shelves of their father's library and grabbed as many books as they could hold. Thane retrieved a couple of overnight bags from the double-door closet and together they stuffed them full. Their choices were based on title alone, and Ghanem had no clue if they'd chosen wisely or if there were even any books within the room that could help him. He had to believe there were, and that one of the many weighing down the bag would answer some of the questions that filled his mind. That Thane would be there to help him decipher some of this was a relief and a fortune he wouldn't undervalue.

"Ready?"

Ghanem looked around, took in his father's domain with a heavy heart, then nodded. His brother's horns receded—a necessary skill learned during youth—before he slapped Ghanem on the back and traced them out of Saharren.

Darkness gave way to a dusting of starlight that steadily increased to a full on blast of intense white light. He reveled in the feel of falling weightlessly. He missed the power of this. Missed the convenience. Getting around in the human world required nothing more than his two feet or the key to a car. This was by far the superior mode of transportation. He hoped Thane would trace them to Italy. With Italy being the closest earth realm to Saharren, Ghanem had frequented the country often in his youth. He felt a kinship to the land and the people. Even the human ones.

They landed silently in the back of a dimly lit bar. A quick perusal showed that, other than a few clusters of people, the place was nearly empty. No doubt due to the stench of bitter beer and cigarettes. "Where are we?" Ghanem asked.

"In a bar."

"Genius. I swear."

"All right, all right. We're in a bar in Milwaukee." Thane chuckled.

He dropped the heavy bag next to the counter and grabbed a stool. The bartender looked over, perplexity evident in his eyes and the tilt of his head. Thane waved a hand and the look passed. The bartender held up a finger indicating he'd be with them in a moment.

"Wait, Milwaukee? As in Milwaukee, Wisconsin?" *So much for Italy.* "And what did you just do the bartender?" Ghanem had watched as confusion changed into acceptance with the mere wave of a hand.

"Yeah, Milwaukee, Wisconsin, and neat trick, huh?" Thane smiled arrogantly and shoved a stray lock of midnight hair out of his eyes. "I've been practicing that for a while now, and I've just about perfected it."

"What did you do?"

"I just added an innocent memory of the two of us coming in the front door. It's no big deal, Ghan, really."

Ghanem wasn't sure about that. Adding memories seemed more than a little wrong. But what did he expect? They were guardians—one of them anyway—and it wasn't as if they lived by a completely moral code. Protect the innocent? Absolutely. But many times the means to do so skirted the edge of immorality.

Thane shrugged and pulled out the stool next to him. Ghanem lowered himself into it before ordering a cognac from the smiling bartender. Thane ordered a shot of whiskey, straight up.

"What are we doing here, Thane? We should be somewhere studying these books. Not sitting in a rank-ass bar in the Midwest sipping drinks."

Thane shook his head. "Is it so bad that I wanted to share a drink with my brother on a Friday night before we get down to some hard-core shit? Need I remind you that I haven't had any contact with you at all, for over two hundred years? And I brought us here because there's less chance of running into other veiled. Plus this is the city I overheard Dominic mentioning to one of his comrades. I figure there's a reason for that."

When Thane put it that way, Ghanem felt like an ass of mega proportions. "Sorry, man. I'm just a little worked up right now." Considering many veiled didn't get along, he could appreciate Thane's reason for this particular locale. The fact that Dominic had made mention of the city by the Great Lake could not be a mere coincidence.

"Don't worry about it. It's understandable under the circumstances."

"Wait. Did you say Friday?"

"Yeah, why?"

"Never mind." Ghanem pinched the bridge of his nose. Drake had delivered his message on Thursday. How quickly he'd forgotten time was but a word in other realms. Minutes could seem like hours. Days could seem like seconds.

Thane nudged him with his elbow. "Why don't you just sit back, drink your brandy and enjoy the view?"

Ghanem choked and had to drag the back of his hand across his mouth to wipe the cognac from his lips. "View? This place is a dive in every sense of the word."

Thane quirked a smile. "Not all of it. Look what just walked through the door."

Ghanem turned his head and felt a sucker punch straight to his gut. "*Merda.*"

"Really? That's your take on shit?"

"Shut up, smartass."

Ghanem's world spun with every step the extraordinary woman took. The blood supply left his brain and went straight to his shaft, something that hadn't happened in too many years to count. He'd never been so glad to be sitting in his entire life.

He couldn't take his eyes off her. She removed her ebony jacket and threw it over the back of a stool. No. Not a jacket, a cloak. The only time he'd seen a human wear one was during their pathetic Halloween celebrations. If only they understood the real meaning behind the holiday, perhaps they would take it more seriously and honor those who had left this plane. She was either a little late or a lot early to be dressing up as a witch, but it didn't matter because when she removed the damn thing, he stopped breathing.

Her long, lithe body had the most feminine of curves. Slim jeans tucked into tall, brown, leather boots clung to her skin like a custom-made glove. His fingers itched to trace along the womanly silhouette. Her pale exotic face tilted as she searched the interior of the bar in the muted light. And those lips. *Fuck me.* Her lush lips begged to be caressed with his thumb before he moved in for a taste. An internal war raged as he struggled to remain unnoticed when all he really wanted to do was look his fill.

He caught her eye for the briefest of moments, and what he saw surprised him. Haunted, strained, tired. Why would such a beautiful woman look as though she carried the weight of the world on her shoulders? His instinct to protect roared to life.

"Maybe I'll invite her over for a drink. I haven't had a human in a while."

Ghanem leveled his brother with a single look. "You will not touch her." The intensity of his words surprised both of them, but Thane backed off.

"Got it. I will not bed this one. But hey, man, just because you live in this world doesn't mean I'll always give you first dibs."

Ghanem shook his head and forced himself to laugh, but the laugh ended abruptly when he snuck another look at the raven-haired temptress with so much sorrow swimming in the depths of her eyes.

*

After a long day of hell, Meera wanted nothing more than to enjoy a glass of wine outside the confines of her condo. What she didn't want was to be alone while doing it. Which had been her reason for choosing this particular bar. Her old hangout. A place she once frequented to meet friends. She just couldn't remember the last time. *Not going there.* Being a Friday night ritual and all, the chance of her friends being there was almost a guarantee. She should have called them first, let them know she'd be here, but feared she'd change her mind and let them down. Again. Insecurities had practically killed her social life.

Anxious, she looked around, and, when she didn't recognize anyone, she pulled her lower lip between her teeth and considered her options. She should just leave, check out the other bars, but the clubs on Water Street would be packed, and she had no desire to deal with randy college boys and perverted middle-aged men who needed to get a life. *Like I have room to judge,* she chastised herself.

A quick scan of the place told her even though her friends weren't there, she did recognize the bartender. Pete had been a mainstay for as long as she could remember. He'd probably been around when they opened the place. She smiled to herself as she pulled off her cloak. There were other people in the bar, but not too many. An oversexed couple sat in a dark corner choking each other with dueling tongues. Hard to tell where one ended and the other began. A few small groups here and there, and two men at the far end of the bar. Hopefully the smoke in the air would obscure their view as much as it did hers. She'd enjoy one drink—maybe two—catch up with Pete, and hopefully make it out without trancing out.

She could handle this. All she had to do was avoid eye contact and stick to her end of the bar. Not knowing when the next episode would hit, she really didn't want to strike up a conversation with a stranger and have to worry about them taking advantage of her tenuous condition. She tried to be patient as she waited for Pete to notice her. Maybe he hadn't heard her come in over the drone of the outdated and scratchy music system barely cranking out the Stones.

"Excuse me," she called. He didn't even look her way. "Excuse me." Pete, dressed in the same plain black tee and jeans he always wore, kept his eyes glued to the Brewers game on the TV above the cash register, the light from the television reflecting off his bald head. Just as she moved to get up, Meera's neck tingled. She turned and realized her calls for service had managed to grab the attention of one of the men at the other end of the bar.

Crap.

So not what she needed.

She pretended she didn't see him when he shot her an awkward smile, and instead looked over the top of his head. She tried not to notice when his strong, angular jaw tightened just before he looked away. She could try all she wanted, but there was no missing this man. Or the way her body responded. Normally chilled, her blood heated beneath her skin. She could practically feel it traveling through her body, excited, pumped, and ready for a little one-on-one action. *Wow.* That hadn't happened . . . ever.

While his black-haired-Fabio friend looked like a model for 'Roids-R-Us, the one holding her attention simply looked like he took care of his body in a shrine-like manner. Deliciously perfect. His pleated khaki pants seemed out of place on a body such as his. Her mind re-dressed him in the perfect jeans and long-sleeved, black, button-up shirt with the sleeves rolled up to expose the muscles in his forearms, and the top three buttons undone to reveal a smooth, hard chest. *Holy testosterone.* Two very fine specimens, the one with the shaved head even more so because he didn't know it even if she did on all levels.

Not that she was interested. Not in the least. *Really? Then why am I sweating?*

Meera snapped her head forward. She'd come here for a drink and a smile and to formulate a plan. Nothing more. She thought back to the nightmare and was surprised she remembered so many details this time. This particular nightmare had been horrific, the morning almost worse. She'd replayed this morning's scene in her mind over and over again, but the confusion refused to waver.

Meera stared into the mirror along the back wall of the bar and still saw the same tired reflection of hours before.

This business with Carrine had her more baffled than ever. Why had she called herself a mentor? What questions did she plan to answer? Who or what was the council? She had never shared her doubts with anyone outside the family—who constantly blew her off—and Carrine, who suddenly claimed she could help even though she'd basically morphed into a stranger overnight. How could someone help when they didn't even know what the problem was? Hell, Meera didn't really know what the problem was. There was so much more to it than just the voices. Deep down, something about her wasn't quite right. Had never been right. So simple and so incredibly complicated.

Meera snuck a look toward the far end of the bar. The time had come to make a plan, and said plan did not and would not include Mr. Delicious down there. No matter how her hormones responded. Boy, did they respond.

When Pete finally noticed her, he made his way down to her with a big welcoming smile.

"Well, well, well. Is if isn't Miss Meera herself. I've missed you, girl."

Meera returned the smile and touched Pete's hand. "It's been too long."

"Too long, indeed. I've been here. Where've you been, stranger?"

"Around." Finding it hard to maintain eye contact for fear Pete would notice more than she was willing to talk about, she flicked her gaze to the TV. "Where is everyone?"

Pete patted her hand and chuckled. "Season tickets. Brewers are having a stellar year."

She hadn't realized, but smiled and nodded.

"Since you're here, you may as well have a drink. What can I get you?"

Mouth completely dry, Meera wet her lips and then did something she hadn't done since college. She ordered a Lemon Drop with a Miller Lite chaser. And quickly amended her order.

"Make that two."

"Of which?" he asked.

"Both."

"Someone joining you?" Pete angled his head, his mouth turned downward.

I hope not danced on the tip of her tongue, but she squashed it. "Maybe." Couldn't have him thinking she had an alcohol problem or worse.

Pete wrinkled his nose, but poured her two shots and slid them across the bar before grabbing two bottles of beer out of the cooler.

Meera downed the first shot, sucked the sugar off the lemon and chugged her beer. She waited a minute or two before repeating the sequence.

Pete raised an eyebrow when she called him over for two more but brought them anyway. "I can't let you drive, girlie. You know that, don't you?"

She smiled, nodded, basked in the warmth of the care in his voice. "I didn't drive," was all she said. Escape. She needed it. Her mind screamed for it. How royally stupid could she be, sitting alone in a bar slamming beers and shots, but today? Today she just didn't care.

Feeling a good sloshing coming on, she lifted her glass and quickly made it through the third round but had to hold off on the fourth. The buzz was nice; her bladder wasn't. No choice but to walk past the delicious one and head to the bathroom.

Meera pushed the stool back from the bar and stood. Apparently a little too quickly. The room spun, and there could have been a slight chance she wobbled. A very slight chance. She planted her feet firmly on the wood-planked floor and held onto the back of the stool until the spinning stopped, furtively hoping no one would notice.

Someone did.

Guess who? No matter, she had to get to the bathroom. Now. She threw her purse over her shoulder and made her way down the length of the bar. She must have tripped over the leg of a stool—or something—in her attempt to be cool, calm, and collected, because before she knew it she fell into none other than the one she had tried to avoid.

He turned quickly and grabbed her arms to steady her. Heat shot through her system so rapidly she swore she'd go up in flames.

She flinched.

He let go.

"Are you all right?"

Meera temporarily lost her mind. Again. Go figure. A sane Meera would have said *fine, thank you,* but no, of course not. "Wow. It's like a blend of new country and old whiskey."

She stood there, gently rubbing her heated arms and ogling the man before her as her body tingled with awareness. For a second—yes, only a second—she lost herself in his gaze, in the barely restrained heat flickering beneath the surface, fighting to break through. The intensity of that heat would melt the chocolate right out of those eyes, and man, she wanted to be there when it happened. Just one taste was all she needed. The Lovers card flashed before her eyes, and she had no problem picturing the two of them locked in an embrace.

"Excuse me?"

"Your voice. It's incredible. I've never heard anything like it." Sanity returned, and an embarrassed Meera swiftly made her way to the bathroom. She was unsteady on her feet. Unfortunately, her mind was stable enough to know she'd just made a major fool of herself. *How freakin' embarrassing.* She gave herself a good tongue lashing while she took care of business in the facilities.

After, eyes averted, she hurried past the inferno, swearing her skin was scorched from his hands. She grabbed her cloak, slapped enough money on the bar to pay her tab with a sizeable tip, and left before she could do or say anything else stupid. Pete called her name, but she couldn't bear to look at him. She'd call him when she got home and let him know she was all right. Leaning against the closed door, she took a deep breath. *What the hell was that?*

Seeing no taxis by the curb, Meera decided to walk home. She didn't live too far from the bar, and it would give her a chance to cool off. Sobering up wouldn't be a bad idea, either. Her whole body was heated, but especially her arms. When he'd touched her, his hands had been so warm, almost hot, as if he had held them in front of a fire. As if he were branding her. The entire encounter had surprised her. The heat and his voice.

She pulled her cloak tight around her face and headed east. If she walked quickly, she could make it home in less than twenty minutes. She wanted nothing more than to crash in her comfortable bed. She prayed this would be a night with no nightmares. No hum. No voices.

The sound of footsteps echoed on the quiet street, bouncing around before fading. She spun around, scanned the street, saw nothing but parked cars and neon lights. When had it gotten so late? Normally there would still be people milling about, laughing and stumbling on the sidewalks. Not tonight. The streets were as empty as a bachelor's refrigerator.

Meera quickened her pace, heard the sound again, and wondered if it could be the beating of her own heart. Deep down she knew it wasn't. The footsteps continued, almost a match for her own. The pace was quick, but the rhythm was slightly off, and her boots had soft soles, causing virtually no sound. She turned again. Shadows crawled up the side of the building and stretched toward the moon. Then they were gone, and once again she doubted herself. Had she imagined it? Had one too many shots?

It didn't take much these days to kick her imagination into high gear. Maybe it was more than that—something closer to delusions.

Headlights from an approaching car almost had her running back to the bar. The blinking *Yellow Cab* sign on top changed her mind. She quickly hailed the cab, then slid into the back seat and gave her address to the man behind the wheel. He didn't turn to look at her, just faced forward and nodded his head. Fine by her. Maybe this meant he wouldn't try to strike up a conversation. She was done talking. Every time she opened her mouth lately, nothing but madness leaked out. Pair that with her delusional mind, and she'd become a total fruitcake.

She stared out the window as the snow started to fall. Just the sight of the white fluff chilled her. Maybe she needed a change of scenery or, better yet, a change of climate. She longed for warm weather. It didn't help that the cabbie didn't have the heat on. "Sir?"

He didn't answer, but his gaze flicked up to the mirror. Goosebumps instantly covered her flesh. Dread hit the pit of her stomach like an anchor, gluing her in place. Something was wrong. With him. His eyes appeared empty. Maybe the darkness of the car caused shadows that played tricks on her mind, but no, it was more than that. Something about the man was dark, evil, and she wanted out. Whispers haunted her mind even though the driver hadn't opened his mouth.

"Stop the car."

He kept driving.

"Stop the car, please." She sat on the edge of the seat, the seatbelt pulled tight across her chest, and watched as the speedometer inched up. "I said stop the car." Her volume escalated with each word. Meera was done being nice. She wanted out now.

He continued to ignore her. She searched for an escape route. She had to find a way to get out of the car before he could take her somewhere remote. The buildings whizzed by. She held on to the door handle as he drove faster and faster, weaving around cars. Meera prayed for a red light. Her heart slammed against her chest and fear grabbed a hold with frigid claws.

Her prayers weren't answered. It seemed as though everything was on his side, working with him to make sure she remained in the car.

Covered in shadow, his hands clutched the steering wheel. She couldn't even make out his appearance. If—No, dammit!—*when* she escaped, she'd never be able to give a description of him to the police. Icy sweat trickled down her spine. Her mind raced. She had to do something.

Meera unlatched her seat belt and slowly reached over the front seat, ready to fight him for control of the car. Fight for her life. She grabbed the back of his headrest just as he slammed on the brakes. Frantic, she scrambled to open the door before falling out onto the curb. Getting to her feet quickly, she turned to run. With a squeal of tires on pavement, the taxi drove out of sight.

Turning a quick circle, she was stunned to find he'd dropped her off in front of her own building. She fished through her purse for her keys and made it to the door in record time. She should call someone. Who was she kidding? There wasn't a chance in Mississippi anyone would believe her. *Yes, officer. I hailed a cab and then he drove me home really fast.* Because, really, that was the extent of it when she broke it down. A hysterical giggle escaped her tight throat. Just another one of her nightmares. She just happened to be awake while this one happened.

She fumbled with the keys, not able to get the door to unlock. Meera looked over her shoulder. More shadows slithered across the sidewalk, inching up the building. She held in her scream though it threatened to rip out of her chest.

Get inside, get inside, get inside. She wanted to shout at her inner voice. Tell it to shut the hell up. She knew she needed to get inside and didn't appreciate the constant reminder. Meera steadied her hand, fit the key in the lock, slipped in, and slammed the door. Flipping on every light, she made her way to her bedroom. She stripped out of her clothes, threw a towel over the mirror so she wouldn't have to look at her crazed eyes, splashed water on her face, and finally lay down on her bed. She forced her eyes to remain open and alert. What if the shadows were real? What if they slipped in while she was asleep? What if?

Meera refused to give into the tears. She was stronger than this. Had to be. With no one to stand guard, vigilance was a must and completely up to her. A traitorous tear escaped and slid down her cheek. She swiped it away with shaky fingers. Exhaustion came in many forms and Meera had been plagued with them all. Tonight would be a challenge.

She angrily swiped at another tear with the back of her hand and fought the fatigue as it fought to take over. Where was her inner voice now? She could really use some encouragement. It remained silent, so Meera opened her mouth and spoke the words aloud. "I am strong. I am strong. I am strong." Over and over she repeated the words she needed to hear. When her eyes began to close, she said the words louder. Before long, she was screaming.

"I! Am! Strong!"

Chapter Four

Realm of Lemra

King Ryken, leader of the slayers, pushed back his chair, stood, and stretched his arms over his head. He leaned over his massive, ornate desk, where he'd been studying the plans he'd worked up over the past couple of months. No detail was too small. Nothing could be overlooked. Still, his mind and body needed the occasional break.

Ryken absently rubbed the tip of his pointed ear, the action soothing his strained mind. While he detested a slayer's true form and never allowed himself to revert back to it—not since his visit with the oracle, anyway—he always retained the pointed ears. They were the mark of a seasoned slayer. One who had been through the painful training and survived the torture of morphing for the first time. He wore his proudly.

He dropped his hand to the desk and focused on the task at hand. First business of the day was to make a decision on what to do with Ninxo Macesinger, a young slayer within the colony. Ninxo had failed, again, to fill his quota. All soldiers within the Slayer Legion were required to bring in a minimum of ten humans a week. Humans were necessary for many reasons, but, most importantly, he wanted the beautiful females. What had started as a craving, a game to appease his evolving appetite, had since turned into a necessity. Those who brought more were rewarded for their efforts. Those who fell short . . . well, that was another matter entirely.

Ninxo had been given ample chances to correct his technique and get the job done, only to be unsuccessful time and time again. So, really, the only question was how to dispose of him. Quickly and quietly, allowing the others to wonder? He'd done that before and got a kick out of hearing the stories mutate into dark and gory tales. The other option would be to punish him in front of the entire colony. This served a greater purpose. No one would wonder what had happened to Ninxo the Failure, and Ryken would gain even more respect. More importantly, those who served him would continue to fear him. Arching his back, he let the feeling of power wash over him. Power and sex. His only two desires.

Decision made, Ryken waved his hand over the plans. The air shimmered and the documents disappeared. He lowered himself into his gilded throne, closed his eyes, and issued a mental call. Mere moments later, a rap sounded at the door.

"Enter."

"You called upon me, my lord."

"Yes, Jayson. Come in and have a seat. We have much to discuss."

Ryken remembered a time when Jayson Nightfinder had come close to suffering the same fate as Ninxo. The difference being, Jayson had learned his lesson and risen above. He'd fought tooth and nail climbing his way up the ranks. Now second in command of the Legion, he served under no one save Ryken himself.

He chose the seat directly opposite Ryken and lowered his glamoured body into it. He stood over six feet tall, and his strong and lean body was that of a warrior. Jayson smoothed his gleaming white hair before placing his hands on his knees. "How may I serve you, my lord?"

Ryken tapped a finger against his lip. "I need you to gather all those who reside in Lemra. No one, including the females and the young, are to be exempt. Ninxo Macesinger will suffer his fate this eve and all will bear witness."

"Is he aware?"

"Seeing as he's an incompetent fool, I doubt he is. All the better, really. The look of terror on his face once he realizes his misfortune will be a sight for all to see, remember, and fear."

Jayson nodded his agreement.

"Now tell me how the Legion is faring." Ryken lifted a crystal glass to his lips and inhaled deeply before savoring the taste of the fine merlot. Even though Jayson was his second, that still didn't warrant an offer to imbibe in the finest with him. No. This bottle, just like the others, was for Ryken alone.

"At this moment, I have several placed near the American city of Chicago. With a population of nearly three million within the city alone, and close to ten million if we include the entire metro area, we should be able to accumulate tens of thousands of their kind before anyone suspects a thing. I believe you'll be pleased to know we have made physical contact with your female interest." Jayson's mouth slowly curved into a smile.

Ryken's gut quivered with excitement. "Excellent. The outcome?" Getting his hands on all that power would give him unparalleled pleasure.

"Crayber took her for quite the ride around her city. As predicted, she is frightened but strong."

Just the way Ryken liked them. "And are the young soldiers blending well?"

"Yes, my lord. None are sent out before proving they can completely morph and blend with the American humans. It's become a competition among the men. Learning quickly and being precise are the only way to top each other."

Fingers steepled, he said, "I would like to see this. Do not let on, but I will be present at the next training session. That is all for now, Nightfinder. Have Ninxo Macesinger and the entire colony ready at nightfall."

Jayson rose from his chair, straightened his green, knee-length vest. "Yes, my lord. As you wish." Jayson bowed his head.

Ryken didn't doubt for a second Jayson would let his own glamour fade the moment the door closed behind him. Just so long as he never presented himself to Ryken in that form, all would be fine. He couldn't—wouldn't—abide anything less.

Ryken drained his glass, waved a hand over his desk, and resumed studying the plans. Everything had to be perfect.

Chapter Five

Meera slept fitfully, the vision of the man with the whiskey voice and the smoldering, oh, so chocolate eyes invading her dreams. She should have been thankful for that, but instead found those vivid pictures almost as disturbing as her nightmares. She shivered, remembering how his hands had covered her body in the most sensual of ways, teasing places only one other had been. His lips had traced an erotic trail from her mouth down to the most sensitive areas of her body, making her tremble with anticipation and need. She was naked. He was fully dressed, just the way she'd imagined him. Even so, she could feel every muscle as he worked his way up and down her body.

Wanting a man she'd really never met and would never see again was enough to make her head throb. Apparently, it was too much to ask for one night of dreamless sleep. One night that wasn't consumed by nightmares and things she could never have or understand.

The smell of coffee roused her. It could only mean one thing.

Carrine was back.

Meera donned her robe and headed to the kitchen to greet her friend—scratch that—mentor.

Carrine smiled in greeting as Meera entered the room. "Would you care for some coffee?"

"I can make my own damn coffee." She stomped to the refrigerator and snatched her favorite bottle of raspberry creamer.

"Sleep well?"

Meera glared at her and held in an exasperated scream. Today could prove to be completely different from yesterday. Deciding to reserve judgment for the time being, she pasted a half smile on her face and sighed. "Peachy. Should we pick up where we left off yesterday, or are you going to leave again?"

"So full of questions, my child. I have no other obligations today. Today you will get some of your answers. Drink up and listen."

Meera rounded the table and snagged the farthest chair from the maddening woman she had, until yesterday, called friend. The tone she'd always found to be tranquil now held an edge she couldn't quite identify. Her kitchen felt more like a boardroom—she at one end of the long table and Carrine at the other. Ally or opponent had yet to be determined.

Carrine's eyes grew heavy with intensity. Her voice commanded attention. "I'm going to tell you a story. A story of long ago. A story the likes of which you have never heard. A story of your history and mine. A story of the past and a story of the future." Carrine threw her hand into the air and lifted her chin. "A story of life . . . "

Meera's jaw practically bounced off the floor. She stared as the room started to fill with mist—mist that emanated from Carrine's fingertips. Her reaction should have been horror, or at the very least disbelief. Instead she found herself amazed, entranced, unable to take her eyes off the hypnotic vapor, unable to draw her attention away from the rhythmic sound of Carrine's voice. She should have been scared. She wasn't.

" . . . and a story of death," Carrine finished. The mist continued to pour from the tips of her fingers, weaving around her arm in a mesmerizing spiral. It drifted in all directions, reaching each corner as if it had no other task than to grow and expand until the entire kitchen was covered in the eerie haze. "Watch, Meera, for it is time."

The chilling words caused Meera to shudder. She gaped at the world flooding her kitchen, a world of intense beauty. A world that glistened in such a way one could only call it magick.

She saw lush, green meadows full of wildflowers and colorful cottages. Snow-capped mountains, thunderous waterfalls, sapphire skies, and towering trees. A world full of women and children so lovely most would pale in comparison.

Her gaze was drawn to two people in particular. A striking woman with fiery red hair and brilliant emerald eyes that were exact replicas of the young child she held in her lap. The child gazed at the woman with such admiration it nearly broke Meera's heart. In turn, the woman stroked the child's cheek lovingly as she crooned captivating words.

"One day you will make a choice; one day you will hear a voice. Follow the light within the wind; shut out the darkness, for it has sinned. Hear me now, oh tiny deara; hear me now, my little Meera."

Meera gasped at the sound of her own name. A yearning she didn't understand seared her soul. She tried desperately to break away. She had to talk to Carrine. Who was this woman? What did her song mean? But she couldn't. She was being sucked in. She grabbed the table in an attempt to root herself. The woman's chanting grew louder. *"One day you will make a choice; one day you will hear a voice. Follow the light within the wind; shut out the darkness, for it has sinned. Hear me now, oh tiny deara; hear me now, my little Meera."*

The darkness consumed her and she was swept away into another world. The wind chafed her skin with its intensity, forcing her body one way and then the next. This had never happened before. This time, there had been no hum, no warning. She struggled to clear her head, to escape back into reality.

Meera. Listen to me, Meera.

The voice circled around her. A hiss one moment, a whisper the next.

Don't fight this. This is your destiny.

She tried to shut out the hiss, but it wove itself around the whisper, strangling the soft, melodic sound. This didn't make sense. None of it made sense. The wind grew more powerful as she fought to make a connection with the softer voice. That voice was the light in this world of darkness, and she had to do everything in her power to latch onto that radiance.

Meera. You are the one. Use the light. Use your hands, your thoughts, your voice. Serenity within the plea.

What did that mean? Use the light?

No! Release us. Such evil, such malice.

She fought with every fiber of her being. Fought against the hiss and the darkness. Fought to stand against the commanding wind. Meera threw out her hands to push away the reptilian voice and the all-encompassing darkness that came with it. She stared as her fingertips began to glow and caught a glimpse of hate-filled eyes within the sea of black.

Use the light, use the light, use the light, use the . . .

The feminine whisper kept chanting as beautiful, white light climbed up Meera's fingers and spilled onto her hands.

The malevolent eyes widened for a split second before becoming angry slits and retreating into the darkness.

She came out of the trance feeling both drained and energized, her hands warm and tingly. She shook her head to clear the fog and remembered she wasn't alone. "What just happened?" Standing quickly, she knocked over the chair. "What the hell is going on?" Her voice sounded shaky even to herself. She took a sip of coffee with unsteady hands and realized it had grown cold.

"What do you remember?" Carrine walked to the faucet and filled a glass with water. She placed it in front of Meera and reclaimed her seat.

Meera drained the glass and moved to refill it. She'd never been so thirsty. "Remember? I—I'm not sure."

"Yes you are. Tell me what you saw, what you felt."

Meera snapped her head toward Carrine's voice as her tone soothed once again. Who was this woman who had somehow changed the kitchen into a magick show? Meera leaned against the counter and tried to recall everything. "I saw a beautiful place with beautiful people."

"Home."

The roar in Meera's ears intensified as drops of sweat slid down her back. "What did you say?"

"You saw home. Your birthplace. Continue, please."

"I ca—can't," she stuttered. Carrine had called that magickal place her home. It couldn't be. Places like that did not truly exist.

"They do exist."

Meera's stomach rolled. "I didn't say that out loud." She slid to the floor, thankful for the cabinets that supported her back.

"No, you didn't. Things are not as they have always seemed. I would have liked to ease you into this world, but sadly, we don't have the luxury of time on our side." Carrine crouched in front of her and placed her hands over Meera's.

"I'm not normal, am I?"

"Not in the traditional dictionary sense, no. But in another place you are far more than normal. You are one of the greatest, or you will be, and I am here to help you. Know this above all else." She looked directly into Meera's eyes. "I am on your side."

Meera couldn't stop the tear that slid down her cheek, slowly descending until it landed on the floor with a silence that belied the agonizing whimpers of confusion in her head. Carrine sounded so genuine. Could Meera believe her? Could she believe any of this?

She looked down at her fingers, the same fingers that had glowed, the same fingers that had held power. She used those fingers to cover her face as she wept for the few questions that had been answered and for all those that remained unanswered. One thing was certain. Her life would never be the same.

Chapter Six

One week later

Meera was not human.

Wow.

That humongous blow, topped with what she'd been told about her *real* family, rocked Meera's already fragile mind. Fragile or not, she had to pull it together. She was in for the fight of her life. Literally.

Sweat spilled from every inch of her body. She paid no heed to the discomfort, was far too engrossed in the next bob-and-weave segment to give it a second thought.

This had become her life.

Before, she'd hated exercise. Now her daily routine consisted of sweat pants and sports bras. Aching muscles. Exhaustion. Kickboxing, Taekwondo, and back alley fighting techniques were being drilled into her day and night. Throw in the magickal power she had to hone and perfect, as well as the spells and chants she had to memorize, and life as she knew it had ceased to exist.

Surprisingly, this didn't really bother her. Yes, she'd been shocked to learn about her heritage, but considering she'd never fit in in this world, she planned to embrace her new life and learn as much as she could in hope that this time around would be different. Preferably in a good way.

Carrine sent her flying with another energy-infused kick. The air left her lungs in one loud *whoosh* as Meera landed hard on her backside. *Shit bubbles.* She'd let herself get distracted for two seconds, and look where it had landed her. On the floor. On her ass. She hadn't seen that one coming.

Carrine offered her a hand. She accepted. At the last second, she pulled hard and flipped her petite assailant over her head. Her mentor-slash-trainer-slash-ninja-like-warrior slid across the floor and straight into the china cabinet. The shelves shook, plates fell, and very expensive pieces of blue glass and white ceramic shattered and added more shards to the ever-growing pile of breakage. Still feeling duped and betrayed by her friend, who was no longer her friend, according to said *friend,* she couldn't help but feel a little satisfaction at seeing Carrine pick herself up and dust off the chunks of debris. Didn't say much for her own character, but whatever. Some things couldn't be helped.

"Nice one," Carrine said, rubbing her hip.

Bent at the waist trying to catch her breath, Meera said, "Thanks."

"We probably should have found another location to begin your training."

"Two things," she said between pants. "One. This location means nothing to me anymore. I hope we . . . break everything. And two. What the hell do you mean 'begin your training'? This is . . . just the beginning? I've been . . . busting . . . my ass . . . for a week." She sucked in air. "I've nailed the *ahp chagi* and the *dwi chagi.* I've chanted from noon to midnight, and I've just about perfected the art of shooting light out of my fingers, even though I have no idea how that would ever help me in anything outside of camping." Meera grabbed the ends of her hair with both hands and pulled her ponytail tighter. "What more could there possibly be?" Tirade over, she sucked in more needed air.

Carrine leveled her with intense, forest-green eyes. "Okay. I've got a couple things for you as well. First—we need to find a better training center. If anyone walked in here, they would assume this place had been robbed and ransacked and call your human police. Personally, this is a problem I don't want to have to deal with and one you're not ready to handle on your own.

"Second—while you've learned a lot in this short period of

time, and I commend you for your effort and determination, you have no idea how much more there is to learn. How much more you'll need to learn in order to survive and to do what you were born to do." She placed her hand on Meera's cheek, her face somber. "You must survive. A lot is relying on that fact alone."

Carrine didn't have to explain the importance of staying alive. Human or not, natural instincts were to preserve one's life as long as possible. To be told Meera may have only a few short months to live was unfathomable. To be told what she would have to endure in her struggle to live was immeasurable. To do what she had to do for herself and for those she'd never even met seemed . . . impossible.

This was her new existence, and one she hesitated to call a life considering the hourglass was headed in the wrong direction at an alarming pace.

Witch.

But not just any witch. No old hags bent over a cauldron while concocting a brew up in here. No horny toads and herbs for her. Not a chance.

Meera was a Luminary witch of the Brennan coven.

Wrapping her mind around that one proved to be no easy task. Carrine had patiently explained—several times—that Meera came from a long line of witches with immense power. Power so unique many sought to capture them to contain the power in hopes of extracting it for their own purposes. Her own mother, Ambra Brennan, had sent her away to try to protect her from what was to come, but in the end, none of them could escape without Meera's help. According to Carrine, Meera was destined to be the most powerful of all, and the only one who could take care of this not-so-little problem currently developing.

Eventually, if she succeeded, she would be expected to lead the coven. Not only that, but as a Luminary she would be expected to help keep order among the veiled—a community of immortals who chose to live amongst, or at the very least, interact with humans. What that all entailed remained a mystery to her. Apparently she'd only get that tidbit of information if she lived past her twenty-ninth birthday. Immortals, veiled, magick? She had so much to learn.

The kicker? Her mother had known it would come to this and still had chosen to stick her in a world where she would never fit in rather than share what might be the only twenty-eight years of Meera's life with her. She could have kept her close and taught her the ways of their world, taught her how to use these powers. But she hadn't made that choice.

Ouch.

That stung.

So far she'd lived in two worlds and not one person had truly wanted her around.

Unbelievable.

She kept thinking that any day now she would wake up and find out this had been just another one of those strange nightmares. It wasn't. One look at her body told her this was all too real. The physical exertion over the past week had caused her body to transform into one of power. Carrine had attributed much of it to genetics. Either way, her long legs were now not only lean but totally ripped. Her biceps could rival any gymnast and her abs . . . rock hard. If she had known this could happen so quickly, she would have donned her running shoes more often.

"I'm starving." One good thing about all the training was getting to eat whatever she wanted without the fear of adding pounds. She'd burn it off and then some in a short period of time. The sessions were that intense.

"Okay. We'll take a short break. Short. I want to work on casting this afternoon." Carrine smoothed her already perfect hair before gliding through the scattered debris to the kitchen.

They had only briefly touched on casting in the last few days. Enough for Meera to note it wasn't only about spells, but also consisted of chanting and power. She'd been told she could use her energy to cast light in all directions. She hadn't thought much of that particular talent until Carrine had punctuated the point that this light potentially produced so much energy it could clear an entire room and cause a lot of hurt in the process. Meera was both excited and nervous to test the theory.

"Would you mind if we went out and grabbed something?" With a wrinkled nose, Meera looked around at all the wreckage, then kicked at a broken lampshade. "I'm starting to feel claustrophobic."

"That's fine, but you have to pick somewhere quiet. I want to discuss a few things." She closed her eyes and a moment later her lavish coat covered her body.

"Showoff."

Carrine laughed. "You can do it, too. You just need to concentrate and focus your energy."

She threw her shoulders back, and, more in tune with her body than she'd ever been, her lashes twined as she squeezed her eyes shut and concentrated on concentrating. Other than that, she sensed nothing. No energy and definitely no warmth from a coat. "Dammit."

"See it, Meera. Visualize what you want. See it."

Carrine's soft words, reminiscent of the soothing whisper Meera so often heard in her thoughts, allowed her to focus. A moment later her eyes fluttered open, and she saw her red cloak hanging midair, two feet in front of her. She squealed, and it dropped to the ground. Didn't matter. Her smile broadened. She'd come closer than ever that time. She picked up the cloak, slid her arms in, and buttoned it tight around her neck.

"Okay, let's go. I'm in the mood for an enormous steak, and I know just the place."

They made their way down to Meera's car. She slid behind the wheel of her white sedan, the buff-colored leather invitingly warm against her backside. Thank goodness for the heated garage. "Buckle up."

"Why? Do you not know how to drive this contraption?" Carrine asked, eyes wide. She pulled the seat belt across her chest and yanked it hard.

Meera shook her head, realizing she had never actually seen Carrine drive. One more topic to add to the odd factor. "It's not a contraption, it's a car. And of course I know how to drive it. I'm surprised you don't. Wait. Don't tell me we fly around on brooms?" Only slightly kidding, she feared Carrine would confirm this. If that was the case, she'd definitely have a custom seat made.

"No, we do not fly around on brooms, although I imagine we could if we had any such desire. Our mode of transportation is much more sophisticated than that."

Meera made a sharp right turn. Her car slid on the ice like a skater destined for disaster. Out of the corner of her eye, she caught her companion gripping the dashboard and smiled internally. Carrine was not the fearless wonder Meera had once thought. Cutting her a break, Meera seamlessly righted the car, avoiding the snow bank.

"You were saying," she encouraged. Carrine slightly loosened her death grip on the dash, changing her knuckles from the shade of a polar bear to that of fading sunlight. "If you don't fly around on brooms, how do you get around?"

"Oh, yes. There are a few words for it. Tracing and shifting are the most commonly used."

"I don't understand."

"No. You wouldn't. You've never done it; and, unfortunately, you won't be able to for a couple more years. It's a gift that comes with your thirtieth birthday."

"Great. I'm two years shy with no guarantee I'll get there."

Carrine turned her head to look at Meera. "There are never any guarantees. Not for any of us."

"I know that. It's just—never mind. So what is tracing?" If they got started down this path again, the conversation would go on and on, and her impending death was the last thing she wanted to discuss over lunch.

"Essentially it's a way to get from one location to another in an instant. We disappear only to reappear in another place and occasionally another time."

"You can't be serious."

"I am."

"You can go anywhere in the world you want to go at any time?" How cool would that be?

Carrine shrugged as if to say the phenomenon was no big deal. "Yes. It takes some practice, but it can be done. Unlike many of the veiled, who can only go places they've been before, our only limitation is that we have to go alone. Some species are able to take others with them, but only if they've been there before. They still have to use human modes of transportation to get to new places. It's a toss up, if you ask me. If I had the ability to trace with you, we would already be enjoying our lunch instead of getting there in this death trap." She clutched her seat belt as the car slid again. "Now that I think about it, I should have just met you there."

Meera laughed. "Oh, come on. This isn't so bad. I'll get you there safely. Imagine how scared I am to find out I'm a witch who has to stop disaster single-handedly or die." Her tone was flippant, but anxiety stirred in her stomach.

"Good point."

She pulled the car into a nearly empty parking lot. Apparently she'd chosen wisely. Carrine wanted quiet, and this place looked to be virtual ghost town. A little too much so for Meera's taste. She preferred surrounding herself with people and noise. Even if she didn't know anyone, at least she wasn't technically alone when she sat in a crowd. "Maybe they're closed." She headed for the door, pulling her cloak tight to guard against the wind.

"The sign says *Open*."

"I guess they're just slow today. You said you wanted quiet. Will this do?" She held the door open.

"Splendidly," Carrine answered, breezing by in her regal way.

The shades were pulled halfway down the front windows to keep the glare from the snow at bay. Meera squinted into the dim interior until her eyes adjusted. A sign posted at the hostess stand noted they should seat themselves. She followed as Carrine chose a table off to the side.

"After we get you sustenance, we'll dive into some training of your mind." Carrine pulled off her gloves and placed them on the edge of the corner table.

"Great. Will there be a quiz?"

"Don't be impish, Meera. You need to take all aspects of your training seriously. If you're not educated on what you're up against, how do you plan to prevail?" Carrine whipped off her coat and flung it over the back of a chair.

"Whoa. Simmer down. I was only teasing. I get it, okay? This is important—more so to me than anyone." Meera kicked at the chair. "It's my life that's about to end, so if I want to make light of the situation every once in a while to keep myself from breaking down, then you'll have to learn to deal with it." So much for avoiding the subject.

"Okay. I'll deal with it. Please sit down. You're causing a scene."

Meera took that moment to check out her surroundings, something she should have done instantly. Her shoulders slumped when she realized everyone in the restaurant had just heard every word of her outburst. Not good. Right now, the crickets were in full effect.

Sheepishly, she lowered herself into her chair, unrolled her napkin, and arranged the silverware. "Sorry about that."

Carrine shook her head. "It's nothing. Let's order a drink. I think we could both use one."

"You can say that again." Meera signaled for a waitress.

Molly, according to the name on her gold nametag, moved at a snail's pace but eventually made it to their table. She gave a half-assed smile and pulled a notepad from the pocket of her burgundy smock before arching a brow. Apparently the gesture was her equivalent of a *how may I help you?*

"Okay then. I'll have a Bloody Mary, loaded, but not super spicy, please." Meera followed her order with a genuine smile. She was going for the kill-her-with-kindness technique—anything to keep Miss Molly Sunshine from spitting in her drink.

"I'll have the same," Carrine said.

Molly sighed, turned on her heel and headed for the corner of the bar.

Carrine chuckled. "She's cheery."

"If by cheery you mean miserable with a dash of extreme boredom and a pinch of go eff yourself, you're right."

Carrine's eyes twinkled with amusement. "You certainly have a way with words."

For just a moment, Meera detected a hint of her old friend coming to the surface. Then Carrine blinked, stealing any proof that the Carrine Meera had met months ago would ever be back. "Thank you, I think." Frustrated, Meera looked around. Something else was bothering her, but she couldn't quite figure out the source. She picked up a spoon and let it swing from her fingers. Then, holding it in front of her face, she stared at her reflection. Her eyes, too, seemed different. Again, just a blink and then nothing.

"What is it, Meera?"

"What? Oh, nothing," she lied. Her body temperature spiked as a sense of awareness tingled through her system. She took a few deep breaths to try to extinguish the fire smoldering beneath her skin.

"What are you feeling?"

"I'm just hot. That's all." She pushed up her sleeves, yet the heat still simmered. She'd do anything to be able to peel off her sweatpants. No hum, though. What did that mean? Would she trance out or not?

"It's more than that. I want you to focus and tell me what's going on. Don't diminish what you're feeling. Focus." Carrine spoke in that soft voice again, encouraging Meera to close her eyes and focus inwardly.

She shut out everything but the fire. She barely heard as Molly approached with the drinks and Carrine asked her for two glasses of ice water. It would take a hell of a lot of ice water to douse the flames consuming her, hell-bent on igniting her core. "Something's coming."

"What's coming?" Carrine reached across the table and placed a calming hand on Meera's arm.

The bell above the door chimed. Meera instinctively opened her eyes. Her temperature blazed the moment she made eye contact with Mr. Delicious Whiskey himself.

Meera sucked in a breath. "Oh, no."

Chapter Seven

Ryken walked the line in front of his legion. Even in this underground world, the sun sat high, illuminating their gorgeous faces in bright light and making them appear to be anything but what they actually were. Some time ago, their kingdom had been shrouded in perpetual darkness, the moss hanging from the trees forming a canopy of shadows. But Ryken had grown powerful and he now controlled everything in his realm. He wanted sun? He got sun. Rain? Torrential downpours. Manufactured or real mattered not to him. It wouldn't be long before he controlled everything everywhere.

The arched structures on their training grounds sat at least five hundred feet behind them and were used only during intense rains. There was no cover on the field. No shelter from the heat. No escape from the extreme exercises. He made sure to make eye contact with each and every slayer. What he saw in return was a mixture of awe, respect, and fear, the fear coming from witnessing the demise of one of their own. The end of Ninxo Macesinger's life had been swift but brutal, something these slayers would not soon forget.

Today, each one had been properly outfitted in human clothing, from jeans and tees bearing rock band logos to business suits. A few even donned clothing befitting the homeless—anything and everything to make them blend. Blending was the first step in his plan for success. Become them and then consume them.

Their pointed ears were hidden beneath caps and clever hairstyles. This attribute was the one thing that would give them away, and they all had been well instructed as to how detrimental this would be to their colony. Each one fought to protect their family. They knew, some from experience and some from horrid tales, if they were ever detected, each and every member of their family would suffer a fate worse than death itself.

Ryken allowed Jayson to make the rally speech. He preferred to sit back and watch the ranks. Earlier he'd had the slups—his personal servants—carry his heavy throne out to the training site. Slups were what this was all about. Humans were captured and then converted. Some were either too weak or too stupid to join the legion. The evaluation process was quick. You passed or you failed. Victors began their training within the legion immediately while slups started slupping. Even now, two of his servants flanked his gilded throne, ready to do his bidding. They would never see the human side of things again. Their thoughts were not their own. They thought what *he* wanted them to think. They did *everything* he wanted them to do. And in turn, he was able to keep his stunning face and body.

"Today is an important day." Jayson's voice boomed with authority. "Now that we have the lay of the land in the human city of Chicago, the time to act has come. All of you are required to bring no less than ten humans to us by the end of this eve."

He paused, waiting for each to assent. As a unit they brought their heads down in a nod.

"Those who can bring more will be rewarded accordingly. Those who fail . . . "

There was no need for Jayson to finish that particular sentence. Ryken arched a brow at the few who dared to cut their eyes in his direction. Those same few would most likely be the ones to fail. He'd cut out their serpent tongues and feed them to the slups.

"Your job is not to convert. Your job is to get them to us without killing them. We will handle it from there."

Pleasure awaited Ryken in just a few hours. There were several ways to convert humans, and he preferred to convert the females. The beautiful ones. A smile curled his lips as thoughts of tomorrow consumed his mind.

He barely noticed when Jayson ended his speech and the slayers of Lemra marched to the portal that would allow them access to the human realm. Only the thunderous sound of the opening of that portal brought his attention from his thoughts of human females. He nodded as each member of the legion bowed at his throne.

Chapter Eight

Ghanem and Thane entered the steakhouse with one thing in mind.

"I'm so hungry, I could eat the entire cow, including the hooves." Not only had they been researching for the past few days, they'd also been training. Extensively. Ghanem considered himself in fairly good shape for the human world, but he'd lost so much of his guardian strength from centuries of neglect.

Actually, that was a little harsh. He didn't exactly consider it neglect, just one of those if-you-don't-use-it-you'll-lose-it situations, and he hadn't had any reason to call upon that strength in almost forever. You couldn't call on what you no longer possessed. Dealing with insurance claims only required enough strength to type.

"Well, let's see what we can do about that. Ghan?" Thane nudged his shoulder. "Ghanem? What is it?"

He felt the nudge but couldn't respond. That woman—the one from the bar—stared him down, and he was utterly compelled not to break eye contact. Ever. Some sort of battle played out here, and he was certain he needed to win. The air sizzled and crackled between them with electricity that was not only dangerous but erotic as hell. What the fuck? His body tensed and hardened at once.

Could it just be coincidence that the two of them had ended up in the same place again? The niggling feeling on the back of his neck suggested otherwise.

"*Fratello*, why don't you just go over and talk to her? You look like you've got a case of puppy love going on here, and it's really not doin' a lot for ya." Thane sighed when Ghanem ignored the comment. "Can we sit down at least?"

Ghanem figured he looked like an idiot with Thane leading

him across the room, but for the life of him he could not—would not—break the connection with the stunning woman. They wove through the tables until Thane shoved him into a booth where he had a clear view of her entire face. He dared not blink. *Yes!* He claimed victory as she finally took a deep breath and directed her attention back to her lunch companion.

"Dude? Get out much?"

"Shut up, Thane. You know who that is, right?"

"Well I don't know her personally, although, I'd like to. Whoooaaa," Thane said as Ghanem drew back a fist. "I already told you the other night. This one is all yours. I'm just saying that—well, I'm just sayin'."

Ghanem slowly lowered his fist and reined in his temper. He shifted in his seat, incredibly grateful they had decided against changing clothes before grabbing lunch. His sweats were just the camouflage his rod needed. Baggy in all the right places.

"Maybe we should go somewhere else."

"No."

"I don't see how I'm gonna get you to concentrate with so much distraction in the room." Thane stuck his menu between the ketchup and A-1 jars and rose.

Ghanem grabbed his wrist. "I said no. I'm fine. We're already here so let's just eat." He'd done a lot of what he liked to call self-therapy over the past few days but still hadn't come up with an explanation as to why her image had been branded in his thoughts. Sexual? Definitely. But there was more to it. He wanted to know her. In every way.

"Fine. Whatever. Maybe if you ever get the balls to talk to her, you could ask her to introduce me to her friend."

He'd also noticed her friend. Hard not to. Their looks were so similar they could be sisters or perhaps mother and daughter. She had one of those faces that made it hard to judge her age. Striking, too, but not in the same way and definitely not in the wrap-your-legs-around-me-as-I-take-you-against-the-wall way. No. He saved all that for the taller one. *Merda*. If only he knew her name. Maybe that would make her more real so he could quit fantasizing about her. He hadn't had a good night's sleep in a week, and it was starting to wear him down.

Thane cleared his throat and Ghanem realized he'd been staring at the woman again. Begrudgingly, he turned to study the menu instead. Eat. Train. Study. That's what he needed to focus on. A quick jaunt off the path, however, and he could focus on devouring her, training himself to go longer so he was sure to please her, and studying all the different positions he'd like to try with her but, yeah, that would be getting a little off track. A little.

"I don't even want to know what you're thinking about right now, but a little hint . . . you may want to try to mask your thoughts. No—" Thane held a hand up. "I wasn't reading them, but this shit is written all over your face. Either do her and get her out of your system or forget about her. We have some very tough times ahead, and you're no good if you allow yourself to get distracted."

Ghanem rubbed his face with both hands. "You're right. I know that, but there's just something about her. Maybe it's just been too long."

Thane quirked a smile. "Really? How long has it been?"

"None of your fucking business. Now, let's go over what we learned this morning." He halted the dicussion when the waitress came over. They quickly ordered two helpings of prime rib, baked potato, grilled vegetables, and the house salad. He corrected her when she repeated the order back to them, explaining they would have two orders each. She looked puzzled but jotted it down. After she left, Ghanem picked up the conversation where he'd left off. "Slayers."

Thane leaned in, talking in hushed tones. "Right. Slayers who happen to have pointed ears. But what we've read so far leads me to believe we're not talking about Santa's helpers."

"No, I should think not. First of all, they stand about six feet tall, and that's both male and female. Second, I believe their strength lies within the manipulative magick."

"Manipulative, huh? Still got a sore spot for magick, I see."

Ghanem arched a brow but said nothing on the subject. Sore spot for magick? Magick ruined people's lives.

"Sorry, *fratello*. I shouldn't have brought that up. Let's just forget I said anything. Okay?"

Ghanem saw the regret in his brother's eyes. "No problem, man. Really, it's no big deal." He probably didn't sound convincing, but at least Thane nodded his head and moved on.

"I think our best bet is to nullify them before they can use their, um, powers."

"Yeah. The problem is gonna be picking them out of a crowd. They blend. They're chameleons. How do we deal with that?" Ghanem smiled at the waitress as she placed iced tea in front of them. She lingered, her gaze going back and forth between Thane and himself. Ping-Pong, anyone? "Uh, thanks."

Still she lingered, adjusting the silverware and napkins.

"We're good," Thane said and blasted her with his toothiest smile.

She blushed, but finally backed away.

"Guess she liked what she saw. Hey, I have an idea. Maybe you could sample her a little. Ya know, get a little somethin' somethin' out of your system?"

"Grow up, Thane."

"Oh, I'm already grown, big brother. Already grown."

Ghanem let him ramble about his conquests over the years. It wasn't that he didn't find the tales interesting. Well, actually, he didn't. No one wants to hear about another's sexual escapades, especially when they haven't had any said escapades themselves. It was just that if he allowed his brother to continue bragging, he could take more time to study the dark-haired beauty.

She'd changed in the past week. Subtle, for sure, but he noticed.

Her face looked a little more angled, her arms slightly more defined. Apparently she'd been working out, too. He liked what he saw. He liked her last week just fine, but the implied power in her body spoke to him on many levels. He could appreciate strength. She would be an equal between the sheets and not one he would have to handle with care, so to speak. Fragile was not written anywhere on this woman's body.

Their food arrived, and Thane continued his boasting between mouthfuls of meat and potatoes. Ghanem ate slowly, methodically, all the while watching as she ate every bit of food on her plate. What a nice surprise. Most women picked at their food. This woman ate and enjoyed it.

She and her friend finished, paid their bill, and headed outside. The moment the door closed, the entire place seemed colder. Darker. He rolled his eyes when his corny-ass brain played the song "You Light Up My Life." *Seriously*, he thought, *get a grip*. He ate faster now. What was he hoping for? To get another look at her in the parking lot? Yup. That was exactly what he wanted.

Thane rose and Ghanem looked up. "Let's go. I already paid our bill while you were ogling the goods, so if you hurry your ass up, you might be able to bump into her outside."

And this was one of the many reasons he liked having his brother around again. Thane knew him. Knew how he thought. Ghanem grabbed his jacket and raced outside. He scanned the parking lot, but she was already gone.

Thane smacked his sagging shoulder. "Sorry, bro. Guess we weren't quick enough."

At the sound of fist on face, they both looked to the left. The sounds grew louder as they headed in that direction. Grunts, groans, garbage can lids hitting a brick wall. They turned the corner. *What the fuck* was the only thought running through his head this time.

*

How the hell had this happened? One minute she and Carrine were walking to the car, and the next minute Meera had spotted three men with what she could only describe as a dark aura around them. The darkness glistened in the sunlight, giving it a magickal yet malevolent appearance. She'd never seen anything like it, and it had her wanting to run in the other direction.

The three approached an elderly couple, and the situation looked anything but good. Thugs harassing defenseless people was so not cool. She'd pointed it out to Carrine who'd instantly taken off at a dead run. Meera followed suit. Big mistake. Now they were smack dab in the middle of a fistfight.

Meera's knuckles cracked as she slammed them into the jaw of one of the men. She shook off the pain and ignored the flowing blood. Obviously that had hurt her much more than her opponent. He smiled a cruel, evil smile as if to say *that's all you've got?*

Hell, no.

She had a lot more in her. She snuck a quick glance to the elderly couple. Damn it. She'd told them to leave but they were huddled in a corner, their arms wrapped around each other, the smell of fear radiating from their pores.

The distraction hurt her. Her head snapped back as her attacker's left heel connected with her jaw. She staggered and fought to remain conscious as her vision flickered like a broken neon sign. She sank to her knees just as he made a run for her.

Diving for the ground, she took out his legs. His head hit the wall and he fell over in a heap. She watched to see if he was still breathing. Relief swept through her when his chest rose. She had no desire to kill anyone, no matter how bad they were.

She caught a flash of something out of the corner of her eye. She spun, fists up and ready. A quick scan told her Carrine held her own against the one dressed in a navy blue business suit, but the homeless-looking thug was gunning for the older couple. The husband shoved his wife behind him and held aged, shaking fists up to block his face.

Hoping she wouldn't be too late, she ran toward them screaming like a banshee. Their attacker stopped inches from them and whispered something intangible. The elderly man appeared dazed and lowered his fists.

Running full out, Meera bent at the waist and rammed her shoulder into the bum's side. She straightened when he fell but before she could shepherd the couple to safety, he got back on his feet.

She grabbed the lid of a metal trashcan and threw it as hard as she could. He ducked. The lid crashed into the wall and then spun on the ground like a child's toy. He smiled, cracked his neck, and walked slowly toward her.

Two things went through her mind in that moment: She was in big trouble and he was not human. The aura progressively darkened as if it were taking over his entire body. Her thoughts traveled back to the taxi driver. Could it be?

Her head ached, her knuckles throbbed and continued to drip blood, but she wouldn't give up. She stood her ground and waited for him to come to her. So close. She readied for a roundhouse kick, swung her leg, and connected with air.

Confused, she dared take only a moment to figure out what happened. She steadied her body and sucked in air as Mr. Delicious pummeled the bum relentlessly. Carrine came to stand beside her, and they waited breathlessly as the two men from the steakhouse took over and made short work of the baddies.

Fists and hair. Fists and hair. That was the only way to describe what they saw when they watched as Carrine's thug fell to the merciless power of a man with beautiful hair rippling with waves. The color reminded Meera of an ocean at night with only hints of blue showing through the darkness. His hands were enormous, his stunning face intent.

His mission complete, he stood back, no worse for the wear, and wiped his hands on his red jogging pants. The gleam in his eye as he watched his friend finish up the other guy made Meera wonder if he hadn't enjoyed every bit of the short fight.

"Ghanem? You need any help over there?"

Ghanem didn't respond, only continued to pound into the kidneys of the guy on the ground as if rage had transported him to another plane.

Meera?

Transfixed, she shook her head, and that was the last she heard from the whisper. For now.

Chapter Nine

Ghanem. Mr. Delicious had a name. *Ghanem.* Her mind repeated it while she scanned every inch of his commanding body. He'd finally yelled at his friend to shut up—and that was putting it in much nicer terms—but other than that, he could not be deterred in the least. His ragged breathing made Meera wonder who was being punished more, the poor guy at the wrong end of a fist, or Ghanem, the one who refused to stop? Unlike the one with hair too pretty for a man, who had practically glowed during his fight, Ghanem seemed to become angrier.

She couldn't let him kill the guy, even though the jerk had kicked the shit out of her and she'd have a ton of bruises to show for it. Maybe the whisper she'd briefly heard had been trying to ask her to stop Ghanem. Meera stepped up beside him, careful of his flying knuckles, and placed a tentative hand on his arm.

He stopped immediately. She didn't remove her hand even though the heat from his skin singed her palm. He let go of the guy's bloody collar and let him drop to the ground. Ghanem turned his head slowly. She released a long breath when his gaze caught hers. His eyes, the color of melted dark chocolate, bore into her, questioning, but she didn't look away. Heat encompassed her. Intense heat. Sensual heat. All-consuming heat.

Everything and everyone else faded into the background. They were alone in a crowd of confusion. The way her body reacted to the sight of him was a torture that held both pleasure and pain in its clutches. Moving away was not an option, as she yearned to feel the fire within. The fire only this man could ignite. Somewhere, deep in the recesses of her mind, she knew this wasn't normal. But then again, neither was she, which had to be the reason she stood there sucking it up like a starved vacuum. She stepped closer, desperate for more contact.

"Ghan, check this out."

She shuddered when he closed his eyes, stepped back, and pulled away from her touch. The loss of physical connection caused a chill to settle deep in her bones. She wrapped her cloak as tight as she could in an attempt to ward off the iciness setting in.

"Yes, Thane? What is it, *fratello*?"

Expensive language lessons had finally paid off. They were brothers? Other than having large statures, they really didn't look alike at all. Thane's hair, so long and dark, while Ghanem's was cut as close to the scalp as possible without shaving it off completely. From what she could tell, if he let it grow it would be the color of dark honey. Thane's eyes were golden, Ghanem's the deepest coffee. Maybe *fratello* was just a term they used between friends, but as she watched them in deep discussion she saw a connection she had never shared with her friends, never shared with the ones who had claimed to be her siblings. This truly was Ghanem's brother.

Instantly jealous of the relationship, Meera shot daggers their direction. Not that she wanted a relationship with him, not really. But she couldn't help feeling jealous he had someone he shared such a close bond with. She had never had that, and since the clock continued ticking on any time she had left, she'd never share that type of relationship with anyone. Life sucked. But dying sucked more, so she better put a lid on the self-pity and figure out what the hell had just gone down in this alley. Besides, letting the green-eyed monster rule over her feelings was petty.

She walked over to the huddled elderly couple to make sure they were okay, and thankfully, though shaken and scared, they were unharmed. She kindly suggested they let her take care of everything here and ushered them to their Buick. The police could not be called—something she'd learned quickly over the last week. It all went the route of *no questions asked* as the husband helped his wife buckle in and then left without a backward glance. She couldn't blame them.

As she approached the only ones who remained standing in the alley, she made sure to stand opposite of Ghanem. Two reasons: She could stay clear of the dangerous heat she'd begun to crave *and* she had a clear view of him should she want to take a peek. Or two. They'd noted the third bad guy, the one Meera had taken down, was no longer with them, but there wasn't anything they could do about that right now.

"I have a feeling about this, Thane." He wiped a hand over his shaved head, leaving a streak of blood down the middle.

Meera wanted to tend to his hands but, um, hello, how inappropriate would that be? *Hey big guy, come over here and let me give you some TLC.* Yeah. So not gonna happen. While that would be one pleasurable diversion, she couldn't afford any diversion at this time in her life. Or should she say . . . at the end of her life?

Ghanem bent down and pulled the cap off one baddie while Thane pushed the hair aside on another.

"Slay—"

"Slayers," Carrine whispered, cutting off Thane.

To say shock flew between the four of them was like saying you shouldn't curse in church. Duh.

Ghanem held up a hand, his eyes narrowed. "Wait. What do you two know about this?"

Meera started to speak, the surprise of seeing the pointed ears disturbing, but Carrine beat her to the punch. "Nothing. What do you know of it?"

Ghanem and Thane both thinned their lips, their resemblance in that moment uncanny. Definitely brothers.

Carrine grabbed Meera's arm and practically dragged her away.

"What's your name?" Ghanem called to her.

"Don't—"

"Meera Brennan," she said, taking no heed to Carrine's warning. This was the first time she'd said her true name aloud, and she liked the sound of it. She watched his lips form her name and swore she could feel his breath on her skin, igniting that fire yet again. Amazing, considering they now stood at opposite ends of the alley.

"Get in this contraption right now."

"Car, Carrine. It's a car."

"What in this realm were you thinking? Do you have any idea what you've just done?" Carrine turned in her seat to glare at Meera.

"I'd say I just helped kick some baddie butt. Aside from that, which is pretty huge, what is your problem?" She threw the car in drive and hit the gas. The car fishtailed right then left. She gently tapped on the brakes until she had it completely under control. "Look. You told me this crap wouldn't start to go down for at least another week, yet here I am with a battered body and a boat load of questions." She split her attention between the road and the passenger seat.

"I also have some questions and will do my best to get us some answers, but we need to focus on the here and now. Those men back there, not just the *baddies,* but the other ones, aren't exactly apple pie. They're veiled. And you just gave them your name. Should have given them your address and phone number while you were at it."

"What do you mean, veiled? Are you telling me they're bad guys too?"

"Not necessarily."

"What the hell is that supposed to mean? What are they?" She flipped on her turn signal and made a right onto Lake Drive. The glare of the sun off the lake temporarily blinded her. Meera quickly grabbed her sunglasses and slid them onto her bruised face. She flinched and slid them down her nose a bit to relieve the pressure.

"You couldn't tell they were different?"

"Different how? If you know they're veiled then you must know what they are. And can we please quit with the twenty questions back and forth?"

"Pull over."

Meera found a pull off and parked the car next to a playground. She followed Carrine over to the bench and gingerly lowered herself into it. Her muscles had already grown stiff. Tomorrow, they'd hurt like a bitch.

Carrine continued, "Not all veiled are bad. There are many amongst us who are truly good. Sometimes exactly what they are is not clear right away. Many have the ability of disguise. However, their true nature can be revealed in many ways. You were the one who pointed out the auras. They were very clear to you. Not many have that ability, the ability to see them as clearly as you did. Yet, other than the initial effect when they first walked into the restaurant, you didn't notice anything off about the other two?"

"Um, other than the fact that they're unbelievably sexalicious, they seemed like two regular guys to me. And I don't know about any initial effect. I was probably just overheated from all these workouts. They look like guys. Plain, ordinary, human guys. Okay, maybe not plain or ordinary but definitely human. The baddies, on the other hand, tried to blend in. That was fairly obvious. But those auras . . . I don't know. They felt evil." The wind picked up, wailing and moaning as if possessed. Meera shivered and wished she had some of that heat Ghanem threw off right about now. The heat she had conveniently not mentioned to Carrine in the alley.

"That's interesting. I'll have to look into that. But back to the other two. You seem particularly drawn to the one. I'm not sure that's wise."

Drawn was about the understatement of the decade. "His name is Ghanem and don't worry about it. I find him attractive, that's all." Heat spread across her cheeks. Meera hoped her blush didn't give her true feelings away.

"I'll trust you on this one, but should we come across them again, I want you to keep your distance."

Rather than make a promise she wasn't sure she could keep, Meera hedged. "I'm sure we won't be running into them again. We'll be leaving soon, right?" The plan had been to stay here for as long as possible and stick to the training regimen. They'd thought they had at least another week or more. Today showed them the training might indeed be complete. Meera was stronger but nowhere near ready.

"Yes. I think you're right about leaving. I'll discuss things with the council tonight, but be ready. We may head out as soon as tomorrow." Carrine lifted Meera's bruised chin with gentle fingers. "It'll be okay. We can do this."

She turned her head and looked out at the sparkling water. "You mean me. I have to do this."

"I'll stay with you as long as I can."

"It won't be long enough."

*

It'd been hours. The sun had set, the moon sat high, and still the two slayers remained tight lipped. So far nothing they'd done had persuaded them to talk. Ghanem's patience was spent. He paced the length of the abandoned warehouse, his footsteps echoing in the emptiness, and left the next session of interrogation to his brother.

While Ghanem dreaded what had to be done to get answers, Thane reveled in it. Chalk that up to being a mighty guardian, a being that stopped at nothing to protect the innocent. Once upon a time, Ghanem would've been having the time of his life. But once upon a time was no longer and watching as another suffered such as this made his stomach churn.

"Buck up, bro. Remorseful eyes won't get us the answers *you* need."

Ghanem stopped pacing long enough to nail his brother with an exasperated glare. "There's got to be another way. Obviously this method"—Ghanem swept his arm toward the slayer's unconscious body—"isn't working."

"Ah, but it will. I'm just getting warmed up. I'm about to go full guardian up in here, and you'll be thanking me for it when we're that much closer to you getting what you want." Already Thane's horns were elongating, anticipation evident.

What did he want? Ghanem walked to the small window and wiped his bare hand across it to remove the grime. He ended up with a small clearing and dirt mixed with dried blood on his hand. He stared out at the dark night and watched as a lone car drove down the snow-covered street. He was just like that car. Or he had been until an opportunity had presented itself. Now instead of being alone, he had his brother by his side and a chance to reunite with the rest of his family and take back what was rightfully his. *That* was what he wanted, and there was only one way to get it.

Resolved, he shoved away from the window and let the years of anger and loneliness wash through his system. The old but familiar feeling started in his chest. It burned through his veins and made its way down his legs and up the corded muscles of his neck. His shirt ripped across his back as the muscles strained against the fibers.

Ghanem threw his shoulders back and roared as pain ripped through his body.

"Aw, shit, Ghan. It's too soon."

Wrong. Not too soon. Too late. The transformation had started. This was what he had waited for, for over two hundred years. Power.

Ghanem went down on all fours, the pain so horrific his features contorted. If he could just make it through, he'd be that much closer to getting back to his true form. Getting back to his sister. And maybe one day getting a chance to make up with his father.

"Breathe through it, *fratello*. Breathe through it. You're not ready."

Ghanem saw the worry in Thane's eyes, but grew too weak to speak. The power began to recede. The pain, too much. He'd failed. His vision dimmed once and then twice. He shook his head, fighting with what little strength he had left. He would not pass out. They didn't have their answers. He would not pass out.

The last thing he saw was the slayer's shoes as they walked up behind his brother. And then he heard a blood-curdling scream tear through the warehouse. Even then he couldn't stop the darkness.

Chapter Ten

He was afraid to open his eyes.

The dreams had been horrible. The screams deafening. He'd just gotten his brother back and now . . .

Hard as he tried, he heard no sounds. They must have left after . . .

He was afraid to open his eyes.

Ghanem couldn't avoid it. The least he could do for Thane was take him home. That was where Thane would want to be for his final resting place. Ghanem owed him that much. He owed him so much more. Dominic . . . Amella . . . How was Ghanem going to explain this to them?

His father hadn't forgiven him for the past. His sister—*gods*— Amella would never forgive him now. He should have waited. He wasn't ready. He'd failed them.

"Dude? You gonna get up anytime today?"

Ghanem's eyes popped open as he sprang to his feet. A wave of dizziness threatened to put him right back on his ass. He fought it and swung around.

"You're alive?" Heart pounding, he crossed the room in two long strides.

"You're so dramatic."

He grabbed Thane's shoulders and clenched his fingers. "I heard the screams. I couldn't help you. You're alive."

Thane laughed. "Naturally you thought I'd be the one on a slab in the proverbial morgue. Such little faith you have in me." He rolled his shoulders then lifted his brows. "Wanna ease up on the grip? I'm not dead, but I am a little sore."

Ghanem dropped his arms. "What the fuck happened? The last thing I remember is you bent over me and one of the slayers coming up behind you." He looked around. They were no longer in the warehouse but instead in a posh apartment that smelled of spice and dripped with sophistication. "Where are we?"

"We're in Chicago, and I got tired of bunking it poverty style, so I decided to upgrade our accommodations. You like?"

"Who wouldn't?" Ghanem stretched out on the white leather sofa. The softness implied quality and soothed his aching muscles. Thane wasn't dead. "Recap, please." Relief swept through him. "Oh, and I'm glad you're not dead." More than glad, really, but he'd already been too emotional and wondered what his brother thought of him. Whatever it was, he could change it. Time to man up.

"So to speak. Thanks, man." Thane grabbed two beers from the fridge and tossed one to Ghanem before reclining in the Lazy Boy. "Let's see. Oh, that's right, your sorry ass passed out, and the two chumps attempted to take me down. I got a little pissed and dare I say went a tad crazy-mother-fucker on the elf fairies."

Ghanem grunted. "Talk about dramatic. Can you just tell the shit without embellishing? And they're not elves."

Thane tapped the neck of the bottle against his lip. "Me, embellish? Never. As I was saying . . . you were taking a snoozer on the concrete and the fairies didn't stand a chance. Elves or not, pointed ears equal fairy in my book, but not only did I nullify them, I got one of them to give up the 411. Which is why we're here in Chicago. This is where it all starts. This is where we need to be."

He had a feeling his definition of nullify and Thane's had acres between them. "If it starts here, why were they in Milwaukee?" Afraid it would sour in his stomach, Ghanem sipped his beer.

"My guess? Rogue. I don't think that really matters. What matters is figuring out how we can detect them, and I think I may have an answer."

Ghanem sat up, intrigued.

"First, we're gonna need some help. I've contacted Father—"

"You what? I have to do this alone, Thane. That's what the letter said. Alone."

"Really? Then why is my ass here with you when I could be hanging with some females? Your attitude sucks. I should have made you bus it from Milwaukee."

"You know what I mean." Ghanem shook his head. "If we ask for help, Dominic won't think I'm worthy." Anguish ripped through his system. He *was* worthy. He just had to prove it to everyone else.

"*We* didn't ask for help. I did. Read the letter again. It states you have to find the source, but it doesn't say you can't have help kicking some dark fairy tail while you look for it."

Ghanem drained his beer. Thane was right. He couldn't do this alone. "Is he sending anyone?"

"He is."

Ghanem arched his brows in question.

"What?"

"Who, Thane? Who is he sending?"

Thane mumbled into his bottle.

"What's that, bro? I didn't quite catch that."

"Drake." Thane stared at the wall behind Ghanem's head.

"For fuck's sake. Couldn't you have asked for someone else?"

"I did. We also get Steffen."

Ghanem fell back and threw an arm across his eyes. "He truly hates me." What other reason would his father have for sending the two guardians he despised most to help him? Could someone please throw some air quotes around the word help? He was too fucking pissed to do it himself.

Drake and Steffen. Un. Fucking. Real. Could it get any worse?

"One other thing," Thane said.

"Great. Can't wait to hear this." He eased his arm back and stared at his brother, awaiting the next bomb.

"We need to find Meera Brennan. She's gonna be our elf detector."

"Excuse me?"

"You know? Your little girlfriend?" Thane waggled his eyebrows. "We're gonna find her, and then we're gonna use her to get you exactly where you need to be. That's how you're gonna earn your way back into Saharren."

Something didn't feel right about that, but Ghanem chose to keep it to himself for the moment. "What makes you think a mere human can help us in this war?"

Thane eased the chair into the reclining position. "She's not human."

"I feel like a broken record here, but excuse me?" True, she might have more fighting abilities than the typical female human, but that was about it.

"Trust me, Ghan. She's not human. I'm a little surprised you couldn't sense it, but she is veiled."

"Are you sure?"

"Positive." Thane picked up the remote and pushed a button. The mirror hanging over the fireplace lost its reflection and became a high definition television. He absently flipped through the channels.

Ghanem ignored the TV and stared at his brother instead. "Then what is she?" He was afraid to hear the answer but couldn't begin to explain why.

"Not sure yet. But I do know she can see those slayers as they truly are, and that's an advantage we must have on our side."

He didn't know what to say and so chose to remain silent. Meera Brennan disturbed him on a level of infinite proportions. How could he be close to her and still function? It wasn't just his dick he was worried about—rusty as it was—but something unexplainable simmered under the surface of his being when she was around. She calmed him. She made him anxious. She heated his blood. She disturbed him.

Ghanem turned his attention to the television and tried to get lost in the football game. His twisted mind turned it into a battle.

Guardian vs. Slayer, with the elf fairies now that Thane had christened them, the moniker stuck winning until the dark-haired temptress walked to the middle of Soldier Field. Both sides froze. She spotted him in his grass-stained football gear. Her eyes pleaded with him. Pleaded for what? Fuck if he knew. The game ensued with Meera right in the middle.

He blinked away the image and shoved off the couch. "I need another beer. Want one?"

"Nah. I'm good. I'm gonna get some sleep. I have a feeling about tomorrow." Thane pushed his chair into the upright position and stood. He stretched his arms above his head before tossing the remote to Ghanem. "Your bedroom is on the right. I suggest you find it soon. First thing in the morning, we need to locate Ms. Brennan."

Ghanem blew out a breath. He watched his brother's receding back and clutched the remote tighter so he wouldn't chuck it at the back of Thane's head. *Locate Ms. Brennan.* He had a feeling his brother knew exactly what happened to Ghanem every time he mentioned her name. He would temporarily excuse Thane's superior attitude. Thane had been second in command for two hundred years though it was Ghanem's rightful place. Old habits died hard, and he couldn't blame his brother for stepping up to the plate. He'd have done the same.

Deciding against the beer, he flicked off the television and then headed for his own room. He closed and locked the door, stripped off his clothes, and slid between the sheets of the king-size bed. Eyes closed, he decided to kick-start a dream and found it easy to conjure an image of Meera wrapped in nothing but a cloak that he would do anything to strip off her.

Chapter Eleven

Dressed in khaki cargo pants and a black ribbed tank, Meera sat cross-legged in the middle of the floor. A sigh escaped from deep within as she took in her surroundings. Only she would feel claustrophobic in such a large, open room. But it wasn't so much the space as it was the realization she'd traded in one high-rise apartment for another.

Granted, the location was different, but the gist of it was the same. Same picturesque views flanked by cream-colored silk curtains, looking over the same massive lake, just in a different city and state. Same top of the line furniture, just in a slightly darker color. Though she preferred the chocolate brown over the taupe she'd left behind, she told herself it had absolutely nothing to do with the fact it reminded her of the chocolate color of Ghanem's eyes. Absolutely nothing.

The council had told Carrine they would find help in Chicago. Meera had no clue if that meant the council would be sending help, or if she and Carrine were supposed to search it out.

Frustrated, she perched her elbows on her thighs and held her hands up in what she assumed to be a proper meditation style. She only had examples from television to go by, and TV was nothing if not educational. *Riiight.*

She'd never tried this kind of deep concentration before, but was willing to give it a shot. Magick wasn't coming to her as easily or as quickly as she'd like. She'd memorized the rhythmic chants, even though she found most of them a tad trite. She even had the voice inflections down, but still . . . she got nothing. Carrine assured her it would come in time, but time was one thing she lacked.

Determination centered her. Meera cracked her neck and rolled her shoulders once and then again. Deep breath in and slow breath out. Eyes closed, posture straight. She visualized what she wanted in her mind's eye, pulled it to her core, then said, "Cloak of mine, don't fail me now. Cover me, I say to thee. Cloak of mine, rise and bow. Cover me so mote it be."

She kept her eyes closed and repeated the incantation three times. Her heart rate hitched and then increased, but she made herself stay calm. She could have been imagining it but swore the air around her changed. Thicker. Heavy. Wishful thinking? *Come on,* she thought to herself. A whisper of cool wind brushed her cheek, just a touch but enough to cause her to shiver. Still, she refused to open her eyes. *Come on.* Seconds ticked by. Just when she would have given up, comforting warmth surround her. Her eyes popped open.

Holy noodle nuts!

She had done it. Her bare arms were now covered with a knit cloak the color of snow. Her smile practically split her cheeks open, and the sound of Carrine's applause behind her just made it spread that much farther.

"I did it."

"You did, indeed." Carrine glided gracefully to the couch and perched on the arm before folding her hands in her lap.

"I can't believe I actually did it." A sense of power raced through her veins, and all because of what she'd just accomplished.

Compared to Carrine's abilities, this was a small feat. She couldn't even begin to imagine the power Carrine held in her small body. How had she missed that for so long? Magickal energy filled the room and practically sizzled when Carrine was around. Perhaps she'd contained it before.

"Believe, child. Believe."

Meera angled her head. "Why is it you always call me child? I'm twenty-eight years old, you know." She snuggled deeper into the warmth of her cloak. Their relationship had evolved so much over the past few days. Gone was the bitter feeling that came along with being betrayed. Meera had chosen to forgive Carrine. This—whatever this was—was so much more than the two of them. Carrine had a job to do. She realized that now.

Carrine smiled. "Compared to me, you are a child. I've been around longer than you could possibly imagine." Her smile faded and her eyes became haunted, hinting at a deep sorrow.

Meera stood, troubled by the expression. "What is it?"

Carrine shook her head and the look passed. She patted the cushion next to her. "Come sit next to me."

Folding one leg under her, Meera adjusted herself until she faced her mentor and then relaxed against the back of the couch. She watched as Carrine waved her hand side to side. Magickal energy caused the fine hairs on her arm to stand on end. The mature witch closed her hand tightly and returned it to her lap.

"I have something for you." She slowly unfolded her hands to reveal a stunning choker. She presented it to Meera.

A gasp followed by rapid blinking was Meera's only response until she tentatively took the exquisite piece from Carrine's hands. "This is for me? Why?" She examined it closely, admiring the intricate design of the white metal that held princess-cut amethysts within the multi-circular pattern. The purple color intensified as the lights above illuminated them.

"Because you have been very brave and accepting of a world you knew nothing about. Most would have run the other direction. You"—she inclined her head—"you have embraced your heritage in a way many didn't expect. You are supreme, Meera. A Luminary, and this small trinket is a token of my gratitude."

Meera blinked back tears as she clutched the so-called small trinket to her chest. This gift she would treasure because it had been given to her by one of her own. Someone she could actually call a friend, and maybe someday Carrine would think of her as family.

"Thank you, Carrine. Thank you."

"You're welcome. Now let me help you put it on." She took the choker from Meera and waited while she turned and lifted her hair. "This is not just a piece of jewelry."

"Oh, I know."

"No. Not yet. But as soon as I clasp this, you *will* know. This ornament will allow you to hone in on your powers more quickly and more precisely. In time, it will give you the knowledge that was robbed from you over twenty-eight years ago. It will allow you to access memories that should have been yours. It is your birthstone. It is power."

Meera shivered at that one word.

How odd. She'd traded insanity—gladly she might add—for power. Some *would* run from it, that was true, but she'd lived her entire life being an outcast and therefore alone. She'd take this chance to find her true self and others who accepted her, and she'd do everything she could to make this last as long as possible.

"Are you ready? Once I click this in place, everything will change."

Meera took a deep breath before closing her eyes. She imagined the woman in her vision, her mother, singing to her with love in her eyes. Perhaps someday she would get to meet her. "I'm more than ready."

Carrine snapped the clasp into place. Meera dropped her hair and exhaled.

"Now, take the cloak off without using your hands. No words either. Just remove it."

Her fingertips tingled. Meera absently rubbed them together. She gasped when sparks the color of the amethysts she now wore dripped from her fingers like Independence Day sparklers, only prettier and definitely cooler.

"The cloak. Remove the cloak."

Somehow knowing exactly what to do, she flicked her wrist. Purple sparks flew out just as her cloak slid off her shoulders, folded midair and came to rest on the couch beside her. "You have got to be kidding me. Did I seriously just do that?"

Carrine laughed. "You seriously just did that. Look in the mirror, Meera."

She didn't question it, just walked across the room and peered into the mirror above the console at the door. She blinked, looked again and blinked some more. *Holy crazeballs.* Gone were her green eyes, the green she'd had her entire life. The color, now an exact match to the amethysts she wore around her neck, shimmered with barely contained magickal energy. *Hot damn.* She freakin' had purple eyes. How cool was that?

"Will they stay like this?"

"Yes. This is your true eye color now. A reflection of your magick.

"That's really cool. How much magick do I have?" Did she need to preserve it? Stock the power away for when she really needed it? God, she hoped not. She wanted to play, to discover her magickal capabilities.

"An infinite amount, really. It will continue to grow as you hone your skill."

Feeling overly energized, Meera held out her hand and wriggled her fingers. Sparks flew, and the sound of disco music filled the air. She flicked her wrist, and the volume pumped up a notch or two. She jumped off the couch and shimmied her way to the middle of the living area. A wave of her hand had her hair up in a messy pony.

She laughed and flicked her wrist toward Carrine, who looked down to see a beautiful purple scarf drape her neck. Carrine smiled and amazed Meera when she stood to join in the laughing and dancing. Who would have thought Carrine could have a good time? Between the two of them, multi-colored sparks filled the air as disco changed to country, and Meera and Carrine donned hot pink cowboy boots for some magickal line dancing.

*

Ghanem growled into the mattress and yanked a second pillow over his head. The hotel Thane had picked for them was upscale, but the soundproofing sucked the big one. Seriously, how long were they going to continue their party upstairs?

He lifted the pillow an inch and turned his head to look at the clock.

One o'clock in the morning. He'd only been asleep a few minutes when the neighbors to the north had kicked off their disco/country/Motown bash. As if their choice of music wasn't bad enough, he'd had to listen to their stomping and giggling for the past two hours.

Enough! He jumped out of bed, slid his jeans on commando style, and slipped out of his bedroom. Thane snored in the other room, which aggravated the shit out of him. His brother had always been able to sleep through hurricanes and earthquakes combined, while Ghanem had been cursed as the light sleeper.

Making sure to grab a key card before closing the door behind him, he took note of their suite number, 1402, and headed to the elevator. He hit the up button repeatedly until the doors slid open. A couple slipped out as he stepped in. The scantily clad woman in four-inch heels stared at him while her polo-wearing man tugged on her arm. Ghanem realized he had forgotten his shirt and shoes but didn't feel like taking the time to go back and get them. He was just too damn tired and too pissed. He hit the button to take him up to floor fifteen and leaned against the mirrored walls.

The elevator came to a stop a moment before the bell chimed and the doors opened. This floor looked identical to the one he'd just left, down to the deep blue carpet and textured beige walls. He took a right toward the room that would be directly above his own. He paused outside 1502 and quietly put his ear to the door. The music had been shut off. Actually the place was extremely quiet. Finally. He started to turn away. Screw that. He'd be an ass instead. They'd kept him up. He'd do the same for them.

Ghanem lifted his fist to pound on the door. Before he connected, it swung open. A wide-eyed woman he recognized instantly stood there. Only her eyes weren't the green he remembered. Lilac? How? He couldn't speak. He couldn't move.

She could. She launched herself at him. He caught her, but the momentum drove him backward. He hit the wall. Hard. "What the fu—"

She silenced him with her mouth. She nipped his lower lip, then bit his upper lip. Smokin' hot. This girl was on fire. Her body was like an inferno. So hot. Too hot. Maybe she was sick. *He* definitely was, because he should have stopped her, asked her if she was okay. Instead he pulled her legs up and locked them behind his back, heel over ankle, as he took control of the kiss.

Ghanem traced her lips with his tongue until she opened her mouth. He slipped his tongue between her lips and explored her mouth fully. She tasted of champagne and, if he wasn't mistaken, a mix of raspberry and chocolate. The combination was intoxicating. He wanted more. Thankfully, so did she.

She wrapped her hands around his head and pulled him even closer. It wasn't hard to oblige when all he really wanted to do was sink into her fully. Their tongues dueled as one of her hands slid from the back of his head to his shoulder and then continued its journey south. She stopped to pet his bare chest, and he thought he'd go up in flames right along with her. Her hips moved in a slow, circular motion. A growl crawled up his throat. She hesitated at the sound, but he encouraged her to continue by moving his hips in perfect rhythm to hers while his hands kneaded her backside.

He turned his head to get deeper access to her mouth. It wasn't enough. He had to have more. The need to drive himself inside her consumed him. Especially when her hand slid between them and found the zipper to his jeans. In his haste to get upstairs, he hadn't taken the time to fasten them. *Good move, Ghan.* Too bad he couldn't high-five himself. Her short nails skimmed his pelvic bone, and his body vibrated with pure pleasure.

He released her mouth to trail kisses along her jaw. He licked her neck, but when his tongue made contact with her necklace they both jumped back. "Shit." His tongue tingled as if something had zapped him.

Whatever it was, he'd deal with it if it meant more time with her. He stepped toward her. She stepped back. He watched her chest rise and fall as she tried to catch her breath. His did the same. "Meera."

"I've got to go." Her hand inadvertently touched her choker. "I've got to go."

He wouldn't force her. She'd been the one to make this move, but had obviously rethought her idea. "Go then, but know I will see you again. Soon."

"We can't."

"We must." He should have left then, but he had no control as he crossed the width of the hall in one step and seared her with another blazing kiss. Her hands stayed at her side, but she sighed deeply when he stepped away. He looked into her eyes, eyes the color of brilliant amethysts. "We must."

*

Oh. My.

What had just happened? She would have thought it was a dream or chalked it up to one of her moments of insanity-induced trances, but no can do considering she'd recently discovered she wasn't insane *and* her lips were swollen from kissing the daylights out of Mr. Delicious, who was currently headed toward the elevator while she stood like a love-struck teenager staring at his gorgeous, bare back.

Not good, Meera. So not good. But really, really good, Meera. Really, really good.

She'd sensed him outside her door moments after she'd shut off the music and Carrine had shut the door to her own bedroom. Her temperature only shot up to a hundred and five degrees Fahrenheit when Ghanem came around. Why? Hell, she had no idea but deny it she could not. She'd only given it a second's thought before opening the door and jumping him. Blame it on the giddiness of finding her magick. Blame it on too much champagne. Blame it on pure, unadulterated lust because she wanted Ghanem more than she'd ever wanted another person.

Sure, she heard Carrine's voice in the back of her head telling her to stay away from him, but try as she might, she feared this was one thing they would never agree on. Maybe he was veiled, but that didn't mean a heck of a lot to her yet. She wasn't afraid of him. She was afraid of not living long enough to discover more about him.

She snuck back in the apartment before he could turn around and see her watching him. She quietly shut the door and leaned against it. She'd yet to question why he'd been at her door or how he'd found her. Dressed the way he was, there was no way he'd come from outside. Even though they were in Chicago, a city known for its frigid winters, it had been uncharacteristically cold this year. Brutally cold. Countless days of below-zero weather took a toll on a person. Maybe she'd stick close to him for that reason alone. She'd never be cold again as long as he stayed within six feet of her. Looking down at her heated arms, she wondered about the redness, but dismissed it as a hormonal blush.

Her eyes flittered closed as she focused on the potential problem at hand. Obviously Ghanem was staying in this building. The fact that they kept ending up in the same place had to mean something. She was doomed. In more ways than she cared to count. *Focus on the good.* Still excited about her magick, Meera wriggled her fingers one last time for the night, and, before she knew it, lilac embers showered her and she found herself make-up free, hair braided, and with silky pajamas on as she slid beneath her cool sheets. She caressed her choker and smiled into her pillow. She could definitely get used to this.

Her plan was to dream of magick and Ghanem. The moment she closed her eyes, her plan went awry.

Chapter Twelve

Meera stood in the middle of an empty cornfield. The hacked cornstalks stabbed at her bare feet, cutting them until they bled. The sun descended rapidly, changing the colors of dusk—oranges, pinks and purples—to the colors of night—gray and black. Dressed in only her silk pajama top, she shivered as chill bumps covered her flesh, forcing her to wrap her arms around herself in an attempt to ward off the cold effects of the wind. Her hair came loose from its braids and became more tangled with each gust of icy air. Shoving the strands away from her face, Meera lowered her head and started walking. With each step forward, the wind pushed her two steps back.

Her mind screamed this was just another nightmare, but she was so cold she could barely move let alone figure out a way to wake up. She headed away from the sunset. Going east would get her closer to the lake, assuming she was still near Lake Michigan, and during the winter that tended to be slightly warmer than the west. Yeah. Like ten degrees made any difference when dealing with below-zero weather.

She jerked her head around at the sound of something—or someone—moving behind her. Nothing other than the outline of the broken cornstalks and the disappearing horizon. The wind howled, becoming more intense by the minute, the thunderous sound playing tricks on her already fragile mind.

Meera's foot slid across a jagged rock. The rock sliced deep, splitting her skin wide open and she fell to the ground. Lying there, exposed to the elements, she knew she had to get up, but the coldness had seeped into her bones, making her limbs numb. Her head pounded as the wind screamed, surrounding her with its torturous volume. Any louder, and her ears would bleed right along with the gaping wound in her foot.

Think, Meera.

Oh, what she wouldn't give for a large, steaming hot cup of vanilla latte right now. *What?* Not exactly her brightest moment. She must be hallucinating if all she could think about was coffee.

If she didn't move she'd be dead in minutes, possibly even seconds. Dead.

That one word was enough incentive to get her moving, albeit slowly. She managed to make it a few feet by dragging herself on all fours across the rough terrain. Her hands were now as cut up as her feet, and her knees weren't fairing any better.

Magick.

Relief swept through her when she remembered the choker Carrine had given her only hours earlier. A vision of her in a Wonder Woman costume had her cocking a half smile. She'd get herself out of this messed-up situation. Right now. She lifted her bloodied hand to her neck, cramped fingers sweeping over her skin. The feeling of relief fled, instantly replaced by dread. No choker. Her neck was as bare as her legs.

Meera frantically searched the ground she still crouched on. Maybe it had fallen off when she'd hit the ground. She crawled backward, continuing her search, patting the ground and throwing pieces of stalk and rocks in frustration. She needed the choker. She needed the magick of it. All her attention was solely placed on finding her lost hope. No wonder she hadn't heard the end of her life approaching until it was too late.

Unable to breathe, she lifted her head with regret in her heart. Regret for what had never been. Regret for the life that could have been hers. Regret at the lost chance of finding herself.

Tears froze on her cheeks, forming beautifully sad crystals. She saw her death in the eyes of the hundreds of men surrounding her. Men identical to the ones she and Carrine, along with Ghanem and Thane, had fought in the alley. Beautiful men with dark auras and long, pointed ears beneath their caps and hair. Men with blood on their minds.

Hers.

She curled up in a ball on the frozen ground and covered her head. If they were going to kill her, she really didn't want to see it coming.

It's not time, Meera. It's not time for you to go.

Meera whimpered at the sound of Carrine's voice. It could only be her mind playing tricks on her. Carrine couldn't help her here. She was alone and she was about to die.

It's not time. Listen to me. Hear me. Come back. It's not time.

If only she could do that, but she didn't know how to get herself out of this icy hell. They crept closer. Their presence was like a knife against her throat.

Someone kicked her thigh, but her legs were too numb to feel the pain. She grunted when another slammed his boot into her ribs. That she felt. She curled up tighter, praying they would leave her alone. It wasn't meant to be. Pain overtook the numbness when their relentless onslaught kicked in.

Come back. Come back.

How could Carrine sound so calm in the midst of this brutal attack? She'd said she would be by her side, but Meera was pretty sure she was the only one getting the shit beaten out of her. A hit to her head had her crying one minute and furious the next. They'd probably kill her, but she'd give them one hell of a fight first.

That's it, child. Come back now.

Meera let out a piercing scream, rolled out of the fetal position, and assumed a fighting stance. She wobbled and fought through dizziness. The baddies laughed in her face and approached from all sides, their auras dark and menacing even against the black of night. She spun around and fell again. Only this time, instead of landing in a heap in the middle of a barren cornfield, she landed back in her bed with Carrine standing over her.

"You're safe now." Carrine brushed Meera's tangled hair away from her face. "Welcome back."

She was too relieved to remember to be upset that she had been alone through the nightmare. She tried to get out of bed but her knees buckled and she fell back. She lifted her hands to find they were covered in blood and dirt. Hot tears gathered in the corners of her eyes. "I thought it was just a nightmare."

"A nightmare of sorts, but all too real nonetheless. They're becoming more powerful. Not good. Not good at all. They shouldn't be able to get to you while you sleep." Carrine pursed her lips, brows drawn tight in concentration, then sighed deeply. "I'll get something to help clean you up. You'll heal quicker than you used to, but it will still take some time."

All she had felt while being beaten in the field rushed back to her. "Where were you?"

Carrine stopped halfway through the door and turned at the strangled sound of Meera's voice with a sympathetic look in her eye.

Meera repeated her question. "Where were you? You said you'd be by my side, but I—I was alone." She choked on her sobs, not caring that she was crying like the child Carrine continued to call her. "I'm always alone."

Carrine hurried to her side and wrapped her arms around Meera's shoulders, careful not to hurt her any more than she already was. "I was right here. I heard you. I felt you. There are rules, and sometimes I can't be there physically. But I was here, child. I still am."

She was so tired of being alone. So damn tired. She held on to Carrine while the sobs racked her body. The physical hurt was bad enough; the emotional pain was pure torture. She feared she'd never have the courage to fall asleep again. The darkness and the wind were more than she could take, and she might not have the strength to continue *that* fight and the one during her waking hours.

Some time later, Carrine helped her into the shower, where Meera crouched on the floor in the corner. The water stung when it hit her body. There wasn't one inch of her that hadn't been battered, bloodied, and bruised. She watched the red-tinged water spiral down the drain and wondered if too much of her was headed down the same path.

Only after the scalding water began to cool did she realize her choices were fairly limited. She could sit in the shower huddled in the corner afraid of her own shadow, or she could take charge and fight for her life. She'd cried more in the last few weeks than she had in her entire life. Time to shut the spigot off.

Decision made, she used the shower wall to push herself into an upright position and carefully shampooed and conditioned her hair. While the conditioner soaked in and worked its own form of magick, she looked down at her black-and-blue body, taking note that Carrine had been right. While nowhere near healed, the bruises were already taking on a yellowish-purple tint.

Thank goodness for small miracles.

She stepped out of the shower, careful not to put too much pressure on her right foot. She'd cut it badly on that rock and felt certain it would be the last thing to heal.

"Feeling better?" Carrine asked, leaning against the opened door.

"Some. Thank you." She wrapped the warm towel around her body and grabbed another to wrap around her hair turban style. "I tried to use my magick. I thought it would get me out of there but my choker was lost."

"It's there now."

Meera's hand flew to her neck and dammit if Carrine wasn't right. "Why wasn't it there when I needed it? I really could have used the help." She didn't even attempt to keep the frustration and bitterness out of her voice.

"I'm not sure. I have to meet the council later today. Find out about this help we're supposed to receive. I have a few other questions to present to them as well, and that one will top the list. Can you walk?"

One of these days she'd convince Carrine to take her to one of these meetings with the council. Something told her now wasn't the time to press the subject. "Slowly, but I can make it. Do you think I can use magick now?"

Carrine lifted one brow. "You're not going to zap me, are you?"

She laughed. "No. But now that you mention it . . . Actually, I was hoping to use it to get dressed and make my way to the couch. I honestly don't think I have the energy or the strength for a major training session today."

"By all means. It is yours to use at will. Our hope is that you won't use it for any evil, but ultimately the decision is yours."

Too tired to worry about whether using her magick to destroy the baddies would be considered evil, Meera rubbed her fingers together and conjured up black, baggy sweats and a teal hoodie. A flick of her wrist brushed and dried her hair, moved her to the couch effortlessly and wrapped her in a white chenille blanket. Even through her fatigue she was proud of her magickal accomplishment. She definitely could have used a little—slash that—a *lot* of magick in that deathtrap corn field.

"Do you need anything else?" Carrine asked with an impressed smile.

"No thank you. I'm just going to lie here and watch reality TV."

"All right then. I need to gather some things and then meet with the council. I'll be gone a while. Try not to get into any trouble." Carrine flicked her own wrist and vanished.

"What trouble could I possibly get into?" Meera said to an empty room.

She couldn't rest. She couldn't get comfortable. Her body ached in parts she hadn't been aware of having. She'd thought Carrine's workouts were vicious. Getting pounded into the ground by about a hundred bad guys definitely trumped that. No doubt she'd be even stiffer if she stayed in this position much longer. Add that to the fact that she was absolutely starving, and she had enough incentive to push herself off the couch and fight a dizzy spell. Her head *still* throbbed where the asshole had kicked her with his steel-toed boot.

Meera stopped to look in the mirror on her way out. She would have cringed if she didn't think it would hurt like hell to scrunch up her face. She waved her hand in front of her to make sure she was at least presentable, but no amount of make-up or magick could completely cover the bruises that spread across her cheeks and jaw. She shrugged. She could do little about it other than stay holed up, but she was desperately tired of being alone.

She slid on black flip-flops and gingerly made her way to the elevator. Yesterday, she'd spotted a small deli on the ground floor. She'd just step outside for a quick minute and allow the cold air to get rid of some of the fog she carried around in her head. A nap would have accomplished the same thing, but that was so not gonna happen. Not when her nightmares left bruises. Instead, she'd hit the deli for a turkey on rye and sit there pretending she was sharing lunch with some of the other patrons. Pitiful.

The elevator door slid open. Empty. *Thank you.* She hoped to make it to the ground floor without having to share the elevator with anyone. Confined in the small space with strangers wondering what the hell had happened to her sounded like tons of fun. Not. At least in the deli she could pretend they were all staring at someone behind her. She punched the button to the first floor and held on to the handrail for support.

Unfortunately, luck was not on her side. The elevator stopped at the fourteenth floor. Meera quickly pulled the hood up on her sweatshirt to cover her face. She realized she was about to get a double whammy when she started to sweat before the doors even opened. *Damn, damn, damn.*

She kept her head down and stared at his silver-and-white running shoes. Maybe he wouldn't recognize her. How embarrassing to have to explain her appearance to the flawless wonder—especially after last night. She waited for him to acknowledge her, but all he did was clear his throat as two more people stepped into the elevator.

Her temperature shot through the roof during the longest elevator ride of her life. The damn thing stopped on almost every floor as more people crammed into the small space. Of course, Ghanem had to step closer each time to make room for the newcomers. If one more person got on, he'd practically be inside her.

Nice. That visual had her temperature rising another notch or two.

Finally the elevator chimed at the ground floor. She waited none too patiently for her turn to step off. She looked up just in time to spot two men coming toward her with definite black auras. Her breath hitched. She stumbled back and bumped into something hard before her world went black.

Chapter Thirteen

Meera stayed silent, having no idea how long she'd been out. She tried to remain calm, get her bearings, but panic set in before she even opened her eyes. Her attackers. Here. She had to get away. More hurt. More pain. She wasn't healed yet. She didn't have enough strength to fight them off. Again. She clawed and kicked, desperate to get up. Something—no, someone—held her down. She struggled against him. She had to move. Had to escape.

Meera fought her way through the fog and literally came face to face with a man.

Ghanem.

In a horizontal position.

Her head twisted from side to side, confusion ebbing away the fear. She was on the couch again, but the heat wasn't coming from the blanket she'd wrapped herself in earlier. This heat came solely from the enormous man currently pinning her arms to her sides and her legs together with one of his own.

At any other time, in a completely different situation, this could have been cozy. Sensual. But after everything that had happened in the past few hours, the timing was all wrong.

Something, perhaps sorrow or pain, flashed in his eyes before he said, "I'm going to let go now. You're not going to attack me, are you?"

Maybe it was the melodic sound of his whiskey voice or the way he restrained her without actually hurting her, but she slowly calmed down, if only a fraction.

"No."

He eased off one agonizing inch at a time until he sat facing her on the opposite end of the couch.

"How did we get here?" Her last memory had been lights out

in the elevator.

"Quickly."

Meera quirked a brow.

"Does it matter?"

"To me it does. How long was I out?" It couldn't have been too long because she was still exhausted. She glanced at her arms. The bruises hadn't really faded at all since she'd last checked. She hated being out of control. Losing precious moments of time when she had so little of it left was a feeling she didn't relish.

He followed the direction of her gaze, but held off on the obvious question. "Interesting that this should be our first actual conversation."

She was thankful for what would probably turn into a short-lived reprieve. Why then did she next bait him with sarcasm? "It'll be an extremely short one if you don't start answering my questions." She crossed her arms over her chest, but dropped them quickly. Her ribs were still too sore.

"I'll make you a deal." He crossed his own arms and leaned back against the arm of the couch.

Meera couldn't wait to hear this. Both eyebrows shot up.

"I'll answer your question and then you have to answer one of mine."

"Childish," Meera mumbled. So much for a reprieve. "Fine."

"You were only out for a few minutes. The elevator closed right after you, um . . ."

The look on his face told her he was trying desperately to come up with the right word. She had no trouble supplying him with a few. "Fainted, passed out, blacked out, lost it? Doesn't matter. Just pick one."

"Swooned?"

Meera almost choked. "Did you just say swooned? I most definitely did not *swoon*, and who even uses that word anymore?"

Ghanem swiped his hand across his head. "Look. I'm trying to be sensitive."

"Don't."

"Noted and filed. Anyway, after you passed out, I pulled back your hood so you could get some air. One look at those bruises told me the only place you need to be is right here on this couch. Which leads me to my question."

Here it comes. How to explain the unexplainable? "I need to get some water." Meera swung her legs off the couch and stood. Pain shot up from the arch of her foot to the top of her head. She fell back onto the couch in a clumsy heap and bent over to examine the damage. "Dammit." She'd opened up the gash and now her foot was bleeding on the ivory carpet.

"Stay here. I'll get a towel and some water." He sprinted to the kitchen and was back before she could even lean back. He handed her a glass of water while he carefully examined her foot before loosely wrapping the towel around it. "You need stitches."

"No way." Meera jerked her foot. He didn't let go.

"Why not."

"Just forget it. I said no."

He lifted his head and she turned away. Ghanem cleared his throat. "Then can I at least bandage it for you?"

"I can do it myself," she whispered. It was one thing to be making out with him in the hallway. It was something entirely different to be comforted by him. She didn't know how to deal with that.

He reluctantly let go of her foot and backed away. "I'll get you some bandages. They must have something downstairs. I'll be right back." He grabbed the keycard from the mirrored console next to the door.

She'd offended him, but wasn't sure how. The flash of hurt in his eyes caused a knot in the pit of her stomach. She'd never met anyone who carried such strong emotions in their eyes. What was the big deal, anyway? She'd take care of this cut just like she'd taken care of all the cuts and scrapes growing up.

Alone.

Her so-called mother and father had never had a tender or

loving hand. She'd learned early on she would get no sympathy from them, just a firm "buck up" and then a dismissal, contrary to the treatment her brother and sister had received. Funny, she hadn't thought about any of them in days and doubted they had felt anything other than relief when she stopped coming around. It shouldn't have hurt. But it did.

Meera limped to the galley-style kitchen for another towel. She opened cabinet after cabinet in hopes of finding some cleaner. This one time, luck was on her side. She found exactly what she needed under the sink. This stainless steel paradise had come fully stocked. Food. Dishes. Cleaners. No doubt Carrine's doing.

Squatting next to the couch, she wondered about the council Carrine so often spoke of. Who were they? What were they like? How many witches made up the council? How were they selected? Carrine had questions for *them*, and Meera rapidly made a list of questions for *her*. She rubbed the carpet with vigor even when her arms screamed. She had to get the blood up. Had to. She didn't need a constant reminder of the stain that had become her life.

*

Ghanem stood at the door and watched Meera go at the stain as if her life depended on it. He walked over and squatted next to her. Placing his hand on top of hers, he gently forced her to stop. "Let me help you."

She snatched her hand from beneath his. "No. I can do it. I've almost got it."

Her voice, laced with desperation, told him he'd better back off and let her complete the task on her own. Something about this entire day had him worried. He silently watched until the last remaining spot of blood disappeared. Only then did she sit back. He wouldn't call her relaxed, but anything was better than the edge of before.

Complicated woman, this one. No doubt about it. But what about his life wasn't complicated? Thane had said they needed to find the "elf detector." Well, he'd found her, but was in no hurry to share her with anyone, even if that meant lying to his own brother about where he'd been.

Thane had called him on his way back up to let him know Drake and Steffen had arrived, and that he should hurry up and get back so they could start formulating a plan. Wanting to delay that meeting as long as possible, he'd told Thane he'd be back soon and he'd bring lunch. Thankfully, Thane hadn't questioned him on his whereabouts. He'd be able to hold off on the lie a little while longer.

Worth it? Absolutely. More time spent with Meera and less time spent with Ding and Dong.

Now what to do about the beautiful and complex Meera Brennan? Last night she'd been a sensual, confident woman. But something had happened between then and now. Presently she looked confused and beaten. Time to get back to their agreement.

"What happened to you? Why are you so bruised?"

Immediately, her spine stiffened and her jaw clenched.

"You want the long version or the short one?" she asked quietly, resigned.

A number of scenarios played out in his head. None of them good. "Your version. I'll take your version." He offered his hand, and she surprised him by taking it. As he closed his fingers over hers, he stretched his legs out in front of him and leaned against the couch. She did the same. They sat there on the floor together for quite some time before she answered.

"A lot has changed for me recently. Most I'm not able to talk about. Mainly because I don't understand it all myself. Remember the alley? Remember those guys?"

Ghanem nodded and stroked her smooth palm with his thumb, his way of asking her to continue.

"I ran into them last night." She closed her eyes for a moment.

They shot open. "So many of them."

Restraint had never been his strong suit. This case proved particularly hard. He had so many questions, but experience told him the second he asked one she'd clam up. Gaze skimming her features—the curve of her neck, the line of her jaw, the edge in her eyes—he simply waited for her to continue. As though she were in a trance, her voice took on a distant, dream-like quality.

"It was cold. There were so many of them. Hundreds, I think. I can't be sure. So dark. So cold. So evil. The wind—"

When she shivered, he grabbed the blanket from the couch and laid it across her shoulders. She leaned into him, and he moved his arm to cradle her neck.

"I was lost and it was so cold. I cut my foot on a rock. I just wanted to go home, but I didn't know which way to go. I still don't. They found me. There were so many of them. Hundreds, I think. They kicked me. Over and over, they kicked me."

Ghanem clenched his fist. He'd heard enough. Hundreds? She'd said it at least twice. What was going on here? His blood boiled with a rage he hadn't experienced in almost forever. He tamped it down before shifting her toward him. "Meera."

She looked at him, distance evident in her eyes. Not hard to see she was somewhere else entirely.

"Meera, it's okay now. You're safe." She looked lost. His throat tightened like a python had coiled its body around his neck. He had no time to question his feelings or his connection to her. Ghanem pulled her onto his lap and placed his lips over hers. A whisper of a touch was all it took to connect and something else he'd question later. Just now he focused on her. Feeling her. The kiss lingered. A kiss wholly different from the feverish one the night before, but no less satisfying.

She pulled back first, just a little, but didn't move away. "I'm afraid, Ghanem. I'm so tired, but I'm afraid to go to sleep."

What had it taken for her to admit that? He knew exactly how she felt. He'd gone decades afraid of the night. Afraid of sleep. Afraid of what he'd see if he closed his eyes. If only someone had been there with him. "I'll stay here. Go to sleep. I promise nothing will happen."

He wasn't sure if she'd even heard him. It didn't matter. Her breathing became soft and even. He wouldn't leave her. Not now. Thane would have to wait.

While they sat together, her resting in his lap with her head on his shoulder, he gaining comfort in the smell of her hair, Ghanem knew there were many questions left unasked—many that needed to be answered. Number one—what was she? They seemed to be skirting around the *don't ask, don't tell* adage. He now knew she was indeed veiled, but his instincts were so whacked he couldn't get a line on what form she could be. Her powers—and certainly she must have some, as all veiled did—had yet to be seen. Was she hiding them? And if so, why?

Her bruises worried him. Not so much in the fact she still hurt physically—he could see the contusions healing at a pretty fast rate—but more so that she'd had to endure the pain and the fear in the first place. All of what she'd told him didn't make sense no matter how much he mulled it over. Such as where had this attack taken place? She hadn't mentioned leaving the hotel, but had talked about the brutal cold. Where could she have gone that a hundred men could attack her out in the open? Had there been no one around to help her? He didn't think so. Fear of being alone shone like a screaming billboard in her eyes.

His thoughts kept going back to Thane's nickname for her. Elf detector. If only they were dealing with elves. Maybe it would be simpler. Obviously, Thane had no qualms about using another being for personal gain. Ghanem's stomach churned at the thought. He wanted to be more like Thane. He *used* to be more like him, so much more of a man—strike that—more of a guardian, but had his banishment stripped him of all his warrior traits? All that had made him who he was? Why else would he feel so guilty about what had to be done?

He breathed deeply, inhaling Meera's scent. A mix of lavender and mint caressed his senses. He closed his eyes and gave in to the moment of complete relaxation. Tomorrow would be soon enough to drown in guilt, and drown he would. The knowledge that, in doing what had to be done, he would in turn be saving the human race should have assuaged some of that guilt, but he wasn't really doing it for that reason. Nothing and no one would stop him from taking back what was rightfully his.

He glanced down at Meera's peaceful features. No matter how much it hurt him to do so.

*

Thoroughly enjoying himself, Ryken smiled. After receiving Jayson Nightfinder's update, he decided to celebrate. Punishing the witch in Midrealm—the realm where dreams took place—had been very satisfying indeed. He hadn't been sure it could be done, but insisted on trying again and again, continually drawing on the dark magick, and this time it had paid off. If only he could have been there to witness it. A small part, buried deep inside, wished he could have taken part in the witch's punishment, but that was beneath him. Fighting was for the commoners, not the king.

Instead he would revel in the fact that he had been the conductor of this orchestrated strike. Attacking someone while they slept was to attack them when they were most vulnerable, and in his opinion, the only opinion that truly mattered, that was the perfect time. Too bad they hadn't killed her. In time they would if she didn't yield to his plan. Of that he had no doubt. He had no room to fail. The Luminary witch, Meera Brennan, must be stopped. She alone could cause everything he strived for to end disastrously.

But right now, they were a few steps in front of her and they'd caused damage. Quite a bit of it, if Jayson was to be believed, and Ryken had no reason to doubt him. He'd proven to be a valuable second.

So, yes, he would enjoy himself with a few beautiful slups who didn't hesitate to do his bidding. Dressed in a scarlet, silk smoking jacket, he stretched across his enormous bed, the coolness of the satin sheets sending dirty shivers of anticipation through his system. He summoned them with a look. One redhead, one blonde, and one brunette approached from separate corners of the room. What could he say—he liked a little variety now and then. They were naked in both body and spirit. Just the way he liked them. He had enough spirit for all of them. The vacant look in their eyes would have bothered most.

Not Ryken. That vacant look was a confirmation of his success.

A wicked smile played across his lips. These slups were all his. Tonight he would celebrate long and hard. Tomorrow he would devise the next step of his plan. Witch Brennan would become his queen or die before her next birthday.

*

One could get used to waking like this. Surrounded in warmth, cloaked in protection, hardness and softness perfectly co-mingled. Meera wanted to stay right where she was but it couldn't be. She heard Carrine down the hall. If Carrine caught her here, in Ghanem's arms, Meera wouldn't hear the end of it any time soon. She tried to ease off his lap, but he wrapped his arms around her even tighter and lifted his head off the couch. He smiled. She squirmed. His smile broadened devilishly.

"I'm sorry I woke you," Meera whispered.

"I'm not," Ghanem said.

"I'm quite aware of how you feel about the situation." She shouldn't have said it, but his hardness was so damned apparent, and she felt impish.

"Sounds like you're feeling better and in the mood to play." He nuzzled her neck.

Carrine's voice grew louder. Any minute she'd open the door and Meera would be busted. Carrine had warned her not to get into any trouble and technically she hadn't, but doubted her mentor would feel the same. The fact she hadn't just *popped* in rather than using the door crossed Meera's mind, but she wasn't one to question a blessing.

"I'd love to play"—*and boy would she*, she thought—"but Carrine is right outside the door. Please let me up."

"Yeah. I hear her and she's not alone. I'll let you up this time." He loosened his hold.

"This time? What makes you think there will be a next time?" His hands cupped her bottom as he pushed her into a standing position. She straightened her clothes and shoved her hair back.

Ghanem stood. She was tall, but he made her feel petite. She loved that. It was hard to find a man who could so easily dwarf her.

"I was right last time, remember?"

Oh, yeah. She remembered. A heated blush covered her cheeks. Her, him, hallway. Definitely something she wouldn't soon forget. "Right. Okay. I don't suppose you know how to disappear?" She glanced nervously at the door and then back at him. There it was again. That look of pain in his eyes. "Are you okay? Did I say something wrong?"

He unclenched his jaw. "No. It's nothing. Why don't you meet her outside and tell her you're hungry. After you get in the elevator, I'll let myself out. Work for you?"

Meera stood on tiptoe and kissed him quickly. "It just might, and thank you for staying." She wanted to stay now, pay him back somehow for what he had done for her. But now wasn't the time.

She sprinted for the door, completely healed thanks to several hours of undisturbed sleep. Just before she turned the handle, she flicked her hand over her head. Showers of purple sparks rained down on her before changing out her sweats for stylish, form-fitting jeans and a fuchsia tunic. She giggled, opened the door, and slid through, completely missing the look of horror on Ghanem's face.

Chapter Fourteen

Meera pulled the door closed, pasted an innocent smile on her face, and turned to greet Carrine. Surprisingly, her mentor wasn't alone, but she couldn't let that deter her even though she was more than a little curious. "Hi. I'm starving. Let's grab a bite to eat."

Carrine lifted one perfectly sculpted eyebrow.

Busted. Totally and completely busted. So there had been a reason Carrine hadn't just popped in. Meera would be thankful for that *after* she figured out a way to get out of trouble. What she needed was a distraction, and the two beautiful women next to Carrine provided just that. She offered her hand to the one standing to Carrine's right, glad she had taken the extra second to spruce up. "Hi. I'm Meera. And you are?"

"Bevva. So, we finally meet. Seems we've caught you at the most inopportune time." She squeezed Meera's hand before releasing it, the twinkle in her eye full of mischief and danger.

Holy wow. What a stunner. A curly mass of fiery red hair nearly took over the entire hallway. If it hadn't been for the diamond-encrusted combs holding it in place, her hair would have been completely and outrageously out of control. Medusa never looked so good. The intensity in her rust-colored eyes only added to the passion surrounding this woman, the epitome of a walking fireball.

"It's nice to meet you." Meera opted to ignore her last comment. A lost opportunity to get to know Ghanem better was a disappointment, but better that than getting on Carrine's bad side. Or so she told herself. He'd done a lot for her in a short period of time, and she'd bailed. She already felt bad enough about it and didn't need for Bevva—whom she'd just met—to cast judgment.

Mentally shrugging it off, she turned to the third woman in the hallway and, trying not to stare, extended her hand. The second Ms. Gothic's hand closed around her own, Meera's attitude shifted, as if she didn't have a care in the world. So what if Carrine was upset, and so what if she'd shirked Ghanem? They'd all work it out one way or another.

"Hello, Meera. I'm Calliope."

She held Meera's hand longer than necessary, a knowing smile playing at her lips, but Meera didn't mind. Not a bit.

"Calliope. I'm happy to meet you." *Happy to meet you?* That was weird and not something she'd typically say, especially to someone wearing black nail polish, ripped fishnets, and blue combat boots, but damn if she didn't feel just that. Happy.

Calliope stood just as tall as Meera, but her hair, carefully styled up and out in all directions, made her appear even taller. She accentuated the onyx color with sweeping bangs the same shade of blue as her intense eyes and graphic dragon tee. Star tattoos formed a cresent shape around one eye. A petite diamond stud twinkled on her perfect nose, and the tattoo covering her entire right arm begged to have its story told. Not everyone could pull off such a funky style, but it suited this one and made her incredibly striking.

Were they witches too? They definitely weren't human. Nobody looked like these women unless they were airbrushed to death in a fashion magazine. She studied them a moment longer, positive she'd never met them before, yet something seemed oddly familiar. She searched her memories, hoping she'd make the connection. Instead she heard tinkling music in the distance, soothing chimes swaying in a mild wind. Confused and disoriented, she knew the sound had come from within her, and she was the only one hearing it. She wanted to know more about these two and their history. Yet it was all too eerie, too intense. In an effort to center herself, Meera briefly closed her eyes.

Carrine interrupted her thoughts. "Now that we've got the introductions out of the way, perhaps we could get you something to eat since you're so very *hungry*. Do you think they'll have something to appease you downstairs? We need to make this quick. We've got a lot to discuss."

Ouch. Meera reminded herself to avoid annoying this new Carrine in the future. The sound of her voice had enough ice in it to make hell shiver. Being a quick study, she wouldn't make the same mistake twice. Lesson learned, memorized, and filed away for quick reference. At least the chimes had silenced. "Sure. Let's go. There's a deli downstairs. I'll grab a sandwich, and you can fill me in on your visit with the council."

"I'm a bit hungry as well," Calliope said.

Bevva chimed in. "I guess I could eat."

Meera smiled. This could be good. With any luck these two would stick around for a while. She could get used to having people on her side. Perhaps she owed the council her gratitude after all.

"Very well," Carrine said. "We'll all eat and then get down to business. We've wasted enough time already."

Meera glanced over her shoulder as they stepped into the elevator. She'd hoped to catch a glimpse of Ghanem to hold her over until the next time. She was just as convinced as he was that there would be a next time. The elevator closed, breaking the connection, though not severing it. His heat wrapped her in a cocoon of warmth. But something else simmered in the air, and it put her on edge instantly.

Anger. Ghanem's heat was tinged with anger.

What was that all about? *Geesh.* Now she felt even worse about ditching him just to save face with Carrine.

*

Ghanem stood like a hundred-year-old tree. The only difference being he was rooted in disbelief. A witch. A fucking witch. The woman who had taken over his every thought and seduced his dormant heart was his worst enemy. Had she known all along what this would do to him? Had she attempted to snare him with veiled magick? For what purpose? What could she possibly want with him? He wasn't the prince. Not anymore.

His head dropped. He felt lower than the floor he stood on. His gaze fixed upon the spot she had scrubbed with an intensity that suggested she had been deeply hurt. Not just physically, but emotionally as well. Had it been an act? He wouldn't have thought so, but that was before she had exposed herself.

A witch.

Suddenly the guilt he'd experienced the night before lessened. Time to meet up with Thane and the losers. Time to take charge and step up the timeline. He was ready. More than ready to take his life back. He had guardian blood, and it didn't matter that he lacked the outward appearance of one. He let the anger sweep through him with each step he took. He'd been fooled—twice now—but not again. Not ever again.

Taking no chances he'd run into her, he opted for the stairs. With his anger came strength and speed. His feet only touched every third step, still it wasn't fast enough. The blaring fluorescent lights cast the walls in a putrid green color, but that paled next to the odor of stale cigarettes and urine. Apparently it didn't matter how upscale a place was, stairwells always reeked and looked like shit.

His breathing hitched with the tightening of his shirt, the pain tolerable, but there nonetheless. His shirt ripped across his back. Furious, he didn't give it a second thought, nor stop to consider why, after all these years, he had recaptured some of his guardian strength, if only in small and painful doses. Rage building, Ghanem slammed against the door, practically ripping it off the hinges, the sound reverberating down the empty hall.

The onslaught of memories promised to drown him in sorrow and regret. A witch. His breathing grew more and more strained, tearing through his lungs in forced puffs as he pounded his way toward the suite he shared with Thane. A few more seconds and he'd be able to fully let go.

Unable to stand upright any longer, Ghanem bent at the waist in front of room 1402 and hammered the door with both fists, not caring that he damaged the glossed wood in the process. A demonic growl rose from his throat, its intensity causing the crystal sconces to shake in time with his own writhing body. The humans would come up with some inane reason to explain it away. They always did.

Hold. On. One. More. Second. He hit the door a final time before it was wrenched open. Wasting no time at all, he pulled his body over the threshold and attacked the first breathing being in sight. Just coming into his first guardian rage in two hundred years, he had little control over his body and mind. A pissed off guardian could do a lot of damage if he lost control. It barely registered he could very well be attacking his brother. No doubt Thane would consider it a workout.

Fighting through the pain of the change, Ghanem relied purely on instinct and strength. A lamp crashed to the floor, and shattered glass flew in every direction. He heard nothing but muffled cursing. He cared not for whoever was on the receiving end of his brutal punishment, nor for the cuts he received when he rolled over the shards of glass.

Someone laughed, then cleared their throat, but Ghanem, too far gone, couldn't focus on where or whom it had come from. His head flew back when a knee slammed into his chin. He roared in anger and, ignoring the pain in his jaw, grabbed the knee and twisted. A painful howl erupted from his opponent.

"Enough."

Fuck enough. It would never be enough. Yet through the pain came moments of clarity. This was what he had wanted. This was what had been missing for the past two hundred years. Power.

"Ghanem! I said enough."

The red haze of fury slowly began to dissipate, melting away like ice on a warm spring day. Thane's voice had cut through the anger-induced miasma. When finally he could see clearly again, he almost laughed. But it wasn't funny. A beginning, sure, but not funny. Maybe he should thank the witch rather than throttle her, because if it weren't for her he wouldn't have beaten the shit out of Drake. Not this soon, anyway.

He gave his unwilling adversary a slight nod. "Good to see you, Derek."

"It's Drake." A tight, bloodied mouth formed a sneer.

"Right. Drake. Why do I always forget that?"

"Because you're an asshole," someone answered for Drake.

Ghanem turned to the voice behind him. "Ah, Steffen. It's been a while."

"Not nearly long enough."

"Finally. Something we can both agree on." Ghanem swiped the back of his hand across his mouth, looked down to see blood, and laughed. He studied the guardian he had never liked, the same fucker who'd pined after his sister longer than he could remember. He would never be good enough for Amella. Steffen, cocky as ever, stood there next to Thane in European-cut jeans and a black, long-sleeved button up. Cuffs open, the sleeves had been rolled back once, but still hung low enough to cover his wrists and the top half of his large hands. His hair was a controlled mess, as if he couldn't be bothered with combing it, when in all actuality he probably spent hours on that alone. He hadn't bothered to conceal his horns. The sting of jealousy hit Ghanem yet again. While his strength had returned, his horns had yet to make an appearance.

"How long have they been here?" he asked his brother.

"Several hours. Where have you been?" Thane narrowed his eyes. "Something you want to tell us?"

"Us? Hardly." No way in hell would he admit he'd been played a fool to Drake and Steffen. They already thought so little of him, why give them more ammo?

"Me, then." Thane turned to Drake and Steffen. "The fridge is stocked. Help yourself. And Drake—"

Drake lifted a brow.

"—you might want to hit the shower and get a change of clothes. You're bleeding all over the place."

Ghanem laughed. Drake did not. "Fuck you, Thane."

"Oh. I see. You're a big guardian now that Dominic's not around." Ghanem couldn't help himself. He'd always loved antagonizing Drake, and one way or another, Drake and Steffen would learn to respect him. As former prince of Saharren, he deserved their damn respect.

Drake lowered his head, but then lifted it and looked Ghanem dead in the eye. "Fuck you." He spun on his heel and headed for the bathroom, visibly trying not to limp.

Ghanem bit back a smile. Maybe he could like, or at least stomach Drake after all, as long as he didn't go back to being a pussy.

Thane slapped him on the back. "Let's go."

Ghanem followed Thane into the bedroom. His sheets, still rumpled from the night before, displayed evidence of his tossing and turning.

"Rough night?"

"You could say that." Sitting on the edge of the bed, he covered his face with his hands. Thane sat next to him, remaining silent. *Smart guy. Knows when to keep his mouth shut.* Ghanem released a heavy sigh. "You know Meera?"

"Yeah."

"I've run into her a couple of times since yesterday."

Thane stood. "What? Why didn't you say anything?" He paced the length of the room. "You know we—fuck 'we'—*you* need her. Did you talk to her? Did she tell you anything useful? Fuck, Ghanem. We're wasting time here."

"Sit down. Your solo waltz is annoying me." He waited until

his brother reclaimed his seat. "Yeah. I talked to her, but not about that. Not exactly." He remembered her story of being attacked by the men. Could they have been slayers?

"Not exactly?"

"Dude. Let me talk."

"Dude? What a human thing to say." Obviously realizing his lame joke hadn't gone over well, Thane said, "Fine. Talk."

"She passed out in the elevator so I carried her back to her room. Yes, she's staying here too, and no, I don't know why." He deliberately neglected to mention how he knew which room was hers. "She was covered in bruises, and, after some prodding, she told me she'd been attacked. I don't know much more than that. She was too upset, too scared to go into a lot of detail."

"If I were able to ask questions, I'd ask what about your conversation with her had you kicking Drake's ass?"

He could do without the sarcasm. Ghanem stared at the ceiling and willed himself not to knock Thane on his ass. "She's a witch."

"What?" Thane cleared his throat. "Shit, man. She told you that?"

He turned his head, not able to take the sympathy etched in the lines of Thane's face. Yes, there was history there. Bad history. So bad, he wouldn't allow his mind to linger there for too long. "She didn't have to tell me. I saw it. Felt it. Fuck. I didn't have a fucking clue."

Thane nudged him with his knee. "She got to you, didn't she?"

He wouldn't admit it to anyone else. But no one knew him like his brother. "Yeah. She did. I don't know, *fratello*. I can't wrap my head around this. Without knowing my past, why would she keep this from me? She would have no idea what this would do to me. No idea at all. What if she knows my history? What if she's part of all this? What if she's working with or for the slayers?"

Now it was Ghanem's turn to pace, and pace he did, certain to wear a path in the lush carpet. "Any of it could be true. All of it, for that matter, but something doesn't feel right. I'm not sure she's all bad, but then I talk myself out of that and wonder if she doesn't

120

have me under one of those damn witch spells." Ghanem shoved his hands into his front pockets. "Obviously I wouldn't know it even if it smacked me upside my hornless head."

Thane stood and ran a hand through his long hair. "You're not gonna like this."

He stopped pacing long enough to shoot his brother a wary look. "Probably not, but go ahead."

"Whether she's with us, against us, or impartial, we need her."

"I know. As much as I want it to be otherwise, I'm not that much of an idiot that I can't see the usefulness and necessity of that."

"But do me a favor, will ya?"

"Perhaps."

"I know this is your gig and you're in charge, but you can't beat up our troops anymore."

He saw the logic, but still. "No promises."

"You'll try?"

He conceded.

"Well, then. Should we congregate?"

Ghanem shook his head. "Big word there, pal."

"I know. You don't have to tell me. I'm a genius." Thane's look was pure conceit, dark eyes shining like tinsel.

Ghanem wanted to supply a witty retort. Instead, he shrugged. "I got nothin'."

They both laughed, easing some of the tension in the room, but none of the confusion he felt about Meera. With any luck, he'd be able to avoid seeing her until his head cleared. That should only take a few centuries. Too bad time, let alone luck, wasn't on his side.

"All right," Thane said. "Let's round up Drake and Steffen. You ready to get this thing started?"

"I'm ready. Let's do this."

Taking the role of leader, Ghanem headed out first. Thane followed him into the large living area. Establishing his position up front with Steffen and Drake was important. Otherwise he could be in a world of trouble if they questioned his authority. Full guardian or not, he would lead this measly horde into battle, and he'd do it with his head held high.

The four of them gathered around the mahogany coffee table, Ghanem and Thane on one side, Drake and Steffen the other. Ghanem pulled out the book that showed the map of Lemra. He smoothed back the pages before saying, "This is where we must go. This map is old, and it's quite possible the underground kingdom of the slayers has changed, but this is all we have to go on right now. Have either of you ever come into contact with them?"

"No," Drake said, studying the aged map.

"Me, either," admitted Steffen. "But they're just elves, right? Should be easy enough. Can't we just step on them?"

Ghanem laughed despite himself. "Yeah, no. It won't be that easy. Thane and I had the pleasure of running into a few of them a couple of days ago. They're not elves at all. The only resemblance to an elf is the pointed ears. Slayers are very strong and stand six to seven feet tall. And those ears? Should be a dead giveaway. Problem is, they disguise them. They look human. Intentionally so. Without seeing those ears, there's no way to distinguish them from any other non-veiled walking the streets. However, I have a feeling there's even more to them than that. Doubt we'll get a glimpse of it in this realm though."

"What are they doing here?" Drake asked.

Thane picked up the remote and flicked on the television. He flipped through the channels until he found the local news. "They've been airing this all day. I'm not certain, but I think this may be their doing."

They listened in silence as the blond-haired, blue-eyed news anchor reported on three missing people. From what the police could tell, the three had nothing in common. Two men, one a stockbroker, the other a delivery services driver, and one woman, a dancer from a local theatre group.

"This is a big city. I'm sure the crime rate is pretty high. What makes you think they had anything to do with this?" But Ghanem's gut told him his brother could be right.

Thane hit the mute button on the remote. "Very similar story for the past two nights. I think it's at least worth considering."

"Without walking up to each man and exposing his ears—which I'm not opposed to, mind you—how do we figure out which ones to follow?" Steffen leaned forward, anticipation rippling off his body.

Ghanem and Thane exchanged a knowing look. "We have a plan."

Chapter Fifteen

The scents of rye, pumpernickel, asiago, and provolone surrounded Meera. She breathed deeply, savoring the aroma. Since meeting Carrine, she'd needed to eat three times the amount of food she normally consumed. She'd attributed it to the strict training regimen, but after a look at Bevva's plate, she had to wonder if it had more to do with being veiled and finally discovering her magick. Well, if that wasn't one hell of a perk.

Her roasted chicken sandwich smothered in mushrooms and crumbles of blue cheese was nothing compared to Bevva's grilled steak sandwich with a double order of French fries. That woman could eat. Looking at them, one would probably think the lot of them were bulimic. Thankfully they'd chosen a booth in the back of the deli, out of the way of prying eyes and any possible eavesdroppers. Though Meera couldn't fathom why anyone would believe any of the tales, Carrine insisted on being careful.

"So you're the Luminary," Bevva said between mouthfuls.

Was that a question or just a statement meant to mock? Meera glanced at Calliope and noticed she'd closed her eyes and placed her hand on Bevva's shoulder. Bevva shrugged it off.

"I'm guessing you're a *witch*." Meera emphasized the last word, giving it the negative connotation Bevva deserved. Two could play at this game.

"Touché." Bevva said before dipping a fry in ranch dressing and sticking the entire thing in her mouth.

Carrine spoke up before she could say another word. "We're all witches, and they're here to help us . . . help *you*." She pointedly looked at Meera. But with her next statement she made sure to hold the gaze of each witch. "This won't be easy, so please, let's all try to get along for the sake of all kind."

"What you really mean is for the sake of keeping this one alive." Bevva cocked her head at Meera as if begging for a fight.

So the council had sent them. Meera decided to hold onto her thank you card for a while.

"Please," Calliope said.

Meera ignored Bevva and studied Calliope. She appeared to grow more tired with every breath she took. Dark circles marred her otherwise flawless complexion, and her eyes grew heavy. "Are you okay?"

Calliope smiled weakly, the effort looking almost painful. "I will be once Bevva learns to behave."

Bevva sighed, the air leaving her lungs full of understanding. "Okay, Callie. I'll play nice. I was just razzing her. You know me."

"Yes, I do, but she doesn't, so could you please lay off for a bit?"

Bevva hugged Calliope. "Anything for you, dahling."

And with that one statement, void of any sarcasm, said with a genuine smile, the circles disappeared and Calliope's eyes became bright once again.

"Somebody wanna fill me in?" Meera asked, completely tired of being left out. Was it too much to ask for a little info every now and then? So much for being the Luminary. One would think that title would come with at least an ounce of respect. *Riiight.*

"As I said before, Meera, Bevva is a witch and so is Calliope," Carrine explained. All witches come with their own strengths, individual and unique to themselves, but we all know even strength can turn into a weakness. Calliope is no exception. She is a *soother*."

"A soother?"

"Yes," Calliope said. "My magick is the power to soothe. But within that power lies my weakness. Negativity drains me, more so when it comes from someone I care about." She arched a brow at Bevva who quickly looked away.

"I see." And she did. No wonder she had felt better the moment Calliope had touched her in the hallway. "How about you, Bevva?

What's yours?"

Bevva stared at her. Meera gasped when she saw the fire in her eyes. Red, orange, and blue flames danced before her and then were gone in a blink.

"I should have guessed." This woman—witch—oozed fire. Any other power would have been contradictory and an injustice.

This was as good a time as any to share some of her own information with the group. She lowered her voice, the whisper barely audible over the sound of clinking glasses and forks on ceramic. "The slayers are here." Meera laughed as they all craned their necks, trying to see any sign of the baddies. "Nice. Very subtle." Even Carrine looked chagrined at being less than her normal regal self. "Not here as in right this minute. But here as in I saw them in the hotel earlier."

Once again composed, her neck perfectly erect, Carrine asked, "And? What happened?"

No way would she tell them she'd fainted from fear. No. Way. "Nothing. I was in the elevator. They were about to get on, but the door closed before they could." Yeah. That was all they needed to know. She could just imagine Bevva's comments if they knew the whole story.

"Let's go." Carrine rose.

"Where?"

"We must train. There's no time to waste. I'm sure they have a gym here. I'll put wards around it so no one will disturb us."

"Wards?" Meera remembered seeing something about that in one of the books Carrine had given her on witchcraft, but her mind was currently on overload, and the exact meaning escaped her.

Bevva rolled her eyes, but Calliope stepped closer to Meera. "I'll explain on the way."

*

The four guardians approached the gym on full alert. Ghanem didn't have all his senses but something was up. His gut was telling him to turn the other way. When had he ever listened to those kinds of warnings? Definitely not then and sure as hell not now. "Do you feel that?"

Steffen groaned, the sound full of dread. "Wards."

"Whose?" Drake asked, his feet slowing as he pushed his way down the hall. "You think it could be the slayers?"

Ghanem gave it some thought, but Thane beat him to it.

"I don't think so. Everything Ghan and I have read so far doesn't lend itself to that. I'm not saying it's impossible, just improbable. Besides, I get a distinctly feminine vibe from these."

Steffen laughed even as he turned to make sure they weren't being followed. He'd changed out of his designer jeans into a gym suit, somehow managing to have just as much swagger in cross trainers as his Versaces. "You can seriously tell a feminine ward from a male ward?"

Ghanem didn't doubt it. Two reasons—Thane knew females, and he'd been trained to detect these things. He quickly squelched his jealous feelings. It wasn't Thane's fault Ghanem had been banished, therefore never completing his own training.

If only . . .

No.

He didn't have time to think *if only*. Yet, more often than not, his thoughts were consumed with nothing but. Thinking of Meera only added to the ever-growing list. *If only* she wasn't a witch. But she was, and Ghanem already knew what Thane would confirm— these weren't just feminine wards, these were witch wards.

Fuck.

Fuck.

And double fuck.

"He can tell," Ghanem said. It had been his suggestion they come down to work out. Riddled with tension and aggression, his body was as tight as a coiled spring. Pumping iron would allow him to take out his frustrations on something other than his so-called team. His muscles were already developing at a faster rate, and he was eager to get back his former body. Steroids had nothing on being a guardian.

But these wards would be the death of him. Already his movements had become more labored than the others'. His thighs burned with each step. He blamed that on lack of strength. They were all struggling, but shit, he had actually started to wheeze. Not that he could see what he struggled against. An invisible barrier. One that would deter humans. They wouldn't notice anything out of the ordinary, only that they suddenly lost their desire to work out. Which was why this hallway was deserted. It worked a little differently on veiled. Depending on the species, it could either be impossible to break through or just appear to be. Ghanem sensed this was the latter. Only those with great purpose would struggle, making their way in ultra slow motion to the double doors that led to the gym.

He tried lifting his right leg, straining against the invisible force that held firm. It was like trudging through quicksand and mud so thick you'd need a chainsaw to cut through it. Sweat beaded on his brow. He swiped at it with the back of his hand. Momentarily giving up—as if he had a choice—Ghanem leaned against the wall and tried to catch his breath. Fucking bullshit. Incredibly embarrassing bullshit. Sure, the others looked a little tired, but they were much closer to the proverbial pot of gold than he.

Drake looked over his shoulder. Ghanem attempted nonchalance, but if Drake's rolling of the eyes was any indication, he was totally busted. "Go ahead. We'll catch up," Drake said to Thane and Steffen. They only nodded and trudged onward.

Ghanem watched as Drake turned around, his legs stuck in an impossibly twisted position before he broke free and jogged up to Ghanem. Too bad the transparent muck hadn't broken his legs.

"I guess it'll be easier to leave, huh?" Drake crossed his arms and leaned against the opposite wall, mimicking Ghanem's stance.

Ghanem dropped his arms to his side. "'Sup?"

"Tired?"

"Naw."

"Really?"

"I'm good."

"That's your problem. It's always been your problem, Ghanem."

Ghanem closed his eyes, silently begging his inner guardian to remain calm. Whatever happened, this was not the time to get all Incredible Hulk-like again. "What are you talking about?" He looked at his brother and Steffen. They'd only made it about five feet since he'd last looked. Another twenty to go. Should make it to the door in, oh, let's say an hour. He hoped Drake didn't plan to keep him company the entire time.

"You've always got to be bigger than life. Big Ghanem never needs any help. He can do it all on his own. Don't get in his way—he'll just knock you down or belittle you in front of everyone. You're not so big now, are you, Ghanem Adamo?" His eyes narrowed, rage causing them to turn a vibrant shade of red.

"Don't stop. You're on a roll." Bigger than life? Yeah. Not the case. So he'd never meshed with Drake. And sure, he'd beat the shit out of him on more than one occasion. That was what they did in their youth. That was what guardians did. Do. Was it his fault Drake had never fought back?

"Does it make you less of a guardian to ask for help?"

Couldn't get any closer to the truth than that. Drake may as well have cut off Ghanem's horns himself. That one statement said it all. *I am less of a guardian.* He never got the chance to respond.

The doors to the gym opened. Thane and Steffen lost their balance, falling against the wall. The wards were gone. The witches were here.

Ghanem's jaw hit the floor before he remembered to be furious. Furious with her. His eyes locked on Meera's. She led nothing less than a runway show featuring four stunning women in cotton spandex.

Cue the music, boys. This was slo-mo, strut-your-stuff at its best. Who turned on the wind machine? Furious or not, he looked his fill. Blame it on being male. Wasn't his fault, but Ghanem shook his head anyway, trying to clear the illusion. It didn't help. No mirage here. Four sexy witches, in the flesh.

Meera smiled shyly, as though she protected a secret. He quickly looked away from the smile, the amethyst eyes, the exposed stomach, instead focusing on the next witch in line. Streaks of blue accented her short hair. The blue was an exact match to her sports bra and—no joke—kick-ass combat boots. Intricate tattoos wound their way around her arm, implying an ancient story only few would know.

The third witch, a complete contradiction to the previous one, held her fiery head high, the crazy curls screaming of a metal pole in a lightning storm. This witch met the gaze of every male in the hallway, challenge on and met. One thing was certain. It would be one hell of a fight.

The witch Meera had called Carrine pulled up the rear, oozing sophistication and wisdom. Out of all of them—besides Meera, for completely different reasons—Carrine scared him the most. Challenging her would be like going to battle with the head nun in a Catholic school, a librarian, and a prison warden all wrapped into one very beautiful witch. No, thank you. Not that he'd ever admit that to anyone. Not in this lifetime, which added up to eternity.

They made their way past the men, Meera slowing as she neared him. Still drawn to her even though she'd deceived him, he held her gaze. She started to speak, but must have noted the look in his eye, because in the end she said nothing. He flinched at the hurt in her eyes. Nothing he could do about that. This was entirely her fault. If only she'd been up front in the beginning. Ghanem shook his head, already fucking tired of the situation, and it had only just begun.

His entire summation had taken less than thirty seconds and a good thing, that. The four witches never stopped, just continued down the hall, giving four guardians an unobstructed view of their backsides.

The first to speak, Steffen asked, "What are they and where can I get one?"

Ghanem growled deep in his throat and lunged at Steffen. Thane stepped between them.

"What? What I'd say?" Realization sparked in his eyes. He looked down the hall and then at Ghanem. "Oh, shit. Is one of those yours, Ghanem?"

Drake chuckled. "Yeah, Steff. Like that would stop you."

"Shut up, Drake." Thane stood his ground, an unmoving wall between Ghanem and Steffen. "They're witches. I'd like to tell you to avoid them, but it looks as though we'll need them. Right, *fratello?*"

Ghanem stepped back. "Just stay away from Meera. I'll deal with her." And he would. One way or another. He walked through the open gym doors, stripped off his shirt, and went to work on the speed bag. He ignored Steffen, who pulled off his shirt and started on the bench press barely two feet away.

"Which one is Meera?"

Ghanem moved away from the speed bag, his attention now focused on the heavy bag. He side-kicked, spun, and crouched low.

Steffen yelled from across the gym. "How am I supposed to stay away from her if I don't know which one she is?"

This he would answer. Meera was his to handle. If Steffen laid one hand on her, he would end up walking around as the one-armed wonder. "She's the beautiful one."

Thane laughed. "That clears it up, bro."

Ghanem pummeled the heavy bag. Punch after punch. Kick after kick. He paused long enough to offer his brother some advice. "You better let them know, Thane. *You* make it clear. Or I will."

Chapter Sixteen

Meera eased back in the chair, a cup of crème liqueur coffee in one hand and a pad of paper in the other. Being this studious wasn't her norm, and Carrine had assured her she'd easily remember the particulars, but no way would she take a chance on forgetting anything. Not when it had everything to do with her mission. Any minute now, she'd finally learn the details of her fate. Finally learn what it would take to live. Only then could Meera step into her role as the Luminary.

She stared at the walls, then stared out the window and watched the twinkling lights of the Windy City and wondered about the quiet mood in the room—too quiet for the symphony of emotions wreaking havoc on her nerves. Was she the only one feeling this? Meera chewed on the end of her pen and tapped her foot while studying her roommates.

Calliope, stretched out on the couch, sans combat boots, looked content and relaxed as she flipped through a stack of tarot cards. She had a tattoo on her left foot, the style similar to that on her arm. For one who repelled negativity energy, she'd had to go through a lot of pain to get those tats. Unraveling the mystery of this soother wouldn't be easy. There probably weren't many up to the task.

Bevva sat on the floor playing a game on her cell phone. Meera hadn't thought of it before, but it surprised her they used them. When she'd asked, Bevva had not so patiently explained they weren't telepathic and how else would she keep in touch with her friends?

Right. Sorry she'd asked.

Bevva clearly didn't like her. Go figure. Nothing new there. Most people didn't like her because after her differences made their way to the surface, they didn't take the time to get to know her. She'd naively thought other witches would consider her one of their own. When Meera had confided in Calliope about her struggles learning certain elements of magick, Calliope had explained Bevva excelled at casting, and had helped many witches in their coven. Meera had wanted to ask Bevva for some tips. Perhaps that could be a way to get to know one another. The permanent scowl on Bevva's face had Meera rethinking that idea.

She looked up to see Calliope smiling at her. Carrine walked into the room and sat in the chair next to Meera. Two out of three wasn't bad. Meera looked over and glared at Bevva. *Challenge on, Ruby Red.* One day, Bevva would like her.

"I apologize for the delay. I had another message from the council tonight and I couldn't put it off. Their messages are always important, but even more so now."

Meera sat on the edge of her seat, sipped her coffee, and readied her pen. Everything she needed to know to save her own freakin' life would be revealed tonight. Her nerves were a mess, jumping back and forth between dread and anticipation. She slurped more coffee and then clicked the pen in and out. *Click. Click.*

Carrine didn't hesitate, instead diving right in. "According to the council, this was fated many years ago. Meera was chosen based on her heritage. This is a curse and a blessing."

"Tell me about it." As far as Meera could tell, the scales were tipped in favor of the curse.

Carrine looked directly at Meera. "If you fail, and I do mean *you* . . . " She stopped herself and smiled, her attempt to assure Meera weak at best. "We are here to help you, but in the end, you must be the one to complete the task. If you fail, you will die and the world—all the realms of the world—will cease to exist as we know them." The inflections in her voice rose dramatically.

Like the dumb girl in a really bad movie, Meera had to know. "In what way?"

Calliope spoke up. "There is a balance. A balance of good and evil. Evil has always and will continue to chip away at the good.

If evil prevails, the world may as well perish. It will be terrible. More horrible than any of us can imagine. Like humans, many of the veiled prefer the darker side of life. The difference is the veiled can do a lot more damage. As a Luminary . . . well, we need your help." Calliope took a deep breath, the negative direction of the conversation already beginning to take its toll.

"She's right," Carrine said. "Anything you've seen in the past will be nothing compared to this. Humans will have no defense, and though some would disagree, we do need humans in this world."

Meera would be one to agree. Maybe humans hadn't treated her kindly, most of them anyway, but she did live among them, and she couldn't imagine watching them suffer or worse, a world without them. She had so much to learn about being a Luminary. So much responsibility. So much pressure. "I get the cursed part." She shuddered. "But where in all this is the blessing?"

"Succeed and find out," Bevva said with a total *duh* tone.

Tired of biting her tongue, Meera snapped. "What's with you?" Bevva had been rude from the get-go. "Did I somehow offend you in the two minutes we've know each other?"

Bevva smiled a wicked *I know something you don't know* smile.

"Enough." Carrine didn't shout. She didn't need to. She had an air about her that commanded respect. Meera had no doubt she'd earned it. Carrine turned to her. "Part of the blessing is your life. Not only will you live, Meera, you will be immortal."

Meera swallowed. The scalding coffee had made her throat raw. The lump of trepidation didn't slide down easy. "If I succeed, I'll never die?" She couldn't wrap her mind around that. Didn't know if she wanted to. Everything had changed so fast. She'd thought she was ready to hear this. Maybe not. Her heart beat frantically as panic set in.

Calliope jumped off the couch and made her way to Meera. She crouched in front of her and eased the coffee cup out of her white-knuckled grip. She handed it to Carrine before placing both hands upon Meera's. "It's okay. Being immortal can be wonderful. You won't be alone."

Carrine cleared her throat. "I know this is difficult, but I must continue."

Meera couldn't speak. She looked down at Calliope's hands and appreciated the magick in them. Meera was still stressed to the max, but the soother had made it so she could at least breathe.

"You'll be fine," Calliope whispered to Meera. "Go ahead and tell us the rest. I'll stay right here." Calliope looked into Meera's eyes as she continued to speak to Carrine. "She'll be fine."

"Immortals can die, though it isn't easy. More often than not, we heal rapidly. We are strong but can be wounded. We can hurt. We can bleed. I would advise not taking any unnecessary risks in the future."

Once again, Carrine had that distant look in her eye. Meera tried to read the pain, solve the mystery, but the look vanished as quickly as it had come. With Calliope still holding her hands, she was strong enough to lighten the dark mood of the room. "Right. Got it. Save the world. Don't take any risks. Damn. I forgot to write this stuff down." She'd dropped the pen and paper long ago.

Even Bevva had to laugh at that.

Carrine smiled. "Maybe I spoke too soon. No risks after you save the world."

"Did the council happen to tell you how I'm supposed to do this? What task am I to complete?" She didn't have a chance of success if she had to figure this out on her own. Maybe she should borrow Bevva's phone and call the damn council herself.

"Yes. I have more information. Meera, I hope you like to travel. You're about to see another world."

Bevva jumped up. "Which one?"

"Lemra."

"Oh, no," Calliope said.

"What is Lemra?" Meera asked.

Carrine folded her hands in her lap. "Lemra. It's the dark kingdom of the slayers."

"Dark being the key word there. As in their energy, not their features."

Meera looked at Calliope and wondered just how much of the dark energy she could take. "Are you gonna be okay?"

"Lollipops and sunshine. That's what I'll be thinking about, and I suggest you all do the same." Calliope gave her a sweet if not encouraging smile.

"How do we get there? Can we trace?" Bevva asked Carrine.

"Unfortunately, no. The council sent scounts who said they've set up their own wards. There's only one way to enter. Through their portal."

"Terrific. Sounds fun. Not. How do we find the portal?" Bevva looked at Carrine, her excitement apparent as flames flickered in her eyes and danced on the tips of her fingers.

"Meera will find it."

"I will? How?"

"We have to follow the slayers. You can see their auras."

She had to pursue the ones from her dream? How could she? How could she not? "When?" Meera whispered.

"Tomorrow." Carrine sighed. "I know this is immeasurably difficult. We are asking much. You can say no, Meera. But you must say it now. Once we go through the portal, there will be no turning back." Carrine's tone echoed the sound of a cell door as it slammed and locked.

What kind of choice was that? "If I say no, then I'll die in two months and ultimately take the entire human population with me?" She'd asked it as a question, but didn't expect an answer. She had no choice. "I'll do it."

The room seemed to breathe a collective sigh of relief. Had they really thought there had been a chance she'd just lie down and wait to die? That she could willingly let innocent people perish? If so, they had a lot to learn about her.

"One more thing the council said." Carrine had their rapt attention. "We won't be going alone. We're going to recruit some reinforcements. Let's go."

*

Ghanem had been about to take a shower when a knock sounded at the door. Steffen was closest and moved to open it. "Put your horns away, idiot."

"Horn this, asshole."

"I mean it, Steffen. Hide them. Now." If they had questioned his authority before, his tone put any doubt to rest.

Steffen allowed them to retract, his hair covering the tips. "You happy?"

"Deliriously so. Open the fucking door." They weren't expecting anyone. Thane and Drake flanked him, ready to battle if necessary.

"How 'bout I stick my eye to the peephole first? Huh, guys? Maybe that would give us a clue." Steffen showed his teeth, baring a smile that held no sign of humor.

Score one for his brains. Ghanem hadn't thought of that. Apparently, neither had Thane or Drake, but rather than admit to it, they all lifted their chins—a unison sign of agreement.

Steffen turned, looked out the eyehole, and whistled low and long. "I'm glad I took my shower. You three dudes reek." He opened the door and leaned against the threshold. "Hello, ladies. What can I do for you?" Steffen's voice dropped a couple of octaves, the bass undertones rumbling from his chest.

Aw, shit. Ghanem sure as hell didn't need or want this right now. He grumbled under his breath. "What are they doing here?"

"No idea," Thane said. "But we're about to find out."

Steffen bowed at the waist and swept his arm theatrically. "Do come in, lovelies. Can I offer you a beverage? A snack? Me?"

"Enough, Steffen." Ghanem's voice, razor sharp, cut through the room. The dangerous edge caused even the witches to hesitate before walking in.

Carrine stepped in first, followed by Meera, who caught his eye. He couldn't mistake her look of hope. *Don't be a fool.* He turned his back, heard her sigh. He glanced over his shoulder only to see she now looked at Steffen with what he could only describe as wonder in her eyes. Steffen smiled broadly. Ghanem moved, but Thane placed a hand on his shoulder, silently restraining him.

Thane gestured to the living area after the last two witches came through the door. "Please have a seat."

Carrine declined. "This won't take long. I'll get right to it. I believe we can help each other."

"How so?" Ghanem asked.

"I—"

Carrine cut Meera off, but he only had a moment to wonder what she'd planned to say before the elder witch had his full attention.

"Previously you mentioned the slayers. Since you're here, I gather you know they are, too."

She'd just confirmed what they'd suspected. Ghanem played along. "We do. What's your involvement?" He'd meant to direct the question at Carrine, the obvious leader of this quartet. Then why had he locked on Meera?

"We could ask the same of you."

Ghanem shifted to the redhead, glad for the distraction. "Since we're going to have this conversation, we may as well make introductions." His tone held as much invitation as a bed of nails.

"I couldn't agree more. I'll start. I'm Bevva. It must be a pleasure for all of you to meet me."

Steffen laughed. "Yes. It most definitely is. I'm Steffen, and since you stopped at the first name, I believe I will do the same."

"I'm Carrine, this is Calliope and Meera. You're Ghanem, Thane, and Drake." She pointed to each one sequentially.

Out of the corner of his eye, Ghanem watched as Meera's head popped up. Obviously Carrine had been keeping her own secrets. Must be a witch thing. Rather than ask how she knew their names, because he honestly didn't give a rat's ass, he skipped to the more important question. "Why is it you think we can help each other?"

"We're sorely outnumbered," the one named Calliope answered. "It'll be hard to beat them, more so if we have to do it alone. I think you can see the logic in that. Plus you're protectors. The humans need to be protected."

There had to be more to it than that. Ghanem smiled at Thane. They needed Meera. She could pick the slayers out of a crowd. May as well let the witches believe this was their idea.

"What do ya think, Ghan?" Thane asked, though he already knew the answer. He enjoyed the game more than anyone else.

Ghanem shrugged. "Maybe we give it a trial run? See how it goes?" This way no one could call him a liar when the guardians dumped the witches at the first opportunity. Not that he cared. The lies were mounting, all parties included. One more couldn't hurt.

Without asking for anyone's opinion, Carrine spoke. "We'll agree to those terms. We'll start first thing tomorrow morning. Let's meet—"

Ghanem stepped forward. "Tonight."

"Tonight?" Meera questioned, her voice full of doubt.

"I said tonight. Is there a problem with that? It's not as if you were planning on a good night's sleep. Right?" Ghanem turned his back on her, but not before he'd caught her flinch at his comment. Good. She deserved that and more. Then why did he feel like such an ass?

He couldn't look at her again. If he did, he'd apologize and that would be a mistake. "Thane, coordinate this. I'll be in the shower."

*

Meera's face stung. Part from humiliation and part from the virtual slap Ghanem had just sent her way. How dare he share her fear with everyone else? He should just rent a billboard. Then everyone in the entire world would know Meera Brennan was afraid to go to sleep.

After his comment, she'd fled the room as fast as her feet could carry her. She'd hoped the sanctuary of her bedroom would offer some solace. It didn't. She thought they'd shared something. Was sure he felt it, too. But something was wrong. Terribly wrong, and she bore the brunt of his anger in more ways than one. He couldn't even look at her.

She wished she didn't care. It wasn't as if they had a long-standing relationship. In fact, quite the opposite. A few steamy kisses, a little pelvic action, and sharing her fears didn't make a relationship. She should just stamp the word gullible on her forehead and call it a day.

And what was up with Carrine? She hadn't let Meera get a word in. And how did she know everyone's names? Her shoulders grew heavy with the load of crap everyone had piled on them.

Ghanem had proved himself to be a fraud. He'd sucked her right in with his caring lines and protective demeanor. It had all been a lie. But for what purpose? To get in her pants? Probably. To get information on the slayers? Perhaps. She'd have to give that one more thought. Was he somehow involved in this? Before Carrine had invited them into the war? She had a niggling feeling he had been part of this all along.

Meera wasn't surprised when her mentor glided into the room and perched on the edge of the bed.

"How long have you known?" Meera threw more clothes in her backpack.

"Known?" Carrine rose.

"Don't play innocent with me, Carrine. This is bullshit. For a mentor—and I use that term lightly—you suck at this. You are not who I thought you were." Not by a long shot. Meera's temper escalated with each word, increasing the volume tenfold. She stopped packing, choosing instead to get in Carrine's face. "A mentor shares knowledge and information. You know so much more than you're letting on, and I'm sick to death of being on a need-to-know basis. This is my life here. And very possibly my death."

Calliope ran into the room and tried to step between them.

"What's going on here?"

Meera ignored her as her tirade gained momentum and readied to barrel right over Carrine. "So if there are any more secrets you plan to keep, like how the hell you knew all their names, you can count me out. Matter of fact, you can kiss your realm and my ass goodbye." She stood her ground, unblinking, and waited for Carrine to utter some sort of explanation. Yes, part of her anger had come from her disappointment in Ghanem, in herself, but it was also time for her to take control of her own fate.

"Well, it's about time." Carrine's tone was calm as a pristine lake, void of any ripples.

"What's that supposed to mean?"

"It means exactly what I said. This is your life. I've been waiting for you to act like it rather than allowing me and others to lead you around blindly. I expected more from a Luminary."

Meera's mouth fell open. "Oh. Is that supposed to be comforting?"

"Not in the least." Carrine took a step forward. "It's reality, and sometimes reality bites you right in that ass you just told me to kiss."

Meera couldn't help it. A laughed bubbled up from her throat. She fought to keep it contained, but it escaped and then refused to stop. She'd never heard Carrine sound so, well, normal since this whole thing had started. Calliope joined in, her shoulders shaking, followed by Carrine. Who knew the mighty Carrine would be able to laugh at herself? Meera fell on the bed and struggled to breathe. The laughter only grew.

"What is wrong with all of you?" Bevva stood in the threshold, hands on her hips.

This only made it worse. Each time Meera gained composure, she'd remember Carrine's words and start giggling again. Somewhere in the recesses of her brain, Meera knew this was no laughing matter, but to go there would be to stand before the gauntlet with no chance of escape. She'd stick with the lighter side.

For now.

Eventually the laughter died down enough for Meera to get a few questions answered. "What's the weather like in Lemra?"

"I believe the weather is controlled by their leader. We should be prepared for anything and everything. I doubt he'll make our stay comfortable."

"That would be too easy," Calliope said. "I'm thinking we should pack light, as in take nothing. We should be able to conjure up a change of clothes and other necessities once we get there."

"Any chance our magick will be blocked?" Bevva asked.

"I don't think so. The council doesn't think he's that strong . . . yet. But we should conserve it if possible. He's been practicing dark magick for some time, and he's learned how to gain strength from humans. Eat and drink from the land if you can. It could make us invisible to them for a while."

Meera began to understand. "You think he'll sense us if we use our magick? Kind of like a tracking device?"

"Exactly. There'll be times when we won't have a choice. If—when that happens, we'll need to move quickly. Try to stay at least one step ahead of them at all times."

"Once we get there, how will I know what to do?"

"Once we get to the portal, I'll explain everything to you."

"But—"

Carrine lifted her hand. "I'm not keeping secrets. I don't know the answer yet. When we get to the portal, I'm supposed to contact the council again. They will read to us what we need to know. I, too, wish they'd be more forthcoming. But this is how the council has always worked."

Meera studied her then looked around the room and saw only truth in the three pairs of eyes that looked back at her. She'd have to believe them. This was her crew. Like it or not.

Meera grabbed her favorite cloak, the one with hidden pockets. She filled it with what she considered necessities—gum, raspberry chocolate, a small tube of toothpaste, and a toothbrush. If for some reason her magick didn't work, at least she'd have fresh breath and her favorite candy.

Meera dressed in a pair of black leggings, a long-sleeved green tee, and kick-ass leather boots. She checked her neck, stood taller when she felt the choker in place. She donned her black cloak and pulled the hood up over her head. "Shall we?"

Chapter Seventeen

Meera shivered. They'd been walking the streets of Chicago for over two hours without so much of a glimpse of a dark aura. Ghanem could have warmed her without even touching her, if only he'd walk a little closer. Nope. He remained distant and stubborn. She hated to admit it, but she missed him.

The sidewalks were busy, even at this time of night. Music from the row of nightclubs wafted out the doors, beckoning for another patron. Many were happy to oblige. Chicago didn't sleep. Most pedestrians gave the eight of them a wide berth, their size and beauty intimidating to the plain Janes and Johns of the world. Even the young and trendy couldn't compare with the looks of Ghanem and his crew and forget about the witches and their goddess-like beauty.

Meera smiled at a passerby. Not as shy as the others, he returned her smile with a dazzling one of his own. A deep, threatening growl came from behind her. The handsome stranger looked above her head before lowering his and rushing by.

Well, isn't that interesting? For someone who didn't want her, couldn't even stand to look at her, he sure had made a sound to the contrary. What was he? Who growled like that? Her ignorance just proved how little she knew of this new world she'd been drawn into. She turned to look at him. He immediately started conversing with Drake. *Wimp.*

She whipped her head to the front, pulled her hands out of her pockets, and blew warm air into them. If they didn't find anything soon, she'd have to take a break for coffee. She was tired and cold, not to mention irritated and cranky. One more street. That was all she would give . . .

Meera stopped. Someone barreled into her. She heard a curse, jolted at the heat, and knew it had been Ghanem. He stepped away and Carrine moved in. She sensed more movement around her, but Meera's eyes had fixated on the sign at the end of the next street.

"What is it, child? What do you see?"

Calliope grabbed her hand. "Did you see them?"

The wind picked up, causing the back of Meera's cloak to billow around her like a velvet eel. She lifted an icy finger, pointed straight ahead. Her hand shook, every bit as much from fear as cold. Calliope's soothing battled that fear, forcing Meera to take a deep breath. "There." She dropped her arm.

Steffen moved in front of her. "Which club? Shadows?"

She nodded, staring at the neon sign.

"Interesting," Steffen said.

Ghanem spoke. "Why do you say that?"

"Let's just say I've been there. A few times."

"And?" Ghanem's impatience made the word come out in a growl.

Steffen shrugged and stepped away. "And it's an interesting club, that's all."

"Meera?" Thane called quietly.

She looked at Thane, his voice soft among the sea of testosterone. Apparently he understood you could catch more flies with sugar.

"How many did you see?"

He seemed larger with each word, as if he was excited at the possibility of a fight, even though he kept his voice low. She shouldn't have been surprised. She'd already witnessed how much he'd enjoyed that alley brawl. "Three. Maybe four. I can't be sure."

"Who knows how many are already in there? Do they normally stay in groups?" Bevva asked, not directing her question at anyone in particular. She rubbed her arms as the wind gusted and wailed around them. "Never mind. I don't care. Let's just get in there. It's freezing."

"All right. Let's go. Try to keep a low profile until *she*"— Ghanem gestured to Meera—"points them out."

So now he couldn't even say her name. Unable to mask her

disgust, Meera rolled her eyes. "Yeah. Good plan. Like the eight of us could keep a low profile."

His gaze scrutinized her from head to toe and back again before he conceded with a tight nod. "Point taken. Let's just get in there before they decide to leave out the back."

He moved past her. She swallowed her irritation at the fact that until she'd spotted the slayers, he'd been more than happy to stick her out front. She tried not to feel used. Hard, that.

The bass hit them first, a strong, steady beat of four on the floor. Not too fast, not too slow. They stopped outside the club. A muscle-head bouncer blocked the door, standing with his arms slightly out to the side as if his sheer size wouldn't allow them to drop. Most would think he looked kinda hunky in his tight T-shirt with *security* stamped across his pecs, but he paled in comparison to the four accompanying Meera and her group.

As they approached, the bouncer quickly stood up straighter and threw his chest out. "Twenty-five dollars. Each." He leaned against the steel door and smiled smugly.

Thane stepped up. "Twenty-five? You want to rethink that, bud?"

"Just pay it," Ghanem ordered.

Meera eyed Thane, afraid he would ignore his brother and throw the bouncer across the street with one arm. He didn't. He retrieved his money clip and counted off not two but three one-hundred-dollar bills. And there were many more where that had come from.

Muscle-head snatched the money and ran a marker across the green paper to check its authenticity before stepping to the side.

Drake grabbed the handle and pulled the door open, pushing the bouncer into an uncomfortable corner. Carrine stepped through first. Meera followed. The intense heat hit her before she made it all the way through the door. This place was hotter than a sauna and not just from the heaters blasting full force. Sweaty bodies crowded the dance floor. Limbs tangled with others in an attempt to get closer to one another, swaying to the beat, hypnotized by the display of lights. The air was heavy. If there had ever been a scent for lust and need, this was it. A mixture of spice, sweat, alcohol, and arousal.

She stripped off her cloak as the men ushered them to a table in a dark corner. She pulled her hair off her neck, caught Ghanem watching her and dropped it. He turned his head. She did the same, taking the opportunity to scan the crowd. The packed club catered to all kinds of clientele. Those who weren't dancing were standing at the bar or lounging in the booths sucking back drinks as though they'd just come back from a trek across the desert. She could relate. The heat was stifling . . . and erotic. Too bad Ghanem had become such a negative Nelson. They could have had some fun here, *if* she weren't fighting for her life and *if* she were in to that sort of thing. Normally, public displays of affection made her uncomfortable. Still did, but in a much different way. The attraction pulled, but she refused to satisfy her curiosity by looking at him, instead focusing on the crowd.

Even though she'd only recently been introduced to power, she sensed magick. A lot of magick. Her skin tingled as the differences in energy washed over her. She wondered how many here were magickal. Had they always mixed so easily with humans? Steffen had called it interesting. *Interesting, indeed.*

*

If Ghanem hadn't sensed her fear, he would have sworn Meera had lied about seeing the slayers just to torture him. It didn't surprise him a bit that Steffen had been in this place before. The entire club was sexually charged from the erotic music, the heat, and the spicy scents he guessed they pumped in through the vents like a drug. A drug he hoped he could resist.

Even across the table, Meera's presence wrapped around him as though she were sitting on his lap and whispering in his ear. She had to remain off limits, but tell that to the friend in his pants. It hadn't been easy walking behind her all those hours, catching glimpses of her backside every time the wind had caught the edges of her cloak.

But her fear had been real. Her heart had pounded like she'd been hanging from a cliff with the tips of her fingers. The man in him wanted to take that away from her. Comfort her. Protect her, though he'd seen her hold her own. Tragic memories made him want to run the other direction, yet here he was, working with her. He had to wonder about that. The witches had been vague, not giving any indication as to why they hunted the slayers. He had his reasons. But what were theirs? Hers? One way to find out.

Ghanem stood, reached out, and clasped Meera's wrist. She sucked in a hiss. He held tight. "Let's dance."

"Excuse me?"

He bent down and spoke softly in her ear. Her pulse quickened beneath his fingers. "I think you heard me. Let's dance."

She turned her head and spoke just as quietly, yet her tone held the bite of a rattlesnake. "And why would I want to dance with you? You've been ignoring me since this morning."

"Well, I'm not now."

She tried to pull her arm from his grasp. He squeezed just enough to let her know he wasn't going to move. "That doesn't work with me, Ghanem."

He realized the others were watching them too closely. "We can't see anything from here. They're probably on the dance floor. Let's go."

She swiveled in her seat and victory was his. As she stood, he slipped an arm around her and guided her through the crowd, his palm dangerously close to the area that had hypnotized him all night. Meera's shirt clung to her back. He wanted to rip it from her and lick the sweat off. Didn't matter that they were in a club full of humans and veiled. Didn't matter that his mind, his memories, screamed no. His body wanted what it wanted. It would take all his strength to deny the urge. They'd barely made it to the edge of the dance floor when the beat became slower, though no less erotic.

"Do you see them?"

Meera turned to face him as he slid both arms around her waist. "No. You?"

He shifted his feet, weighing his answer before deciding how much to let on. "Not yet, but they're in here. Somewhere." This wasn't the time to give her the upper hand by admitting he couldn't tell a slayer from a human unless one walked up and bit him in the ass.

Using the growing crowd as an excuse, Ghanem pulled her closer and placed one leg between hers. Her back stiffened and he counted ten heartbeats before she finally relaxed in his arms. The sway of her body in time with his was like nothing he'd ever experienced. He closed his eyes, breathed in her scent, and then remembered. "How much do you know about me?"

Her dark lashes fluttered, exposing that seductive shade of purple when she tilted her head. "Not much, and what I thought I knew?" Her voice grew weary. "I guess I don't know you. Not at all." The last few words were said on a whisper.

The music screamed, yet he heard every syllable as if they were they only ones on the floor and wondered, not for the first time, if he'd heard what she had thought rather than what she might have said. "I could say the same for you."

She snorted. "Hardly. I'm not the one who pulled a one eighty today."

Ghanem arched a brow and laughed. "Didn't you?"

Meera shoved against him. He pulled her closer. She pinched her lips together and grunted.

"Well, didn't you?"

"No. I didn't," she said speaking through her teeth. "You were the one who was all sweet and caring before you turned into a jerk."

He had been a jerk. He wouldn't apologize for it. "Why didn't you tell me you're a witch?"

"That's what this is about?" Meera dropped her arms, slapping her thighs with balled fists. "Man, do I have a lot to learn about this veiled shit. I don't even know what you are, though they tell me you're not human. What are you, Ghanem? Other than a prejudiced jackass?"

"Nice language, babe. Does your mama know you speak like that?"

She flinched. "Fuck you. How's that for my language?"

They were attracting an audience. It wasn't because of the language or the content of the conversation—no one could hear them over the blaring music—but the fact that they were no longer dancing had caused more than a few to take notice. He grabbed the back of her neck and pulled her to him. Her lips parted on a gasp. Ghanem ducked and took full advantage. This kiss, so different than any other they'd shared, was full of anger, resentment, and the forbidden.

Meera's fingers dug into his triceps as she returned the kiss with just as much passion. He eased his hands down her back, cupped her bottom, and pulled her to him. They were as close as two beings could get while clothed. As long as his hands didn't linger on her skin, he didn't burn her. He'd like to blame it on the music, the ambience, such as it was, but it was more than that. She was more than that. To him, it was akin to having money to spend at the candy store only to find out you got there too late. All locked up. Access forbidden.

He broke the kiss, and exhaled a quiet breath when she leaned her head on his shoulder. He thought about kissing her again, wanted to, but he wouldn't—couldn't. That had to be their last kiss. If his lips touched hers again, he wouldn't stop. And, gods forbid, if that happened, all the walls of Saharren would come crashing down on him. He'd never get another chance at redemption.

They stayed that way, swaying in time to the pounding music, for what seemed like eternity and a fraction of a second at the same time. Her temperature rose steadily as they remained in contact. Before he could do much about that, every muscle in her body became rock hard.

"What is it?"

"They're here." Her voice wavered. "There's three—no, four of them. More are coming in the door."

Ghanem held on to her. "Okay. We need to get the rest of our group. We'll follow the first ones to leave. Keep your eyes on them." He slid his palm down her arm, grabbed her hand and moved them to the edge of the dance floor. "I'll be right back." Ghanem bent to eye level. Saw the clouded courage within them. He gave a tight nod, turned and took off to get Thane.

*

Meera's hand shook as she lifted it to her mouth. Her nerves trembled like gelatin beneath her warmed skin, and not just because she'd seen the slayers. While watching them through hooded eyes, she traced her swollen and tingly lips. How stupid to let him kiss her after he'd voiced his feelings about her being a witch. So, she was good enough to get all hot and heavy with, but not good enough to treat with respect? Dumb. Dumb. Diggity-dumb.

She'd asked what he was, but never got the answer. He'd silenced her and devoured her at the same time. Dumb. Dumb. Really dumb. She shouldn't have let him, should have demanded to know who and what he was. And she damn well shouldn't have acted so impulsively in a crowd. But, no, she'd tilted her head and given him full access.

She'd questioned herself more than once about the veiled. She'd accepted it only as truth and with mild curiosity when Carrine had explained them to her. Was it an ingrained memory or just relief that she wasn't either crazy or alone in her complexities?

She shifted her weight from one foot to the other and back again, and quickly looked over her shoulder. No sign of Ghanem or any of the rest, for that matter. Attention back on the slayers, she followed as three of them moved through the crowd toward the back of the club. They weren't alone. Each of them had a woman draped on his arm. These women appeared to be well past the drunk stage and moving rapidly into the *I have no idea what's going on and won't remember most of this night come morning* stage.

The beat of her heart rivaled that of the bass drum. She refused to chastise herself for being scared. Witch or not, this was all new to her. Before Carrine had come into her life, she'd never even punched a pillow, let alone socked someone in the jaw with a garbage can lid. So what if she was magickal? Maybe if she had another year—or ten—to get used to it and perfect it, she'd be able to use it in situations like this.

Right.

Maybe then she wouldn't worry that each day brought her closer to her last.

Meera picked up her pace. She wasn't about to lose them. They moved steadily toward what she assumed would be a door leading to the back alley. What was it with them and alleys? She glanced over her shoulder again. If she got stuck battling these three alone, she'd be royally pissed. No doubt about it.

A thought edged its way into her mind. What if Ghanem had no plan to get the rest of them for help? What if his prejudiced nature was so extreme, he'd actually leave her to fight alone, knowing she didn't stand a chance?

The music clashed with that of the surrounding clubs when they opened the door. The women's feet were barely touching the ground. They'd probably been drugged, which really ticked her off. Not wanting to be seen, Meera waited a dozen stuttered heartbeats and then followed them through the door. She unintentionally kicked a rock, sending it skidding across the blacktop. *Craptastical.* She ducked behind the Dumpster. The stench made her gag. She chewed on her bottom lip and held her breath. The wind carried the slayers' voices straight to her.

"Did you hear that?"

"What?"

"I heard something."

"I can't hear a thing over the ringing in my ears."

Go, go, go. Meera willed them to leave, but never heard the sound of retreating steps. Certain their attention remained focused in her direction, she crouched lower. There wasn't a chance in Tahiti she'd poke her head out to check. She looked back at the club for what seemed like the hundredth time. As much as she wanted backup, she prayed they wouldn't choose this moment to come through the back door.

"There's nothing there. Let's get these slups to the portal. Ryken will be very happy with these three. Pretty delicious, don't you think?"

Slups? Ryken? Meera repeated the words over and over in her head until she was certain she wouldn't forget them. If the others didn't hurry, she'd have to go through the portal alone. Everything she'd read told her to expect the unexpected. Traveling through a portal could have different outcomes depending on what realm awaited on the other side. One gateway could lead to a fantastical world full of goddesses and unicorns—now that she'd like to see, though she doubted unicorns really existed—while others could put her smack-dab in the middle of an ancient battlefield with warriors on both sides and no way to defend herself. You had to be prepared for anything and everything with so many possibilities and no way to predict the outcome.

The space of time between one realm and the next could be a heartbeat away or feel like several hours. Either way, she'd learned it left one drained and quite possibly ill, especially in the beginning. She'd never been through one. Yay, her. Total newbie. What would it feel like? What would *she* feel like?

Finally, the baddies walked away, and she mustered up the courage to leave her hiding spot. Though she wondered if she smelled as bad as the Dumpster, at least she hadn't had to hide in the foul metal box. *Way to look at the positive, Meer.* She followed at what she hoped would be a safe distance until someone grabbed her from behind.

Meera flipped around and, using the heel of her hand, connected with her captor's jaw. His teeth banged together before she realized it was Ghanem. He didn't utter a word. If she wasn't mistaken, he actually looked impressed. Still, she should apologize. One for hitting him, and two for doubting he would come after her.

"Sorry, I didn't know it was you."

He rubbed his jaw. "No apology necessary."

"Did I hurt you?" He shifted his eyes, the flash of pain fleeting yet unmistakable. What was that all about?

He didn't answer the question, instead saying, "You shouldn't have left the club."

She wouldn't take the bait. They didn't have time to argue. Three women were in desperate trouble. Meera could only imagine what would happen to them once the slayers got them to their world. Before she could block the horrid visuals out, a sick shudder rocked her body. They'd wasted valuable time, and she was beyond impatient. "We've got to go. Where is everyone else?"

"They're around. Hiding in the shadows."

Meera squinted into the darkness, and then shrugged. She'd have to take him at his word. The temperature steadily dropped as each minute passed. Meera shivered. Damn. She'd forgotten her cloak and it was too late to run back and get it. She reached for the cold metal around her neck, touched it and smiled. She'd just conjure up another cloak. This time she'd give Ghanem fair warning, though she doubted he deserved it.

He ran his tongue across his teeth. "What are you up to?"

"I'm about to do something very witchy. Feel free to turn around." She waited, then grinned when Ghanem continued to stare at her.

Meera pursed her lips and gave careful thought to the words she would say next. Keeping it simple would be best, but the creative part of her insisted it rhyme. It didn't take long before she came up with a summoning incantation. "Cloak of mine, rise and flee. Cloak of mine, soar to me."

Meera raised her arms in the air, ignored the chill bumps gathering along her skin, closed her eyes, and rubbed her fingers together. Within moments her favorite cloak slid over her hands and down her arms until it rested on her body. Purple embers sparkled before falling to the ground. Much warmer, she hesitated only briefly before lifting her head and looking at Ghanem. This was who she was, and he could take it or leave it.

Her gaze met air. She spun around, but he was already twenty feet ahead of her. Guess that answered her question. He'd left it.

Meera pulled up her hood and jogged to catch up and then matched each of his long strides with two of her own. She could still see the slayers dragging the women. She focused on that. Focused on something she might be able to change. Screw Ghanem. She couldn't change who she was nor did she want to. There were other men out there. Men who would accept her. All of her. If she lived through this thing, she'd find one of them.

Face obscured by her hood, she looked over at Ghanem, at his strong jaw set firmly in place, at his shaved head with faint scars, at his chocolate brown eyes with dark honey lashes.

Too bad she didn't want anyone else.

Chapter Eighteen

A small pocket of wrinkled air churned in the distance. Meera figured out what it was before Ghanem uttered a word. She simply nodded when he confirmed her thoughts.

"That's the portal."

She'd been walking close to him—really close—as they traipsed through the back alleys and dark corners of Chicago. The conditions were colder than an Eskimo's nose, and heat continued to pour off him. His warmth had to be a trait of his species. Part of being veiled. Perplexing. Thane was his brother, yet she didn't feel any warmth when she stood near him. Just Ghanem, the walking, talking space heater.

Meera inched closer when the wind blew her hood back and whistled past her ear. For warmth, for protection, for a number of reasons, she stuck to his side like a Siamese twin. He noticed the invasion of his personal space, but never said a word. Her only indication Ghanem paid any attention was his sharp intake of breath whenever she brushed up against him. Hard to tell if her touch annoyed or aroused. With him? Who knew?

Ghanem lowered his head, pointed toward the slayers. "Do you see it?"

"Yes," she said, her voice mimicking the sound of the chilly breeze.

He arched a brow, his face so close, his lips a breath away. She quickly recovered. Meera pulled her hood up and held it closed around her neck. "The air is different. Almost wave-like." It rippled in a diagonal pattern about a hundred feet in front of them. She'd seen the effect many times in her life, normally in the heat of summer when it danced off the hoods of hot cars and blacktops. Now she had to wonder.

Had those waves been entryways to other worlds and dimensions? How many times had she walked by one and completely ignored it, completely ignorant of what waited on the other side?

How incredibly cool!

"You're excited?"

She stepped back, tripped and caught herself. "How do you know that?" This wasn't the first time he'd been aware of her feelings. If she had been jumping up and down clapping her hands, she would understand his astute perception. But she hadn't flinched. Not until his words. She took another step to distance herself from his uncanny ability.

"Easy." He gestured to the slayers inching closer and closer to the portal with a tilt of his head, obviously afraid she'd alert them and they'd hurry through the gateway. They'd have already crossed through if it weren't for the fact their cargo had become dead weight and had to be dragged.

She stopped backing up, but no longer sought the comfort of his heat. She clenched her jaw to keep her teeth from chattering. The cold did nothing to chase away the feeling of being exposed and violated, only exacerbated it. She glanced at the slayers then slid her narrowed eyes back to him. "Can you read minds?"

"Not usually."

She studied his face, the crease between his brows. He looked as confused as she was. "Can you read mine?"

He shoved his hands in his pockets, his arms tight to his side. "Not exactly."

"What does that mean?" Her voice sounded as sharp as the icicles hanging from the roofs; her soul was just as chilled.

Ghanem looked over her shoulder, quickly shook his head before reaching for her hand. He caught her arm as she turned to see who hid in the dark. Sure as flowers in spring, he'd silently told someone not to approach. Peering into the darkness, she tried to sift through the shadows only to come up empty. He brought her attention back to him by rubbing the inside of her wrist in a circular pattern with the pad of his thumb. Her lips parted. Whether she wanted it or not, a delicious heat spread throughout her body and zeroed in on her core. Meera squirmed. He'd intentionally distracted her. Maybe she would have appreciated it under other circumstances.

Maybe yesterday. Today? Not so much.

Before it got out of hand, Meera snatched her arm away and stomped off toward the portal. "Stay out of my head." *And out of my heart.* The last part she kept to herself.

Stupidly, she hadn't thought of the noise her stomping made and had to dive for the shadows—again—when one of the slayers stopped and turned. She silently swore like a pirate when she whacked her elbow on the corner of . . . *Oh, for the love of . . .* Another flippin' Dumpster. She'd barely managed to calm down once the slayer turned back around, but only after berating herself for being an idiot. Going off half-cocked through a portal wouldn't be her brightest moment. One of the few things she could be sure about. That and the fact she needed Ghanem.

Exactly what she needed him for remained a question. Not a chance in Mississippi she'd admit to anything right now, even to herself. Instead, Meera shut down the voice in her heart as it had an all-out debate with the voice in her head and waited for Ghanem to catch up. This time he wasn't alone. Her little army had regrouped.

If the situation were anything other than dire, she'd have to laugh. The six of them were paired up as if it were date night. Steffen and Calliope, Drake and Bevva, Thane and Carrine. Make that eight if she counted herself and Ghanem. Had they picked their own partners? Interesting. She would have totally put Bevva with Steffen. But this wasn't date night, she wasn't Cupid, and Ghanem wasn't hers.

"Where have all of you been?" She waved her hand. "Forget it.

It doesn't matter." Meera pulled Carrine to the side. "You need to contact the council now. I have to know what to do." Panic edged its way into her voice like a lost child.

Calm as ever, Carrine said, "I know. Calliope? Come stand next to me."

Ghanem shifted. "Who are you contacting? We don't really have time for this. I don't know if anyone else noticed, but the portal will be closing any minute now."

"I noticed," Thane said. "They're moving faster. They must be on to us."

They all turned to look. The second slayer had already made it halfway through. The woman he carried never stirred.

Meera gasped, grabbed Bevva. "Hurry. Give her your phone, help her summon or whatever it is she needs to do. Just do something."

Bevva's eyes flared. She shrugged off Meera's hold, but stuck her hand in her pocket to retrieve her phone. Calliope groaned. Meera spun on her heel to ask her what was wrong. She didn't have to. Calliope saw the same thing she did. Meera's jaw dropped faster than a piano falling out of a third story window.

Ghanem, Thane, Steffen, and Drake were nearly to the portal. The jerks must have sprouted wings to have made it there so quickly. The slayers were already through, and the portal began to shrink. A knot the size of a baseball seized her stomach, causing it to cramp. Ghanem had ditched her. Her heart pounded in her chest, too soon to shatter, but bruised nonetheless. He'd used her.

"I'm sorry, Meera," Calliope said, though her voice did nothing to soothe Meera this time.

Meera took off at a dead run, hoping the others would follow. She had no plan. No guide. No map. Just an instinct to conquer and live.

Her heart thundered in her ears as each foot pounded the pavement. Carrine's voice drifted to her like a whisper on the wind.

"Go, Meera. We'll find you. Remember your magick. Remember the light. Use the light."

The last three words were repeated over and over again, sucking Meera back in time. Back to the beautiful land with the cottages, mountains, and waterfalls. Back to the woman who sang to her. Back to her mother.

Use the light. Use the light. Use the light.

She pulled herself back to present time, zoned in on the shriveling portal. Drawing in what could very possibly be her last earthly breath, she gauged her target, and, with as much speed and courage as she could muster, Meera launched herself through the portal.

Her heart skipped, and then she was falling. Rather than flailing her arms in an attempt to right her body, she wrapped them around her middle and held on to the one thing she could count on.

Meera.

The fall seemed endless. Minutes, possibly hours ticked by and still she continued to drop. Her body twisted, turned in the darkness. One moment she plummeted headfirst for so long she blacked out, only to awaken an indeterminate amount of time later in an upright position. Her stomach rolled. Her breath caught in her throat. She blacked out again. Woke. Heard hissing as rough hands slid over her skin, shoving her down, trying to push her up. No light. Not even a glimmer.

Meera prayed she'd black out again, stay that way so she wouldn't have to hear the hiss. The ugliness of it. She fought to cover her ears, but her hands wouldn't cooperate. Someone—something—held her arms down, forcing her to listen to the evil hiss.

Her mind was just playing tricks on her. That was what she kept telling herself. If she admitted any of this was truly happening, she'd go insane. The hiss grew louder. Meera struggled to break free from her unseen tormenters. She ripped her arms from their clutches and covered her ears as tightly as she could. Her hands barely muffled the sound.

The falling didn't stop. She dry heaved from the nausea. Tears leaked from her eyes and not just from the wind hitting her face at gale force. This was the end. She cried not because she was going to die, but because of how she would die.

In the dark.

Alone.

*

Ghanem found Lemra to be everything and nothing like he'd thought it to be. He'd imagined darkness; he saw light. He'd imagined desolation; he saw lushness. He'd expected to be surprised—the one thing he'd had right. The magick of the land coursed through the earth beneath his feet. He heard it whistle overhead though no breeze disturbed the calm air, and felt it rolling off the branches of the trees draping overhead like a canopy of gloom. He stood alone, but someone—or something—watched him.

Passing through the portal had been quite a ride. Definitely not one for the faint of heart. It had been years since Ghanem had had to cross into another realm, but still, he'd been prepared. He thanked the gods Meera hadn't been with him. Witch or not, he had a feeling she was fairly inexperienced. Most likely that ride would have killed her. Mad as he was, he couldn't bear to have that on his conscience. He carried more than enough anyway.

He assumed Thane and the other two guardians had made it through. He had no way of knowing for sure. They'd become separated during the fall and probably ended up in other areas of Lemra, but they were stronger than him. He had to believe they were fine.

He thought of Meera again, imagined how pissed she and the other witches were right now. They'd ditched them. That had been the plan all along. So what if it ate at his gut? He'd get over it and so would she. They were both better off this way. Cut the tie before it became impossibly knotted. If that happened, he wouldn't have a chance at resisting her. Now he had worlds between them, and still it didn't seem far enough. He could feel her as if she were next to him. He only hoped time would help to break the connection. A connection he had yet to comprehend.

This wasn't the time or place to dwell on the subject. He needed to focus on the task and the land at hand. It had been late when he'd left Chicago. He couldn't say the same for this realm. A freezing night had been replaced by a sweltering hot day here in the underground kingdom. He tilted his chin up. His initial surprise at the lack of an actual sun had been fleeting. He was underground, after all. Any light here had to be completely manufactured by some form of magick. Ironic that this light came from dark magick.

Ghanem stripped off his shirt and tucked it into his pocket. Unfortunately, heat wasn't the only thing he had to contend with. He turned a full three sixty, his body on alert. Dense forest as far as his eyes could see. Fuck. This would be no easy trek. He'd need a machete to cut through this shit. He didn't even have a pocketknife. Which way should he go? With no other tool than his gut, he turned and started the long journey through the hot jungle.

Begrudgingly, he admitted he could use a witch right about now. He pictured Meera rubbing her long fingers together and conjuring up not only a machete, but a fuckin' bulldozer to plow through the thick foliage.

As sweat dripped from his forehead, he grabbed the shirt from his pocket and tied it around his head like a sweatband. The edges of the plants cut into his skin like razors. He couldn't stop now. If he could just get through this, maybe the terrain would cut him a break. The odds were stacked against him, but anything was possible. He hoped Drake and Steffen were fairing worse than this. The two deserved to be tortured for a while. Thane? Ghanem pictured him sucking back piña coladas with some female he'd run into. He'd never been very discriminating in his tastes.

He'd find them, and together they would defeat the menacing slayers. If he could find a way, he'd return the humans to their world, though he doubted they would ever be the same. A kinder end would be death, but he wouldn't be the one to deliver the blow.

Sixth sense kicking in, Ghanem stopped dead in his track as if he'd just slammed into an invisible wall. He listened. But it wasn't what he heard—more what he sensed. Definitely something he should not have felt in this realm. *Ah, hell.* Was this a trick? He should turn away from it. What if it wasn't a ploy? He couldn't chance it.

Moving as quickly as he could, he barreled through the sea of green as it cut and slashed his arms, ripped through his jeans, and tore at his face. The farther he got, the stronger the feeling became. He needed to fly, but his legs wouldn't propel him any faster.

Hearing movement nearby, he slowed and crouched low. Ever wary of a trap, he crept closer. The pace went against everything he felt, though he understood the feelings were not his own. Panic, regret, anger, and sorrow. He felt the sorrow so deeply; it tore at his heart and screamed in agony. Inch by inch, Ghanem crawled toward the despair, hoping he was wrong, certain he was right.

Meera. He fought a wave of dizziness at the sight of her curled up in a ball at the edge of a brook. She wasn't moving. *Fuck.* She shouldn't be here. He'd left her, had been certain she wouldn't make it through. Wouldn't risk it. He sat, frozen in place, and listened to the sounds around him. The only sound was that of water as it ran downstream over rocks and plants.

Only when he knew for certain they were alone did he close the distance between them. He pulled her limp form onto his lap. Relief left his body in a gush of air when he as her heart beat beneath his hand. Barely. Her skin was so pale it had taken on a gray hue. Her brow, covered in beads of sweat, spoke of a fever. She was burning up, yet her skin was clammy to the touch. Unwilling to release his hold on her, Ghanem pulled off one sleeve and then the other, moved her heavy cloak to the side, and laid it on the ground next to them.

"Meera? Can you hear me? Meera?" Leery of causing her any more distress, he kept the panic out of his voice as best he could. Her clothes, completely soaked through, had left small pools of sweat on the ground. He placed his hand on her cheek, moved it up to her forehead once more. Certain she had a fever, he lifted her off his lap and placed her body on her cloak. Untying the shirt from his head, he dipped it into the cool water, then wrung it out and wiped her brow repeatedly. His eyes scoured her body. Still drenched. He didn't have another option. If—no. He couldn't think like that. *When* she woke, she'd be spitting mad, but he'd deal with that then.

Keeping one eye on the perimeter and the other on Meera, he carefully removed her sodden shirt. Even with her pale, clammy skin, his body hardened at the sight of her green lace bra, the cut of it low and barely containing her breasts. He turned away, re-soaked his shirt and laid it over her stomach. Next, he removed her boots and then pulled her pants off one leg at a time. Surprised he could get any harder, Ghanem shifted uncomfortably. Of course her underwear would match her bra. He'd always considered himself a thong type of guy, but the cut of these was almost more than he could take. Whatever they were, she needed more of them. In every color imaginable.

This time he used her own shirt to cool down her legs, soaking it in the cool water before wiping down her thighs, her calves, and then her red-tipped toes. Her body completely undid him. He wanted her to get better, fight with him, kiss him, feel him. *Dammit, Meera.*

She moaned and all sexual thoughts left him. He lifted her head, cupped his hand, and scooped up some water. He tasted it first to make sure it wasn't toxic. One never knew when in another realm. Nothing was a given. He scooped up more of the clear liquid, put his hand up to her lips, and tried to get her to drink.

Meera moaned again and tossed her head to the side. Her hair, clinging to her face in sweaty tendrils, reminded him of a tangled web. She clenched her fists and jaw so tightly he feared she'd pop her bones. He held her legs down as she kicked out, even as the pain she was experiencing racked his body. He'd take it all away from her if he could. Clamping his hands on her thighs, he held tight as her fever burned strong. He had to do more to help her. But what? How? If he didn't figure something out, she would die, and her death would be entirely his fault.

Ghanem sure as hell didn't need any more blood on his hands.

Chapter Nineteen

"What are you waiting for?" Meera's throat felt like old plaster flaking off a wall, raw and cracked. An attempt at licking her lips proved she had no moisture to give the thirsty desert. Yet the pain of that small movement revealed she'd made it through the portal. Alive. Surrounded now by a group of slayers, she wondered if death lurked just around the corner, dimming the spotlight on her fleeting triumph. Especially since the smiles they flashed held anything but friendly undertones.

They possessed such beauty, almost blinding in its intensity, but all she could see was the clear ugliness of their souls. None carried even a hint of kindness in their eyes. Their auras melded together until it seemed as though the entire world became shrouded in darkness.

A rumble of laughter drifted her way, and she narrowed her already sleepy eyes. Meera sat upright, her back supported against a large tree, the rough bark irritating her sweaty skin. If not for the tree, she had no doubt she'd be flat on her back.

"You're here to kill me, right?"

One slayer stepped forward, his confidence evident in his posture. White, thick hair hung straight as a board, carefully tied in place with two strips of leather on each side of his head. He looked down his nose at her with sharp eyes, a pillar of malevolence. When he spoke, his voice resonated as though it came from all directions. "Wrong."

Usually hope would be the emotion one experienced after being told they weren't about to die. All Meera had was dread sitting in the pit of her stomach like two-week-old meatloaf. That and about a hundred invisible icepicks stabbing at her brain. Killer headaches must be a side effect to portal hopping. She made a mental note to load up on ibuprofen before she jumped through her next portal. If there was a next time.

"Ryken wants to play with you first." A half smile arced across his pale face. "Do you want to play, Luminary?"

They knew. "Never." Meera dug deep, collecting what little strength she had left. One of the slayers made kissing noises at her. The leader back handed him, sending stringy spittle flying. Bile rose, and she turned her head to relieve her stomach. Nothing. There would be no relief. Not now. Only a gut-deep desire to live.

"Not feeling well, witch? Don't worry too much about that. This is nothing compared to how Ryken will make you feel."

"Who are you?" Her lip split open as she formed the words. She tasted blood and welcomed the wetness.

With his chest puffed out, conceit dripped off his tongue when he said, "Jayson Nightfinder, second commander of this legion."

Second commander. She assumed Ryken must be first.

"Grab her. Let's go." Jayson barked out the order and several stepped up to do his bidding. He turned and strode into the forest, evidently confident the matter would be taken care of to his satisfaction.

Several pale hands grabbed her at once. If the slayers thought she had no fight left, they were dead wrong. She held it in, biding her time and carefully restraining what little energy she could muster. She heard a hiss—several hisses—and wanted to rip her own ears off, but she couldn't. Not if she wanted to win.

The hissing suddenly stopped, and she wondered if she'd imagined it as even more hands grabbed for her. *Enough.* Meera twisted her body, thrashed her head, and ignored the pain. Kicking and screaming, she vowed to take at least one or two of them down with her. She nailed one of them in the shin. He cried out, bellowing like a little girl. Meera smiled at her triumph. Her small victory was short lived.

More slayers poured out of the dark forest and flanked the others. No words. Just action. They dragged her across the ground. Her limbs burned from being tugged so brutally. She kicked. Someone grabbed onto her legs and held them down. The slayers continued to pull, but she'd become fixed to that spot by an invisible force. They yanked; she remained rooted. Her thighs heated and smoldered as if the force holding her down possessed fire, and that heat made her think of Ghanem.

Ghanem. He'd left her. She wanted a chance to tell him what she thought of that. Thought of him. Her mind screamed as they wrenched her arms over and over again nearly pulling her limbs out of their sockets. Still, she didn't move. Darkness flickered across the outer edges of her vision. Meera blinked repeatedly to clear her head. Ultimately, she lost that battle as the shadows rallied and pulled her under.

∗

Meera woke feeling cold, clammy, weak and . . . *oh, please, no* . . . naked. Maybe not completely, but close enough. She shivered in the cool air and wondered what it had taken for them to finally move her. Somehow they had managed to break the invisible force. Though there was little sound, she knew she wasn't alone, knew someone watched her and waited for her to open her eyes. She could practically feel eyes boring into her skin. In no hurry to face Ryken, she kept her lashes twined and weighed her options.

She could lie still and hope this had all been a bad dream, or she could open her eyes, face her captor, and figure out exactly what and who she was dealing with. Meera swallowed. Her choker tightened reassuringly. Besides, plan B seemed much more proactive than wishing it all away.

Meera opened her heavy lids, twisted her head to the side, and gasped. Unless Ryken could take on the appearance of someone else, Ghanem sat about ten feet from her, his head down, picking at the grass. He resembled a broken angel with the light illuminating him from behind and casting shadows over his tawny body.

Too relieved to stay mad at him, she opened her mouth to

speak. Nothing came out. Not even a squeak. Meera swallowed. "Ghanem?" The sound croaked out as if someone had their hands around her throat in a stranglehold.

His head shot up and chocolate eyes connected with hers. "Hey."

The defeat in his voice almost undid her. "Come here. I'm cold." Meera's voice cracked again on the last word.

"Are you sure?"

What happened to Mr. Confident? When did he become so unsure of himself? "Please, I—"

He moved quickly now, was by her side in a heartbeat. She marveled at his speed, hoped she'd recover at the same pace. Sweat covered his torso, glistening like tiny crystals, yet she shivered. He reached out to touch her, then quickly dropped his hand.

With questions flooding her brain, her voice came back in a rush. "Where are my clothes? Did they take them?" She couldn't remember anything after she'd blacked out. Meera jack-knifed and patted the ground on both sides of her body, her hands flying over the grass and dirt. "Where the hell are my clothes? God, what did they do?"

"Who?"

She didn't answer. He grabbed her hand. Released it when she flinched.

"Who, Meera?"

"The baddies, um, the slayers. They were trying to take me back to their leader. Ryken. That's what they called him. They were dragging me, hurting me. Did they undress me?" Her ragged voice hitched.

Ghanem cradled her face with both hands. "No, no. I undressed you. I had to. You were burning up with fever," he quickly explained. "You were kicking and screaming, and I had to hold you down. I'm sorry if I hurt you."

Meera closed her eyes, carefully slid back to the ground, and then stared at the sky while collecting her thoughts.

"Meera?"

"No. It's okay. I'm just relieved it was you." She exhaled slowly.

"I couldn't remember. Where are they? I want to get dressed. I'm really cold."

"It's actually hot out here. Your fever must be breaking. It's just been you and me here, so I'm guessing you had a nightmare or maybe even a hallucination brought on by the fever."

Meera's teeth chattered. Ghanem must have been the force holding her down. But the slayers had seemed so real. Just like in the field in her dreams. If they could find a way into her dreams—and obviously they had—the ramifications were . . .

She didn't want to think about that or anything else right now. Not the nightmare. Not the portal. Nothing. "My cl-clothes?"

"They're soaking wet. I'm afraid they would make it worse." Ghanem shook his head, mumbled under his breath. "I can't believe I'm about to say this, but can't you just do your magick thing and conjure something up?"

"Hmph." *Get over it already.* "Maybe. I'll try." She rubbed her fingers together. Sighed. Tried again. "I think I'm just too weak."

Eyes to the sky, Ghanem said, "Try saying one of your rhymes." He barely concealed the flippancy in his voice.

"I can't do it right now. All right?" she said through clenched teeth.

"Yeah. I'm sorry." His brow creased in thought. "Do you want me to lay with you?"

"Do you want to lay with me? I'd hate to put you out." She was so freaking cold she swore her lips were turning blue, and her damn teeth kept doing the jackhammer dance in her mouth.

"Shut up." He edged closer and stretched out beside her.

Meera rolled into him, seeking the heat only he could give. She wrapped her arms around his muscled torso and tucked her head under his chin. "Just don't try anything, okay?"

He chuckled. "I don't know if you've noticed, but you're the one who wrapped your body around me like a *polipo.*"

"A what?"

"A *polipo,* an octopus."

His chest shook with laughter. So what if she'd tangled her legs around his? "Whatever. I'm just cold."

"Umm hmm."

Figuring she had him right where she wanted with no chance to evade, she asked the questions that had been on her mind. "Why did you leave me—I mean us?" *Crap.* She'd meant to keep it casual.

"Wondered when you'd get around to asking that. I'll answer, but first I need to ask you a question."

His fingertips stroked her back, the action making her very supple and agreeable. "Hmmm?" She liked the change in him. He'd gone from defeated to sarcastic to loveable faster than a getaway car at a bank robbery.

"How long have you been a witch?" The timbre of his voice was low, sensual, though it still held an undercurrent of disdain.

"Apparently all my life."

"Let me rephrase that. How long have you known?" He continued to stroke her, his fingers following the concave line of her spine.

Meera could sleep for a hundred years, so long as he continued touching her this way. Completely relaxed, she shifted. Her body glided over his as she sank into him. "A couple of weeks. Why?"

He groaned, low and deep. "Even more recent than I thought. Damn. That, Meera, is one of the reasons I left you behind."

Lifting her head, she looked at him. "What do you mean?"

"I figured you were relatively inexperienced." He smiled when she stiffened. "I don't mean it in a bad way, only that going through a portal is not easy. Especially for those who are just coming in to their power."

She relaxed and laid her head on his shoulder. Her body temperature steadily heated up. Not normal yet, but getting closer. "You can say that again."

"You could have died." He whispered this.

Now she understood. This was why he'd looked and acted so defeated. He definitely loathed what she was, but he cared for her. Cared whether she lived or died. "You said that was one of the reasons. What else?"

He sighed. "I'm anti-witch. Remember?"

Yep. She remembered. That message had come through loud and clear, more than once, though she doubted that was really why he'd chosen to leave her behind. She'd get it out of him sooner or later. "Where's my cloak?"

Several moments passed by.

"Ghanem?"

"Yeah. It's next to the brook. I'll get it for you." He started to move out from under her.

"No. Stay here. I can get it." Her heart soared with possibilities. Even if he couldn't accept what she was, maybe he could get used to her. For a while. Maybe he would like her enough to help her. Heaven knows she'd need all the help she could get. And it wasn't as though she was using him. She genuinely liked him. Yes, even when he was being a silent, brooding ass.

Meera extracted her limbs from his, sat up, and waited for her equilibrium to even out. Her mouth tasted like she'd swallowed dirty cotton. Hopefully some of her necessities had made it through the fall. She stood and walked slowly to her cloak, the grass tickling the soles of her bare feet. Each step made her head pound, but at least she'd stopped shivering. Crouching next to her discarded clothes, she noticed they were all lined up to dry. She looked over her shoulder to thank Ghanem, caught him with his head propped up on his arms checking out her backside. Meera flushed in embarrassment.

"Stop staring." She turned back around and rooted through the pockets of her cloak. *Eureka!* She'd hit pay dirt. Forgetting her state of undress, she shook her body with a little happy dance.

"Not a chance. What are you wearing, by the way?"

"Are you trying to be funny?" What was she wearing? Her skin and little else, thanks to him.

"No." His voice dropped, the tone hitting the bottom of the

musical scale. "What kind of underwear are those?"

"Boy shorts. I'm sure you'd prefer a thong."

"Not anymore. Boy shorts, huh?"

"Yep. Hungry?" She saw the wicked glint in his eye. Of course his mind had gone somewhere completely different than she'd intended with her question. Well, maybe not completely different. Her senses reeled. His heat did more than just boost her energy, and she had every intention of getting more of it.

"Ravenous. Why? Got something for me?" With lightning fast speed, he caught what she threw at him. He opened his fist and burst out laughing. "You brought chocolate?"

She held up her finger, asking him to wait as she brushed her teeth and gulped down water from the stream. He laughed some more and shook his head. That sound alone had the last remnants of her slayer ordeal slithering away.

Thirst quenched, mouth clean, Meera recapped her toothbrush, shoved it back in the pocket, and walked over to him. "Not just any chocolate. This is the best. Raspberry chocolate. Try it." She folded her knees and sat next to him.

"You first." Ghanem unwrapped a piece of the chocolate and held it out to her.

Afraid the moment would pass and they'd be back to arguing or, worse, silence, Meera leaned down, wrapped her mouth around the candy, and took it from him. It wasn't her fault her tongue snaked out and licked the tips of his fingers. A mixture of raspberry and milk chocolate combined with the salt from his fingers burst to life on her tongue. She closed her eyes and savored the flavor. Moaning, she slid her eyes open and found him watching her intently. "Do you want me to get another one for you? It really is good."

"I can tell. Come here."

Meera slanted her head in question.

"I want to taste it on you."

There wasn't a chance in Toledo she'd let this invitation pass her by. "Okay, but first you have to warm me up again." She arched one eyebrow seductively. Ghanem quickly scoured their surroundings and Meera appreciated his alertness. She'd almost forgotten they were in a strange land full of ticking time bombs waiting for her to misstep. Meera sighed as reality bit down hard and burst her bubble.

Ghanem dragged a knuckle over her shoulder. "Oh, no you don't. There won't be any mind changing going on. We're alone."

Meera pulled her hair to the side, then rubbed the back of her neck. How could she possibly do this—whatever this turned out to be—with him, when the world could come crashing down on them at any minute? So absolutely, incredibly unfair.

"I promise, Meera. No one else is here." Ghanem opened his arms to her.

She didn't hesitate. Meera flew into his arms and wrapped her body around him once again. If this was the end, she couldn't think of a better way to go out.

Ghanem laughed low and deep. "That's my *polipo*."

"I think you need to work on a new nickname. I'm not sure that's very endearing." But she liked it and he knew it. She could tell by the glint in his eye and the lopsided grin on his face. "Too bad the octopus ate all the chocolate."

Meera laughed as Ghanem growled, flipped her onto her back, and stared down at her with the most devilish look in his eyes. "Uh oh. I think I'm in trouble," she said, then licked her lips, grabbed on to his arms, and slid her fingers over his sculpted triceps.

"You have no idea."

*

Ghanem dipped his head, brushed her lips with his own. Slowly, methodically, all the while consumed with troubled thoughts. He tried to squash them. This was neither the time nor the place, but turmoil rarely picked favorable conditions. She'd be the death of him. No matter how much he fought it, he was losing the battle.

His heart had practically been wrenched from his chest when he saw her lying there, motionless. He'd told himself he'd left her behind for all the right reasons. That he had to distance himself . . . from her. From her magick. Had to focus on his mission. He had to get back to his family, not alienate them further, or worse, cause the same kind of unforgivable harm he had centuries ago.

Meera kissed him back, sighing against his lips, her breath a mix of mint, chocolate, and sweet red berries, and his thoughts went in the opposite direction. He should have kept her close. Protected her. Helped her endure the ordeal of her first portal experience. He should get to know her rather than hanging on to past prejudices. But who could blame him? Magick—to be more precise, *witch magick*—had stripped him. Left him bare and raw.

Meera arched her back as if craving his touch. Bias aside, he needed this. Desired it just as much as this sexy witch, if not more. Her knee came up, grazed his shaft, and he was lost. Ghanem slid his hands under her head, tangled them in her long hair and sank. Sank so deep he didn't know where his tongue ended and hers began. The taste of her was like a mind fuck. Complete, utter eroticism consuming his every thought.

He moved to her neck, pushed her hair aside, and traced her skin with his mouth as she wrapped her legs around his hips setting off nerve endings that hadn't been stimulated in more time than he cared to count. He growled in her ear. She laughed, the sound of it deep and throaty. She was hot, sweaty, and his chest slid over her like they were covered in oil. Now that was a visual he could get used to.

"You're so hot," Ghanem whispered. Meera's skin grew hotter with each breath. When he'd found her, she'd been cold, her skin almost gray, then her temperature had risen and he'd been sure he'd lost her. Permanently. He straightened his arms to get a better look. Her skin was tinged pink, flushed with heat and desire. She looked good. Too good.

He waited until she opened her eyes. Smiled down at her.

"You're not so bad yourself." She returned the smile, grinning sinfully.

"Thanks. And don't get me wrong, you are hot . . . but, Meera—" Ghanem brushed her skin. "You're really hot. Are you okay?" It was too damn soon. Her fever had spiked again.

"I'm fine. It's you. You do this to me." She propped herself up on her elbows, kissed his chin, his neck.

Ghanem sucked in a breath, went in for a quick but scalding kiss. Fire bloomed between their lips. "What do you mean?"

"You haven't noticed? How could you not? It's always hot when we get close. Always. Trust me. I'm okay with this." She chewed her lip, lifted a brow in invitation.

He couldn't resist. His body swelled with need. In one swift movement, Ghanem flipped her over so she straddled him. He wanted to feel her on top of him. She began to move, grinding her hips in a slow, sensual dance. "Wait—I can't believe I just said that, but please, just wait a sec, okay?"

She pouted, but obliged.

"In the hallway, the other night, I thought you had a fever. And the club? It was just plain hot in there. Yes, I agree, the temperature spiked when we danced, but I assumed it was the crowd. You're telling me it wasn't?" Ghanem groaned when she moved again.

"It wasn't. Now shut up. Okay?"

For now. He'd get his questions answered soon. "I can do better than that."

She rocked back and forth in a teasing dance. "Can you?"

He'd teach her not to challenge him. A guardian never lost, and with her sitting astride him, he felt more like his old self with every second that passed. Ghanem started at her shoulder, used two fingertips to mark a heated trail. A faint red line formed where his touch seemed to singe her skin. He studied Meera, sensed her pleasure as her lashes fluttered, then twined. Assured the heat caused no pain, Ghanem continued his path. When he was done, there'd be no doubt she'd been touched and by whom. This pleased him more than it should have.

She shuddered when he reached her elbow. He lingered there, aware of the sensitive area, before moving on to her wrist, enveloping it with his hand. His fingers dropped to her thigh as she continued to rock in place against him. He had to touch her. Ghanem reached the edge of her lace, slid her boy shorts to the side. Her wetness teased him before he even touched her core. She wanted him. Wanted this. He didn't need any more encouragement than that.

His fingers sought her center. Ached every bit as much as his manhood did for their chance to feel her surround him. He knew he'd connected when she froze, locked her gaze on his. He waited, torturing himself, though his only goal was to make her ask for it. Beg.

She didn't have to. Her body trembled with anticipation, and he could wait no longer. Ghanem slid his finger in and almost spent himself, the pleasure too much. She felt so soft against his rough skin. He held his hand still in an attempt to get his body under control. She wasn't having that. Meera pivoted her hips, drawing him in even further. "*Merda*. Don't move. Let me pleasure you before I lose myself."

She continued her rhythmic dance, her voice breathy, sure. "I'm already lost. I want you to join me."

"I will. I promise. Just let me do this." He held on to his control by a fraying thread. He gripped her. Made her stop the frantic pace, but every breath she took moved her body just enough to make him even harder. She had to feel it. Had to know what she did to him. Ghanem withdrew slowly, loving the feel of her body clenching.

Her eyes pleaded with him when she couldn't find her voice. He gave her exactly what she craved. He rubbed his thumb over her slick folds, confident he'd send her over the edge. He wanted to be inside her when that happened.

Ghanem reached between them with his free hand and unsnapped the button of his jeans. The moment he released his hold on her, she moved against him with a quickness that spoke of urgency, danger. He kept his eyes locked on hers, drowning in the depths as he watched her desire spike right along with her body temperature. He had a moment of reservation, wondering if he marked her skin everywhere he touched her. Wondered if it had anything to do with his guardian heritage. This hadn't happened before. Ever. He'd have to ask Thane about it. Maybe his brother could shed some light on the situation.

Meera sighed, urged him on by moving his hand out of the way and lowering his zipper. She used her legs to push off him just enough that he could lift his body off the ground to shove his pants down. He'd prefer to have her in a comfortable bed. He'd prefer to be naked rather than have his pants down around his ankles. He'd prefer for his brain to shut the fuck up so he could get back to pleasuring Meera and finally himself.

"Are you going to fulfill your promise now?" The teasing lilt in her voice held its own promise. "Or do I have to take matters into my own hands?"

As if she hadn't already tried. His turn. He would be the one to set the pace. Ghanem grabbed her and brought her in for a scorching and demanding kiss. She was a temptress for sure and kissed him back with just as much fervor as he gave. Bed or no bed, he would have her. He reached behind her to unhook her bra, craving the naked feel of her breasts. Meera cried out and slumped against him. Hot, sticky fluid ran over his hands. He lifted his hand and saw red.

Blood red.

Chapter Twenty

What the—They had to move. Needed cover. They were exposed as much as two people could be. Literally.

After her initial shock, Meera fought through the pain and jumped off Ghanem, who was still desperately trying to cover her with his own body. Her shoulder bled, though she didn't know why. Maybe she'd been shot, but wouldn't that hurt more? It hurt. A lot. Like someone had stuck her with a hot poker and then twisted. But she could handle it. "I'm fine. I'm fine. Let me up. We've got to get out of here."

"You're not fine." Careful not to touch her shoulder, he moved her behind him as he struggled to pull his jeans into place.

She could have laughed at the picture they painted, looking like two teenagers caught in the back seat with their pants down. Ghanem's pants were tangled, and he couldn't manage to right them with one hand while trying to shield her with the other. She almost laughed, but then something whizzed past her right ear. The fine hairs of her neck stood on end. "Crap. Let's just go." She scrambled to gather her clothes, clutched them to her chest, and took off for cover in the looming forest with Ghanem right on her heels. He swore and Meera hoped he hadn't been hit too.

She glanced over her shoulder to see he'd shed the jeans rather than pull them up. The image of his muscled legs propelling him toward her caused her to lose focus. She tripped on a rock, struggled to right her body as the ground drew closer. With her hands tangled in the wet clothes she carried, and no way to brace for the eminent fall, her body tensed. Just when she would have done a face plant, Ghanem scooped her into his arms and picked up the pace.

"Be careful." His low voice was laced with shrapnel.

"Careful?" she hissed in question. "You cannot be serious. Put me down. I'm not a toddler."

"Well, you certainly run like one."

Meera catapulted out of his arms, shot him a deadly look before she took off deeper into the woods. She only remembered her own state of undress after her foot hit another damn rock that sent waves of pain from her heel to her spine. Her shoulder burned too. Whatever hit her must have only grazed her skin. She hobbled another few feet before stopping. She evened out her breathing and listened to the sounds around her. She didn't know what she did or didn't want to hear, but it seemed like the right thing to do. Ghanem had also stopped nearby and silently edged closer.

Neither of them said a word, just stood together in their skivvies behind a massive palm tree. The sheer size of the tree was an anomaly. She'd never get her arms around it even if they were twice their current length. She didn't focus on that. Instead, she listened. The sounds of the forest were eerily quiet. No birds, no crickets, no rustling leaves. Just quiet.

Dead quiet.

"This is odd," she said.

"That it is. It's too quiet." He looked down, glanced at her shoulder before meeting her eyes. "Are you all right? It looks like it's healing."

"Fine. You?"

He seemed unsettled by her question, merely creasing his brows rather than answering.

"I thought you were hit, too."

A quick shake of his head and then, "I wasn't."

"Then why were you cussing?"

"Can't recall. We need to keep moving, Meera. We're sitting targets here."

They'd been sitting targets before, yet had let themselves get caught up in the moment, setting all danger aside. They'd paid the price. Her body tingled where he had touched her so intimately only moments before and she wondered if it had been worth it. Even now, looking at his nearly naked body made her want to do it all over again. Oh, yes. So worth it.

"Are you ready?" he asked as if he were reading her mind again, his tone beguiling.

"Shut up. Just give me a minute." Meera took a deep, calming breath. "Give us cover for our skin, for the quest that we begin. Give us shoes for our feet. Make them swift, make them sweet." She repeated her verse even when Ghanem walked away. She caressed her choker and rubbed her fingers together as the air shifted and changed around her. Purple embers surrounded her and Ghanem like sparkling tornados. While her body relaxed, Ghanem's stiffened, making him appear all angles and tension rather than smooth and sculpted. And then they were covered from top to bottom in gear befitting a trek through the Amazon jungle.

Meera wriggled her toes in her new green-and-gray cross-trainers and smiled approvingly. These shoes were both swift and sweet. Just as she'd ordered. Her legs were covered in camouflage cargo pants similar to the style Ghanem now wore. She nodded toward his fatigues. "You like?" She already knew the answer, but pursed her lips and waited.

His eyes narrowed. His gaze, so full of anger and resentment, told her more than words ever could. He spun on his heel and stalked off. Meera watched the fury ripple off his tank-covered back. So the witch thing totally irritated him. He'd get over it and eventually thank her for the convenience of her gift. Maybe.

Not eager to debate their differences, she hung back. She wasn't stupid though. She stayed close enough that she could catch up if she needed to. The space, though, allowed her a few minutes to work up her own temper. And boy, was she getting worked up. Way up. She jumped over creeks, climbed over logs, slapped away foliage as though it were her worst enemy. Still, her anger escalated. On a scale of one to ten, she'd soared way past eleven on her way to infinity.

She reached down, picked up one of the infuriating rocks and launched it straight at Ghanem. It hit him right between the shoulder blades with more *oomph* than she'd thought she was capable of. She almost gloated, but settled for a smirk even as an inkling of regret settled in her heart. He whirled around in a blaze of rage and advanced on her, seemingly bigger with each step he took.

He stopped inches in front of her, but close enough that she could feel his breath on her skin. "What the fuck is your problem?"

She wanted to turn and run. He didn't even look like himself. His veins bulged, and his shirt began ripping apart at the seams. She swallowed audibly, the lump of fear tasting sour in her throat. "Wha—what?"

"I'll ask you one more time. What the fuck is your problem?" With each word he uttered, Ghanem's voice took on a menacing, almost beastly quality that resonated through her body and took up residence in her bloodstream as it pounded its way through her veins and arteries.

Meera took a step back, stumbled, and fell to the ground. She scrambled backward, her eyes wide. What was happening to him? To her? He continued to advance on her, stalking her like a lion after its prey. His eyes flashed red. She blinked. A short time ago she had been willing to give her body to him—now he threatened to take it from her.

Her lips trembled when his eyes turned yellow and his head started to distort. Meera stifled a scream as two charcoal horns emerged from the faint scars on his shaved skull and elongated until they curved around his head like a mighty ram. "You're a monster."

He paused at that. It wasn't much, but long enough for her to get her footing. She didn't hesitate, just took off. She headed back the direction they'd come, willing to take on the slayers with their weapons rather than the creature Ghanem had become. She covered her ears at the roar behind her. The entire forest rushed by her as if a hurricane had ripped through at record strength, careening her body into another tree. Meera clung to it as the wind lifted her feet off the ground. She held strong until the roar and the wind died down. Then she ran for her life.

*

Ghanem had felt her anger. Felt her confusion and rage mounting, consuming her every thought, coursing through her system. It mixed with his own, melding them together like a braided cord until he could no longer contain it. He'd waited centuries for this. Long, agonizing centuries wanting to be the guardian he was born to be. He'd tried over and over again to call to the inner beast, each time ending up defeated and in pain.

Not this time. This time the beast had called to him, transformed the mere shell of a man into an ancient warrior. He'd grown taller—several inches so—stronger, a mass of pure, lean muscle. He breathed in the scents of the forest, all more clear to him now. Breathed in her fear. Let her run, get a head start. He would find her. No one could hide from him when he was in this state. He would enjoy the pursuit and teach her to never again use her witch magick on him.

Ghanem lifted his hands, touched the tip of his powerful horns, rubbed the length of them. They weren't stunted like in his youth. They were fully matured, complex in their spiraling design. A weapon more powerful than any blade or firearm, for within these horns lay eons of knowledge passed down from a millennium's worth of forefathers. He caressed the tips and called out. His roar was full of pride, authority, and strength and left no doubt to anyone in Lemra that he was here.

His shirt hung in tatters around his waist. He ripped it off, meant to throw it aside, but the scent stopped him. Her scent. He hadn't even touched her while wearing it, yet it was saturated with Meera. Meera and something else. Something spicy and electric. Magick. His body hardened against his will, but not just that. No. So much more than that. The pull of lust was strong, but not alone. His chest ached as if a two-ton truck were sitting on it, slowly crushing the life out of him. It was the witch and her magick doing this to him. It seemed wrong. Wrong on so many levels, yet the combination called to him. Begged to be taken. His body wanted release, and there was only one way to get it.

The hunt was on.

Raising the shirt to his nose, he breathed deeply before tucking it into his pocket. Determination doubled with each step he took as he trekked through the forest with only one mission in mind. Find, conquer, own. She would be his. What he would do with her after was a question for later. Much later. Ghanem planned to take his time. She had tried to rush him before. Make things go her way. He'd almost let her. Probably would have if they hadn't been interrupted.

He quickened his step, every nerve ready to respond. Danger was imminent, and Meera had headed right back into the thick of it. As he neared the clearing he could feel her close. Ghanem launched himself into the trees knowing the vantage point would give him the best view, show him what he was up against. His judgment was cloudy, blurred around the edges, but his sight and senses were acute, honing in on everything around him, not missing the slightest detail.

He saw her then, edging her way around to the opposite side of the brook. His eyes narrowed, on full alert. He wanted her, but first he had to make sure no one else got her. *Protect.*

He moved from branch to branch, testing each one to make sure it would hold his weight. He traveled quietly, methodically, imperceptible to the witch below. Ghanem crouched low, saw

184

movement coming from the east. A lot of movement. An army of slayers made their way through the dense foliage. They'd traveled far. They'd left behind a trail as their boots stomped and trudged through the tall grass. Any moment they'd descend upon Meera. She wouldn't even know what hit her. *Protect.*

He jumped to another tree, barely touching his feet to the bough before moving on to the next one. Determined to get to her before the slayers did, he launched himself through the air just as the world became shrouded in darkness and Meera let out a blood-curdling scream.

He heard her struggling. The sound of her shoes clambering against the ground as she attempted to fight them off nearly sent him over the edge. *Fuck.* Ghanem froze, let his eyes adjust to the night. Patience. It went against every fiber of his being. His mind silently screamed along with Meera, though she cried out in fear while his was rooted in anger—primal and all-consuming anger.

They couldn't have her. She was his. Fortune must have been on his side—at least for that moment—because the slayers carried a kicking and screaming Meera straight toward the tree he hid in. He had to give it to her—she fought with everything she had, including her blasted magick. The sky rained purple. He had a feeling if she ever learned to center her energy and draw from within, she'd be unstoppable. But right now, she needed help.

Biding his time had never been his strong suit. Didn't matter. He didn't have to wait another second. Blessed or damned, depending on how one looked at it, Ghanem had better night vision than the most advanced goggles in the military. Fortunately, he could see Meera amongst the slayers that trooped through the pitch-black forest. Unfortunately, he could see Meera *and* the blood that covered her.

With a growl starting in his chest and erupting from his throat, he leapt. Ghanem curled his body into a ball so his shoulder would hit the ground first. He rolled before standing and facing the enemy. "Let her go."

Rising to his full height, he met each of their stares with a deadly one of his own. While he couldn't make out the exact color, they were all dressed in uniform. He caught a glint of something metallic on their tunics. Buttons, perhaps, or maybe medals. They'd stopped, formed a group that covered Meera and kept her from his view. He didn't need to see her. She was close. And she was scared, but not only that. Her fear mixed with just enough anger and determination to make her his ally—at least in this situation. No matter how she might feel about him personally, she was too smart to deny his help. At least he hoped that was the case. He'd help, and then they could get back to whatever discussion they had been about to have.

One of the slayers spoke up. "You." He looked Ghanem over, cocking his head to the side when he spotted the horns. "You think you can stop us? You are one. We are many."

Ghanem watched the punk lift his head in confidence, noticed he had more of the metallic emblems than the others, and figured they must be an accolade of some sort. He held the leader position here. That much was clear. Ghanem admired and pitied him. The shower of purple continued to fall around them. Though the intensity had lessened, it still illuminated the shadows, allowing him to make a head count. Outnumbered. Vastly outnumbered. "I can and I will. Have no doubt about that, fairy." The last word caused the slayer to flinch. A slight movement, but Ghanem noticed and would use it to his advantage later. This slayer didn't care to have his manhood questioned.

Like a bull, he charged the slayers by stepping forward with his right leg, stomping the ground as a sign of intimidation. He smiled when the entire group moved back. They regained composure immediately, pulled themselves together, and moved forward as a unit, obviously comfortable and trained as an army.

He may have appeared nonchalant to the mass in front of him, but inside he had already assumed the fighting stance, in body and spirit. Every muscle flexed. Every thought geared for battle. No matter how long it took, he'd wait for them to make the first move. If he could keep the focus on him, he should be able to keep them from hurting Meera further.

Ghanem stood his ground, aware of the almost imperceptible movements the men on the farthest ends made. They planned to surround him, come at him from all directions. They'd never get that far.

Keeping himself rooted, he reached out, snatched one of them by the neck, and held him off the ground. The slayer kicked his legs, his heavy boots nailing Ghanem in the shin. He swore softly, but held tight. The others held back, waiting to see what he would do. Whatever move he made here would be the turning point. Let the slayer live, walk away, and go back to the life he'd led for the past two hundred years? Or kill him, start the riot, fight the battle that would wage a war in an unknown land, maybe give him the life he wanted, the life he deserved?

A turn of his wrist set everything in motion. Neck broken, the dead man slumped forward like a rag doll. Ghanem discarded him as if he were no better than Tuesday's rubbish. In an instant, twenty slayers pounced on him. He flung them off one by one while taking hits to his head, torso, knees, and everything in between. He felt it all. Took it in. Drew upon it. Anger and pain made him stronger. For each hit he received, he gave ten in return. He never stopped moving forward. Never detoured from his path to Meera.

He could see her now. He started to yell, warn her to watch out, but she ducked right before a blow would have hit the back of her head. She leveled one of them with a side kick, then swung to do the same to yet another. The distraction cost him. He swore with a vengeance when a boot caught the side of his head, sending shock waves from his ear to the tip of his left horn. He grabbed the perpetrator with both hands and pulled him close. "You'll die for that."

With the strength of ten warriors coursing through his body, Ghanem threw him, watched him soar fifty feet through the air, the speed causing his long white hair to obscure any view of his face, before slamming into a massive tree. The slayer slid to the ground, back broken, each shallow breath drawing him closer to death.

Jumped from behind, Ghanem stumbled forward. The slayer clung to him with a strength that beguiled his fairyness, wrapping his arms around Ghanem's neck and squeezing. Ghanem tried to shake him off, staggered again before regaining his balance. He used his elbow to gouge his ribs, heard the crack. Still, the slayer held tight, crushing his forearms against Ghanem's larynx. This time, Ghanem threw both arms back. The slayer cried out when several ribs broke. He fell to the ground, writhing in pain. Ghanem sucked in air then turned and stomped on the slayer's chest for good measure before kicking him to the side.

The battle continued. For how long, he didn't know. He was too consumed by rage, taking it out on every creature with sharp pointy ears. Ghanem fought to kill. Fought for the years he'd lost. Fought as a guardian, using his fists, his legs, his head, and his horns to overcome the imps of this army. He took them down one by one, overpowering them with his brute strength. He used his horns to ram them, lift them up, and then flip them over his head, all the while keeping Meera in his sights.

A trumpet sounded in the distance. Tenor notes floated through the air. Hard to tell where it came from, but the slayers that could stand retreated, picking up those who still lived but were too injured to walk. They threw the injured over their shoulders before disappearing into the foliage and the darkness.

He let them leave. It was possible they wanted him to follow. Draw him into a trap of sorts. Another time, maybe. He'd had enough for now. He waited, made sure they weren't coming back. After several minutes, he walked over to Meera where she sat next to the brook, using the water to rub the blood off her arms.

He touched her shoulder. "Are you okay?" She jerked away. Was it his voice? It still held the deep rumble that came with his altered state. Was it his touch? She'd called him a monster earlier; maybe she couldn't stand to look at him. When she didn't answer, he moved away.

The darkness dissipated enough for him to see the carnage. There were at least twenty dead slayers, broken and bloodied, strewn amongst the land and trees. They weren't beautiful anymore. In death they were repulsive, with gray peeling skin and forked tongues. He tried to focus on the land around him but found it just as repulsive. Gone was the brown of the earth. In its place was a vibrant red. A bloodbath. He'd done that. All of it.

Maybe Meera was right. Maybe he was a monster. His mind had been human-like long enough to realize the damage he'd done. He wouldn't lie to himself and say he'd done it all to protect Meera. A lot of it, yes. But the need to prove himself had joined along in the ass-beating party. *Monster.*

Before he could consider the pros and cons of the moniker, a wave of nausea had him doubling over. Ghanem fell to the ground and retched.

*

Meera heard the retching. She wanted to be mad, wanted to stay scared. He was a monster. She'd witnessed it; saw the transformation as it happened. His horns had been the clincher. She'd stared in amazed horror at the sight of those horns spiraling out of his head. If not a monster, definitely a beast. But was he really? In the truest sense of the word? He'd protected her when he could have hurt her. The slayers had appeared more human in their appearance than the changed Ghanem, and they *had* hurt her. Repeatedly. She had no doubt Ghanem could have chased her down in the woods moments after she'd fled. Sure, he could have ulterior motives, but he hadn't hurt her—not physically, anyway.

Ghanem heaved again. The sound ripped through her and made her chest ache. She couldn't stand it. Meera turned, made out his shape within the shadows. She slowly approached, afraid he would turn on her. She hadn't been kind. But in her defense, she was new to all this. Used to dealing with humans, not creatures she couldn't even name. Not pointed ears, auras, magick, and now . . .

She avoided the dead and rotting bodies, shuddering at the horrid sight they created and going out of her way to make sure she wouldn't have to step over any of them. Death, twisted and mangled among the dirt and trees, cast an ominous stench. She should feel bad. A normal person would definitely feel bad or, at the very least, feel something. She didn't. Not for them.

She squinted into the night, trying to make out the shape of his horns. The horns were gone. His body had returned to the Ghanem she recognized. A knot formed in her stomach. Was she disappointed? Certainly not. She'd been terrified. Had run from him. Run for her life. Then why did she feel as if she had missed something? Missed a chance? What was wrong with her?

Before she could even think to answer that question, Ghanem moaned, clutched his stomach, and emptied it into the grass again. Crouching, Meera placed a tentative hand on his back and rubbed in slow circles. They stayed like that for a long time. Neither spoke a word. He never looked up, just continued to get sick. She wondered if this was some sort of side effect that would happen every time he changed. Changed to what, she didn't know. He'd yet to tell her what he was. What he'd become.

She thought back to how strong he'd been. His muscles had bunched beneath his skin, making him appear larger than life. He'd cut through the baddies like they were nothing, merely ants under his feet. But they weren't ants. They were strong, powerful creatures. Yet Ghanem had been stronger. Much stronger.

She stepped away, walked over to the brook. Meera quietly conjured a cup, dipped it in the fresh water. She walked over to him, sat by his side, and then silently offered it to him. He finally looked at her, despair in his eyes. They analyzed each other before he finally sighed and accepted the offered cup. He filled his mouth, swished the water around and then spit it out.

In a raw voice, Ghanem inquired, "It pains me to ask, but you wouldn't happen to have an extra toothbrush, would you?"

She wasn't offended when he didn't look at her again. He hated her magick, and she knew what it cost him to ask. "Sure," she said. "No problem." Meera turned her back to block the purple embers from his view trying her best not to add to his obvious pain. Touching her middle finger to her thumb, she rubbed them together. Before she could even speak a rhyme, a toothbrush and toothpaste appeared in her other hand. *Well, isn't that something?*

Holding them out to him, she waited for him to accept before releasing her breath. He'd asked for it, but that didn't mean he'd willingly take something from her—not when it came from magick. She took this as a good sign. A small one, but still good. Meera sat quietly, watching the trees and bushes for any sign the slayers were back. She sensed nothing other than Ghanem scrubbing his teeth by the brook.

She laid back, exhausted, but couldn't sleep. As tired as her body was, her mind warned her to stay awake. Every time she fell asleep, the nightmares returned. So far, they'd been just as bad, if not worse than her reality. At least when she was awake, she had Ghanem with her to help fight the baddies. Asleep? She was alone. She wouldn't run from him again. Stupid, stupid move.

Easy to say that now. He wasn't a monster anymore. He was the man she fought with, played with, talked to, kissed. The same man who had touched her so intimately just a short time ago. Even now she craved his touch. He didn't know that though, and there wasn't a chance in Tallahassee she'd be telling him.

191

Lost in her thoughts, she jumped when he cleared his throat. "We can't stay here, Meera." He extended his hand.

His voice had returned to normal. Gone was the almost evil-sounding resonance. In its place was the smooth, melodic tone she loved so much. She lifted her hand to his, shivered when his closed around hers and heat enveloped her. As soon as she stood, he released her. She sighed inwardly. They kept going backward when all she really wanted to do was wrap her arms around him and hang on. She didn't. It was as much her fault as his. Maybe more so. "Where should we go?"

"Your guess is as good as mine. I don't have a map, though I wish I did. But we're too exposed here. We need to move."

"Okay, then. Let's move." She turned a full circle, took in the landscape. The towering trees made the forest even darker. "We're going to have a very hard time navigating in the dark."

"I know, but we have to. We'll walk for a while. See if we can find a place to hole up for the night. We'll need to sleep."

Meera turned to stare at him, her eyes wide. "I'm fine. I could go for hours."

He quirked a hesitant smile. "We'll see."

She followed as he picked a direction and headed toward an opening in the outcrop of trees. This time, she kept up. She didn't want to distance herself from him at all. She wanted other things. So many other things. Things she shouldn't desire at times like this. She had no control over how her body responded to this man, and respond it did. Every time he was near. And when he wasn't, she yearned for the sight of him.

But right now, her blasted vision wouldn't adjust to the night. She couldn't see a damn thing so she held on to his arm. First of all, she didn't want to bust her ass. She kept tripping and used his solid frame to keep herself on her feet. Second of all, she liked the feel of him. Loved the texture of his skin beneath her fingers.

He chuckled. "What's so funny?" she asked.

"Not funny, per se. Just interesting."

Meera wondered what his expression would tell her. She couldn't gauge his mood from his voice and that really bothered her. Now it was her turn to chuckle when a memory wormed its way into her thoughts. She remembered sitting in her kitchen. Remembered the energy in her hands and how they had started to glow. If she could do that then, she sure as hell could do it now.

She held tight to Ghanem's arm as they continued to trudge through the black forest. Since she couldn't see anyway, she closed her eyes and concentrated. Instead of focusing on the panic that wanted to take over because she was all but blind, she centered her energy just like Carrine had taught her.

Her abilities took form inside her. She was beginning to understand how this worked. It all came from her core. Easy peasy, so long as she could find her core. Slow, even breaths brought her closer. Her fingers tingled. She kept concentrating, kept focusing on the light within her. It was there—she just had to project it. Meera lifted her free arm, cracked her eyes open, and watched as her fingers started to glow. The light, white and bright, illuminated every shadow in the forest, every shadow on Ghanem's scouring face.

She beamed. He didn't.

He cracked his neck, then shook his head. "We need to talk."

Of course we do.

Chapter Twenty-One

Whether he realized it or not, Ghanem had stopped at the perfect resting spot. The blackness of the night had lifted a bit, almost as if someone were playing with the dimmer on a light switch, allowing her to see the layout of the area. They'd made it to the base of a mountain with several crevices and sturdy footholds.

The different landscapes were quite interesting. Dense forest to their right. Rock-hard mountain to the left. Vines, stones, logs, and stumps everywhere in between. With his insistence, they'd climbed until they'd come across a ledge they could rest upon. It was perfect, actually, as though it had been cut out of the side of the mountain for this very purpose and made the effort of climbing worth it. The ledge had more than enough room for the two of them to sit comfortably—as comfortably as one could sit on a hard rock—and they could even stretch out if they wanted. Maybe Meera could convince him to let her whip up some blankets and pillows. But that would make her want to sleep and she wanted anything *but* that. Scratch the idea; she'd just let her backside suffer.

It appeared as though they were relatively safe up here. With nothing but solid rock at their backs and no way for someone to approach without them hearing, Meera finally released a semi-relaxed sigh. Until she remembered he wanted to talk. Then she sighed for completely different reasons.

Meera rolled her neck, stretched out the tight muscles. Stress was a killer on the spine. "You know what?" She didn't wait for him to answer. "Let's just do this. You wanted to talk. So, talk. Matter of fact, I've got some questions myself."

He shifted next to her, long legs dangling over the ledge. "Such as?"

"As if you don't know. I've asked the same question repeatedly, yet you don't seemed inclined to answer it. Why is that, Ghanem? You expect everyone to do as you say, when you say it, yet you give nothing in return." She couldn't keep her anger in check. She wasn't even sure who she was mad at, Ghanem or herself. "So?"

He stared straight ahead for a full two minutes. Frustration had her tongue itching to lash out but she held it in check. Finally he straightened his shoulders and turned to her. "I deserve that. At minimum, some of it. I've not been forthcoming. There are reasons for that, Meera. Did you ever consider that?"

Well, call her thoroughly put in her place. She swallowed, started to speak, and then clamped her mouth shut. Maybe it would be better just to shut up and listen.

He seemed to accept her silence as some sort of peace offering because he smiled, sort of. More like the corners of his mouth refused to stay in line with the rest of his lips. "My life is complicated. What do you know of the veiled?"

"Unfortunately, nothing. You said your life is complicated. Mine is that and more. Maybe we should swap war stories." She leaned back on her elbows, stared up at the sky. A blank canvas. No moon, no clouds, no stars. Just the eeriness of the night.

"Maybe we should."

He stayed quiet for a long time. So long she almost fell asleep, lulled by the sound of his breathing. She jerked to attention. *Uh, uh.* Couldn't let that happen. Meera sat up, turned her body so she could face him, and sat cross-legged. She studied him while she finger-combed her hair. The tight set of his jaw told her he was in deep thought. She didn't want to intrude on his thoughts. That wasn't quite true. She could at least be honest with herself and admit that she *did* want to intrude. She wanted to know about other veiled, about him, about his complicated life. She wanted him to look at her. To see her, and talk to her.

Meera tried to smother her surprise when he did finally look her way. His eyes were different, scary, almost hypnotizing. She bit down on her lower lip to keep from crying out and didn't let up when she tasted blood. She wouldn't run. Not this time.

"What color are they?"

"What?" She wasn't intentionally being obtuse. She honestly hadn't heard him, so focused on trying not to panic. Deep breath in. Slow breath out.

"My eyes, Meera. What color are my eyes?"

"Orange. Only not."

"What do you mean?"

"They're orange, but unlike any shade I've ever seen. It's like all the colors of a sunset are there, only deeper."

"Mmm."

"That's it? Mmm? I tell you your eyes are freakin' orange and you say, mmm?"

"Precisely. My eyes change colors with my emotions."

"Since when?" She slapped her thighs then waved her hand to clear the dust that rose from her dirty clothes. "I've known you for a little while now, and I've never seen them change colors. Well, shoot—actually, I thought they had earlier today, but I assumed it was a trick of the light." *Hoped* was more like it.

"It wasn't. I'm certain they were red earlier."

She gasped. "How do you know? It's not as if you can see your own eyes. Not without a mirror, anyway."

"Were they red?"

"Yes. But—"

"I was angry." Ghanem shrugged. "They turn red when I'm angry."

She swallowed audibly. "Why is this just now happening? You've been angry with me before, and none of this happened then."

He rubbed his scalp, then pinched the bridge of his nose. "I'm not sure. I—I honestly don't know."

She considered it. "But you do know what you are, right?"

"Yes."

Meera wanted to scream. This was worse than getting information from Carrine. "And?"

"And nothing. I'm not sure you want to know. I'm really not sure you can handle it."

"That's bull, Ghanem. Total bull." Sorta.

"Is it? You couldn't get away from me fast enough when I changed. Remember that?"

"Oh, don't even. That was so not my fault. I had no warning. Zero. It's not like I see people like you roaming the streets of Milwaukee."

"Point taken. You were unprepared."

Meera nodded smugly. About time he conceded a point.

The edges of Ghanem's mouth turned up. A wicked smile presented itself. "And now? Are you prepared now?"

Her heartbeat kicked up a notch. "What do you mean?"

"Exactly what I said. It's simple, really. If I were to change now, right now, would you be? What was that word? Oh, right. Prepared?"

*

Ghanem knew he taunted her. He watched her gaze dart around. She attempted to look at anything but the top of his head, and she completely avoided his eyes. She was so easy to read. Her confusion was mixed with more than a touch of fear. He'd become comfortable, maybe too comfortable with the way he could sense her feelings. They were linked. He didn't know how or why, but he could no longer deny it or label it as a fluke.

So he taunted her, not because he wanted to start a fight, not because she was a witch, and certainly not because he wanted to scare her off. Indeed, it was the opposite.

He enjoyed her company, liked bantering with her. Sitting next to her on this ridge seemed almost like a date. Could have been a date if not for the current situation. Even more than that, his past was ugly, full of mistakes and regret that hung over his head like a black cloud, a constant reminder. All because he'd become too wrapped up in a woman. And not just any woman. No. She, too, had been a witch, and she'd thrown around promises wrapped in magick. He'd bought into her tale, the romance of it, and it had cost him.

Dearly.

And here he was, getting sucked right back into the magickal abyss. But this time he was different. Meera had called him a monster. He could be. The evidence of that was back in the clearing. Maybe she was right. He'd wanted this, but when he thought about what he'd done, how he'd broken and killed those slayers as if they had no value in this realm or any other, the nausea came back with a vengeance. Guardians didn't care a lick about who they killed because there was always a reason they killed. Always. It wasn't just for sport as many believed. They were honorable. They were noble. They were warriors. So he'd killed because he felt threatened. Because *she* had been threatened. If he was to believe what he'd been told, the entire world was threatened because of the slayers.

So he killed. He should be proud. His churning stomach told him otherwise.

Maybe he'd lived too long in the human world. All he'd been able to think about since he'd massacred the slayer army was if there had been another solution. Could he have detained rather than killed?

Meera punched his shoulder. "Just get on with it, would ya? Just tell me what you are so we can move on to the next topic."

Ghanem admired her spunk and attempt at courage. She couldn't lie to him, not when he could tell exactly what she was feeling at any given time, but she didn't know that. He rubbed his shoulder, feigning pain. Might as well tell his story—the condensed, Swiss cheese version—so he could start learning hers. She hadn't told him much about herself, either. Such as why she was here. What was she after? He hadn't thought of it before, but maybe she'd been placed in his life as a test. Did someone want to know if he could resist? He wouldn't blame them if they did. He'd screwed up, and now he had a chance to make amends.

He turned to Meera, ready to accuse her of tricking him. His mind played out all the different scenarios; her scheming with his father to lay out an elaborate yet easy plan to snare him. Thane as a co-conspirator?

Ghanem growled in frustration, then berated himself for allowing his imagination to create the lies. If there was one thing in this world he knew for certain, it was his trust in Thane. That meant one theory destroyed and laid to rest. Good riddance. That still left the other one.

"Ghanem?"

"I'm a guardian, a warrior created by the gods."

*

Impossible. No way had she heard him right. Ghanem didn't look like a warrior—not how she pictured a warrior, anyway. In that other state, he looked like a monster, a demon. And his eyes were red again, full of more anger than a being should possess. The air sizzled with intensity. Her breath caught in her throat, and she struggled to breathe as his persona threatened to take over, consume her. Wrapping her mind around the fact that she was immensely attracted to a being who looked like pure evil . . . well, she just couldn't. How would she ever manage to handle all his anger?

She tore her stare away from his wicked eyes, forcing herself to concentrate on his head. No horns. Yet.

"Stop it." He wasn't a monster. He just wasn't.

His eyes narrowed as he edged closer. Meera refused to back up, refused to cower. She could bring him back to himself. She could get Ghanem back. And then what?

Using a softer voice, she attempted to soothe what she thought of as the monster with whispers instead of aggression. "Ghanem, I'm not scared of you." It took everything she had to relax her breathing and soften her features. "I'm not afraid."

"Aren't you?" His voice altered between a growl and almost normal.

The red of his eyes slowly turned burgundy then brown. Maybe he hadn't been that far gone. Besides, she really hadn't done anything to ignite the anger. Not that she could think of, anyway. They'd just been having a conversation and then, *wham*, out of nowhere came the monster, or at least the beginning stages of it. "No. Not anymore. You're not a demon, Ghanem. Stop acting like one. That's not you. Don't get me wrong. You have your moments. But for the most part, you're a pretty decent guy." She tried to lighten the mood with a lopsided smile but couldn't tell if it worked. While not red, his eyes carried just as much intensity.

He laughed, though the sound offered no pleasure. "I'm not a demon, Meera. Though I could see why you'd think that. I'm a guardian. There are more differences than similarities between the two species."

"Evil similarities?" She couldn't get past the horns and his anger. Definitely demonic in appearance and attitude. She had enough on her plate to deal with, what with her Luminary tasks and all. Time wasted trying to tame someone who would ultimately leave her was time she couldn't afford. He would leave. She didn't doubt it one bit.

"Not all demons are bad. Many are protectors like the guardians. You shouldn't scoff at what you don't know."

Flicking a pebble over the ledge, she said, "Maybe. But all I've ever known about demons and monsters . . . " She waved her hand. "Now you throw guardian into the mix, and I'm to believe you exist only to protect? I call that one scary-looking protector. Children would run screaming. Shoot, I ran screaming. I just don't see it, Ghanem. Not when I look at you like this."

Ghanem couldn't help how his body transformed. It hurt that he continually judged her, and here she was doing exactly the same to him.

Both worlds, veiled and real, had her more and more confused with each passing minute.

"Trust me, I may not be a full guardian now. But, Meera, I can assure you I was once, and I will be again. It is all I want."

She flinched at his last remark, unable to stop the disappointment that hit her. Whatever he was didn't matter. But she would never tell him that now. He'd just made it perfectly clear he didn't want her and confirmed her earlier suspicions. She shouldn't be surprised. She wasn't, really; she'd just hoped he would be different. He'd given her more reasons to think he would dismiss her just like all the others, but still she'd held on, convincing herself those moments when he'd shown her tenderness and passion would start to outweigh everything else. If she could run, she would. Not because she was scared. No. She wasn't. She'd run because even though they were sitting here together, she was still totally alone.

"Did you hear what I said?"

She looked at him, really looked at him. Stared right into his chocolate-brown eyes. "Oh, yes. Loud and clear. And I was wrong."

"About what?"

"You truly are a demon." She turned away from him them, curled up on her side, and scooted to the back of the ledge, closest to the wall. She had nothing left to say to him, didn't want to hear anymore of his guardian, protector-of-the-innocent crap. He was only interested in himself. And she sure didn't want to waste any more of her time getting to know him. It would be nothing but wasted effort on her part. As soon as he fell asleep, she'd leave and somehow figure out a way to find out what she had to do and how she would do it. Shouldn't be too hard. *Riiiight.*

*

It could have been a kiss. The wind blew gently across Meera's cheek like a lover's caress. Her eyes fluttered open in surprise. She couldn't believe she'd fallen asleep.

She pushed her hair out of her face and held it to the side. The wind blew stronger, calling to her. She stood and stepped over Ghanem's sleeping form, taking care not to wake him. Her feet were light, her spirit heavy. She walked to the edge of the cliff, gazed up into the starless sky, and, while she wouldn't call it comfort, she'd grown used to the wind.

It was her summoner. Constant beckoner. Calling her to do its tainted bidding.

She stood with her toes gripping the edge and wondered what it would be like to let go—let the wind take her and lift her into the air. Would it let her soar through the trees, over the mountain? Or would it send her into an awaiting hell? Only one way to find out, and she was ready. So ready.

Meera stretched her arms out to the side, hesitated slightly when she heard the whisper within the wind.

Meera.

The wind blew harder and threatened to push her over the cliff. She'd go, but on her own terms. She pushed all the weight onto the balls of her feet and stayed rooted. A hiss sounded on her left. She jerked her head toward it, but before she could find the source the hiss moved to her right.

Meera, the whisper called again.

The hiss grew louder as though angered by the competition. A hiss, a whisper. One after another called to her, the weaving of their voices like an ancient tapestry in her mind. An angry symphony orchestrated by the wind.

The hiss lashed out at the sweeter voice. The whisper didn't falter. It called to her over and over again, beckoning her toward a light she had yet to see. It was only in these moments that she was confused, uncertain where she belonged in the battle between good and evil. Was it wrong to let the wind decide? Let it carry her to the side she was meant to help?

Only one way to find out. Meera lifted her hands over her head and then back down. Her arms mimicked wings though she wouldn't need them. The wind would make her fly.

Or would it?

She glanced back at Ghanem and wondered how he slept through all the noise. Maybe he didn't hear it. It made sense. No one had ever heard the voices she heard. No one shared in her torment. She wanted to go to him, tell him goodbye, but he had already made his choice, and it didn't include her.

She closed her eyes, took a deep breath then allowed her eyes to reopen. She wanted to see. See the faces behind the voices. Meet her destiny. She leaned forward and her feet lifted off the ground. The wind made a sound like a triumphant sigh. She continued to fall forward, the weightlessness causing her to lose her breath. The current caught her and lifted her higher. Her relieved smile didn't last.

Meera screamed when something grabbed her ankle and yanked her back onto the ledge. She slammed against a wall so hard she would have fallen to her knees, but the wall held her up as its arm snaked around her ribcage and pulled her even closer. Ghanem was the wall, and he was unmoving.

As though angry for being interrupted, the wind wailed like a banshee, screaming as it whooshed by. Its intensity should have blown them over the cliff, but the sheer size of the being holding her kept them both in place. She lifted her chin and their gazes locked for what seemed like an eternity. Meera wanted to yell at the wind, tell it to stop, but she couldn't speak, too lost in the depths of Ghanem's eyes as they changed from blue to green and then the most beautiful amber. She wondered what they all meant. He'd said the color changed depending on his mood. How could he feel so much, so differently, in the space of a few breaths?

Though they barely touched, it was as if he were almost inside her. Though fully clothed, she felt naked, exposed as though he could read her darkest fears and her deepest desires. For a minute, she truly thought he could and that scared her. She hadn't shared anything with anyone in forever. And now, with just a look, just a stare, he could take her secrets? She wasn't ready for this. Not when he would take those secrets and then leave. Pulling away was so hard to do, but Meera had no choice.

The wind seemed to guess her intention. It helped push her back as she pried Ghanem's grip off her arms. He held strong, but she had self-preservation on her side. Either he let go or adrenaline had given her the strength she needed to escape his hold. It didn't matter. All that mattered was bracing for his anger. It was coming. Of that she had no doubt.

While his eyes slowly changed from amber to blazing red, she silently chanted. Over and over, the words repeated in her head. *Give me strength. This I need. Give me power. For this deed.* Over and over and over she chanted, barely able to hear the soundless words over the commanding wind, but feeling the power build in her body.

When Ghanem leapt forward, Meera threw out her hands and blasted him with white-hot power. He slammed into the mountain, and she swore the earth shook beneath her feet. His look of shock only lasted a moment. She glanced behind her, confirmed she had nowhere to go. She stood on the edge of the cliff about a hundred feet off the ground. No chance she could jump and remain alive. Even with the witch blood that allowed her to heal quickly, a fall like that would surely kill her. What had she been thinking? She hadn't been. Not her own thoughts anyway. Each trance was sucking her deeper into the dark shadows of a world she wanted no part of.

Seconds ticked by while she searched for an escape route. She could go up, but he was faster. Ghanem jumped at her again so she hit him with more light. He staggered back, but this round didn't have nearly as much oomph.

Ghanem roared her name, his voice rivaled the thundering sound of the wind.

Meera screamed back. "Stay away from me. I don't want to, but I will hit you again."

She hoped it wasn't an empty threat. Hitting him with the light twice had worn on her. She was completely drained, as if her energy had been sucked out with a vacuum leaving only bits of particles behind. The last thing she wanted to do was fight. The one thing she couldn't do was give in. He'd said all he wanted was to be a guardian. He'd never said a word about how she fit into that scenario or if she even could. With nowhere to go, Meera sank to the ground and covered her face with her hands. "Please, Ghanem. If you're in there, please, just leave me alone. Go away."

Her sobs came quickly. She was physically spent and emotionally at odds with herself. Was it too much to ask that she go one day—one night—without some sort of turmoil? One wouldn't think so, but the past year had been just that. Night after night and day after day of crap. She could only put up with so much and had to wonder if the constant fighting was worse than the silence of before. She'd definitely had enough.

She cried until the tears ceased to flow, until that particular river had run dry. It was only then that she noticed the wind had died down and simply existed as a faint, fluttering breeze. And it was only then that she lifted her head and opened her eyes. Meera had gotten her wish.

Ghanem was gone.

Chapter Twenty-Two

"You failed." Ryken ran his hands through his hair while his slup lightly ran her fingernails along his back, a constant motion, up and down. The action should have soothed him. But he didn't feel soothed. Far from it. He shrugged off her touch. "Go."

Without a word, the redhead left his bed and walked out the side door. He didn't watch her go. When he was ready, she'd be on the other side of that door awaiting further orders. He'd allow nothing less.

He narrowed his eyes. "Well?" Ryken demanded.

Jayson stood before him, flashing back and forth between his true self and the beautiful creature Ryken preferred. Extreme fatigue made it difficult to remain in the desired form. Ryken would punish him later. Right now he wanted answers.

"Almosssst . . . had . . . her." Winded, Jayson bent at the waist and gulped air. Flashed from hideous to angelic and back again. His forked tongue flicked out to grab the spittle at the corner of his mouth.

Ryken nearly gagged. "Almost isn't good enough. I expected more from you." He watched as Jayson's eyes widened, as his skin blanched and peeled. "Pull yourself together." He didn't have to yell. Barely above a murmur, his voice dripped with promise—the promise of death.

"I understand."

Two words. Words without a hiss. Ryken figured Jayson could manage no more as it took every ounce of strength to pull his body into an erect position and force the beautiful side to hold. He tried to appreciate the effort, but he couldn't. He didn't. Anger at Jayson's failure clouded any other emotion. To fail was to be weak. A weak leader meant weak soldiers.

"I can fix this, Ryken. I *will* fix this. I'll get her and bring her to you. I won't fail again." He held his shoulders back, lifted his chin.

Ryken considered this. Should he give him another chance? Time was running out. If they didn't capture the witch soon, everything he'd worked for would be for naught. It would be over.

"If you don't succeed this time, I will do it myself. Fail and die, Jayson . . . fail and die." He turned his back on the weak slayer. "Find a slup and take what you need, then get me the witch."

Jayson already forgotten, Ryken walked to the side door, placed his white hand on the carved wood. The handle turned and the redhead, still dressed in gauzy white, presented herself. "Bring three more and then join me." She turned to do his bidding and he walked to the bed, discarding every stitch of clothing along the way. He stretched out, his beautiful, naked form beyond ready for the game he was about to play. He released the anger and replaced it with anticipation.

Moments later, four beautiful women stood before him. Though their souls were long gone, he wondered if there was even an ounce of hope left somewhere in the recesses of their minds. It didn't matter. He linked his fingers behind his head and spread his legs wide as a smile full of sin emerged.

"Worship me."

Chapter Twenty-Three

Never in his life had Ghanem experienced anything like the chaos this woman incited in him. He hadn't gone far, but he'd left her alone like she'd asked. Meera's tears had practically ripped his heart from his chest. And what had she been thinking? Was she suicidal? He hadn't been asleep like she'd thought. He'd watched the entire thing play out. Yet he didn't understand it. Any of it.

Who the fuck had she been listening to? He'd heard nothing, but there wasn't a doubt in his horned head that she had. And if that weren't bad enough, she'd jumped. She'd fucking spread her arms like wings and jumped off the side of the mountain. He shouldn't even care. Caring would get him nothing but trouble and heartache. He'd had enough of that to last a hundred lifetimes.

Dammit. He did care. If he didn't, he wouldn't be crouched in the bushes at the bottom of the mountain waiting. Waiting for her. She'd called him a blasted demon and when he'd corrected her, she'd shrugged it off as if a demon and a guardian were one and the same. Both in her mind equaled monsters.

He'd never thought in those terms, never thought of his horns as scary. Never until he'd met her. So here he stooped, hoping she—the witch who'd called him a monster—wouldn't send him away again. Hoping she'd tell him exactly what she was dealing with and why she was here. And what if she did tell him? Would it matter? He had to finish this. He had to defeat the slayers. He had to get his life back.

Ghanem reached into his pocket and pulled out the scroll. He read the letter for what must have been the thousandth time. Guilt washed over him, and then the hope that always followed. What if he could make this right? Somehow make up for the choices he'd made?

His mother thought he could. He found the passage, heard her voice as if she were right next to him, speaking to him:

You are strong. You are mighty. You have intellect that has yet to be revealed. You must be the one to find the source, the source they value above all else, and you must destroy it.

Somehow he would do it. No matter the cost.

"What are you reading?"

Ghanem jumped to his feet, quickly rolled the scroll before stashing it in his pocket.

"I didn't hear you coming." How the hell had that happened?

"Obviously." Meera shrugged and turned to walk away.

"Where are you going? You shouldn't be alone, Meera. It's not safe."

"Why do you care?" She leveled a gaze on him that reflected a world of hurt.

Ghanem closed the distance in two strides and placed his hands on each side of her face. He tilted her head up, forcing her to meet his eyes. "I shouldn't. I don't want to . . . I really don't want to." Her breath hitched and he wanted to give her more, ease her mind, but he couldn't. Not with words that could turn out to be a lie.

"Ghanem, I—"

He leaned in, stopped her with a brush of his lips. Heat raged under his hands, between their mouths. He had to taste more of her. He slid his fingers through her hair, letting them tangle in midnight bliss. He cupped the back of her head. "Open for me, *polipo*. Open for me."

She gasped at the familiar nickname as he pulled her closer, intent on ravishing her full lips. She pulled back.

"Someone's here."

He turned on his heel and shoved her behind him and held her there. "Who is it, Meera?" He couldn't see anyone in the darkness, though he tried damned hard.

"I'm not sure." Her voice trembled. "But someone is out there watching us."

"Just stay behind me. Can you see them?"

"No—no, I can't see anything but you. But they're there. I can sense magick."

Of that he had no doubt. Of course she could sense it. She *was* magick. "Light or dark?"

"What?"

He tried to inch around him. He held her firmly in place. "The magick. Is it light or dark?"

"How would I know?" Though said on a whisper, her voice dripped with frustration.

"You know. Just focus. I need you to help me out here. I can't sense it. Never have been able to. Focus, Meera. Is the magick light or dark?" He slowly backed up until there was no space between Meera and the mountain. Unfortunately, there were still three more directions to cover. Her breathing evened out, slow and easy. He just hoped she'd hurry the hell up. He had to know what they were dealing with here.

Again, her skin heated beneath Ghanem's touch. He let go of her right arm and grabbed her left. She'd said he wasn't burning her when they touched, but he'd seen the marks, and, in this case, he didn't like it.

Meera let out a squeal behind him.

"Shhh, woman. Just because we can't see them doesn't mean they can't see or *hear* us."

"No. It's okay. It's light, Ghanem. The magick is light, and I think I know who it is."

"I'm impressed, child. You've come a long way since I last saw you."

The voice had drifted in from the darkness. Ghanem had also figured out who it was, and he hoped she'd brought reinforcements. "Show yourself, Carrine. And you better be with Thane."

"I was enjoying the show, Ghan. Too bad little miss witch knew we were out here. This could have been better than Netflix."

"Where the hell have you been?" Ghanem watched as not only

Thane and Carrine but the entire crew emerged from the shadows. A quick once-over assured him they were no worse for wear. He was beyond relieved. No chance he'd be sharing that with any of them.

"Did you miss us?" Steffen asked.

"Hardly."

"I did." Meera said from behind him.

He'd forgotten to let her go and still hesitated to do so. Why was that? They were safe—for the moment. He'd let go, but if she went too far, he'd just have to pull her back again. Back to him.

*

Meera waited for Ghanem to let go of her arm. For someone who couldn't wait to get rid of her, get back to his wonderful life, he seemed awfully possessive all of a sudden. She didn't want to feel encouraged by that, and she definitely wanted the butterflies to stop dancing in her stomach. Definitely.

She squeezed around him so she could hug Carrine and Calliope. As always, Bevva acted chilly and actually stepped back as Meera moved toward her, but she didn't let it ruin the reunion. She just bypassed her and moved on to the boys.

Seeing everyone safe relieved some of the tension stored in her shoulders. She chose to ignore the growl behind her when she hugged Thane, Drake, and then Steffen. Ignored it outwardly. Inwardly she beamed big time and then chastised herself for letting him have that effect. Stepping back, she stood next to Ghanem as the questions started to fly. His growl ceased the moment her skin touched his.

"Was that you we heard, Ghan? Never mind. Don't even answer that. I'd recognize that roar anywhere." Thane beamed at Ghanem.

Meera tilted her head up to see Ghanem's expression. Proud didn't even begin to describe it. The cloud she had been floating on moments before started to sink as if someone had shot a million arrows through it.

"Meera thinks I'm a demon," Ghanem said through a laugh.

Meera's spine stiffened. "You totally missed my point."

"Demons?" Drake asked, laughing.

"Hell, no," Steffen said.

Meera would have smiled had the comment been the least bit funny. "Nice word choice, Steffen."

"Oh, please. You can't actually believe that." His brows drew together. A lock of stray hair fell between his eyes. He shook the hair out of his face. The action allowed a glimpse at the tips of two horns hidden under the mane.

Meera shrugged. Ghanem had acted like one so she'd called a spade a spade. She refused to be sorry about that. Red eyes? Excuse her for being human. Except she wasn't human. She had so much to learn.

Calliope looked from Meera to Steffen. "Believe what?"

Thane walked over and stood next to Calliope. "I think Meera is under the impression we're demons from hell."

He then turned his gaze to Meera. She flushed but couldn't explain why. "I know you said you're guardians. I get it, okay? Can I help it that my mind processed the word demon when I saw his horns and heard that roar?" Why was she even asking? She should just keep her opinion to herself. Obviously they found it insulting to be considered demons. She looked at Ghanem again, tried to read the expression in his eyes but couldn't decipher the meaning.

Bevva laughed. "Are you that clueless? Seriously? That's like calling me a sorceress. Or a wizard a warlock."

Carrine placed her hand on Bevva's arm. "Enough, child. She's not clueless. Not at all, in fact. She just lacks the information that has been denied her. Ghanem will clear this up for her. Won't you, Ghanem?"

Meera swallowed audibly. She wasn't sure she wanted to hear what he had to say any more than he probably wanted to tell her. Which was not at all. She just had to wonder if her attraction to Ghanem was just another tug from the darker side of magick.

"We are not demons. Not. Demons."

"Okay, already. I said I get it." Though she didn't really.

She edged away from Ghanem and closer to the other witches. She refused to heed the warning of the rumble in his chest.

"I think we could all use some sleep." This from Calliope the Soother.

Steffen sidled up next to the gothic witch. "I couldn't agree more. Shall we?"

Color instantly covered Calliope's cheeks. "Um. I don't think so."

"Too bad," Steffen said with a shrug before narrowing his gaze at Bevva. "How about you?"

"Get real, jerk. I'm no one's second choice." Her eyes were ablaze. She whipped her head around, sent her curls flying, and stomped off while fire danced on her palms.

"I'll go with her." Calliope followed Bevva into the darkness.

"What the fuck is their problem?" Steffen looked baffled.

Thane laughed. "You just don't get it, do you?"

"Get what?"

"Come on, Stef. Let's go. Drake and I will explain this to you."

One by one they all disappeared into shadows of the surrounding forest. Meera hoped they wouldn't go too far. Now that they were all together again they'd finally be able to decipher the puzzle—figure out what she had to do to defeat the slayers and win her life. At least she hoped they could.

"Carrine?"

"Yes, child?"

"I know there wasn't time to call the council before I went through the portal. Any chance you were able to contact them after?" She looked directly into Carrine's eyes and hoped she would hear good news.

"Yes. I did speak with them."

Meera steadied her breathing. Whatever it was, whatever information Carrine could give her, she would take. "And?"

Carrine glanced from Meera to Ghanem and back again. "I think we should speak privately."

An internal war raged within her, surprising her. She wanted to know what Carrine had to say. Oh, how she wanted to know. But the pull toward Ghanem proved to be just as strong. Moments ago she'd wondered if he was trying to steer her toward the darkness and now? Now she wondered if the dark side would be worth it. At least she would get to experience life. Experience him. But for how long?

But if she died, there would be nothing to experience. No light, no dark, no Ghanem. Nothing.

She turned to him. "I need to go with Carrine."

She expected him to turn his back on her. She expected his eyes to flash red. What she didn't expect was the gentle hand that cradled her chin and tilted her head up. What she didn't expect was the softness of his lips as he brushed a swift but thorough kiss across her mouth. What she didn't expect was the four words he uttered . . .

"I'll be right here."

Her lips tingled and her chin burned, but the burn felt good, a reminder of his heat, a foretelling of so much more. "Okay," was all she could manage before Carrine guided her through the darkness and into the woods.

Her sense of foreboding grew stronger with each step she took, but it was too late to go back, too late to run the other way. So she followed. Though the forest was pitch black, somehow her feet conquered the terrain. Not once did she trip over a root or a rock. Not once did she feel the urge to pick up said rock and fling it at Carrine's back. No. All of that was saved for Ghanem, who seemed to relish twisting her emotions, turning them this way and that until she was dizzier than a three year old on the teacup ride at Disney World.

She almost wished for the feelings of insanity to come back. Who would have known they'd be easier to deal with than the emotional roller coaster she rode now? Meera steered herself away from that confusing road and took the fork right on over to the next one. "Haven't we gone far enough?" She wasn't aware Carrine had stopped until she plowed right into her. "Geez," she said while backing up. "Give a girl some warning, will ya?"

"Pardon me. I thought you said we'd gone far enough."

Meera put the lid on her temper. She wasn't really mad at Carrine. Just pissed about her present circumstances. She rubbed the back of her neck and wished she could rub away the feeling that things were about to go from bad to really messed up in the space of a very short conversation. "Just tell me what you know."

"I think we better have a seat."

*

He'd watched Meera walk into the woods until the darkness swallowed her up. It killed him, absolutely killed him not to be included. Not only did he want to know, he *needed* to know what was going on, and he needed that information yesterday. But he'd meant what he said. He would be right in this very spot the moment she returned from having her little conversation with Carrine. He hoped giving her privacy would make it easier for her to open up to him. *Fat chance.* When was the last time something had been that easy? Oh, yeah. He remembered. Never.

He sensed his brother before he saw him. Being around Meera messed with that particular ability. He'd been so into her, he hadn't sensed anyone before. Now those once-dormant senses were wide awake. "'Sup?"

"I could ask you the same thing. Using her for a little more than detecting the slayers?"

"Don't."

"Don't what? I saw you just now. I've seen that look before."

Ghanem clenched his teeth until his jaw threatened to pop out of its sockets. He didn't want to do this, but if Thane said one more word about Meera, he'd forget all about the brotherly love shit.

"What?" Thane asked. "You wanna throw down? That witch mean something to you? That wasn't supposed to happen. Did you forget what you're here to do? Dammit, Ghanem. This could ruin everything. Is that what you want?"

Sometime during his tirade, Ghanem had tuned Thane out, too focused on his brother's emerging horns to give a fuck about the bitch-out session. Whatever it was, he was probably right. Thane usually was, but he didn't want to worry about who was right and who was wrong just now. Ghanem wanted a fight, and if Thane's stance was any indication, he was about to get one.

So rather than answer any of the questions his brother threw his way, Ghanem allowed his own horns to surface and heated energy to flow through his veins. He squared his shoulders and growled low in his throat. Thane's red horns were a sight to see as they jutted straight out of his head at a forty-five degree angle. But there wasn't a doubt in Ghanem's mind he could take his brother. Two days ago? Maybe not. Now was a whole other story. They were about to see what was what.

"Hey, boys. Let's calm down."

Out of his peripheral vision, Ghanem saw Calliope slowly approach, followed by Fire Head and the two asses. "Stay back." If they didn't heed his warning, someone would get hurt. Maybe all of them. Not his problem.

"You're brothers. Feel the love," Steffen taunted.

"Stay the fuck back, Steffen. This is none of your concern." Thane kept his eyes on Ghanem as he issued a warning of his own to the gathering crowd.

"Whatever," Bevva said. "Let 'em mess each other up. Anyone got popcorn?"

"Bevva . . ."

Ghanem heard not only the pleading in Calliope's voice but the almost hypnotic rhythm of her breathing. He couldn't let her near him. He didn't want to be soothed, and, from the look in Thane's eyes, neither did he.

Thane pulled his already ripping shirt over his head and threw it to the ground. Ghanem one-upped him by tearing his own down the middle with a low roar. So what if it looked like a battle of testosterone. So fucking what.

The redheaded witch laughed. Man, there were times when he wanted to throw her off a mountain. Maybe he'd let his horns accidentally gore her. It wouldn't kill her, but it wouldn't be pleasant either. Something to think about, but right now he had more pressing matters to deal with. One of them had to make a move or this would turn into a battle of who could glare at whom longer rather than the bloodshed he itched for.

"What are you waiting for? Need Meera to give you a good-luck kiss first. You're sure gonna need—"

Ghanem cut off Thane's words and his wind when he rammed Thane low in his gut. His brother stumbled backward about a foot before coming to life with a roar of his own. He launched forward fist first and clocked Ghanem in the shoulder. The fist had been meant for his face, but he'd seen it coming. He just hadn't been fast enough to completely miss it. Still, his shoulder hurt like a bitch. Completely dislocated.

Ghanem popped his shoulder back into place, and nailed Thane in the chin with a side-kick. It landed hard, but Thane took it like a man and, rather than going down, he grabbed Ghanem's leg before he could swing through. His first thought was *nice move*, but Thane twisted his leg and something exploded in Ghanem's knee. The pain of that motion shattered any coherent thoughts Ghanem had.

He heard a hiss behind him and a low *damn* from Drake. Yeah. It hurt, hurt so bad he was almost incapacitated, but he could handle it. The question was could Thane handle what he was about to do? Ghanem wrenched his leg from Thane's hands and tackled him like a linebacker sacking a quarterback. They landed hard on a bed of rocks at the foot of the mountain. He gave Thane zero chance to flip their positions. His fist met Thane's face once and then again and again. Over and over, he pounded into Thane's head. The force of the blow radiated through his clenched hands, up his arms, and into his back. It wasn't enough. His brother swore and tried to protect his face, but Ghanem didn't let up. His anger and confusion wouldn't let him. Not when Drake and Steffen grabbed his arms and tried to pull him off. Not when Calliope laid her soothing palms upon his shoulder. Not when Bevva shot a fireball that hit him in the middle of his back. And not even when Thane repeatedly told him it was enough.

His *monster* had completely taken over, and there was no stopping him. Not until it had death on its hands.

Chapter Twenty-Four

They made their way back through the woods, each keeping silent in their own thoughts. Meera shouldn't have been surprised by everything Carrine had told her. Not really. It wasn't all bad news, but the bad outweighed the good by about two tons or so.

Find the source. Stop the source. End it. Or else. Could the source be Ryken himself, or something else, an item or a place, that gave him such dark power; something that made him so full of evil he would kidnap people and do God knows what with them? She really wished she were able to speak to the council herself. Not that she didn't trust Carrine to ask the right questions; it was just that she was used to doing things for herself, and hearing her fate first hand from those who supposedly were all knowing seemed . . . well, it seemed right.

But what was right about any part of this situation? Zip, that was what. Carrine had wanted to act quickly. Her reasoning? Ticking clock. Well, no one knew that better than Meera, but this was her fight, and she needed to at least attempt some semblance of control over it. One thing she did know, she—scratch that—*they* would have to find where Ryken and the slayers lived so they could observe them. Preferably from afar until they became clear who or what the source was. Then *she* would have to stop it.

So much to take in. So against Carrine's advice, Meera had decided to take tonight to digest everything and hopefully between herself and the other witches, they could formulate some sort of a plan. Any plan would be better than the current one. *Oh, right. What current plan?*

She'd been looking at the ground, watching her step when what seemed to be the sounds of an out-and-out brawl brought her head up with a quick snap.

"What the hell?" She stopped and stood dead still. If the slayers were back, she didn't want to run right into them. Not until she figured out exactly where and how many. If it was them, and the others needed help, she'd do whatever she could. Yeah, what a change. She was used to doing things on her own and being alone, but she'd started to think of the crew—even the demonic-looking ones—as friends. And friends didn't leave friends to fight alone.

"It certainly doesn't sound like a friendly spar, now, does it?"

Meera listened closely and moved as quietly as she could manage, placing one foot in front of the other. Carrine followed suit. When she heard Calliope begging Ghanem to stop, she grabbed Carrine's arm and raced toward the noise. The sights and sounds that awaited Meera when she approached the makeshift camp were not what she had expected. At all.

She had no idea what had started it, only knew she had to stop it. Soon. If she didn't, there would be two dead brothers—Thane from being pummeled to death and Ghanem from guilt. When had she started thinking of Ghanem and his monster as one and the same? She had to quit doing that. He wasn't a monster.

This wasn't the time to argue with herself. Ghanem appeared to be in full guardian form and didn't even know what he was doing. At least she hoped he didn't, but he loved his brother and if this ended badly, the ramifications would be staggering. Of that she had no doubt.

She grimaced when Ghanem's fist made contact with the side of Thane's head, sending an arc of blood onto the nearby rocks. From the look of things, this had been going on for some time. Thane's horns were half receded, and his oversized stature had ebbed with the loss of blood and strength.

She quickened her step, but paid heed to the flying fists. She wanted to stop the fight, not become part of it. One wrong step, and two angry guardians would take her down. Permanently.

"Ghanem." She'd hoped just hearing his name would slow him down. No such luck. And what did she expect when Steffen and

Drake couldn't manage to pull him off, when Calliope the Soother had had no effect? She had to keep trying, and, hopefully, she could make a difference. This time she raised her voice. "That's enough, Ghanem. He's your brother." She waited a split second but knew she hadn't penetrated the anger. She had to be more assertive.

Meera rubbed her choker with two fingers and then let her hand drop to her side as the magickal energy began to build. The intensity, and the quickness in which it came, continued to surprise her.

The familiar tingle started in Meera's fingers as Carrine stood next to her and grabbed one hand while Calliope took the other. Bevva sighed before joining them on Carrine's right. The sign of solidarity was enough to make Meera swallow past tears. She could definitely use their strength.

She swallowed again before starting the chant. The other three witches joined her during the second recital. Their voices melded together in a harmonious tone that was both beautiful and haunting.

"Blood of blood. You are one. Cease the fray and step away. Blood of blood. You are one. Cease the fray and step away."

They continued the incantation as Meera stepped forward with her hands outstretched. Her fingers took on a luminescent glow. This time it wasn't the white-hot heat that would hurt. This light had a healing quality and managed to quiet the panic consuming her. She let the calming light build in her hands.

Ghanem's fists slowed, but they had yet to completely stop. While working, he still retained enough strength to fight the power of the chant. He proved that with each connection to Thane's jaw.

Come to me, Ghanem. Let me help you. She didn't say the words aloud, too afraid for anyone to hear them. She desperately wanted to help, and, even more than that, she wanted his beast to rest so Ghanem could emerge. She needed him. No denying that. The light turned to brilliant shades of purple as it left her fingertips in a slow, fluid motion. It reminded her of a beautiful winged bird gently gliding through the air, making its way home.

Home?

What did Ghanem have to do with home?

It took just seconds, but to Meera, time stood still. She held her breath while the words around her blended beautifully. One moment in unison, the next holding amazing notes of harmony. Her lips stopped moving as she focused all her energy on the healing light. All her energy on Ghanem.

Steffen and Drake stood at the edge of her light. Maybe they were afraid of what would happen if it touched them. But they didn't go too far. They would step in if necessary.

The light reached the tangled brothers and covered them like a security blanket, weaving its way between them as if it had a mind of its own. The movements were almost desperate—or maybe Meera had projected her own emotions through the light—as it swayed back and forth, picking up momentum and forming a barrier. The more it separated the guardians, the more powerful it became until it became an impenetrable wall. A wall that made Ghanem's punches futile.

Meera waited. She had forgotten to breathe, forgotten everything but Ghanem. He blinked. Once. Twice. His horns receded. He blinked when the light dissipated slightly. Certain he saw the blood that covered Thane's face, she watched as he looked down at his own bloodied hands, and then she ran as his knees buckled.

She reached him just before he hit the ground. Somehow she found the strength to hold him up. Calliope sobbed softly but Meera chose to tune them out. Steffen came up beside her and tried to take Ghanem's limp form. "Don't. I've got him." She looked up. "I've got him, Steffen. Just go help Drake with Thane."

She took a deep breath before easing Ghanem and herself to the ground. He'd passed out. She didn't know if fatigue, shock, guilt, or a combination of the three had caused him to lose consciousness. None of that mattered to her. He'd taken care of her. More than once. She would do the same for him.

Meera placed his head in her lap and stroked her fingers over his skin. She found the motion to be soothing and hoped it would in turn soothe Ghanem at least a little. She addressed everyone without lifting her head. "Leave us. All of you. Please. Take care of Thane. Make sure he's all right." A tear slipped from her eye, slid down her cheek and landed on Ghanem's head. Meera absently wiped it away with her continuing caress. "Please. Leave us for tonight. We only have a few hours to rest."

She said nothing else. Not out loud anyway. Inside she said a million and one prayers. Prayers that Thane would heal, and that he would forgive. Prayers that Ghanem would wake up, and that he would also be able to forgive. Himself.

*

Ghanem woke with a groan and an ache in his heart so painful he could barely breathe. He didn't panic though. He couldn't panic until he remembered what had happened.

His body was stiff from the rocks, but his head was cushioned on what had to be the softest bed of grass he'd ever felt. He breathed deeply. Meera. His head was cradled between her hands and her lap, her grip soft but secure.

He would've smiled at that, but agonizing thoughts riddled his mind. Something had happened. Something bad. He blew out a long breath and thought back. *Oh, shit*. What had he done? Ghanem lifted his hands. His knuckles were scabbed over and his fists slightly swollen. He wanted to deny it, chalk it up to a nightmare, but he could do neither. The memory of the truth had slapped him with a reality he couldn't escape.

Ghanem extracted his head from Meera's lap. She opened her eyes and looked at him. Neither said anything for quite some time. He broke the silence. "Is it as bad as I think?"

She bit down on her lower lip and nodded.

Ghanem leaned against the rock, slammed his head back. He welcomed the pain.

"Ghanem, stop."

Even in the blanketed darkness, he could make out her features. Concern swam in her eyes, and fear rippled just beneath the surface of her skin. He didn't deserve the former but understood the latter. "I am the monster you think I am."

Meera moved to crouch in front of him. She placed her hands on either side of his face. "No, you're not. I was so wrong about that."

He turned his head. With a gentle hand, Meera directed his gaze back to her. "I am, Meera. I know what happened. He's my brother and I disregarded that. I should have let his comment slide. I should have been able to control my anger. Is he . . . is he dead?"

"Oh, my God, no. He's not dead. They're taking care of him. I won't lie to you. He was in pretty bad shape when they left, but I'm sure he's fine—" She trailed off, looked over her shoulder and then back at him. "Or he will be. You guys heal fast. I've seen it myself. Look at your hands. Already they're so much better than they were just an hour ago." Meera nodded. "He's fine, Ghanem. I'm sure of it."

She wasn't sure. What if? What if he had killed Thane? His own brother. "I have to know." He stood and pulled Meera up. "Where are they?"

"They went that way." She pointed. "Not sure how far, though."

It didn't take long to find the others. They had made camp about a quarter of a mile away. His eyes scanned the sleeping bodies until they landed on Thane. He watched for the rise and fall of his chest and breathed a long sigh of relief when he saw the evidence of life. But just because he still breathed didn't mean Ghanem hadn't caused damage. Irrevocable damage.

Calliope lifted her head, spotted the two of them and proceeded to make her way over. She had been resting closest to Thane. He figured they'd been taking turns. Ghanem couldn't quite meet her eyes. She reached out, but he stepped back. He didn't want to be soothed. Calliope dropped her hand.

"How is he?"

It should have been Ghanem who asked the question, but he couldn't bring himself to ask. Thankfully Meera could.

"He's resting comfortably now. The physical damage is starting to heal. If we can get him to sleep for a few more hours, he should be okay."

The *physical* damage. Calliope had phrased it perfectly. Sometimes emotional damage would never heal. He'd found that out first hand and now had even more layers to add to it. No matter what Thane had said to provoke him, he should have been stronger, should have been able to control himself. But it had been so long, so many years that his guardian had been dormant, maybe he no longer had control. Maybe he never would. Could he live with that? Live with the knowledge that Thane may never forgive him? He couldn't bear it if Thane looked at him the same way Dominic did. His brother *and* his father? That would be the death of him.

Lost in his thoughts, he didn't realize Calliope had reached out to him again until she placed her hand on his forearm. He looked up.

"Go with Meera. Both of you—all of us need to rest. Tomorrow will be soon enough to deal with this. A new day is a new start."

Whether it had been her touch, her words or his own guilt, Ghanem agreed with her. He needed to get away from Thane, away from the evidence of his own betrayal. He would do whatever it took to get his brother to forgive him, even if it meant keeping his distance for a while. Yes, tomorrow he would start the long road back. Meera took his hand. He squeezed back before turning to her. He shouldn't ask, he realized that, but he needed her just now. Badly.

"Help me. I need to forget. Just for a while."

She nodded, turned and led him back in the direction of the mountain. At this moment he needed her more than he had ever needed anyone. Even as the turmoil of the earlier events wreaked havoc on his system, the underlying anticipation of touching Meera, experiencing Meera, made its way to the surface. He should fight it, but once again he had no control.

Would history repeat itself? Would tonight be the night he allowed another witch to destroy his life? He had no one to blame but himself.

Each step brought him closer to fulfillment and very possibly his ultimate downfall.

Chapter Twenty-Five

Meera picked her way through the dense forest, leading Ghanem away from the others. They needed privacy. If she thought about it, really thought about it, this probably wasn't the best decision right now. Ghanem would use her to forget. The thing was, she didn't care. Not in the least. Maybe she was using him, too. They both had reasons to shut out the world, close the door on everything and everyone. Their problems were mounting, and if they could use each other as an escape, even for a brief moment, a moment they may never get the opportunity to share again, she was all for it.

The proof of that was in the beating of her heart, the nervous energy bouncing beneath her skin. She could feel it in his, too. He had her hand in a death grip and while the heat they created singed her skin, she wasn't about to complain. There wasn't a chance in Topeka she'd allow any distance to come between them. She feared he would change his mind.

She also feared she had fallen in love with him. All of him. While she'd slept with his head in her lap, she'd dreamt of him as Ghanem and then as Ghanem the guardian, and she wanted him in both forms. In her dream she had run her hands from the base of his horns to the tips, following the curve every step of the way. She'd taken her time, and, when she'd looked into his eyes, she'd known it had turned him on just as much as it had her. She longed to see that look again, to know she was the reason behind it.

Neither had said a word in so long, but sometimes words only got in the way and the silence didn't bother her at all. But she couldn't go much longer without seeing his eyes and searching their depths. Even if what she found proved to be fleeting.

Ghanem didn't say anything but he sensed the direction of her thoughts. His breath hitched, and he growled doftly behind her.

That sound sent a shiver of anticipation dancing across her skin. Not long ago, she had considered that not only an intrusion but also a violation. No longer. Now she reveled in the thought that he was so in tune with her feelings. She probably wouldn't feel that way tomorrow, but tomorrow didn't matter. As she had quickly found out, tomorrow wasn't promised. Not to anyone.

Meera searched for a soft patch of ground and thought she spotted one not too far off the path that would lead back to the mountain and then to the others. Just a little farther should be good. She should conjure up a bed—one with plush, down-filled pillows and soft sheets. Wouldn't that be something? But with her magick came magickal sparks and those sparks could be seen by anyone. She wanted privacy, not an audience, and definitely not an audience of slayers.

Their last scrimmage with the slayers had been some time ago, and they hadn't seen a glimpse of them since. Surely they were out there. They had to be. This was their land after all. Were they rebuilding their forces? Gaining more strength? Maybe they were just waiting for a prime opportunity. She just hoped it wouldn't be within the next hour or so. She and Ghanem deserved this escape.

Escape or not, she had to talk with the other witches. Soon. Formulate a plan. Should they include the guardians in their discussion? Would they even help? They were obviously here for their own reasons, though Ghanem had yet to share those with her. But she hadn't been forthcoming either for that matter.

Later, Meera.

Yes. All of this could wait. She hadn't realized she'd stopped until Ghanem released her hand. She whipped around, afraid he would leave . . . but he didn't. His eyes sought hers. Questioning. Burning. And more than that. Even if his irises weren't the shade of coal, she'd know what he was feeling. Sorrow. A sorrow so deep she feared he was standing on the brink of hell fighting to find his way back. He was there now, at the edge of the flames as they licked and teased, threatening to consume, and yet he wasn't.

Reaching up, she placed her hand on his cheek. He closed his eyes and leaned into her palm. Meera stepped closer, closing the short distance between them until he enveloped her in his arms. She sighed deeply and rested against him. If this was all he could give, she would take it. But she wanted more. God, how she wanted more.

"Are you afraid of me?" he asked, his voice low, barely more than a whisper.

"No," she whispered back. She should be. Go ahead and call her a fool, because with him she felt safe. Safe and sane.

"I won't hurt you."

She wouldn't cry. No way. "I know," she choked out.

Ghanem stepped back and looked down at her. She moved forward and tucked her head into the side of his neck.

"Meera, why are you crying?"

She sniffed. "I'm not. I'm totally not crying."

"Okay. You're not crying."

She wanted to stop, but the tears continued to flow. The harder she tried the worse it got. "I can't quit crying."

He held her tight, gently rocking back and forth, one hand caressing her back while the other cradled the back of her head. "I know. Care to tell me why?"

"Not a chance in Toledo." *I'm scared of what I feel for you.*

Ghanem laughed soft and low. "You say the strangest things."

She pulled her head back, finally able to look at him and thankful for the lighter tone, even if it wouldn't last. "So I've been told." Her lashes, heavy with tears, fell until her eyes completely closed. She didn't have the emotional strength to open them. Not before he answered her next question. "Can you distract me? Please?"

"Distract you from what?"

Her eyes opened, and she hoped the look she gave showed how much she needed this. "From myself. From life. From death. From where we are—shoot, who we are. I want to . . . I want . . . " Meera trailed off, unable to voice her deepest desire.

"You want to forget. You want to lose yourself. You want—"

"You, Ghanem. I want you." There, she'd done it. She should be relieved now that it was completely out in the open. Instead, her nerves bundled into a knot in the pit of her stomach. Would he reject her? Everyone else had. He'd asked her to help him forget, but that had been earlier. Maybe he'd changed his mind. *Please don't let him have changed his mind.* Who was she praying to? The god of fornication?

"And I want you, *polipo*. More than that . . . I need you."

*

Meera shifted. The tension left her shoulders as she once again laid her head against Ghanem's neck as if her body had released a sigh. He liked the way they fit, almost as if they were meant to stand like this, nestled against one another. But if he had anything to do with it, they wouldn't be standing long. And wasn't he one fortunate guardian that she obviously felt the same?

Her lips sought the skin beneath his ear and made a path along his jaw until they found what he'd hoped they'd been looking for. Regardless, he couldn't wait another second to taste what she offered. He moved in for the most blazingly erotic kiss of his long life. His tongue traced her lips, retreated until she leaned into him.

He gave her exactly what they both needed. A teasing dance of give and take played out. He pulled back, just for a moment, and then with one hand still on the back of her head, the other tangled in her hair, Ghanem pulled her in, tilted his head, and devoured her. The taste of her was completely intoxicating as their tongues battled. A combination of mystery and magick. The promise of even more with each sweep of his tongue. The magick should have repelled him. Instead, he let it roll off her tongue onto his own, the energy of it sending sparks through his system. He hadn't expected it but couldn't deny he liked the way his body responded to it. He wanted more.

She moaned, he growled. He reached down and lifted her off the ground only to ease her back onto it, but this time she ended up horizontal with him looming over her. She tried to reverse their positions. Not a chance of that happening. He needed to have total control right now, and if he allowed her to get on top, shit, he knew exactly what would happen.

"Please."

"No."

"Let me up, Ghanem," she pleaded breathlessly.

He looked at her, deep into her eyes. He hadn't scared her; she just wanted to be on top. *Maybe next time,* he thought to himself.

"Later, Meera. We're doing this my way."

"But—"

"Uh-uh. Shhh." Ghanem placed his finger against her lips and then smiled when her tongue snaked out to lick it. *Naughty little witch.* "We're taking this slow. Don't worry. You'll enjoy it. Every. Agonizing. Second. Of. It." With each word, he inched closer until he was a breath away. He closed the fraction of space and sucked her lower lip into his mouth. He felt the pull of her smile, then eased back. "I promise." It had been such a long time since he'd last pleasured a woman, but the chemistry between them was undeniable. That alone gave him the confidence to make that promise.

He waited. Yes, he was in control, but would do nothing until she acquiesced even as his blood pounded through his system. His need was almost unbearable, yet he would endure the exquisite torture if it meant they would have this one night together. "Well?"

She chewed on her lower lip and he imagined doing the same. She had no idea what she did to him. Then again . . . The twinkle in her eye told otherwise. Well, he could play too. Ghanem rolled off her and threw his arm over his eyes.

"Ghanem?"

"Hmmm?"

She punched him. He laughed at her weak attempt.

"Ghanem, come on."

And there she was, sounding all breathless again. "Say it."

She punched him again and he laughed harder. Man, she was stubborn. The throbbing between his legs had moved past the point of uncomfortable. Nonetheless . . . "Say it, woman."

Through gritted teeth, she said, "Fine. You can be in control."

His groin tightened in response to those words, but he refused to look at her. "You sure? I want you to be sure."

One breath. Two. Three. And then, "Very."

Say no more. He was on it and on her, certain she never even saw him move. The surprise shone in her eyes when he straddled her and ripped her shirt down the middle in one swift motion. Her surprise didn't last long. She grabbed the back of his head and pulled him to her breast. He nudged the lacy fabric aside, then licked and teased one breast and then the other while his hand slid down her body. She arched her back when his fingers skimmed along her rib cage. He made a mental note to make sure there wasn't an inch of her skin left untouched.

His hand continued its journey until he found the sweet spot between her thighs. Her body jerked at the contact before she melted into him. He could feel the heat that lay beneath the fabric. The next several moments became a blur of tangled limbs beneath a canopy of trees and a sky that held no moon and no sun. She was everything he needed and yet everything forbidden. Perhaps that was what made the connection so incredible, because every touch of her body against his ignited needs and desires he had never possessed.

Her body was solid yet lithe, her touch soft yet sure. She drove him to the brink of sanity with one touch and then pushed him even farther with the next. All this and they were still clothed. The need to feel her flesh against his own became his lone goal. Most certainly he would find another goal after he achieved that one. Making sure his touch never left her for too long, he quickly removed her clothes and then his own. The warmth of her body increased three-fold. "We'll have to be careful, Meera. I'm afraid the heat we create this time will cause you to combust."

"Mmm . . . I sure hope so." She grabbed the back of his head and pulled him back to her.

He kissed her again, knowing he would never tire of her taste. He found her center again. The softness enveloped his fingers until all he could think about was sliding into her. Their bodies became slick with sweat. The heat reminded him of a nagging fly buzzing around his head. It worried him. She seemed to enjoy it. Oh, yeah, he thought as she groaned, she enjoyed it, but their bodies had yet to unite fully, and her temperature rose steadily. He'd promised not to hurt her.

"Meera? This isn't going to work." He couldn't believe those words had just left his mouth.

"I'm fine. Really, I'm fine."

*

Ghanem looked torn and Meera appreciated his concern. But, seriously? He could just stop? She was on fire, but it was from more than just the fact that his skin touched hers. Every desire she'd ever had and repressed had come to the forefront of her thoughts. She had to figure out something before they lost this connection. "Okay, tell me this. Do you want to be with me?"

He looked down between them at the clear evidence of just how much he wanted her. "You know I do."

Meera licked her lips. "Then please permit me to try something. And before you agree, I should warn you that it entails a bit of magick." She pulled his hand to her mouth and kissed his palm before trailing a path with her tongue to his wrist. A bit of magick and a bit of seduction never hurt anyone.

He watched her through hooded eyes. "At this point, you could bring in a whole magickal circus and I would applaud. Whatever it takes, witch."

She beamed, her smile full of mischievousness. "All right, guardian, repeat after me . . . *The fire is building from within. There's no need to singe the skin. Give us this time to be together. Do it now, change the weather.*" Okay, so she could use a little help in the incantation department. Who cared as long as it got them back to the feely-touchy stuff?

She smiled as Ghanem pinned her with an incredulous stare. "What? Am I asking too much?"

"Ya think? I am not saying that."

"Fine. I can do this alone."

"Do what alone?"

Oh, poor boy thought she meant something else entirely. "The spell, silly. What did you think I meant?"

"Nothing. That—what you said." His voice cracked on the last word.

"Right. Let's get on with it." She closed her eyes and simply felt. His breath on her skin. His need, a need equaling her own. *"The fire is building from within. There's no need to singe the skin. Give us this time to be together. Do it now, change the weather. The fire is building from within. There's no need to singe the skin. Give us this time to be together. Do it now, change the weather."*

The shift in the air started with the first phrase, and by the last, she practically quivered as huge snowflakes fell from the sky and landed on her naked skin. She'd done it. She'd really done it. Would she ever become accustomed to this magick? Her magick? Meera lifted her face as the snow continued to fall, promising to cover them if they didn't get moving.

"How's this for cooling me off?"

"I'll admit I'm impressed. And I'm freezing. Get over here."

Before she could move, Ghanem reached out and pulled her onto his lap. She wrapped her legs around his waist just as his mouth found hers. The fire continued to grow inside her, but the snow kept her skin from burning. Who knew a winter wonderland could be so much fun? And so incredibly sexy?

They moved as one, urgent, hands everywhere, mouths intimately connected. He shifted, stretching her body beneath his, and this time she didn't feel powerless, just cherished and needed. This time instead of fighting him, she took the opportunity to enjoy his body as it slid over hers.

The muscles in his back bunched beneath her touch. She moved her hands lower, pressing his backside closer until he gave her exactly what she wanted. She arched against him as he slid into her. The heat of that connection seared her, sending tingles down her legs. She wanted more. Now fully buried inside, he stopped and she cried out.

Meera arched her back again, felt his pulse deep within her as he slowly withdrew and then moved against her again and again. Leisurely. As if he wanted this to last forever. He seemed to grow larger with each measured stroke. His fullness almost sent her over the edge, but every time she came close to her release, he stopped, waited, kissed her, and then started again.

Words weren't needed. Not when actions spoke so much. She clung to him as he quickened his pace, pumping into her with a ferocity she had only imagined existed. This was just as good, just as raw as the slow thrusts. She matched his intensity as the burning inside threatened to consume her.

"Let go, *polipo*. Feel me and let go."

His words were a rumble against her ear. The sound of his whiskey voice completely undid her. She cried out as wave after wave of electric orgasm ripped through her. Purple embers fell parallel with the snowflakes. Ghanem shuddered, then growled deep in his throat as his release matched her own. His lips sought hers, and she kissed him deeply, held him tight around her until the convulsions slowed and then eventually stopped. They were both breathless, both sated, and she wanted nothing more than to lie in his arms for the remainder of the night. She could only hope his sigh meant he wanted the same.

"We need to talk."

Her heart lurched. Their moment of contentment had only lasted a few seconds and already he wanted to talk? Somehow that seemed like role reversal to her. "Now?"

"Is there a better time?"

"Yes, actually. Any time after my nap. I'm really tired, Ghanem. I feel like I haven't slept in a year."

"That's one of the things I want to talk about. Your sleep is disturbed with dreams, or perhaps I should say nightmares. Why are you not at peace when you sleep? What are your nightmares about?"

He had been stroking her hair, soothing her with his caress. But now he stopped and she felt the loss.

How much could she tell him? How much *should* she tell him? Carrine hadn't been clear about that. No surprise there. Maybe she could evade for just a bit longer. She really was tired. She'd hoped with him next to her, the nightmares would give her a break. But now that he'd brought it up, that certainly wouldn't be the case. At least not tonight. Or was it today? This no sun or moon crap really ticked her off.

"It's a simple question, really. After what we just shared, I wouldn't think it would be that big of a deal to answer a couple of questions. Unless . . . "

"Unless what?" Her heart rate kicked up a notch, and, for reasons she couldn't explain, she was on the verge of major panic mode. She forced her voice to stay steady. "What were you going to say?"

Ghanem dragged his hand down his face and then sat up. He reached for his shirt and pulled it over his head. "Unless what just happened between us didn't mean anything to you. It didn't appear that way to me before. But now?" He snatched his jeans out of the snow and stood to pull them on. "Now I just don't know."

A deep cold that had nothing to do with the foot of snow surrounding her seeped under her skin and into her bones. She couldn't believe this was happening to her again. Another person casting her aside and somehow making it seem as though it were her fault. She should've known, should never have let herself get involved with him in the first place. He'd despised the fact she was a witch from the get-go. He'd been more than upfront about that, yet she'd let herself get sucked in, let herself believe this time would be different.

She wished she could disappear, but all she could do was stare at him in disbelief. No, that wasn't the right word. Deep down, she could admit she knew all along this would happen. She'd been so hard up for a relationship, or any kind of affection for that matter, she'd forgotten how it would end. Poorly and with her being alone.

Again.

"You really want to know what my nightmares are about? Do you really?" She, too, gathered her clothes. The only difference being all she had to do was rub her fingers together and they magically fell into place, right along with the green, down-filled cloak she had just conjured. Yes, she was hurt, but she was also mad and had every intention of rubbing her *witchness* in his face.

Ghanem didn't answer. He turned his back to her as if he couldn't stand to watch anymore of her magick. Emotional wall firmly in place, she didn't allow his action to hurt her. Instead, she silently sent blasts of icy wind his direction and watched as he struggled not to shiver. Before, she would have conjured up a coat for him. Not anymore. Not after he made her feel used and angry. It didn't matter that he didn't answer, didn't look at her. More than ready, she planned to tell him exactly what her life, awake and dreaming, was like.

"I dream about light and dark and the battle they wage against each other—a battle I don't understand. In my dreams, they pull me in opposite directions. They both need me, and I don't know which way to go. The wind calls to me, hisses, and pushes me toward the dark. The dark beats me and rips me apart. You've seen the evidence of that yourself. And then the light . . . the light whispers in my ear constantly, as if without me it would cease to exist. Those dreams, Ghanem, tell of a story I should know and a life that may or may not have been mine. In my dreams, I'm attacked for what I am. And now I see my dreams are no different from reality. I was never accepted as a human, so when Carrine told me I was a witch, a Luminary no less, I embraced it in hopes I would finally be able to connect with someone, anyone who would understand what I've been going through. But there is no difference. I'm still completely alone."

Ghanem had turned toward her, his eyes flashing from brown to blue and back again. He reached out for her. "Meera—"

"Don't. Don't touch me." She stepped back but refused to wrap her arms around herself, even though all she wanted to do was shut down. That would show weakness, and weak was something she would never be again.

"I—"

"No, Ghanem. You don't get to explain yourself. You've said more than enough already. And just so you don't have to wonder anymore . . . I'm here"—Meera threw her arm out and gestured to the scene around her—"in this godforsaken place to fight for my life. *I* must find Ryken and be the one to stop him and his source or *I* will die. The time is growing near. I can feel it. So you can go to hell. Or maybe I should say, go back to hell." She spun on her heel and took off in a dead run away from him and his judgmental eyes.

She slipped on the snow and landed hard on her hip. She wanted nothing more than to sit in that crumpled heap and pray things would be different. It wouldn't help. Never had. She got up and took off again. She sensed him behind her though she didn't think he had left his spot. She could almost feel the fire of his gaze.

There wasn't a chance in Alaska she'd stick around to see what he had to say. Already embarrassed enough, she couldn't deal with him, and she certainly couldn't deal with all this snow. *From this point on I need a path. Clear the snow so I can run fast.* It no longer took time to come up with an incantation to fit the circumstances. Thoughts came to her as if the answers had always been there. Perhaps they had been, just locked away for safekeeping until her time had come. Meera kept running as the snow melted and sapphire embers cascaded around her.

She had no idea where to go. She just wanted to be alone. What a change. She couldn't remember a time when she had actually made the choice to be by herself. And now when she could have run to Carrine, Calliope, or even Bevva, she didn't.

Her vision blurred. She swiped at her eyes relentlessly. These were tears she would not shed. He wasn't worth it. If she had any chance at all to save her life and actually make something of it, she couldn't spare another thought for the jerk. Even if she could feel her heart splintering into a million pieces because of him.

Movement sounded behind her. *Ghanem.* She turned but wasn't quick enough to dodge the rock that hit her shoulder. Not Ghanem. They'd found her. She'd been warned about this but had chosen to use her magick anyway. She'd led them right to her. She looked right and then left, ignoring the pain the rock inflicted. She turned again. The slayers had surrounded her and were moving in, their auras casting enormous shadows and darkening the forest around her. There would be no more running.

She'd sensed it earlier. Impending doom.

She searched for an escape route and when she saw none, her thoughts betrayed her one last time. In her mind, she saw Ghanem as the man and then as the beast and then the two of them together. Why did she think of him when her only thoughts should have been how to save her own life?

The slayers advanced and she kicked out, nailing one in the chin. His head snapped back, the crack audible amidst the chaos. He shook it off while his aura shimmered with dark anger. He came at her swinging. He kicked, she dodged. He punched, she blocked. She called to the light, collected it in her fingertips, and then pushed it out with everything she had left.

The air reeked of burnt flesh. Her stomach rolled. She'd managed to hit quite a few of them. On the ground, broken, they writhed in agony. Their moans were almost childlike. Guilt gave her pause.

That indecision cost her. The others quickly advanced, and she hadn't taken the time to gather more light. She doubted she could even if she tried. Her energy and strength waned as unexpected fatigue set in.

Meera stumbled and watched in horror as the slayers she'd zapped morphed into hideous creatures. Their skin turned ashen gray and began to thin and rip apart at their cheekbones. One smiled and licked his lips. The sight of his serpent-like tongue sickened her enough that she gagged. She stumbled again, lost her footing, and fell.

The air left her body in a rush as she slammed to the ground. She gasped, fought to breathe. The only thing she could hear over the pounding of her own heart was the leaves rustling above her. On her back, Meera opened her eyes just as two more slayers swooped out of the trees, knives in hand.

She didn't even have a chance to scream as her world, once again, went black.

Chapter Twenty-Six

Ghanem kicked the ground as uncertainty tore through his mind. What had he done? He'd lashed out at Meera because of his own insecurities and not because of anything she'd done to deserve it. He'd honestly wanted to know more about her. He could only blame himself that what should have been a casual, take-it-to-the-next-level conversation turned into an interrogation riddled with accusations.

Not one of his proudest moments.

His heart tightened beneath his ribs. She could die? Of course she could die. Even immortals lost their lives at some point. But that wasn't what she had meant. She'd made it seem imminent. Of all the reasons he'd thought up for why she had to fight the slayers, this hadn't been one of them. The source? *Fuck!* What were the chances of that? As if the situation weren't complicated enough.

He'd seen the look in her eyes—pain, hurt, anger—when he'd reached out for her, felt the emotions as if they were his own, and maybe they were. What tore at him most was the underlying fear. He'd wanted to embrace her, comfort her. But the damage had already been done. Once again, he'd made the wrong choice. Would he ever learn? Could he fix this? Thane would help him figure this out . . . The fist squeezed tighter around his heart. He couldn't go to his brother. Not after what he'd done.

There must be a way to—to what? Repair the enormous wound he'd created between him and Thane? Save Meera's life? Still get what he wanted?

What did he want? At one point in his life, he would have talked this out with Amella. Guilt opened the door and stomped its way into the mix of emotions. He hadn't even thought of his sister in days. But wasn't she one of the reasons he was here now?

He hadn't seen her in so long. Had no idea what type of woman she'd become. She'd always been his voice of reason. She and his mother. It would be impossible to speak to or even see his mother again, but Amella? He could see her and become a part of her life again. He just had to finish this.

Ghanem pulled the scroll out and gently unrolled it. Sinking to the ground, he braced himself against the trunk of a large tree. The tree blocked some of the wind Meera had created. He didn't want that. He shifted until the wind whipped around him. He welcomed the cold. It helped clear his head. Maybe he'd missed something in his mother's words. He sincerely doubted that. He'd read the letter at least a hundred times. Nonetheless, he had to read it once more.

The fate of all lies on your shoulders. You are strong. You are mighty. You have intellect that has yet to be revealed. You must be the one to find the source, the source they value above all else, and you must destroy it.

Only one can finish the task.

But know everything is not what it seems. Don't be quick to judge, as hard as that may be. Be patient, be diligent, be the warrior you were meant to be. Then and only then will you have everything you seek.

Don't be quick to judge? Everything is not what it seems? This was true yet hadn't heeded his mother's words. He'd judged Meera from the onset. Based his beliefs on a mistake made long ago. A mistake that had nothing to do with her.

There was so much at stake. So much he had to do, and yet the sand continued to steadily trickle through as the bottom of the hourglass filled.

He hadn't realized he'd started walking, making his way back to the others. Not until the sweat dripped off his forehead into his eyes. The snow had melted. He missed it. Missed why it had been created. He pulled off his T-shirt and wiped his head, then tucked it into his back pocket. The sound of Thane talking gave Ghanem a moment of relief. *Alive.*

He did a head count as he approached the edge of the camp.

The talking ceased as they all turned. The small fire crackled in the silence. A soft breeze pushed the smoke toward him as if it wanted to shove him away. He wasn't welcome here. Not right now.

"Where's Meera?" His question blended with the words of Carrine and Calliope as they asked the same of him.

"She's not here?"

"Do you see her?" Bevva rolled her eyes.

He didn't care for this particular witch's tone. She had a superior attitude and could stand to be knocked down a few pegs. He started to react, but Calliope placed her hand on his arm. He breathed deeply and turned away from Bevva. "I thought she would have come back here. Obviously I was wrong."

He hadn't failed to notice Thane had stepped away from the group. He should say something to him. But what? What could he possibly say that would make it right between them? He took a deep breath. Something was better than nothing. "Thane, I—I—"

"Don't, Ghanem. He's not ready. Just leave him be for now." Calliope squeezed his arm.

She was right, but he didn't have the luxury of time. He patted her hand before removing it from his arm. He walked to his brother, glaring at Drake and Steffen as they moved to flank Thane. The three of them united? Not surprising, but it still stung.

Thane stood with his arms to his side, his posture as stiff as a body in the morgue. His eyes flashed red, then green. Ghanem could understand the anger, but jealousy? Not all colors meant the same to each guardian, but he was well in tune with his brother's moods, and Thane's eyes reflected the true emotions of the colors. Red—anger, green—jealousy, blue—sorrow, white—hope. It had always been that way with him.

Ghanem swallowed past the lump in his throat. "I was out of control. I never expected that would happen with you, and for that I am truly sorry. I'm messed up, Thane. Beyond messed up. I don't know what to do now. I no longer know what's right. I want to be able to go back to Saharren, whether I get the throne or not. That is no longer important. Family is. You are. I must complete this. I need to find the slayers' source and destroy it." Ghanem scrubbed his face with both hands. He lifted his head and looked Thane in the eye. "But if I do, Meera will die. And I don't know if my soul can bear to be the cause of yet another death." *Nor can my heart take losing her.* He kept the last thought to himself.

*

The darkness wrapped itself around Meera like a cloak of evil, smothering her just as much as the stale air she breathed. She was alone. And thanked God for it. But where and for how long?

Pushing fear to the side, Meera took stock of her surroundings as best she could. Maybe she couldn't see, but she could use her other senses. The air smelled damp. The slight scent of mold mixed with something else. Something she recognized but couldn't quite place. It reminded her of dirty pennies. The ground she lay on was hard and cold with a layer of dust that left her hands feeling gritty. It could be cement, though she didn't think so. Hardened earth, perhaps?

She tried to sit up. The throbbing in her head forced her back down. An image flashed in her mind. Slayers. The knife.

She frantically searched her body for any stab wounds, then took a deep, calming breath when she didn't find any. Maybe they had hit her in the head with the hilt of the knife. That would certainly explain the golf-ball-sized lump that accompanied the throbbing. If only she had some ibuprofen and a tall glass of water.

A smile tugged at the corner of her mouth. She didn't have medication, but she had something better. Much better. Magick. Hope flared. She could use her magick to ease the pain and then get some light in here so she could see what she had to deal with.

Make it stop. Ease the pain so I can feel all right again. She waited for the bass drum to stop pounding in her head, but it only intensified. She grabbed her head with both hands and pushed against her skull. The pain ripped through her like a jackhammer on pavement. *"Make it stop. Ease the pain so I can feel all right again."* Speaking the incantation aloud only made it worse, almost as if her voice had screamed through a megaphone within her mind.

She tried repeatedly to call her magick—incantations in her mind, then spoken aloud, rubbing her fingers together over and over. She stroked her choker, tried everything all at once. Nothing worked. Time stood still and yet seemed to go on and on. The pain along with the darkness . . .

Something had bound her magick. Or someone. This seriously pissed her off. And scared the bejeezus out of her.

She scooted her body until she came up against the wall, then laid her head back down.

Icy tendrils crawled up her skin, covering her body and reaching up toward her throat. A million arctic pinpricks forced her into a ball.

Her imagination went crazy every time she heard the slightest sound. Mice, spiders . . . inhuman creatures. She remembered how the slayer had changed into a grotesque monster, how his eyes had become crazed, his tongue forked. Her stomach cramped as images assaulted her fragile mind.

Something small scurried past. She curled into herself even further and prayed it wouldn't touch her. Still . . . She scratched at her skin, feeling as though all the creatures her mind had created were crawling on her. She tried to still her hands and quiet her thoughts. Silence fell upon her like a scratchy wool blanket, warm but uncomfortable.

Her stomach rumbled with a sound that seemed to echo in the hushed room. Even if they presented her with a seven-course meal, she wouldn't be able to consume it.

The longer she sat there, isolated and shrouded in complete darkness, the more she suspected she was being watched.

Closely.

*

They found the cave almost by accident. Ghanem and the others had been searching for hours, possibly days. In this realm he had no sense of time, only a feeling of urgency that drove him forward, drove him past the fatigue and fear promising to bring him to his knees.

Earlier, after much debate, they'd decided not to split up. Maybe that had been a mistake. Maybe they could have found this place sooner. Pointless to argue about it now. They were here, and his gut confirmed this was the entrance to the underground kingdom.

The mouth of the tunnel loomed in front of them like a grizzly about to devour its prey. Razor-sharp stones shaped like oversized shark teeth jutted out along the circumference in a clear warning to any who didn't belong.

"This should be fun. Know any contortionists? Cause they'd be the only ones who could fit through there." Steffen shook his head and laughed, though the sound held no joy. "Maybe we should see if there's another way in."

"No. This is it."

"And who made you all-knowing, Ghanem?"

"He's right. This is the only entrance. Maybe the three of us"— Carrine gestured to Bevva and Calliope—"can manipulate this somehow. Stand back."

"No."

Carrine's spine went ruler straight. "No?"

"If you use your magick, they'll know we're here."

"You think they don't already know? Seriously, Ghanem, don't be a fool."

Ghanem took a step toward Bevva. "If you don't shut up . . . " His jaw locked in anger.

"You'll what? Huh, big boy? What?" Bevva took two steps forward as if to call his bluff.

"Leave her alone."

Ghanem swung around to look at Thane. These were the first words out of his mouth all day, and they were in defense of the fire-breathing bitch? The only expression he could read on Thane's face was that of determination. Determined to do what? Ghanem sighed internally. Who was he to judge?

He turned back to Bevva and didn't miss the flash of interest in her eyes. Thane and Bevva? Man, he hoped not. "You're probably right." He ignored Bevva's smug smile and continued, "They have the advantage and probably know we're here. We're sorely outnumbered, have no idea what we're stepping into and no clue as to the layout of this place. The only thing we might have on our side is the element of surprise. If there is that chance, are you all willing to give it up?" His eyes made contact with each member of the group as he waited for their answer. *Too many fucking leaders in this club.* "Well?"

Thane cleared his throat. "What do you suggest?"

"The witches can trace themselves inside. One of us will have to go through first"—*the hard way*—"and then come back out and trace the others in one by one."

"You volunteering? I'm not fucking up this body on those rock teeth." Steffen put his hands out in a *look at me* gesture.

Calliope groaned but said nothing. Bevva laughed. She would. She had probably thought the same thing about herself. Those two were meant for each other. Scratch that idea. Too much conceit between the two of them. They'd probably fight each other for a turn in the mirror.

"I can try it, but to be honest, I'm not sure if I can trace," Ghanem said. And it really wasn't something he wanted to attempt in front of the others. He could already hear the remarks if he failed.

"I'll do it."

Surprise, surprise. Drake volunteering for the job? Ghanem hadn't thought he had the balls. Times had certainly changed.

"You sure?" He didn't question Drake's aptitude; he just wanted to make sure he was okay with it. This was going to hurt. Bad.

Drake cracked his neck on both sides. "Yeah. I'm sure."

"We'll go through first. You know, just in case . . . "

Calliope didn't have to finish her sentence. *Just in case* Drake needed some medical attention once he got through. Ghanem had no doubt Calliope would have to use her soothing capabilities soon.

Ghanem walked to the mouth of the cave and crouched low. He squinted into the darkness and listened. It seemed to be clear, but one never knew.

"All right. We better get going. It looks empty. At least in this section. Carrine, go ahead and go through with your girls." He stood to the side of the cave. Not because they needed him to get out of the way, but because he didn't want to feel them going through him. Every entity was different, and he wasn't exactly sure how a witch traced, just that they could only do it alone.

He watched as Carrine, Calliope, and Bevva faded one by one and then reappeared just inside the mouth of the cave. They peered out and seemed no worse for wear. He suppressed an eye roll as Bevva whistled an eerie tune. So much for keeping her quiet. That would probably never happen.

Drake would be the next to go. There was no other way. If—no, when—he made it through, he could come back out and get the rest of them. He looked at the jagged opening again. He did not envy Drake in the least. But he did respect him. Ghanem shook his head. Respect was the last emotion he ever thought he would feel for Drake. Just goes to show how wrong he'd been to judge.

Dressed in black camos and a black tank, Drake approached Ghanem on his right. "Are you sure you want to do this?" Ghanem kept his voice low.

Drake cocked his head. "You think I can't?"

"Not what I meant."

Drake sniffed. "Isn't it?"

"No, Drake, it wasn't. I know you can get through there. It'll hurt like a bitch, but you won't say a word about that. You'll suck it up and take it, and then you'll get the rest of us through." Ghanem shoved his hands in his pockets. "But this isn't your fight. Meera isn't anything to you, nor do you care if I get the throne. I know that. I get it. I'm giving you an out."

"Are you joking, man? I don't bail when it gets a little rough. And you're wrong. She's in trouble and I can help. I will help. And no matter what happened between us back in the day, we're brothers. Maybe not blood like you and Thane, but brothers in kind. I get that. I'm sorry for you that you don't."

Speechless, Ghanem did nothing but stare as Drake crouched in front of the cave, looked at it from all angles, and then shrugged before lifting his right leg and carefully stepping through the opening. The rocks snagged the fabric of his pants and ripped them from knee to groin. Drake pulled his leg back through.

Ghanem sucked in a breath at the close call. Too close to the nads, if you asked him. Drake didn't flinch. He really had misjudged him. Shit. His judgment sucked. Period. If they made it out of this messed up realm in one piece, he would have to do some major internal reevaluation.

Steffen laughed behind him. "You're gonna sing like a girl, Drakina."

Drake cracked his neck, twisted and tried the other leg. Almost the same result—just add blood. He hissed but said no more.

Ghanem wanted to help. Started to speak, but Drake held out both arms, took a deep breath, and then launched himself through the opening headfirst. The tip of each rock grabbed his skin and held on, puncturing the skin before shredding it.

"Fuck. Did you see that?" Steffen ran to the cave, peered in, whistled low.

Thane moved up, too. Shook his head.

Ghanem closed his eyes, mentally called Drake every name under the sun, and then admitted to himself he was indeed impressed. Took some major balls to do what that Drake had just done. Had to be major damage. As in brain damage. "You good, Drake?"

Drake coughed from inside the cave, then poked his head out. Blood dripped from both temples and above his left eyebrow. He blinked hard. "All good."

Yeah. Right. "Then could you please quit fuckin' around and come out here and get us? Time's a-wasting." Sure, he was impressed but not enough to make a major deal out of this. Besides, that would only embarrass the guardian. Not true. He really did need to make some changes. Small personal changes. Starting now. He waited until Drake traced himself back out of the cave before slapping him hard on the back. "Nice job, man."

Drake winced. "Shit, Ghanem. Watch the back."

Ghanem winced, too, once he got a look at Drake's torn body. "Sorry about that."

"No problem. Short on time, right? Let's go." He placed his bloody hand on Ghanem's shoulder and traced him into the cave. "Be right back." He disappeared again.

"He's in pretty bad shape, but he wouldn't let us heal him," Calliope said.

Ghanem shrugged. "Pride."

"Stupidity." Bevva arched a brow.

He refused to nibble on Bevva's bait this time. He turned his back on her and waited the brief moments it took Drake to bring in Thane and Steffen. Already Thane had started to heal, but it still had to hurt like a mother. "Let's go."

As a unit they moved deeper into the cave. The light faded almost immediately, and the opening narrowed. Tight quarters. What fun.

Bevva conjured a few torches and then used her eyes to light them. Once again, despite his opposition to magick, he was impressed. Difference being, this time there would be no compliments. They were forced to walk single file and before long most had to duck. He had a feeling they would all be feeling a little claustrophobic if it weren't for Calliope. He could sense her soothing presence. "Thanks, Calliope."

Though farther back in line, she heard him. "No problem. Just doing my thing."

Maybe, but soothing seriously drained her. Hopefully they would get through this section soon. If she collapsed, someone would have to stay with her. He couldn't afford to lose anyone at this point.

They squeezed around a tight corner. Ghanem wouldn't call it luck—his luck had run out about two centuries ago—but the cave was ending. The walls widened until they had enough room to stand elbow to elbow. One by one, they moved up and formed a tight line. Lemra, the underground kingdom of the slayers, awaited. He'd expected medieval accommodations. He got that but with a contemporary flair.

Floral fields, weeping juniper trees, and a gentle river overflowing with brilliant teal water flanked a castle that would rival those of the past and have the kings and queens of yesterday forming armies to attack and claim it. In the center, a drawbridge and shimmering moat beckoned and forbade at the same time. Everything here seemed contradictory. Beautiful, yet it held an underlying repulsion he couldn't pinpoint.

At least a quarter of a mile stretched between the end of the tunnel and the fortress. Whoever built it had known their craft. The only way to get to the castle would be to walk straight to it. They would be exposed.

A trickle of awareness tiptoed up Ghanem's spine. Their being there was no secret. Most likely had never been one. Bevva had been right. Any plan he could have come up with went out the door as the sound of metal against metal screamed across the open field. The drawbridge slowly lowered, and he saw several slayers just beyond. Fantastic. A fucking welcoming party.

He heard the sound of knuckles being cracked. The guardians were excited and ready to brawl. The witches combined their energy, creating a sizzle of electric magick. His own horns elongated with the promise of a gruesome fight. Sorely outnumbered? Hell, yeah. Did he care? Not in the least.

"I'm gonna torch some of these nasties."

Ghanem looked at Bevva and saw the flames leaping in her eyes like a war dance. Now this he liked. "Light 'em up, Red." His voice sounded ominous even to himself. Good. He'd need every ounce of terrifying he could muster.

"Ghanem?"

At the sound of his brother's voice, he pivoted his head. "Yeah?" Thane's horns hadn't resisted the call either.

"We'll do our best to hold 'em off. Do what you can to make your way through the doors. Meera needs help, and I don't think we'll all get through them anytime soon."

Ghanem swallowed hard, then gave a tight nod. Thane hadn't forgiven him, but he had done the next best thing. He'd acknowledged what Ghanem felt for Meera. He had to get her out of there. More than that, he planned to help her find the source and then let her destroy it. In a short period of time, he'd come to value her life so much more than any throne. Even if it happened to be a life that she wouldn't be spending with him.

More and more slayers poured out of the castle and over the bridge. They stood in rows, combat style. Well trained but fearless? He couldn't tell. The warrior in him didn't care.

"I think I can shield us," Carrine said. "I don't know how long it will hold, but at least it'll get you closer, Ghanem."

Relying on magick? Man, things really had changed. "Do it, Carrine. Hold it for as long as you can. We'll move closer. When you can't hold it anymore, give the signal." Ghanem faced his small but powerful team. "Guardians, rush in and break some balls. Bevva, torch these mothers. Calliope, save your strength. We're gonna need you before this day is over."

The ripple of magick flooded his senses. He couldn't see it, but could feel the push of the barrier Carrine had created. He took a moment to watch her, but for the life of him couldn't figure out how she'd done it. Serenity smoothed Carrine's previously tight mouth. She stared straight forward, but it wasn't with any more intensity than was normal for the elder witch.

Awestruck, he could only imagine how old she was to have perfected her craft this much. He felt a tug in the pit of his stomach and then a squeeze on his heart. Looking at Carrine was like seeing Meera a thousand years from now. Only they called Meera a Luminary, and though he didn't know exactly what that meant, he had no doubt her power would make Carrine's seem like dollar-store magick tricks.

Carrine blinked and then flashed her gaze on him. "Go."

He did as instructed, placing one foot in front of the other. He wanted to run, barrel through the approaching slayers, but the barrier held him back. He could only walk as fast as Carrine since she controlled the invisible wall. He hoped there was a method to her madness, because dammit, slugs crawled faster than this. Meera couldn't have much time left.

Refusing to allow himself to think about what they slayers could be doing to her, he focused on the mission. Right now his only goal was to help her live so she could become the witch they needed her to be. He scoffed at their ignorance. They had no clue. Meera was already perfect in every sense of the word. Mind, body, and spirit. Too bad it had taken him so long to figure that out.

"They're almost here," Steffen whispered.

Bevva sighed. "Way to state the obvious. As if none of us has eyes." She smacked Steffen on the back of his head.

He growled deep in his throat.

Thane grabbed Steffen's left horn and pulled his head around until they were eye to eye. "I wouldn't do what you're thinking, Steff."

Steffen whipped his head out of Thane's grasp. "Then tell your bitch to keep her hands off me."

Ghanem gritted his teeth and backtracked to step between the two of them as Thane's eyes glowed violent red. He nodded to Calliope. She walked behind Thane and placed a hand on his shoulder. The red faded, but not as quickly as they all would have liked.

Smack!

The feud disintegrated immediately as the first line of slayers bounced off the barrier and landed hard on their asses.

Drake, Steffen and Bevva laughed until the slayers transformed. Their perfect and almost heavenly appearance disappeared.

Steffen cocked his head. "What the fuck?"

Chapter Twenty-Seven

Meera kept her lashes twined and her breathing even. Through the narrow opening of her lids, she saw a pair of tall, brown boots laced up the front. The sound of her pounding heart echoed in her ears if not the room. An open door let in just enough light for her to make out the details of her jail. The coppery smell she couldn't place before no longer remained a mystery.

Blood.

Blood, not all of it dry, covered every inch of the room. She had to wonder if any of it belonged to her. Why hadn't she noticed how sticky the floor had been? Maybe more than just her magick had been restricted.

"I'm not obtuse, witch. I know you're awake. Get up." The voice bounced off the walls and surrounded her with its evil timbre.

She squeezed her eyes shut. They popped wide open as that boot came crashing down on her hand. Like putting out a cigarette, he moved his foot side to side until her bones crunched.

Having no idea if her tormentor got off on fear or strength, she rolled the dice and assumed the former. Even with shock waves of pain shooting up her arm, she bit down on her lip to keep from crying out.

"Get. Up."

Finally she lifted her head. "I can't. You're standing on my hand," Meera gritted out between clenched teeth.

He smiled. Even more beautiful than the others, this slayer's aura was the darkest of all. His hair hung over his shoulder in a long, white braid bound by leather. His blue eyes sparkled nearly as much as his perfect white teeth. His clothing screamed quality, and his stance exuded superiority. "You must be Ryken." Though she hadn't meant it as a question, he answered.

"King Ryken."

He placed so much emphasis on the word *king* she knew she'd hit a sore spot. Maybe she could find a way to make that work to her advantage. "Well, Ryken, if you would get your boot off of me, I'd—"

His hand connected with her mouth, cutting off her words. Once again, she refused to cry out but couldn't stop the blood that flowed from her split lip. Obviously, sarcasm wouldn't work to her advantage. What would? Probably begging. Would she stoop that low? No. Not yet, anyway. She hoped not. Funny how her conviction had already begun to wane. A little throbbing in her hand and some hunger pains, and already defeat seemed forthcoming. She hated that. Hated *Ryken* for making her feel that way.

Ryken wrapped his hand around her hair and pulled her up until she stood on her feet. She'd always loved her hair. Now she wished she'd shaved it bald.

He leaned in, whispered in her ear. "You smell bad and you're filthy. But I can see the beauty beneath it all. We're going to get you cleaned up. Then you'll give me exactly what I want. You'll be the best yet."

His forked tongue licked her lobe. Meera gagged. *Oh, God.* It had been him all along. Watching. Her instinct had been dead. What a skeev. When this was over, she'd stand under hot water until her skin peeled off. Maybe a skin graft or two would make her feel clean again.

Ryken kept his hand entangled in her hair as he dragged her out of the blood-soaked room. She could only imagine the horrors that happened within the confines of these walls. Her broken hand must seem like child's play to him.

The difference between the room she had just left and the hallway was staggering. Gilded walls and white marble floors set the tone. Mirrored doors were spaced about every twelve feet or so. The image of Ryken pulling her behind him mocked her with each passing door. How very reminiscent of caveman days. He had her body turned so her back was to his. He pulled hard and she tried to plant her feet, but the slick marble made her attempts useless. The only satisfaction she had was watching the blood trail she left behind as it practically poured from her lip onto the pristine floor. Not so pristine now. Her satisfaction didn't last long.

Two women dressed in white stepped out from another room. One had a bucket, the other held two mops. Both briefly lifted their heads long enough to look at her before dropping their gaze and cleaning the floor with sure, even strokes.

One look had told so much, though. Eyes void of any emotion, any spirit. Soulless. Dead. Sheer terror raced through her system. Would that be her future?

Not if she had anything to say about it. Reaching up with her good hand, she tried to pry his grip out of her hair and then resorted to scratching at his hand with her nails. He laughed. His hand didn't budge. She kicked and screamed, called for help. The two women never gave her a second glance. No one came.

Ryken stopped and opened another door. He shoved her inside with enough force to send her flying to the other side of the room. She hit the far wall and collapsed in a heap.

"Undress," Ryken commanded. Rather than enter the room, he stood on the threshold eyeing her.

"No."

"Must we play this game? While your spirit is captivating, your attitude is tiresome." He crossed his arms and leaned against the doorjamb.

Ghanem had been the last person to see her naked. While still seriously pissed at him, she didn't want anything to taint that memory. There had to be a way to get out of this. Somehow making a deal with this beautiful but evil creature no longer held any sort of appeal. How had she ever thought she might actually welcome the dark side?

Ryken shifted his weight and stepped back. Cold water dripped onto her head. She looked up. Icy water began to pour from a shower system reminiscent of a gas chamber. She drew her legs up and wrapped her arms around them. Her teeth chattered. His idea of cleaning her up equaled torture in her book. No way in hell would she strip in front of him. No freakin' way. "L-leave and sh-shut the door. I'll undress and sh-sh-shower."

He smiled and shook his head, but did as she asked. Once the door clicked, she tried to stand. The force and temperature of the water made it difficult, and her legs had already been shaky. She wasn't the idiot he thought. Just as she knew he had watched her before, she also knew even though the door had been closed and there were no windows, he still watched. At least she didn't have to see his ogling eyes. Oh, how she wanted to get this over and done with.

Meera quickly stripped, covered her breasts with one hand and forearm and the apex of her thighs with her broken one. Miraculously—or not—the water warmed. Her body relaxed against her will, and some of the tension left her tight shoulders. Having no idea what view Ryken had, she didn't know which way to turn. Didn't really matter. She removed her hands and let the water rinse away most of the grime. She scanned the enormous stall and found the soap in the corner. She grabbed it and then used her good hand to lather her body, instantly feeling a little better after removing the smell of him from her body. She paid special attention to the ear he'd licked. *Gross.*

But even acid wouldn't cleanse her of the fact that he stood on the outside watching. Probably getting off. *Sick perv.*

She forced the horrid image from her mind and focused on her hair, having found the shampoo in the same corner as the soap. Funny she hadn't noticed earlier. In fact, she was fairly certain it hadn't been there when she'd reached for the soap. Apparently, she was the only one of the two who couldn't use magick, which really pissed her off.

The warm water continued to lull her tight muscles, but her hand refused to stop hurting. The throbbing only intensified as the water pounded down. So much for quick healing. She lifted her arm and watched the colors of a bruise take form—yellow, purple, black, and then a deep blue. She held the other hand up for comparison. The broken one looked twice the size.

As soon as she rinsed the last suds from her hair, the water shut off. More proof he lurked out there. And if not him, someone. When she would have reached for her wet clothes, a veil of steam approached as if it were an actual entity, enveloping her in a type of cocoon. It swirled around her body in eerie waves, taking form before slinking away and then back again.

It is time.

She whirled. "Who's there?" The steam continued to swirl. Became thicker. The mist obscured her view until she saw nothing but the white sheet it created.

It issss time. The voice, different this time, hissed instead of whispered.

An image of Ryken's tongue, slayer tongues in general, invaded her head, and she finally knew whom the dark voice belonged to. It had been them all along. They needed her for something. Something dark. Surely, the council must have known this, yet they still sent her here, to the very place that had been threatening her sanity. What kind of game did they play?

The steam began to dissipate, thinning and then fanning out to the edges of the room before completely disappearing as if being sucked out by a vacuum. Her gaze darted around the room, finally landing on her own body, which had somehow been covered in a sheer white dress. She shuddered. It reminded her of the women she'd seen in the hallway. Only Meera's dress had crystal jewels adorning the neckline in a halter-like fashion. Her choker lay flat and useless against her skin.

The door swung open. Three slayers, in their true form, stepped into the room. Squeezing her eyes shut and pretending this was all part of a sick and twisted nightmare was not an option. She couldn't fight if she couldn't see. She had no weapons, no magick, and no backup. It shouldn't have hurt or even be a surprise to feel so alone, but it did. Painfully so.

Meera straightened her shoulders and lifted her chin. Their ugly orbs roamed over her body. Nothing remained hidden behind the transparent gown.

Slayer number one stepped forward. Flakes of dead skin fell off his body like the bark on a peeling white birch tree. He didn't flinch. "He issss ready for you, my queen." He continued toward her until he stood only inches from her body. He reached out with both hands.

It took every ounce of determination she could muster, but Meera didn't move a muscle.

He reached behind her and pulled a sheer hood over her head. Odd. If he wanted her covered, he needed to put her in something a bit more substantial. Then it hit her. Ryken had adorned her in his sick version of a cloak. One a witch would wear on her wedding night. And the slayer had called her queen. *No, no, no, no, no,* her mind screamed, and her body flew backward, desperate for escape. Yet there was nowhere to go.

Number One grabbed her wrist. Two and Three grabbed her other wrist and her ankles, lifting off her feet and carrying her from the room. She kicked, thrashed, and cursed them to high hell, all to no avail. Her dress parted and cool air met her damp skin. The throbbing in her hand moved up her arm.

Meera turned her head and threw up all over Number One. Or was it Two? Whoever it was dropped her arm when he jumped back, throwing them all off balance. She went crashing to the floor and took three slayers with her.

*

Ghanem had made it through the onslaught of slayers. Once he'd seen them in their natural form he'd gone full guardian. Carrine had gotten him as close as she could before her power had been stressed to the limit. She'd nodded for him to go, and that was exactly what he he'd done, charging through the masses, tossing many over his shoulders, slamming his fists into their throats. The sounds of battle were behind him now, though he didn't know for how long. The count was six to hundreds, maybe even thousands. He felt guilty about that but had to move past if it he was going to save Meera.

Pressing his back firmly against the inner wall, he paused to catch his breath. He had crossed the drawbridge and now hid just inside the entryway. Hard muscles bunched beneath his skin with each ragged breath he took. More than anything he wanted to charge through the halls and demand to be taken to Meera. Instead, he took stock of his surroundings. Exposed, whitewashed stone walls surrounded him. Several branching corridors he assumed led to the different wings of the structure bordered the entrance. Which one to take?

He turned to his left, took a deep breath before repeating the same action to the right. She'd shared her body with him. He could track her. The gods had given them that gift as yet another way to protect loved ones.

When Meera's scent permeated his nostrils, his heart jerked a second before he took off. He rolled his eyes at the overdone opulence of the décor. Hell, this was only the hallway, and you could practically peel the riches off the walls. Though if he had to live a life looking like one of the creatures he'd just fought, he too would surround himself with excess beauty.

He'd turned a corner to follow her scent when a thought popped into his mind. How were the slayers transforming themselves from gross to angelic? Magick could never be enough without . . . there had to be some sort of ritual or . . . *Shit*. He couldn't believe it had taken him so long to figure it out.

Whatever they had to do to convert themselves would be considered the source, and said source had to be destroyed. In Chicago, they had been able to lure the human women away from the club because they looked like humans. Unbelievably attractive humans. And they brought the women here. Why? And where were they now? For that matter, where were the slayers? They couldn't all be outside. Any good army would leave enough men on the inside to protect the women and elders. And of course their leader.

But he hadn't seen any women, elders, or humans since they'd arrived in Lemra.

Meera's scent hit him full on as he passed one of the mirrored doors. He staggered back from the intensity of it. He smelled more than just her. He smelled her blood. His hand shook as he grabbed the knob and turned it to open the door. The sight of the bloody room was like a knife gouging his heart. It appeared to be some sort of torture chamber without the machines. No tools, no chains. Just a bare room covered in blood. And some of it belonged to Meera.

Ghanem refused to believe she was dead. He'd have to see her body with his own eyes to believe that. Backing out of the room, he slammed the door shut. He continued down the hall, past the mirrored doors and came across two women as they cleaned vomit off the marble floor. They'd ignored him even as he stooped next to the mess to smell it.

He wouldn't have thought the contents of someone's stomach would relieve him, yet this did. There was no doubt in his mind Meera had passed through here and gotten sick on her way. In his mind, this proved she lived or at least had been alive after she'd left that hell room.

"Where is she?" he asked from his crouched position.

When no one answered, he looked over his shoulder at the two women. They stood to the side with their heads down, obviously waiting for him to move so they could continue their task. They could have been twins with their long, dark hair and bronzed skin. The way their shoulders hunched made him feel sorry for them. He stood, grabbed one by the shoulders, and gave her a gentle shake. "Please. I need your help. Where is the one who did this?" He looked into her eyes but there was no one there. Not really. They should have at least shown fear. Most did when coming face to face with a guardian. But only emptiness stared back at him and he knew, *knew* he no longer only had to help Meera, but had to help all these innocents.

"It's okay," he told her. "I'll try to get you out of here." But was it too late? This thought he kept to himself. With a last nod, he continued down the hallway.

He hadn't gone much farther when he heard gothic organ music somewhere in the distance. With each step, the music grew louder. Though he couldn't quite make out the tune, it seemed oddly familiar.

Rather than give everything away, Ghanem retracted his horns and took several even breaths to bring his body down. He would go in as Ghanem. When it became necessary and would work to the most advantage, then and only then would he unleash all his power and go full beast on them. He rounded another corner and the music intensified, filling his ears with resonating chords of that song that continued to elude.

Double doors with ornately carved cherry wood were the only things standing between him and seeing Meera again. He believed this to be true with every fiber of his being. What he didn't know was what shape she would be in.

He fisted his hands around the long steel handles of the doors. The coolness of the metal couldn't soothe his heated blood. He pulled and was forced to step back as he opened them.

The huge room held rows of wooden church pews flanking a long aisle. A gold-colored carpet had been rolled out and covered the length of the walkway. Ghanem took in the seemingly endless rows of slayers—young, old, women, some in the grotesque form he had seen outside the castle and some in the human-like form he'd continually encountered. At the end of the gold carpet, he saw a white, gauzy dress—indecent in its transparence. He swallowed past the huge lump forming in his throat as his gaze followed the silhouette of legs he knew all too well.

Finally his eyes met hers. If it weren't for the door handles he still held in his hands, he'd have fallen to his knees.

"Ah. The fallen one has chosen to join us."

Ghanem shifted his attention to glare at the being next to Meera. The other slayers had been attractive, but none compared to the beauty of this one. His features, so intense, almost blinded Ghanem. He wore his blond hair in a twisted pattern atop his head and had adorned it with a jeweled crown. Dressed in a white tuxedo and white Italian loafers, this had to be the leader. Ghanem actually laughed inside at the audacity of the slayer's style.

He laughed until he looked at Meera again. No amusement twinkled in those amethyst eyes. No sadness. No fear. Resignation swam in the depths, and that tore at his soul. Why hadn't she used her magick to get herself out of this horrid situation? Her choker answered that question. The amethysts no longer sparkled with power. The necklace, once vibrant and full of endless potential lay against her pale flesh, tarnished and dull, echoing what he had seen in her eyes. Her magick was gone.

His gaze flew back and forth between Meera and whom he now knew to be Ryken. She wore a white gown. He wore a white tux. She held a bouquet of dead roses. He held a smug smile on his perfect face. And then the song that had continued to elude Ghanem started up again, and he had more clarity in that moment than he had ever had or ever wanted.

The organ music swelled with the overused bridal march song played in church after church, weekend after weekend. *Dum, dum, dee-dum. Here Comes the Bride* screamed through his mind. And even though this was a bogus-ass wedding, jealousy consumed him. She belonged to him. He should be standing beside her.

"Meer—"

An object pressed against his neck a split second before his body convulsed with each volt of electricity. His head flew back and his back bowed. His hands slid from the door handles as he fell forward. They continued to shock him. He tried to summon his guardian. They increased the voltage until he spasmed on the floor. Ryken laughed and Ghanem sensed Meera drifting even farther into herself, and there wasn't a damn thing he could do about it.

The next thing Ghanem knew, his arms and legs were bound, the stretch of his shoulders hot with pain. They'd tied him like this, wrists to ankles, so he would look submissive and he hated them for it.

"Wakey, wakey." Ryken clucked his tongue. "You're delaying our beautiful ceremony. It's rather rude to black out for so long. We can't proceed without you being one of our witnesses."

Ghanem looked around. Same room, same scene. The organ, which sounded more like background music now, continued to play, though the song was different. *Thank you.* Meera stood in the same spot. He tried to make eye contact, but someone behind him held the Taser to his neck. If he didn't lower his head, they'd squeeze the trigger and zap his ass again. *Fuck.* He wasn't a submissive, but being almost catatonic wouldn't help Meera. So, yeah, he lowered his head and played the part, all the while trying to come up with a way to get them both out of this messed up situation.

"I am King Ryken, and this lovely creature next to me is about to become the Queen of Lemra. Initially that wasn't my plan, but as they often do, plans change. Originally I planned to have you both slaughtered. But then I saw her, really *saw* her, and all this beauty should not be wasted."

Ghanem wanted to jump out of his skin and strangle the motherfucker.

"Add the power in with the beauty, and we finally have someone worthy of sitting in the throne next to mine. Right now she's confused. Has been for some time. While I don't understand it, she's torn between the light and the dark. It's an obvious choice, really. One that is no longer hers to make. Once we are wed, all decisions will be mine to make, and she will do my bidding."

Keep talking, you sick fuck. The longer he talked, the longer Ghanem would have to gather his strength. He could feel the urge now, just under his skin. A current, a ripple of awareness as his inner guardian clawed its way to the surface. *Not yet.*

"That's how it works. The wedding is a mere formality. It's the sexual binding that will change her. She will be mine to do with as I please. The humans? I'll still need them. Yes, I can't stand to see my brethren as less than perfect. The humans are a necessity to my wellbeing. But my queen? Ah, yes, with her I will be the most powerful being in all the realms."

He stepped forward, nudged Ghanem's head up with the toe of his boot. "Because I prefer to be honest, I can't have my queen coming into this partnership with any questions or doubts." He stepped back and withdrew a knife from a sheath at his side. "Why don't you tell the witch why you were banished? It's a great story. Please, please, tell us all about your dirty secret." He wrapped his arm around Meera's neck and held the blade to her jugular.

Chapter Twenty-Eight

"Tell us, guardian, or she dies." Ryken flicked the blade enough to draw blood. The tip of his forked tongue quivered as he lapped up the droplets from Meera's skin.

More than a little shell-shocked, she shuddered internally and watched as Ghanem's gaze turned crimson. Even if she could call out to him, she wouldn't. She hadn't seen a way out, and rather than bear witness to the dark path being chosen for her, the path she now realized was wrong and evil and totally not for her, she'd done the only thing she could do to protect herself. Retreat. She'd withdrawn so far, searching for a place where she could find even a semblance of comfort. Anything to get her away from him. But Ryken had known. He'd watched her closely, pushed at her until he'd backed her so far into the corner she was almost on the other side of life.

Death.

Only this existence wasn't as clear-cut as that. She didn't cease to breathe, cease to exist. Instead she'd become a shell, and Ryken now had free rein to manipulate her and, she assumed, her magick.

But like in death, she felt the cold. Where Ghanem had given her so much heat, Ryken was his polar opposite. Even as he held the blade against her throat, ice crystals in her veins stabbed her with frosty tips. She prayed for numbness that never came.

She looked out through eyes that now belonged to a stranger, yet what she saw wasn't a stranger at all. Ghanem. She'd already forgiven him. Over and over again. He didn't know. She couldn't tell him. So he'd judged her? Big deal. In the scheme of things, he'd done no more than the equivalent of rolling his eyes at a bad joke. Not that she considered herself a joke. Not at all. But when she put the fight into perspective against the being they now fought against, that was exactly how she felt. And hadn't she done the same to him? Casting judgment by comparing him to a demon when she really understood so little about any of the veiled beings?

She looked at him now from behind the mask, behind the edge of death, and almost wished Ryken would pull the thin metal across her neck, because worse than being stuck within this shell was seeing Ghanem tied up and on his knees in front of Ryken. So wrong. Those roles should have been reversed. Ryken was less than nothing. Ghanem was more than everything. And now Ryken would force him to tell his past. She wanted to know. Had always wanted to know. The difference was, she wouldn't have forced it out of him. The story was his to tell when he was ready. Just as hers was. If she could go back . . .

His gaze searched for her now, a desperate longing in the depths of his once-chocolate eyes. Yes, she could see him, but he didn't know it. No, thanks to Ryken, who earlier had been kind enough to place her in front of a mirror, Meera knew exactly the image Ghanem saw, and it wasn't pretty. Vacant eyes had stared back at her as her soul struggled to remain hers. Ryken and his black magic crushed and tortured minds until there was nothing left but an unoccupied and used body. Meera's mind might have been fragile, but she'd refused to let him suck her soul into a black abyss, no matter how hard he probed. Instead, she'd run internally, fled the mind torture. Ultimately, that small glimpse into his mirror had sped up her retreating process.

But she'd seen something else, too. Ryken hadn't been aware she wasn't quite *gone* when he'd shoved the curtain aside to reveal a floor-to-ceiling mirror. No, not quite gone, but almost . . . She had seen so much. And what she'd seen had hope hanging on for dear life when what she feared most was retreating too far and not being able to pull herself back. Struggling to remain balanced and not teeter over the edge to a totally catatonic state, she silently pleaded for her captor to leave Ghanem alone.

"I will tell her. Lower the knife, Ryken."

He wrapped his free hand around her hair and tugged, exposing the length of her neck. "King Ryken," he said between clenched teeth.

Her spine made an odd popping sound as he twisted and held her head at an angle. No pain. Just cold. She supposed that was one advantage to retreating. Maybe the only one. To distract herself from the dark thoughts, Meera focused on the pulse beating in Ghanem's throat. As long as he breathed, she would do whatever Ryken wanted.

Still, the urge to fight rallied. From within, her tiny safe place tried to wrap her in warmth, a feeling of lukewarm liquid sliding by, but the effort cost her, and she slumped against Ryken. His knife slipped.

Ghanem's veins bulged in his neck, exposing the accelerated beat of his pulse. There must have been more blood though she couldn't feel it. The words poured out of his mouth of their own accord. Her mistake had cost him.

"I was young. Young enough to think I knew it all. Cocky enough to be a fool. Her name was Antonia and I was enthralled. Thinking with my cock, which at the time was synonymous with my heart." He swallowed. "I now know the difference."

Satisfied his pulse was steady, Meera focused on the intensity in his eyes as they silently pleaded with her. *I hear you.* She had to believe he knew that. Ryken kicked out with his boot, landing a hard blow to Ghanem's shoulder.

Ghanem continued without flinching. "She wove her tales as beautifully as she wove black magick. Those around me knew what she was doing. Tried to warn me. I wouldn't listen. Not to any of them . . . " He trailed off.

"Get on with it. Your story is dragging. Let's kick it up a notch, shall we?" Ryken emphasized the word *kick* with another of his own. This time to Ghanem's jaw.

Something inside Meera snapped. Anger coiled around her safe place, widening it, allowing her a little more room to breathe. But it wasn't enough. Not nearly enough.

She screamed for Ghanem to stop. She didn't need to hear

what had happened. Obviously, it pained him to remember the details. Her screams went unheard to anyone on the outside. But Meera heard every one of them as they whipped around inside her head, searching for an escape. *I'm here. I'm here.*

"Dominic, my father, had ordered me to watch over my mother and sister while he was away on family business. When he returned, my training would resume. I was to take over his throne when I came of age. I am the eldest son. It is . . . was my right."

He dropped his head.

Please don't give up on me, Ghanem. I am here.

"I hadn't planned to be gone long. Antonia sent me a message. Wanted me to meet her in the meadow. How could I resist? A tryst? In the middle of the day? I went. I met her and we made love. Not once. No, that wasn't enough for her. She begged me for more and I felt larger than life. I gave her everything she asked for in that meadow. I could see our home. I knew everyone was fine."

"Ah, finally. This is where it gets good. Tell her. Tell her what you found when you returned from your *tryst*."

She didn't want to know. Already prickles of dread teased her senses.

"I floated across that meadow, high on lust disguised as love. The air seemed thick, different somehow, but I paid no heed. I was a man on cloud nine. When I reached the edge and stepped onto the path that led to our entryway, I heard a pop and the thick, heavy air vanished. Our front door . . . I was certain it had been closed. Certain. But it stood open. An invitation I wanted to decline, but I couldn't. I ran . . . ran up the steps and into the house. Furniture was overturned, paintings torn."

Nausea hit Meera full force. She needed to comfort him. Reassure him he wasn't alone. She couldn't move. If she could have, she would have held her hands against her ears and run. Run away from this ugly tale, this ugly world. She'd take Ghanem with her and help him forget. Instead she was forced to hear the rest . . .

*

"I pushed through the destruction until I reached my parents' room." Ghanem took a moment and tried to distance himself from the memories. The images were so clear, as if a movie played before him in high definition. A horror movie in which he happened to be the star. Bile seared his throat, leaving a thick residue that tasted of death.

"Blood flowed from beneath the door. I saw my reflection in the puddle at my feet and wondered why I didn't quite recognize the eyes looking back at me. Already they were haunted, and I had yet to enter the room. Didn't yet know what I would find beyond the closed door. But I did know. I knew it would be horrible, and that I would never be the same. None of us would.

"I pushed the door open and stared into my mother's lifeless eyes as my sister held her on the bed, rocking her like *she'd* been rocked as a babe. They had taken nothing other than my father's most prized possessions. His wife and the innocent heart of his only daughter. And where was I?" Helpless to stop them. The tears fell. He hadn't cried in a century, and he hated Ryken for making him remember. But he hated himself more.

"I was fucking a warped witch a hundred yards from the house while my father's enemies came in and butchered his wife while his daughter stood watching. Her power was illusion and I fell for it. And she'd done it all for a handful of fucking trinkets."

He hadn't spoken of that day in almost two centuries. It could have happened yesterday. The pain. The guilt. He'd seen how lost Amella and Thane had become with the knowledge their mother was no longer there. Not just gone. But dead. Tortured and dead. Amella had screamed for days. And then Dominic. The crushing blow of his fist had been the least of what Ghanem had deserved. He'd taken it. Would've taken it over and over again for the chance to remain with the family. But Dominic had been unable to look at him again. Unable to forgive. Ghanem couldn't blame him. To this day, he couldn't forgive himself. The fact that Amella and

Thane had was something he'd never understand. Never.

"So you killed your mother for a romp between a witch's thighs. Pitiful, don't you think, my queen?"

Ghanem's eyes flicked to Meera with the word *queen*. A queen, yes, but not Ryken's. He hoped she understood that. His fists clenched when he noticed her lips had moved. This was the first movement he'd seen from her since he'd been carried through the door.

Even as he tried to squash it, hope bloomed in his chest. It didn't make the memories any easier, but if he could ensure Meera had a future, maybe then he could start to make amends to others. To himself.

No sound escaped, but he tried to read her lips. Nothing made sense until . . . *Yes*. He had heard something. A whisper. Just a whisper.

"What's that, my queen? Is there something you'd like to say?" Ryken wrenched her head back.

Anger surging, Ghanem had nothing but death on his mind. The bastard held Meera so close his breath made her blink. His guardian called to him, and this time he didn't even try to hold it back. No. This time he encouraged it.

"I. Am. Not. Your. Fucking. Queen." She pulled back her head and slammed it into Ryken's.

Ghanem roared to life as Ryken stumbled back, a look of surprise on his pale face. His knife tumbled to the ground. He hadn't released his hold on her hair, but Meera didn't let that stop her. She head-butted him again and brought her knee up at the same time. Ryken fell to the ground, bringing Meera with him.

Atta girl. He silently cheered her on. His horns elongated and twirled over his head. He twisted his neck until it cracked. The slayers behind him gasped.

Taking a page from Meera's book, he rammed his head backward, making contact with whoever happened to be there. The spatter of their blood hit the back of his head.

Ghanem threw an elbow. Welcomed the sting. Heard the moan. He kept his focus on Meera as she struggled to untangle herself from Ryken. Fucker had a death grip on her hair, and it didn't look as though he would relent anytime soon, even though he was in obvious pain. At least she had nailed his ass.

Still hogtied, he wouldn't be able to get to her unless he could release his bindings. Ghanem twisted his arms this way and that, yet the rope wouldn't budge, only sliced into his skin more and more. Magick. Had to have been reinforced with magick. That would be the only reason he couldn't break free. In full guardian state, breaking the rope should have been as easy as a child snapping a twig. Could Meera undo this magick with some of her own?

"Meera?" Ryken had her on her knees and held his hand inches from her face as some sort of power coursed through his hand in bright white waves. He couldn't tell if it came directly from Ryken or if he was siphoning it from Meera.

"Meera. I know you can hear me. I know you're in there. I need you to help me so I can help you. Find your magick, Meera. Find it and use it." He continued to fight against his bonds as he spoke to her. He kept his voice low, soothing, encouraging.

Someone grabbed him. Pushed his face to the ground and held him there. It nearly tore his skin off to do so, but he turned to his side so he could keep his gaze fixed on Meera. Her skin turned pallid and blood continued to flow in a slow but steady stream from the knife wound on her neck, dripping onto the floor and pooling in front of her. He felt her tiring, fading, submitting.

"Damn it, witch. Don't you dare leave again. Find your magick. You are the strongest one here," he yelled. "I need you, *polipo*." Scream, kick, fight. He didn't give a fuck what she did as long as she did something. Anything to keep her from giving up and dying. If Meera died, he would, too. Without her he would be nothing. Nothing but someone who constantly failed those he loved. He did love her. Probably had since he first saw her in that dingy bar. It seemed a lifetime ago.

She stopped fighting, slid off her knees and onto her side. They lay not two feet from each other on the gold carpet stained by her blood.

He stared hard into her eyes, begging her to stay awake. Stay with him. He never anticipated the blow. Darkness faded in and out like a neon light on the fritz. On, off. On, off. They hit him again, and he knew he might not recover from that hit. The darkness consumed him, making him very tired. Still, he fought. Fought for her to live. "Find your magick, Meera. It's . . . in the light. I . . . love—"

*

Follow the light within the wind; shut out the darkness for it has sinned. Follow the light within the wind; shut out the darkness for it has sinned.

Beautiful singing. Two voices. One feminine, one masculine. Their voices were like a bandage to her wounded soul. One was her mother. The mother she had never met, yet she could hear her clearly, and, for a moment, it was almost as if she had always been there. Always been a part of her life.

The other voice was that unique mix of new country and old whiskey. Before the singing had started, he'd been trying to tell her something. She wanted to listen, but had only heard bits and pieces. Something about finding her magick and love. What did one have to do with the other?

A breeze skimmed her cheeks, and her eyes fluttered open. Ryken was no longer there, but Ghanem so close she could almost touch him. Meera reached out to do so. She was so tired, as if she'd been sick for years, bedridden. She took a deep breath and stretched her fingers. She could just touch the tip of his horn—a horn that had once terrified her enough she'd run. Now she wanted nothing more than to cradle his head in her lap and caress his horns.

He didn't move. At all. Frantic, she focused on his chest. Counted to twenty. It rose and fell. She counted again. This time she made it to forty before he took another breath. *No, no, no.* She couldn't let him die with his last thought of a mistake he'd made when he'd been young. The mistake was not his. Terrible people had done terrible things to his family, but he was not to blame. They'd not only taken his mother from him, they'd also taken everyone he loved and, in the process, stripped him of his very life. They were at fault. Not the man before her. He had a brother and sister who loved him very much, yet he hadn't been allowed to see them. She could only imagine how that tortured his soul.

Her breath quickened, racing from her chest in ragged pants. He'd never once told her why he was here to fight the slayers. She had her reasons and had only recently shared them with him. But, really, there could only be one reason he would be here, with the brother he hadn't seen in more than two hundred years. He was here to get his life back. She could only assume if he defeated the slayers, stopped the source, he would get to go home. Maybe even get the chance to seek forgiveness from his father.

Why hadn't he told her how important this was to him? Had he tried? Had she not listened?

She had no family to go back to. He did. "Wake up, Ghanem." Her voice sounded raspy, as if she had swallowed gravel. "Please wake up. I can help you." With one finger, she stroked his horn and considered how she could help him. Having had a glimpse at the source, an idea of how to destroy it began to formulate. Ryken had showed her a simple mirror, and she had seen so much more than just her own battered body. She had seen the room beyond. The room with the cocoons. The room in which ugly slayers entered, but only beautiful ones left. That room smelled of fear, sex, and victory, so much of it the walls actually throbbed.

With her finger touching his horn, she used her energy to push her body closer to his. Where had Ryken gone? Did he think they were both dead? She couldn't worry about him right now, nor could she worry about the slayers seated in the pews talking amongst themselves.

Meera pushed her face through the warm blood that lay between her and Ghanem. Breathless, she gave a final thrust and grabbed for Ghanem's hand.

Heat flowed through their joined hands and up her arm the instant she made contact. She welcomed the burn that gave her hope he still had life left in him. Holding tight to his hand, she pulled her body closer.

"Tsk, tsk. What do you think you're doing?"

Meera froze. The condescending voice of Jayson was unmistakable.

"Ryken is ready for his bride in the other room. He's had something made just for the two of you. You better appreciate it."

She didn't dare speak, instead concentrating on the emotions coursing through her. Ghanem had always been able to sense her feelings, and now she would do everything she could to let him know what he meant to her. Fire blazed under her skin but she didn't let go. What she did do was bear down. Meera forced the magick furling deep in her belly to uncoil.

Seemingly out of nowhere, a gust of wind whipped through the room and knocked Jayson off his feet. He landed flat on his back on top of Meera's legs. Ignoring the pain, she held tight to Ghanem and tried to push her love into his heart.

Out of the corner of her eye, she watched Jayson gather his wits and stand before reaching down and wrapping his arms around her waist. He planted his feet and pulled. Meera's dress ripped across the middle. She held strong. Another blast of wind rolled past her body. Where the hell had it come from?

Jayson swore out rapid commands as yet another gale blasted through the room. He held his ground this time and lifted her off the floor with some help from members of the army. Meera's fingers began to slip.

"Ghanem!"

They tore her from him and shoved her toward the door. The

wind swirled around her like a cyclone, causing her hair to shoot out from her head in Medusa-like waves. The locks tangled above her head, the wind nearly pulling the hair out of her scalp.

She broke free and lunged for Ghanem. Falling next to him, Meera wrapped her body around his. If they took her, they'd have to take him, too. Intense heat ripped through her body. Her choker crackled and sizzled against her neck. The metal threatened to sear her skin. Inch by inch, she pulled herself closer to his motionless form while slayer after slayer pulled and tugged on her body.

Legs wrapped around Ghanem's hips, one arm around his neck, the other his torso, she brought her face to his. "I love you, warrior," she whispered before touching her lips to his.

The wind wailed and lifted her and Ghanem's limp form off the floor while knocking down every slayer within ten feet. Meera didn't stop kissing him, pressing her mouth against his until finally his lips began to move. The swirling air stole her breath away as she gasped when he deepened the kiss. They rotated in the wind. Anxious, she kissed him back as if there were no tomorrow, because chances were, neither of them would survive the next hour.

Dizzy and breathless, she begrudgingly broke the kiss to stare into chocolate-brown eyes.

"You love me?"

Purple embers swirled within the cylcone. Her magick was back. Ghanem had given her back what the others had stolen. "I do love you. Very much." The wind howled relentlessly, but they only had to whisper to hear each other.

"I killed my mother, Meera." He touched his forehead to hers. "I don't deserve your love."

"You didn't kill your mother. Even if you had been there you couldn't have stopped them. There were too many. They were too strong. You were just a boy."

He didn't say anything so she continued. "If you defeat the slayers, do you get to go home?"

Tortured eyes locked on hers. The intensity threatened to break her heart; his words threatened to take her soul. "It doesn't matter. You will destroy the source. You will live. That's what's important."

Refusing to be deterred by words that meant so much, Meera asked, "What does the letter say about the source?" To be having this conversation in the midst of a tornado normally would have seemed impossible or fantastical. Yet, now, after everything they'd been through, she wasn't shocked in the least.

"It says one. Only one can destroy the source."

Her heart plummeted. For a moment, she had allowed herself to believe there would be another way, a way in which they would both win. But it wasn't to be. Resolve washed over her as she kissed Ghanem again. When she pulled back, the wind stopped and they drifted to the floor like feathers from a pillow.

"I know where the source is, and I think I know how to stop it."

Wide eyes flashed orange. "Take me there. I'll help you as much as I can. But you have to finish it, *polipo*. Finish it and live." He cradled her face. "Your life has only just begun."

Let him think that. It would only waste time to argue. Time neither of them had. Sure, she could destroy it and live and perhaps, for a time, they could be happy together. But he couldn't be truly happy without his family, and in the end, he would only resent her. No. She'd made up her mind. She would take him to the room, and he would destroy it and everything in it.

Chapter Twenty-Nine

Sprinting down the aisle, Meera led the way as they left the makeshift chapel with pews and slayers turned upside down and inside out. There would be much more destruction before they were done. Ghanem didn't worry about that. His mind raced, playing out different scenarios. All of which ended with Meera alive. That would be the only outcome he'd allow. Now that he knew what real love felt like, he called himself all kinds the fool for ever believing he'd felt anything for Antonia. Even after her twisted mind had worked with the other veiled to massacre his family, he'd nursed a broken heart and tried to deem her innocent in his mind. But she wasn't innocent. She had been every bit as guilty as the ones who had murdered his mother.

Fingers wrapped around Meera's, his heart swelled, nearly exploding with the need to cherish and protect the one who had fought for him. Meera believed in him even after he'd told the sordid story of his past. While he could never wipe the slate clean, he could at least dust it off.

They had yet to run into Ryken, but it was just a matter of time. Where was the doomed fucker, anyway? Ghanem practically drooled thinking about ripping the bastard apart.

Though he didn't doubt Meera knew where to go, he breathed a sigh of relief when, just a few turns and several hallways later, she stopped in front of a room. The doors stood open, and he couldn't squelch the feeling of déjà vu. The scene reminded him too much of his past. In his mind, nothing good came from open doors. Meera glanced back at him. Squelching the regret of the past for the time being, he nodded, moved around her, and then stepped inside.

"This is it? There's nothing here but a mirror." Ghanem pivoted on his heel in a full circle. Except for the tall, gilded mirror against the far fall, the room appeared barren. Papered walls in a baroque pattern told more of the lavish style Ryken preferred. Now that he'd seen the slayer's true form, he understood Ryken's need for the opulent. But Ghanem wasn't here to admire or debate the slayer's style. "What am I looking for?"

She shook her head. "Not here. Beyond."

He didn't see anything beyond the four walls. Perhaps there was a hidden doorway. He moved deeper into the room and began patting the walls, listening for a hollow sound.

Meera stepped in front of the mirror and pointed. "There. Past the mirror."

He moved behind her and placed his hands on her hips. What he saw was the two of them and a future he hoped they'd share together. Maybe with her magick, he could find a way to visit his family. The throne didn't mean much to him, but Amella and Thane did. His father, too, if he were being honest.

His elongated horns tingled as her eyes locked on their image. While he liked the look of her body, he couldn't stand that she still wore what the snake had chosen for her. "Can you conjure up something else to wear?"

Her cheeks reddened. "I—I think so, yeah."

"Oh, baby. Don't be embarrassed." Still behind her, he caressed her cheek with one hand and rubbed her bare arm with the other. "If you had chosen this, I'd love it, but you didn't. He did."

Her chin jutted forward. "You're right. I'd rather be naked than wear this another minute."

Ghanem's groin hardened at her words. He pressed it against her backside and smiled at her in the mirror. She blushed again, but this time the tinge came from arousal. "There will be plenty of time for that."

She looked away and fondled her choker idly.

In the mirror, Ghanem watched white light dance across her fingertips. Her amethyst eyes sparkled, and within a blink she'd changed to jeans and a purple ribbed tank. Much better.

He kissed the top of her head. "Take me through, Meera, so we can end this."

She held his hand and squeezed before she stepped to the mirror and then through it. One minute he could see her, the next he could only see the hand that held his. Freaky. She pulled. He stepped through with one leg. A feeling akin to jelly passed through his limbs. Sluggish and a bit unsteady on his feet, Ghanem pushed the rest of his body until he stood on the other side.

Caught up in the scene before him, he forgot all about the odd feeling of passing through the mirror. The large, dark room held glowing, oversized cocoons that hung from the ceiling. Within each cocoon were two silhouettes. Grunting. Gasping. Crying. It didn't take a genius to figure out what was going on inside.

So many sounds filled the room. Lustful moans, tortured cries, and a throb he couldn't quite get a handle on. Full of questions, Ghanem scanned the interior until he spotted the source. In the middle of the room, beneath the sex chambers, was a pedestal. A throbbing sphere full of dark, malevolent energy pulsed with each grunt. Power surged through the air around the orb. He'd only seen one of these before, and it had been much smaller. He'd heard tales, though.

"Fuck me—I—"

*

Meera covered his mouth and pulled him back in the shadows as a haggard-looking Ryken stepped through the mirror. His skin had turned ashen, thinning and drooping on his body like someone who had lost a hundred pounds.

"Out," he ordered.

The grunts ceased and, one by one, the cocoons descended from the ceiling until they rested upon the floor. Beautiful slayers emerged from the chambers followed by women who had probably been quite pretty, but now looked like soulless sheep. The aura around each slayer appeared to be larger and more ominous, as if they were shadows that would and did consume all the beauty and life out of others. The slayers left through the back of the mirror while the women walked single file through a dark hole in the opposite wall.

Meera's heart pounded against Ghanem's back. Now that the cocoons were void of life, they had lost their reflective quality and looked like tattered rags. Other than the sphere, there were no adornments in the room, as if nothing could compete with its power. The sheer size told him it had been used for some time. This type of sphere, an Illumine, grew larger with each use. Good or evil mattered not to the Illumine, but the singular course would be set after the initial request. Good had never touched this particular sphere, which made it all the more dangerous. When he'd thought of the source, he'd never imagined it would be this. His gut soured with the impossibility of the situation.

Ryken turned as Jayson, bloody and bruised, entered the room. "Where is the witch?"

Jayson appeared frazzled, his pale eyes darting around the room. "I'm sorry, my lord. The guardian woke, and there was magickal wind. I tried, but I couldn't get her."

Ryken's fist sent Jayson flying.

Meera jumped reflexively when Jayson smacked his head against the wall. Ghanem eased her further into the shadows.

"You're sorry? I gave you one task. One. And you failed. Go find her. I . . . need . . . her." He staggered back. His eyelids fell away, drifting to the floor like dried leaves on a blustery fall day. "Do . . . it."

Jayson quickly got to his feet and tripped through the mirror.

Ryken waved his hand in the air, and, within seconds, three women entered the room.

Meera flinched. Ghanem turned to her and said everything he needed to say with a look. They just had to wait for the right opportunity. He touched his fingers to her lips and then turned back so he could watch Ryken.

Ryken's intent became clear when he motioned to the women and they disrobed. Three women, all flesh and curves, stood before him. But not even their bodies were as naked as their eyes.

Ghanem could have puked. Meera had possessed that vacant look not long ago. That this could have been her future nearly knocked him to his knees. Stealing a line from Meera, there wasn't a chance in Saharren he'd let this slithering motherfucker get away with raping another woman. Biding his time, he watched as Ryken limped toward them.

"Make me beautiful."

The Illumine began to pulsate when Ryken stepped closer to it, dark red light thumping from within like the beat of a heart. He held his hands on either side of it, careful not to touch the orb. As deadly as it was magickal and fortified by a group of ancient mages, the sphere could never be touched.

The women surrounded Ryken. He moaned when their hands touched his body. His skin tightened. His eyelids grew back. A brunette woman moved in front of him and sank to her knees.

"No."

Ryken swirled around as Meera cried out. A wicked smile spread across his face. "You are here. Come out of the shadows and join us. With you I will have eternal beauty." The woman on her knees repositioned herself and took Ryken into her mouth.

Ghanem stepped out before Meera could. He understood why she had yelled. He'd been on the verge of doing so himself. Fuck timing. Neither he nor Meera could stand to watch him demean these women one more second.

*

Meera didn't know what the hell to do. She couldn't just blast Ryken. Her skill wasn't quite as honed as she'd like. If the women weren't in the room, that would be another story. They'd already been hurt enough. She refused to be the cause of any more of their pain. If she could just get Ryken talking, Ghanem could get the women to safety.

"I'm here," Meera said. "What happens next?"

Ghanem flashed unbelieving eyes at her. A slight shake of her head was the only response she gave. If she wanted to succeed, she had to get her hands on that sphere and get it to Ghanem so he could destroy it.

Ryken laughed. The ominous resonance echoed in the room. Still, the brunette continued her task as if her mouth were a machine and she'd done this a thousand times before.

Meera shut out the disturbing sight and instead divided her attention between Ryken and the sphere.

"You are a Luminary. When your white light combines with my dark energy, I will be unstoppable."

Inching closer, she moved past Ghanem and flicked his hand away when he would have stopped her. Apparently Ryken knew more about being a Luminary than she did. "And how do we combine our magick? You'll have to forgive me. I'm rather new to this."

"Meera, stop."

Ghanem's command came out as a growl. She couldn't heed his warning, though she did hesitate.

"Your warrior tries to hinder you. He's not a fan of magick. Can't say I blame him, but do you really want to be with someone who despises your very essence?" Ryken shoved the brunette to the side and stepped closer. "I will help you cultivate your gift."

Meera stayed rooted in place. True, Ghanem didn't like her magickal ways, but in the short time they'd known each other, he'd grown more tolerant. She couldn't blame him for being jaded. Was she foolish for thinking he would eventually love all of her? *Wait.* There wouldn't be an *eventually.* If she allowed Ghanem to destroy the source, she only had a short time left. But her mind had united with her heart, and she would take one day with Ghanem over a lifetime without him.

Shoulders back, she once again shrugged off Ghanem's hold. She deliberately placed herself between Ryken and the other two women, creating her version of a wall. The sphere crackled as she drew closer.

"Don't touch it," Ghanem shouted.

She jumped back and Ryken laughed.

"Yes, my queen, don't touch it. You don't need to. Can't you feel it drawing out your light?" Ryken's sinister smile practically split his face.

Meera started to nod, then stopped herself. The sphere seemed to crave her magick. Her fingers extended toward the orb as if it were a magnet and her fingertips were made of metal. She balled her fists repeatedly in an attempt to keep her magick inside. "What is this?"

"It's power." Ryken's tongue flicked out. He pulled it back in and bit his lower lip.

Talk about lack of restraint. Just the word *power* had him drooling.

"It's an Illumine," Ghanem explained.

He'd somehow moved behind Ryken without making the slightest sound and now rocked onto the balls of his feet, ready to spring. His eyes widened slightly, and she caught his meaning. She kept her focus on the sphere as Ghanem continued.

"It feeds off magick, and it doesn't care if it's on the giving or receiving end. But one touch will prove fatal, so don't get any closer."

"Is it alive?"

Ryken glanced back at Ghanem, then shrugged as if the guardian were no threat at all. "Let's just say it's enchanted. Shall we?" He extended his arm in invitation.

The urge to accept reared its ugly head, but Meera wasn't falling for it. Ryken and the Illumine had paired up and were calling to her. It had always been them. Both needed her. But like Ghanem, Meera had learned to understand her magick in a very short time.

She'd also learned that ultimately the choice was hers to make.

She smiled slowly, wide and sensual. Ryken took it as victory. Ghanem took it for the sign she'd meant it to be.

He grabbed Ryken from behind and lifted the slayer king off the ground. The third women fell to the floor, and Meera quickly helped her up and ushered the women to the back of the room before pushing them through the hole. Hopefully they would stay put until Ghanem destroyed the Illumine. She raced back to Ghanem and skidded to a stop in front of Ryken. His eyes bulged as he struggled to breathe past the chokehold Ghanem held him in. *Take that, asshole,* she thought to herself.

Shoving a finger into his chest, she said, "This is what happens next. I am a Luminary and I am a queen, but I will never be yours. Consider yourself overthrown."

Spittle foamed at the corners of Ryken's mouth. Meera stepped back and nodded. With a roar, Ghanem tightened his hold and twisted, breaking the slayer's neck. In less than a blink of an eye, Ryken's body slumped and Ghanem threw him to the ground.

Careful not to touch the crackling sphere, Meera closed the distance between her and her warrior and rushed into his arms. "Thank you," she said.

He chuckled, slid a hand through her hair. "You're thanking me for killing that sonofabitch? I'd liked to have prolonged his agony."

Meera eased back, searched his eyes. "I'm thanking you for everything. For the first time in almost forever, I don't feel alone." She blinked rapidly.

Ghanem pulled her back to him and tucked her body against his. His chin rested on her head. "Don't cry, Meer. I feel the exact same way. I've been alone for so long, I'd almost forgotten how to care for someone. You've changed that for me. You've changed a lot for me."

Face pressed to his chest, she gave in and sobbed, let the soft fabric of his shirt soak up the salty tears. "I've never cried so much in my life." She sniffed. "I'm so sorry I ever thought you were a monster."

"And I'm sorry I ever thought you were a conniving witch."

This had her laughing. "Well, you have at least half of that right."

They stood in silence for a few moments. As the seconds passed, Meera grew more somber. "You have to do it."

He stiffened. "Do what?"

She pushed away and held him at arm's length. "The world needs more guardians like you. More protectors. With you as king, you can train other warriors to help keep the world safe."

He pinched the bridge of his nose, then let his arm drop. "Not all warriors are protectors. Some are the monsters you were always warned about."

"Yes, some are. But you're not. You need to go back home, Ghanem. Be with your family. Rule alongside your father." The Illumine hummed as if it tried to repel her words. Just to be safe, she took another step back.

"No."

"No what?"

"I know what you're trying to do, and it won't work." Ghanem also backed away, but he was all about putting distance between the two of them. "You will destroy it, Meera. You. I'll find another way to be with my family." He cocked a half smile. "In fact, I think you can help me with that."

"No."

"Now you say no? Not happening." He lifted his hands and took another step back. "You blast the fucker, and then we'll blow this joint together."

Was he serious? What right did he have to make such a monumental decision? The fact that she'd planned to do exactly the same crossed her mind, but she flicked it away. "Blast the fucker? I don't think so. Maybe I should blast you."

"And that would solve what?"

Pursing her lips, she considered his question. "Nothing except making me feel better." Her shoulders sagged with the weight she carried. "Please do this for me. I want to know that you'll be back with your family, surrounded by those who love you. I want to know that you'll be doing what you were born to do." The last word had been but a whisper. Knowing Ghanem would do just that gave her a semblance of peace.

Crossing the room in two strides, he lifted her chin with his finger and dragged a knuckle across her cheek. "You say all this as if you won't be around."

Solemn eyes blurred as she looked at him. "You know what they said, Ghanem. Only one . . . "

"I won't let you die. Dammit, I won't let you." His voice grew urgent, louder in an attempt to be heard over the hum.

"And I won't have it any other way." She, too, had to yell. The drone became so loud the ground beneath them trembled. Her fingers extended again, and this time she didn't fight the pull.

"Blast it, Meera. Now!"

The walls around them splintered. Pieces of cement broke away and smashed on impact. Cracks formed beneath their feet as the quake undermined the structure of the entire castle.

"Do it now," Ghanem roared. He moved in, gripped her shoulders, and shook.

Meera's eyes flashed between a very angry Ghanem and an even angrier Illumine. Focusing inward, she let her magick coil inside. It grew, readying for release. She stepped back and stretched her arms to full length. She saw the triumph in Ghanem's eyes. He thought he'd won. Ultimately he had.

Meera released her magick. Blinding white light fled her fingertips with such staggering power it knocked her off her feet. Her aim was golden. She blasted her intended target and hit the bullseye.

Ghanem lurched to the side, but wasn't quick enough. Her light hit him full on, sending him crashing into the pedestal holding the Illumine.

"Noooo," he yelled as he tried to steady the teetering base.

The Illumine didn't stand a chance. She'd hit Ghanem with so much power, there was no way he could stop the sphere from falling to the floor. As if in slow motion, the magickal orb rolled along the edge of the pedestal, hung precariously over the side. Meera held her breath, stared into Ghanem's accusing eyes.

"What have you done?"

Finally, the Illumine fell. Silence filled the room for one breath until the sphere hit the floor and shattered. The tortured screams of thousands of souls rose from the shards. She heard one voice over all the rest.

"Why, Meera?"

Chapter Thirty

The castle crumbled around them. Now that Ryken's magick had died along its wielder Lemra seemed to be quickly reverting back to the land's original state. Plaster fell from the ceiling. Ghanem dodged a hefty chunk as Meera flittered from one side of the room to the other.

"We have to save them."

She was right, but all Ghanem could do was stand there and stare. His own soul had been ripped from his chest and now dashed around the collapsing room along with all the others who'd escaped the Illumine's prison. He'd had it all figured out, down to the happily ever after shit he'd dreamed about for so long. With one blast of her magick, she'd destroyed any chance they'd had.

"I have to know. Why did you do it?"

She crossed the room and wrapped her arms around his neck. "Because I love you, and because the rest of the worlds need you." Meera leaned in and pressed her lips to his. Such tenderness seemed out of place with all the madness happening around them.

Ghanem had a hard time thinking it was anything other than a kiss goodbye. He inhaled her scent and vowed to fight her fate, even as his lips moved of their own accord. Meera wasn't dead yet. Until she drew her last breath, he'd fight any higher being who threatened to take her away from him. Being First Prince of Saharren had to count for something.

Hope once again surged, though this time he held it in check. Sinking deeper into the kiss, he crushed Meera to him and allowed himself to escape into the comfort she offered. His tongue danced across her lips, then dashed inside when she opened for him. The taste of Meera intoxicated like no other, and he longed for a time when they could laze away hours just enjoying the flavor and feel of each other.

Her moan, so full of hunger and despair, nearly had him collapsing along with the room. Instead he reluctantly pulled away, kissed the tip of her nose, and whispered the only three words that mattered.

"I love you."

Her smile told him all he needed to know. Somehow, they would find a way to be together. Even if it had to be in the afterlife.

"You didn't burn me." Her brows drew close together.

He'd realized that. The heat hadn't been as intense in the chapel, either. Another thing he couldn't explain.

"I feel warm but not burned."

"Consider that a good thing, Meera." But was it really? He never wanted to hurt her, but did the dying flame mean exactly that? Death?

She only shook her head.

Shouting drew his attention to the mirror. The forms on the other side were distorted, but he recognized the voices.

"Looks like the crew made it in. Let's get the women and get the hell out of here." He pulled Meera in for a chaste kiss and squeezed her hand.

"I couldn't agree more."

Together, they worked quickly and efficiently, drawing each woman out of the dark hole and through the mirror before presenting her to Thane and the others. There wasn't much time. Even though the women's bodies were being led to safety, their souls continued to scream. Ghanem wondered if he would ever get the sound out of his head.

Only after the last woman had been ushered out did Carrine step through the mirror. A smile tugged at the corners of her lips, and, for the life of him, he couldn't figure out why. The world was literally crashing down around them, and chances were those victims would never be the same. He doubted they'd be able to save any of them. They couldn't very well escort them back to their homes in the condition they were in now. Carrine had to realize that. Then why the smile?

On alert, he watched as the elder witch glided to Meera, arms outstretched. Meera ran to the security of the embrace. Her choked sobs tore at him. Again, he vowed to somehow make this right.

Brushing a hand over Meera's hair, Carrine spoke in whispers. "Why the tears, child? You did it. You destroyed the source."

"I—"

Stepping up, he said, "She didn't. I did."

Carrine waved her hand in dismissal even as her brow furrowed. "Impossible. I would feel if she were going to die."

That bitch, hope, made another appearance. "What do you mean?"

Half of the ceiling took that moment to crash at their feet. Dust flew around the room, seemingly chasing the anguished screams.

"No time to explain now. I came in to collect the souls. We have to get out of here." She gently shoved Meera into his arms. "Take Meera and the others and get outside. I'll join you soon."

Questions scorched the tip of his tongue, but he trusted Carrine to do what she had to do and then shed light on the situation. As it stood now, he was more in the dark than if he'd resided in the black hole.

Meera tugged his arm. "Let's get out of here."

A quick glance over his shoulder, and then he and Meera pushed through the back side of the mirror while Carrine spread her arms wide and turned in a full circle. He heard the whisper of a chant but couldn't make out the words.

Thane and Bevva were the only ones who had waited. Thane lifted a brow, then strolled through the debris and out the door. Ghanem expected nothing but sarcasm from the redhead. His jaw hit the floor when Bevva embraced Meera, albeit awkwardly.

"Glad you're okay, sis."

Meera stopped back, angled her head.

"What do you mean, *sis*?" Meera asked, her tone guarded.

"Oh. Did I forget to mention that?" Bevva shrugged in a *whatever* move. "My bad." She tossed her curls over her shoulder and turned. Just before she walked out the door, she added,

"Calliope's a Brennan, too."

Ghanem could only imagine how Meera felt in that moment. She'd finally found a family. Even more reason to keep her alive.

*

What the fudge had just happened? Sisters? Was Bevva for real? Meera struggled to make sense of this latest revelation. Why hadn't they said so earlier? And if they were sisters, why did Bevva harbor such anger toward her? Only time would reveal these answers and more. Too bad she wouldn't be around to hear them.

Sighing, Meera reached for Ghanem's hand as the foundation continued to rock. Her knees practically knocked from the vibrations beneath her feet. "Let's go," she said, her voice deadpan. Other than being witchy, she couldn't think of anything else she had in common with Bevva or Calliope. Sure wasn't any family resemblance going on. Not unless you counted Bevva's red curls. Meera's only memory of her mother had revealed she, too, had fiery hair, though Ambra Brennan's had been more wavy than curly. Calliope's hair was as dark as her own, but Meera had attributed that to a good dye job, especially since she'd played it up with blue streaks. Maybe she'd been wrong.

Ghanem squeezed her fingers reassuringly as he said, "We'll figure this out."

One brow arched. "What's to figure out? What's done is done. I know what you're thinking."

Ghanem smiled and led her into the hallway, his steps swift and sure as he maneuvered around the wreckage. "I doubt it, but go ahead. What am I thinking?" he tossed over his shoulder.

Meera jogged to keep up and prayed once they hit the outdoors, the rumble would quiet. "You're thinking," she yelled over the sound of crashing debris. "If I'd had known they were my sisters, I'd have done things differently back there."

"I—"

"You're wrong. I'd still have played it the same way. Knowing I have a real family makes this difficult, but in my heart, I know I made the right choice. Besides, there must be some reason they kept it a secret."

Ghanem yanked her arm and pulled her against the wall just as a beam fell. Heart thudding madly, Meera sucked in much-needed air. That one was a bit too close for comfort, but it had managed to pull her out of her mini pity party.

"Thanks."

"Don't thank me yet. We've still got a ways to go."

The twinkle in his eye, hinting at a zest for life, was a picture she'd take to her grave. That and the curve of his sexy horns. This was what her warrior was born to do. Protect. He was totally in his element when it came to saving someone. Trying to keep hope under control had turned out to be the equivalent of wrestling one wily beast.

Was it wrong to think Ghanem would somehow be able to keep her breathing? That thought she wouldn't say aloud. He didn't need that kind of pressure. Not with everything he'd been through in his life. Ironic that the end of her life was the first time she truly felt alive.

Ghanem jumped over the beam and then turned to help her. Gripping her waist, he easily hefted her over the obstruction. Though she could have managed on her own, Meera didn't say a word, and instead basked in the warmth of his touch.

After rounding two more corners, they made it to the entrance and rushed through the gate. The sight before them was akin to a war zone. The fake sun had disappeared. In its place lay a dark and damp world, more like what one would expect underground. Thousands of injured slayers littered the grounds around the crumbling castle, moaning and wheezing. With dazed expressions, many wandered as if in search for direction. Now that Ryken was gone, who would they turn to? Meera couldn't help but feel for them.

"Don't."

"Don't what?"

Ghanem reached out and pushed her tangled hair out of her eyes, let his touch linger. "Don't feel too sorry for them."

"How did you—never mind." Though the connection only flowed one way, she'd miss the feeling of being understood.

Out of nowhere, a body slammed into her. Tensing, she braced for the fall that never came. Feelings of comfort washed over her.

"I'm so glad you're okay." Calliope squeezed tight.

Meera hugged Calliope back with an intensity that startled even her. She could forgive the secrecy—had already done so. All she wanted was a chance to get to know her sisters. She pulled back and eyed a glaring Bevva over Calliope's shoulder. Yes, she even wanted to know the bitchy one.

"Why does she hate me?"

Calliope smiled. "Because you were first-born, of course."

Well didn't that just explain everything and wrap it up in a glittery bow. "And this is my fault how?"

Her dark haired sister gave her one more squeeze. "Somehow to Bevva, it just is."

Ghanem had stepped away to speak to the other guardians. She kept one eye on him at all times. With such little time left, she couldn't risk missing a second. He slapped Thane on the back, and, though Ghanem's brother didn't return the smile, he didn't back away either. This alone gave her hope their fractured relationship would one day heal.

"So you did it, huh?"

Distracted, Meera fought to bring her attention back to Calliope. "Did what?"

Wide *duh* eyes mocked her. "You destroyed the source. Otherwise this place wouldn't look like the aftermath of war."

"Yeah. About that. Not exactly." She couldn't even look at her sister, certain she'd see disappointment.

"What happened, then?" Calliope scrunched up her nose.

She lost the chance to answer as Ghanem stormed past her with purpose in his heavy steps. Carrine had just exited what remained of the battered building. Weariness shadowed her beautiful face, making her appear decades older. She'd collected the souls, and Meera could only guess where she'd stashed them.

Ghanem approached Carrine. Tension hung in the damp air like a heavy fog. Strong hands gestured and even though his back faced her, Meera could guess at the depths of his emotion.

It seemed as though everyone could. As a unit, the entire crew—Thane, Bevva, Steffen and Drake, along with Calliope and Meera—closed the distance until they all stood in front of Carrine. Somehow they knew she would be the one to lead them out of this place, the one with the answers. She'd said she would have felt it if Meera were going to die. What did that mean?

All along, Carrine had guided her with the council's instruction. Her mission had been clear. Meera had to be the one to destroy the source. Only when it came down to it, she'd chosen love over life. She wouldn't be able to act as the Luminary, but maybe Carrine and the council could find someone else to keep the peace in the realms. Surely, Ghanem and the other guardians would step up to help.

Meera sidled up to Ghanem, wrapping her arm around his waist and tucking her head into the crook of his neck. His muscles bunched and then he leaned into her.

"Follow me."

Carrine stepped between Thane and Steffen without another word. They had no choice but to follow. The seven of them, along with a long line of Ryken's victims, trailed behind a somber Carrine as she led them into the woods.

Complete darkness shrouded the world beneath the canopy of trees. With darkness came heightened hearing. Meera heard every breath her friends and family took. A symphony of inhalation. Another time it would have been relaxing. Like if she were at home in bed and needed to wind down. Just now, the sound made her claustrophobic. And what would they do with all these casualties? She inched away from Ghanem only to have him drag her right back to his side. Her only other choice was to light up.

Keeping the light to an ambient glow, she cast the beam only as far as a few feet in front of Carrine. The elder witch spoke as if the light were an invitation to break the silence.

"Tell me exactly what happened."

Between the two of them, Meera and Ghanem relayed the entire story of how not only the Illumine but also Ryken had been destroyed. The questions had to have been adding up, yet everyone held their tongue.

As they neared the portal, a fist closed around her heart. This realm had been awful, but it had also been the backdrop for memories she would cherish.

"Don't give up, *polipo*." Ghanem's breath tickled her ear.

To never experience his touch again, to never hear that whiskey voice of his, to never feel the type of love destined to last several lifetimes . . . Just thinking of this had her knees buckling. She wanted to speak, to tell him everything she felt.

"I already know. I feel it, too," he whispered.

Even Calliope's gentle touch couldn't ease the pain in Meera's heart, though she appreciated the effort.

"I wouldn't have taken you for someone who'd wuss out." Bevva shook her head. "You know, you being a Luminary and all."

Before Meera could respond to Bevva's snide taunt, Carrine lifted her finger. "Enough."

Just beyond Carrine, the air shimmered. The portal between this realm and the next beckoned. Meera remembered her last trip and swallowed past the lump in her throat.

Though it never quite reached her eyes, Carrine smiled. "This time will be different. This time you won't be alone. In fact, you will never be alone again. Someday soon you will even meet your mother." She moved to stand in front of Meera and Ghanem. With steady hands she laid Meera's shaky palm over Ghanem's fist. "The council has found a way to help all these people. Thanks to you. You have destroyed the source. Both of you."

Meera closed her eyes and waited for Carrine to finish. Was this the goodbye speech? The close-but-no-cigar rally? Neither seemed to fit Carrine's tone. She'd said Meera would get to meet her mother. But she didn't want to meet her unless she would have time to get to know her. Ready to face whatever fate threw her way, Meera opened her eyes and clung to Ghanem. She focused solely on him and the love they shared.

"Yes, both of you destroyed the Illumine, but you did it as one."

Ghanem spoke first, though his gaze never strayed. "I don't understand."

Calliope squealed. "I do! Please, Carrine, let me tell them."

Carrine dropped her head in agreement.

Calliope shifted from one foot to the other, barely able to contain her excitement. While Meera appreciated her enthusiasm, she really just wanted her to get on with it.

"L. O. V. E. Looove. You guys have it. For each other. One heart. You united and became one." By the end of the sentence she was jumping up and down. "Don't you see? You both win."

"Does that have anything to do with why my touch doesn't burn her anymore?"

She'd wondered the same thing, but Ghanem beat her to the question.

"Yes," Carrine said. "You, Ghanem, cannot hurt if you love completely, if you accept everything about who that person is. It's not in your nature."

Meera's heart expanded two-fold and dislodged the fist holding it hostage. Tears formed, and this time she didn't care. So she'd turned into a crier. Big deal. She bit her lip and waited for Ghanem to say something. Anything. When he didn't she began to panic.

What if this wasn't what he really wanted? Oh, for the love of witchery. "Thinking about ditching me?"

A wicked half smile threatened to melt her heart. His words did just that. "Not a chance in Mississippi, Witch."

About the Author

Elle J Rossi grew up in rural Indiana surrounded by great people, a huge family and more animals than she could count. But the sites and sounds of the world beckoned, so she left her small town to escape into a creative world full of music. As a full time singer she was able to lose herself in a thousand different songs in a hundred different places.

After meeting the love of her life and settling down, she yearned to find a new and fulfilling creative outlet. Overly fond of the happily ever after, she wondered what it would be like to have her own characters lead her down dark and twisted paths. The very first word on the very first page sealed her fate. She'd found a new love. She'd found her escape.

Now along with weaving haunting tales about the journey to love, she's creating cover art for authors around the world and loving every second of it. For fun, she cranks country music to take her back to her roots, and sings karaoke anytime she gets a chance. Her husband, two children, and a cat that rules the roost keep her company along the way and guarantee she doesn't get lost in the enchanted forest. She wouldn't have it any other way.

In the mood for more Crimson Romance? Check out *The Peacekeeper's Soul* by Candace Sams at *CrimsonRomance.com*.

17751409R00161

Made in the USA
Charleston, SC
26 February 2013